"*Hell Divers* is action-packed, gritty, and wholly original. A rare combination of a high premise, solid storytelling, and heart."
—DANIEL ARENSON, *USA TODAY* BESTSELLING AUTHOR

"Relentless action and danger...*Hell Divers* is one hell of a page-turner!"
—BOB MAYER, *NEW YORK TIMES* BESTSELLING AUTHOR

"Literally skydiving into the apocalypse, *Hell Divers* delivers more of Smith's trademark breakneck action and suspense. Amazing settings, great characters, the end of the world shouldn't be this much fun!"
—MATTHEW MATHER, BESTSELLING AUTHOR OF *CYBERSTORM*

"A terrific blend of high-concept and wild action...A must for fans of smart postapocalyptic storytelling."
—SAM SISAVATH, BESTSELLING AUTHOR OF THE PURGE OF BABYLON SERIES

"I love it! The whole book was awesome... It was creative and intense and there was never a dull moment... You should definitely give this one a try!"
—*HOOKED ON BOOKS*

HELL DIVERS

NICHOLAS SANSBURY SMITH

BLACKSTONE
PUBLISHING

Copyright © 2016 by Nicholas Sansbury Smith
Published in 2016 by Blackstone Publishing
Book design by Kathryn Galloway English

Printed in the United States of America
First edition: 2016
ISBN 978-1-4551-1598-3

1 3 5 7 9 10 8 6 4 2

CIP data for this book is available from the Library of
Congress

Blackstone Publishing
31 Mistletoe Rd.
Ashland, OR 97520
www.BlackstonePublishing.com

To my agent, David Fugate, who provided excellent feedback and encouragement, and the Blackstone Publishing family for believing in my story. I'm lucky to work with such a talented team.

There is no death, only a change of worlds

—Chief Seattle

ONE

The average life expectancy for a Hell Diver was fifteen jumps. This was Xavier Rodriguez's ninety-sixth, and he was about to do it with a hangover.

He waited outside the doors of the launch bay in silence, head bowed, palms against the cold steel. The armed guards standing across the hallway might have thought he was praying, but he was just doing his best not to puke.

The night before a dive was always fraught with tension, which sometimes led to poor decisions on the *Hive*. Normally, Captain Ash turned a blind eye to the diver teams' debauchery; after all, she was dropping them into the apocalypse to scavenge for parts on the poisoned surface of the Old World. Rarely did all the divers come back. A bit of booze and sex the night before was practically a given.

"Good luck, X," one of the guards said.

X sucked in a long breath, tied the red bandanna with the white arrow insignia around his head, then pushed open the double doors. The rusted metal screeched across the floor, drawing the gaze of Team Raptor's three other members. Aaron, Rodney, and

Will were already suiting up near the lockers.

At the far end of the room, past the dozen plastic domes of the launch tubes, stood a few divers from Team Angel. They were easy to spot in the crowd of technicians and support staff gathered along the wall. Engineers, soldiers, thieves: divers had a wide variety of skill sets, and they would stand out like a flame in the dark even without their red jumpsuits.

He gave the room a quick scan. Team Apollo hadn't shown up this time. That was fine with X; he didn't like being watched anyway.

"Nice of you to make it, X!" Will shouted. The newest member of Raptor threw on his dented chest armor and looked X up and down as he walked over to his locker.

"You look like hell, sir," Will said, chuckling.

"Nothing a few stims can't handle," X replied.

He didn't need to look in a mirror to know that Will was right. X looked much older than his thirty-eight years. Crow's-feet had formed around his eyes from too much squinting, and his habitual frown had carved its way into his cheeks and forehead. At least he still had most of his teeth. But for his unusually white smile, he would have looked a good deal worse.

X stopped at his locker for another ritual. Tracing a finger over his name tag, he took a moment to remember the divers who had come before him. It was growing more difficult by the day. Some days he couldn't remember some of their faces at all. But today that was partly a product of his pounding headache.

Opening the door to his locker, he searched

the top shelf for a bottle of the stimulants he had discovered on a dive a few months back. The precious tablets—one more thing that was impossible to make on the *Hive*—were worth their weight in gold.

X felt the burn of eyes on him as he swallowed the tablets. The tall, lean figure of his best friend, Aaron Everhart, filled his peripheral vision.

"Just say it," X said.

"I thought you said you were cutting back on the 'shine."

There was no point in lying; Aaron would see right through it.

"Haven't gotten around to it yet," X said.

Aaron held his gaze and frowned. "You sure you're up—"

X held up a hand, as if about to scold a rookie diver. "I'm fine, man."

After a tense moment, X went to check on Rodney, who was pushing one dark brown foot through his black bodysuit. He glanced up, his blank, emotionless gaze seeming to look through X rather than at him. He was the third most experienced diver on the ship. The work had hardened him over the years, and sometimes X had the passing thought that Rodney *wanted* to die. One of the doctors had asked X the same question after his last health exam. But who could say? Deep down, all Hell Divers must have at least some hint of a death wish.

"Listen up, everyone," X said. "I just came from Command. Captain Ash said the skies look good. No sign of electrical storms over the drop zone."

"What's on the list this time?" Rodney asked.

"Nuclear fuel cells. That's it. The captain was very clear."

"Man, what happened to searching for other shit?" Will said. "I miss the days of scavenging for real treasure."

X glared at him. "You should be happy that today's dive is over a green zone—less chance of radiation on the surface."

"I guess I could get used to these green-zone dives," Will said. "Maybe I'll live to become a legend like you someday." He flashed a grin that evaporated under X's scowl.

Will was about as young as X had been when he joined the Hell Divers, and just about as naive.

Hard to believe that was twenty years ago. X wasn't a legend by any stretch of the imagination, but he did have more successful jumps under his belt than any other diver in history. The only one who came close was a guy named Rick Weaver on their sister ship, *Ares.* Last X heard, Weaver was still diving.

Throwing back his head, X swallowed two more stims. He washed them down with a swig from his water bottle, grimaced, and faced Aaron.

"How's the little man doing?" he said. "I haven't seen Tin for a few weeks."

"Michael's growing up way too fast," Aaron said. "He just got accepted into engineering school a couple of weeks ago. They took him two years early." X caught the trace of sadness in Aaron's sharp blue eyes, but he wasn't sure what it meant. Was it because he hadn't made an effort to see Tin lately, or because Tin had decided to become an engineer instead of a Hell Diver?

"You didn't think he would want to follow in *your* footsteps, did you?" X asked.

"Aw, hell no!" Aaron said. His blond eyebrows scrunched together. "Would never want this life for my boy."

"Can't say as I blame you."

Aaron hesitated, his lips forming a thin line. "I wasn't going to mention it, but you missed his birthday."

"*Shit,*" X muttered. "When did he turn nine?"

Aaron's brows scrunched again. "He's ten."

X looked at the floor. "I'm sorry. I'll make it up to him after we get back."

Aaron shut his locker. "I won't hold my breath."

There was nothing else to say, really. X needed to prove himself, not make another hollow promise. He grabbed his well-worn bodysuit from his locker and slipped his legs through. The internal padding conformed to his musculature as he zipped up the front. Aaron handed him the black matte armor that shielded his vital organs. The piece felt light in his hands, but the titanium outer shell could stop a shotgun blast. The chest plate had saved him from broken bones or worse on countless dives.

Sliding the armor over his head, he sucked in his stomach and fastened the clasps on both sides. It was snug, molded to fit the body of a much younger man, long before his metabolism slowed and his bad habits caught up with him.

The titanium leg and arm guards didn't fit much better. He clipped them over old muscle covered in a layer of fat that seemed to cling on no matter how many push-ups or laps around the ship he did.

After affixing the guards, he slid the helmet on. He completed the routine by inserting his battery unit into the socket on his chest plate. It flickered to life, spreading a cool blue glow over the dull black armor. The equipment was old, like just about everything else on the ship, but the pieces fit together perfectly and protected him from the hostile conditions of a dive.

"Tubes are ready!" a voice yelled from inside X's launch tube. Ty, the team's technician, climbed out, wiping grease onto his yellow jumpsuit. He chomped nervously on a calorie-infused herb stick. No matter how many of the damn things Ty ate, he stayed thin as a whippet.

X grabbed a vest stuffed with flares and shotgun shells, slung it over his shoulder, and headed for the drop tubes, scanning the porthole windows as he walked. Nothing to see but swirling dark clouds. The divers from Team Angel made room as X and his men reached their tubes. Rodney and Will hurried over, but Aaron paused, as he always did, and nodded to X. It was more powerful than any words. Despite the tension from earlier, they trusted each other with their lives.

One by one, the divers climbed into their metal cocoons.

Even after all these years, X still felt the lump of fear as Ty closed the plastic dome over the top. It took a few moments of squirming before he settled into a comfortable position. His mind quickened, and the hangover fog began to clear—the stim tablets were finally kicking in.

X breathed out and tapped the minicomputer on

his right forearm. Behind the cracked glass surface, the control panel flickered. He punched the button activating the Heads-Up Display (HUD). A green translucent subscreen emerged in the upper right corner of his visor, and digital telemetry scrolled across it.

He flicked the monitor on his forearm a second time. Another translucent subscreen emerged above the data on his HUD and solidified into a rectangular map. Four blips emerged, one for each member of Team Raptor.

X chinned the comm pad in his helmet to open a line to his team. "Raptor, systems check."

"Ready, sir," Rodney replied.

"Everything's looking good," Will said. A second's pause, then, "Ready to dive."

The faint quiver X heard in Will's voice didn't surprise him. This was the kid's fifteenth jump, and according to the numbers it should be his last.

Fuck statistics, X thought. If the numbers told the whole truth, he himself would have been dead eighty jumps ago.

"Systems look good, X," Aaron said. "See you on the surface."

"Dive *safe,*" X replied, putting emphasis on the second word.

A new voice crackled in his helmet. "You're mission clear, X." Captain Ash's voice, clinical and characteristically smooth.

"Roger that," he replied. "We dive so humanity survives." It was the Hell Diver motto, and his typical response—a reply that reassured the captain she could count on him.

As the *Hive* slowed to a halt, X flipped up his mirrored visor and pressed the thin polymer mouth guard against his upper teeth. The ship was now at hovering altitude, but he waited for Ty to confirm what he already knew.

"We're in position," Ty said a moment later. "I'll launch the supply crate to the surface in a few seconds."

X flashed a thumbs-up, and Ty locked the plastic dome over the top of the cylinder. He patted the translucent ceiling, removed the herb stick, and mouthed, *Good luck*.

A siren wailed in the launch bay. The first warning.

X felt the familiar tingle of anticipation building. It was a messy, addictive combination of fear and exhilaration—the feeling that pushed him to jump again and again. Although he would never admit it to a soul, X lived for this rush.

Every drop was risky, often in its own new way. You couldn't jump twenty thousand feet from an airship, plummet through electrical storms, and land on a hostile surface without risk. And this wasn't a normal salvage mission. The fuel cells Ash had ordered them to recover weren't easy to come by. Only a few known locations on the continent remained where they could find the nuclear gold. Without the cells, the *Hive* wouldn't be able to stay aloft. If they failed …

X clamped down on his mouth guard at the thought. He wouldn't fail. He never failed.

The seconds ticked down on his mission clock. His senses were on full alert now. He could smell the worn plastic of the helmet, feel his hammering heart and the rush of blood pulsing in his ears, and see the soft blue glow from the interior LEDs of his helmet.

A second siren screamed right on time, and the emergency light bathed his pod in red. The sound of creaking metal, then a loud pop as Ty launched the supply crate from another tube.

One minute to drop.

X skimmed the data on his HUD a final time. All systems clear. Rodney's, Will's, and Aaron's dots were all blinking, their beacons active. They were good to go. The final minute ticked down in X's mind. He squeezed his knuckles together until they cracked.

Thirty seconds to drop.

The sirens faded to a faint echo, and the red glow shifted to blue—the last calm moments before the tempest. The clouds seemed momentarily lighter beneath his feet, but that had to be an illusion. Command had said no electrical storms in the drop zone.

The voice of Captain Ash, dispassionate yet soothing somehow, crackled in his helmet. "Good luck, Raptor."

Five seconds to drop.

A shiver ran up X's spine when he saw the unmistakable bloom of lightning across the clouds below. The distant flash waned and died, leaving only traces of fuzzy light.

Bumping his comm, X screamed, "Delay launch! I repeat ..."

He reached up to pound on the dome just as the glass floor whispered open. His gloved fingertips raked the metal surface of the tube as he fell, his voice lost in the shriek of the wind.

For a moment, he felt weightless, as if he were nothing but pure consciousness. Then the wind took him, sucking him into the black void. Anger boiled up. How could ops have missed the storm? A faulty sensor? A negligent officer too busy playing grab-ass with some cute trainee? He didn't know, and none of that mattered anyway right now. He had to focus on the dive and getting his team to the surface alive.

X surrendered to the forces lashing his suit and flinging him earthward. Stretching his arms and legs out, he broke into a stable free-fall position. The smooth, beetlelike shell of the *Hive* floated overhead, the turbofans flitting like insect wings. Far above the ship, deep in the meat of the clouds, he glimpsed something he hadn't seen in a long time: a plank of golden light. The sun, struggling to peek through. Then, in the blink of an eye, it was gone.

He shifted his gaze back to his HUD. They were already down to nineteen thousand feet. In his peripheral vision, he saw the blue glint of Aaron's battery unit. For a millisecond, he wondered what was going through his old friend's mind, but he probably had a fair idea. Aaron dived with the weight of more than just his chute and armor. He had a son waiting for him above.

X had no one waiting for him or weighing on him. And that was what made him one of the best divers.

Feeling the cool mattress of wind pushing up on him, X reached outward a few inches with his left arm—just enough to make a slow rightward turn and check on the other divers. They were closing in, working their way into a wedge formation at three-hundred-foot intervals.

He angled his helmet downward, peering into the clouds again. A dazzling web of lightning forked across below them at fifteen thousand feet.

Static crackled from the speaker in his helmet as one of the other divers tried to speak, but the garbled words were impossible to make out. X trained his eyes on the swirling clouds. The darkness masked the size of the storm, but he wasn't deceived. If it was already screwing with their electronics, it had to be huge.

As he cut through the sky, the sporadic lightning intensified. A pocket of turbulence jerked him suddenly to the left at twelve thousand feet. The wind whistled over his armor and rippled across his bodysuit. He focused on centering his mass and holding his stable free-fall position.

Ten thousand feet. Halfway there.

He shot through a shelf of cloud as black and flat as an anvil and watched in shock as the entire sky lit up with flashes of electric blue. Experience immediately took over. Bringing his arms back into a V, he tilted his nose down, and narrowed the V into an arrow point.

His team had vanished in the clouds, but they would be doing the same thing. The wind shears and electrical disturbances would render them deaf and blind, their electronics useless. That was why X had trained his team to calculate their altitude and velocity by time in free fall, aided by whatever they could glimpse of ground or horizon, without the assistance of a computer program.

But running numbers while falling through a lightning storm was next to impossible. The wind beat every inch of his body, and the lightning strikes seemed to bend the darkness and warp the space around them. He hadn't seen a storm this massive and deep in a long time. It spread across his entire field of vision. There was no getting around it. They just had to punch through as fast as possible.

He split through the clouds like a missile, his body whistling as his velocity increased. A scrambled HUD reading, "*8,000*'," flickered on his visor right before he slipped into the dark heart of the abyss. He was falling at one hundred sixty miles per hour and counting. Every fiber of muscle in his body seemed to quiver in readiness. The screaming wind gave way to the rifle crack of nearby strikes, and the bowling rumble of those more distant. The constant shears threw him this way and that, forcing him to stiffen his legs and adjust constantly with his hands as rudders to maintain the nosedive and avoid spinning or tumbling.

An arc of lightning streaked in front of him. With no time to move or even flinch, he felt every hair on his body rise as one.

The mere fact that he was having this thought meant the strike wasn't critical. He could still see, and his heart was still hammering away. The strike hadn't penetrated the layer of synthetic materials in his suit that was designed to offer a degree of protection against the electrical jolt. Still, he was bound to feel some of the burn before long.

Six thousand feet.

Bringing his arms out to his sides and bending his knees, he worked his way back into a stable position and finally felt the heat. His skin was on fire. He bit down harder on his mouth guard, tasting the plastic.

Five thousand feet.

The digital map on his HUD had solidified again. One of the blips had vanished, a heartbeat gone. It was Rodney, lost to the darkness.

"*God damn,*" X whispered. He clenched his jaw, fighting to compartmentalize the anger swirling under his burning flesh. Someone would pay for this stupidity, but it would have to wait.

Four thousand feet.

Lightning flitted through his fall line. This time, he didn't even blink. He was almost down and was focused completely on gauging the time between himself and the surface. The suits had no autodeploy system—the engineers had removed them years ago at X's request. He didn't want a buggy computer system as old as he was determining when his chute fired.

A blinking dot in the welter of data on his HUD pulled his attention back to his visor. Will's beacon had veered dramatically off course.

X tilted his helmet, searching the darkness for the blue glow of the battery unit, and glimpsed it spinning away into the whirling black mass.

Will's beacon blinked off a moment later, his heart stopped by a fatal jolt of static electricity. The kid had ended up precisely on the statistical mean after all: dead on his fifteenth jump.

X felt a tremble of anger. The two divers had been

so close, almost out of the storm, almost through to the relative safety of a toxic earth. And now they were dead. A waste of precious human life that could have been avoided if the officers in ops had done their fucking jobs. How could they miss a storm a hundred miles wide?

Screaming in rage, X burst through the cloud floor at terminal velocity and bumped the pad in his helmet to activate his night-vision goggles (NVGs). Below, a decaying city exploded into view. The rusted tombstones of skyscrapers rose out of the metal-and-concrete graveyard. Those buildings that hadn't crumbled stood leaning against one another like a forest of dead snags. Their tilted girders, showing vivid green, filled his visor, growing larger with every thump of his heart.

Three thousand feet.

Clear of the storm at last, X tucked one arm and made half a barrel roll, then lay on his back, legs and arms spread. The glow of a battery unit came into view, and two seconds later a diver shot through the clouds above. Having confirmed that it was Aaron, he rolled back into stable position and pulled his rip cord. The suspension lines came taut, yanking him upward, or so it felt. Reaching up, he grabbed the toggles and steered toward a field of dirt to the north of two crumbled buildings.

With the drop zone (DZ) identified, he pulled the left toggle, turning the canopy to scan the sky. Aaron came back into view a heartbeat later, but something was wrong. He was still in a nosedive and screaming toward the pyramid of ruins.

"Aaron, pull your fucking chute!" X shouted into the comm.

Static crackled, and a second passed. Another two hundred fifty feet closer to the ground.

Aaron's panicked voice boomed over the channel. "I can't see! My night vision isn't working!"

X squandered a half second checking his DZ. He was still on course for a clear landing. He returned his gaze to the sky, locking on the blue meteor that was Aaron.

"Pull your chute! I'll guide you."

"I can't see nothin' but rooftops!" The flurry of static couldn't hide the fear in Aaron's voice.

"Pull your chute, God damn it, unless you want to *eat* one of those rooftops!"

X breathed again as Aaron's canopy finally inflated. He still had a chance to slow down, a chance to live. X would guide him. His eyes would be Aaron's eyes.

"Steer left!"

Aaron pulled away from the towers, but there were so many. *Too* many. He plunged toward the jutting bones of what had once been a magnificent high-rise office building.

X rotated for a better view, his ears popping from the change in pressure. Dizziness washed over him. He blinked it away, keeping his eyes on Aaron. He was slowly gliding away from the stalks of broken buildings.

"I can't see, X!"

"Keep pulling left. You're almost clear!"

There was a pause.

"Remember what I told you about Tin?" Aaron's voice was softer now.

X's heart caught for half a beat. "Yes."

"You have to take care of him. Promise me!"

"Aaron, you're going to make it! Keep to your fucking left! You're almost clear."

The canopy pulled Aaron away from the jungle of steel and glass, but X couldn't see a clear landing zone. He squirmed in his harness, eyes roving frantically across the desolate landscape for a way down.

"Promise me, damn it," Aaron repeated.

X sucked in a measured breath. "I promise. But you're going to—"

Before he could finish his sentence, the blue silhouette swung around and smashed into the side of a building. X watched helplessly as the chute caught on jagged metal. The force tore it free, and the blue glow plummeted into darkness.

The lonely crackle of static washed over the comm. An eyeblink later, he lost sight of Aaron, but he heard the crunching thud over the comm as his friend's body smacked into the pavement.

X stared at the ruined buildings, the air seized from his chest, unable to process that Aaron was really gone. He had only seconds before he had to flare his chute and hit the ground himself, but he couldn't pull his gaze away from the towers or bear the thought of finding Aaron's mangled corpse. Not now, not after surviving this many dives.

At some point, he snapped out of his dazed state, jolted alert by his promise and his duty. Humankind was counting on him. Aaron had died, and Will and Rodney before him. But X *couldn't* die. He still had two things to do: find the power cells and see Tin through to adulthood.

The square of dirt was rising up to meet him.

Bending his knees slightly, he pulled on the toggles to slow his descent and performed a two-stage flare. A halo of dust billowed up around him as his boots connected with the poisoned ground. He tried to run out the momentum, but with no grass or leaves to flutter in the breeze, he had misgauged and approached crosswind. His knees folded, and he lost his balance.

X hit the ground hard, his body tumbling and then skidding across the bare dirt. When he finally fetched up, he was on his back. He lay there for a few seconds. That horrible crunching sound still echoed in his ears. He couldn't see or breathe. He had lost his entire team in a single jump, in what was supposed to be a *green-zone* dive.

Furious, he thrashed at the risers and cascade lines wrapped around his midsection and legs. The loose low-porosity nylon rippled in the toxic breeze. He squirmed and pulled it away from his armor, tripping and falling again in the process. Pulling his knife, he sliced through the harnesses, finally freeing himself. He swore again and kicked at the dirt from a sitting position.

The wind had calmed, and the roll and clatter of thunder was far away. He sheathed his knife and lingered on the ground before finally pushing himself to his feet.

Wobbling as the blood rushed from his head, he looked through the bees swarming in his field of vision at his HUD. The beacon of the supply crate Ty had dropped was a half mile away.

Reaching down, he activated his wrist computer. A map rolled out across the screen. He flicked the surface with a fingertip and dragged a navigation marker to the crate's location.

At least he wouldn't have to trek across the wasteland for hours to secure his gear. He checked the map for a second time to search for the main target. The *Hive*'s records put the nuclear fuel cells in an old warehouse two miles from the supply crate. He set a second nav flag to mark the location.

When he had finished plotting his route, he checked the radiation readings. His heart skipped when he saw the digital telemetry on his HUD. Something had to be wrong. The numbers were astronomical.

Green dive, my ass!

He hadn't the time right now to curse Captain Ash's team. He had to get moving. His layered suit wouldn't keep out all the radiation, so the clock was ticking. He pulled his blaster from the holster on his right hip and cracked the triple-barreled break-action open to expose two shotgun shells in the breech. It was good he checked; he had forgotten the flare. He plucked one from his vest, inserted it in the top barrel, and snapped the action shut with a click.

The training and experience he had acquired over ninety-six dives kicked in. He scanned the devastation all around him, framed on either side by hundreds of skeletal buildings, and at the top by the swirling storm. It was a sight other Hell Divers had seen countless times, but this time X was the only man left standing to see it.

TWO

"Please Maria, there's still time," Mark Ash said. "Jordan can take over. You've done your duty to the *Hive*. It's time you looked after yourself."

Captain Maria Ash hunched over the sink and spat blood into the bowl. She shivered and gripped the cold metal to steady herself.

"Jordan's not ready," she said. "He has a lot to learn before he takes the helm." She closed her eyes and waited for the dizziness to pass. She opened them to her husband's reflection in the mirror. What little brown hair he had left formed a crown around his skull, like a monk's tonsure. He positioned his glasses farther down, against the bulb of his nose, then smiled when he saw she was looking at him.

Even though she should be accustomed by now, she still gasped at the sight of the woman next to him. Her pale skin accentuated the bags under her green eyes, and her tailored white uniform couldn't hide the weight she had lost. Her face was haggard, and for a moment she wished she could buy makeup off the black market. But she had to set an example, even if it meant looking like a walking cadaver.

She ran a hand through her bright-red hair. At least *that* had come back. Her hair had always been a defining feature, and losing it had been like losing part of her identity. Two days ago, when one of the *Hive*'s doctors told her the throat cancer had returned, the first thing she had done was touch her hair. It was her one luxury, the one bit of femininity she could still show to the world. She deftly twisted it into a bun and secured it with a handful of pins.

Mark put a hand on the back of her shoulder. "I love you, Maria, since the day we met nearly twenty-five years ago. I don't want to lose you."

She turned away from the mirror to face him. "And I love you, but you know how important my dream is to me. I have to find us a new home. I know there's a place out there for us—a surface area that's habitable. I will find it."

He gave a little sigh. "You want to believe it's out there, but even your own staff doesn't think such a place exists. Please, I'm begging you. Let Jordan take over. Accept treatment again. I almost lost you once already."

Maria shook her head and turned back to the mirror. She was a fighter. Always had been. Before she was captain, she had been a lieutenant in the Militia. She always wore her uniforms with pride.

"The ship needs me, now more than ever. We just dropped Team Raptor into an electrical storm, for God's sake!"

Mark crinkled his nose—something he did when he wasn't sure what to say.

"There are only two airships left in the *entire*

world," she said. "I will not abandon my duty now."

"Okay, I understand." With a defeated nod, he opened the bathroom door and left her staring into the mirror.

Maria picked her wedding ring up off the sink and twisted it back into place. It was loose on her bony finger, and she had to curl her hand into a fist to keep it on. Mark was right. Most of her staff didn't believe there was anywhere on the poisoned surface where humanity could start over, but she had to believe. Most days, that small ray of hope was the only thing that kept her going.

An undecipherable voice broke across the PA speakers outside, recalling her to the bridge. After losing contact with Team Raptor, she feared the worst. They needed those nuclear fuel cells to keep their home in the air, and to stiffen her resolve to keep looking for a new home. It wasn't often that they came across potential locations for nuclear cells—which made today's mission even more vital.

Maria flicked off the light and walked back onto the bridge. Mark had returned to his shift at the water treatment plant, but her stone-faced executive officer, Leon Jordan, was waiting for her at the entrance of the room. She studied him from afar, trying to get a read before he broke whatever news he had. He was a stoic young man with stern features that she might expect from someone twice his age. His strong jaw and dark brown eyes revealed no hint of anxiety, only strength. It was partly why she had selected him as her XO. He was smart, loyal, and ambitious, and like her, he cared about the *Hive* and its passengers. He would make a fine captain someday—maybe someday soon—but she wasn't ready to hand over the reins just yet.

Maria stepped out of the shadows and gripped the railing, looking out over the room below her. "Any news on Raptor?"

"Afraid not, Captain," Jordan said. "But engineering did fix the faulty sensor."

"Doesn't help X and his men, now, does it?" Her tone was harsh, but she wasn't mad at Jordan or engineering—only at herself. The damage was already done. She had likely sent an entire team to their deaths. Hell Divers were a precious resource. Of every five recruits, only one made it through the training alive. And the life expectancy of those who did was only a few years. X and Aaron were the exceptions. To think she had lost them because of a faulty sensor made her throat hurt even worse.

Maria made herself breathe deeply. The faint scent of bleach lingered in the air. The entire bridge was spotless and bathed in clean white light. The tile floor, walls, and even the pod stations matched the white uniforms of those who worked here. Keeping the room immaculate and bright was a tradition handed down through the generations. The bridge was a beacon of hope, and Maria wanted her staff to embody that hope at all times.

With Jordan in tow, she walked down the center ramp that bisected the room. Passing operations and navigation, she asked him, "You got a sitrep from engineering?" She stopped beside the oak steering wheel in the center of the platform and rested her hand lightly on it.

Nodding, Jordan continued to the main display at the front of the room and activated it with a flick of a finger. A close-up of Chief Engineer Roger Samson's bald head filled the screen. The cam pulled back to a short, burly man, scratching his scalp and staring at another monitor offscreen.

"Samson," she said, "Jordan says you have a sitrep."

Startled, the engineer looked up. "Yes, Captain. We have a major fucking problem. The electrical storm caused severe damage to the pressure relief valves on two of the reactors. Both are stuck, and I had to shut them down. Luckily, we didn't have any radiation leaks."

Maria breathed a sigh of relief. "Radiation" and "leak" were the last two words a captain wanted to hear, since even a small leak could kill everyone aboard.

"I have to keep them offline until we can get a crew to fix them. Probably be a couple days. We're running at half power now, with two others already offline. I need those fuel cells from Team Raptor, and I need 'em yesterday."

"Can't you take cells out of the damaged reactors and put them in the two that are offline?" Jordan asked.

Samson snorted, then caught himself and said, "Doesn't work like that, sir."

"So what do we do?" Jordan folded his arms across his chest.

"We pray X comes back with cells," Maria said. She knew her ship inside and out. Without the reactors, they were dead in the water—*air*, actually. The thermal energy they produced converted into electrical energy that fed through a network below decks. Some of that energy was stored in a backup battery the size of an entire room. When it was gone, the helium gas bladders would keep them in the air, but without power, the ship's systems would fail. Everything, from the water reclamation plant where her husband worked to the massive farms where they grew their food, would shut down. The rudders and turbofans would be useless, and the *Hive* would drift helplessly through the sky, dark and dead, until an electrical storm or a mountain peak dealt the final blow.

"How are the gas bladders holding up?" Maria asked.

"We lost another two," said Samson. "Down to sixteen of twenty-four. I was able to revert the helium back through the network, and we've diverted energy from all nonessential sources, but I'm running out of options. Pretty soon, we're going to have to start shutting off lights."

Jordan shook his head. "If you do that, we're going to have to worry about more than just riots. We'll be dealing with pure chaos and anarchy from the lower-deckers."

"Would you rather crash?" Samson glared at them from the screen. "I don't know if you realize this, Lieutenant, but the *Hive* is dying. If we go down, there's only *Ares* left—and frankly, that bucket of rust is in worse shape than we are."

Maria held up a hand. "I'm painfully aware of this, Samson."

The fat engineer wiped his forehead and said, "Sorry, Captain. It's just …" He paused and locked eyes with her. "Unless you find us a magical place to put down, we're going to have to start making some very unpopular choices if we want to stay in the air."

She exchanged a glance with Jordan. His features remained unchanged, unemotional. He would tell her his opinion in confidence, away from the ears of the other officers. Talk spread quickly through the *Hive*, and she didn't want to feed the rumor mill with a note of raw panic.

"Keep this quiet," Maria said. "That's an order, Samson."

"Understood."

The feed sizzled to darkness. She had a sour burn in her throat. She could almost feel the cancer cells, chomping away at her insides. The *Hive* had a sort of cancer too: a shortage of power. Samson was right. The ship was dying, and if X didn't return with more cells, it would be a matter of when, not if, they crashed to the ruined surface like all the other airships before them.

*   *   *   *   *

Two hours of trekking through the dead city gave X ample time to think. He carried more than the assault rifle he had retrieved from the supply crate. As he trudged through the wastelands and climbed to the top of an overlook, he felt the weight of every diver's death over the past twenty years. Will, Rodney, and Aaron were just three more bodies on the pile.

He could almost make himself believe that it was an accident, but the combined gut punch of anger and grief still made his insides roil. What the hell had Command been thinking? Dropping a team through an electrical storm was a disastrous mistake—one that his team had paid for with their lives. And now, on top of that, he was trudging over radioactive dirt in what was supposed to be a green zone.

Humanity was three deaths closer to extinction, and if he didn't get those power cells, half the rest would die. Twenty thousand feet overhead, 546 men, women, and children were counting on him.

But if he made it back to the *Hive,* he would find the people who had made his best friend's son an orphan. If he needed it, that gave him one more reason to survive this.

The distant boom of thunder pulled him back to the present. He raised his binos and glassed the ruined city. Sporadic flashes of lightning backlit the husks of towers with a pulsating glow.

He clicked off his night-vision optics and saw the world for what it was: gray and brown and dead. No matter how hard he tried, he couldn't imagine the thrum and bustle of this metropolis before the bombs dropped.

The boneyard of ruins stretched as far as he could see. Even in this vast openness, he suddenly felt trapped, suffocated by his suit and the narrow view through his visor. Ironic for someone who had lived most of his life in the cramped confines of the *Hive*. Usually, diving allowed him an escape from the controlled, regimented, stifling environment.

But now he just felt isolated and lonely, like a fish in a small bowl.

He swept the binos over block after city block of rubble until he found a cluster of four buildings still standing amid the destruction. Checking his minimap, he confirmed his location. He was at the target.

The aboveground vaults were warehouses of Industrial Tech Corporation, the same company that had built the *Hive* and her sister ships. The engineers had designed the floating warships to last ten, perhaps twenty years. No one had ever imagined they would end up becoming humanity's home for almost two and a half centuries. The ships should have fallen to pieces long ago, and they would have if not for the Hell Divers.

X took his duty seriously. Sure, the little perks like extra rations and private quarters were nice, but those weren't why he dived. He dived to keep humanity in the sky. Every decision he made on the surface affected whether they lived or died. And right now he was wasting time.

Peering down the long incline of brick and metal, he found himself weighing another decision. He could climb down and risk a tear to his suit, or find a way around. The radiation readings made the decision simple: a tear would result in a lingering, painful death.

He stepped closer to the edge to look for a way down. The darkness hid all sorts of traps that had claimed the lives of countless divers. He had watched teammates swallowed by sinkholes, crushed inside unstable buildings, shredded in dust storms that stretched for miles. Hell, he had even seen them torn apart by mutant things that had adapted to live in the radiation zones—zones like this one.

He reactivated his night vision and searched for signs of life. No motion and no heat signature—nothing to suggest that anything had crossed through here lately.

A strong gust pushed him back, and he stumbled to the side. He planted his boots, but the slight movement changed his view. A hundred feet to the west, a path that he had missed earlier curved to the bottom.

He worked his way over to the trail and picked his way down to the cracked street. There wasn't much cover between him and the buildings. Although he didn't see any movement, that didn't mean he was alone.

After making a final sweep of the area, he took off at a dead sprint across the open stretch. A blast of wind laced with dirt hit him a few feet from the building. He fought it, head tucked to his chest, and propped his back against the wall.

Hot breath fogged the inside of his visor as he rested for a few moments, eyes roving for threats, ears searching the whistling wind for anything out of the ordinary.

A brilliant delta of lightning streaked overhead, the thunderclap barely half a second behind. He waited for the noise to pass, then stepped away from the building to look at the double doors looming above him. They were sealed—a good sign that the building hadn't been raided yet.

Hugging the wall in a low crouch, he slunk to the

alleyway separating the cluster of warehouses. Another flurry of wind slammed into his suit as he stepped out into the narrow passage. He took a cautious step across to where the alley grew darker. Dust eddied and swirled through the narrow defile as he slowly worked toward a steel door pocked with rust.

X quickly brushed off the security panel, pulled a small cord from his vest pocket, and patched the cord into his minicomputer. Numbers flickered across the display, freezing in place a digit at a time. The access codes downloaded, and the security panel chirped. A series of hollow clicks sounded as the locking mechanisms worked for the first time in over two centuries.

He slowly pushed the door open with one hand, keeping the rifle leveled in the other. The metal creaked open to reveal a space about the size of the Hell Diver launch bay. He stood in the stillness, playing his weapon over the space and listening.

Row after row of shelves, stacked with boxes and metal crates, rose to the ceiling. A staircase to his right led to two mezzanine levels that extended over the aisles of storage. The ceiling sagged and bulged in one corner. He paused to examine the hole. It looked large enough for a man to crawl through, but he spied no sign of life.

The darkness always hid something, but he didn't have time for a full search. He grabbed the railing and took the stairs two at a time to the first landing. A catwalk stretched down the first aisle: shelves stacked with electrical cables. He continued up the stairs to the second platform. The shelves here were piled with what looked like computer parts and monitors.

He loped up the final stairs to the third platform. His heart leaped at the sight of stacked metal cases bearing the international radiation symbol.

Jackpot.

He hurried over, pulled a case from a shelf, and flipped the latches. The lid clicked open, and he felt his lips twist into a half grin. Five cylindrical power cells. He lost the smile, though—it didn't feel right. Three of his men had died for these. The cells would power the ship for years, but no matter how he looked at it, X couldn't see it as anywhere near an even trade.

Closing the lid, he grabbed the handle and traversed the catwalk. The cases were heavy, at least forty pounds. He would have to come back for more after he dropped the first at the supply crate.

X hurried across the mezzanine, footsteps clanking over nonskid metal, but beneath the echoey sound was another: a buzzing, almost electronic whine. He slid to a stop, ears on full alert, wondering whether he had tripped some sort of alarm.

The noise stopped abruptly, but the sudden silence only put him more on edge. He waited a beat, then walked on. His ears had played tricks on him in the past, picking up phantom sounds in a world of darkness. That was probably the case now. *Too keyed up, that's all.* He picked up the pace.

A second buzzing screech sounded when he was halfway along the platform. Not his imagination. Not an alarm, either. This was a cold, shrill noise.

And it was organic, not digital or electronic. In all his dives, he had never heard anything like it.

X bolted for the staircase. He grabbed the railing and swung down, two rungs at a time. He hit the second landing hard, stumbling and nearly toppling down the bottom flight.

Movement below pulled his gaze toward the floor. There was a wide crevice in the ground at the far end of the room—an entire missing floor section he hadn't seen earlier. A rookie mistake that could cost him his life—could cost *everybody's* life. He scanned the room more carefully now, looking for anything else he might have missed.

And he had.

He wasn't even sure what that something was. A trio of bulblike cocoons, covered in thick bristles and scabby tissue, like half-molted snakeskin, hung from the upper left corner of the ceiling, over the exit door. The shadows had disguised them when he entered the warehouse, but he could see them well enough from the stairs.

X took a step closer. Not cocoons, but nests, with openings at the crest and center. An outer rim of the coarse skin, like hardened lips, surrounded the ridges of the holes.

He took another step, accidentally banging the fuel-cell case against the guardrail with a loud clang.

A shrill screech sounded in response. He cursed in his mind, eyes flitting to the wall in the darkest part of the room, where a blob of flesh fell from one of the nests and dropped to the ground.

What in the hell … ?

X ducked down and held his breath. Through the gap in the railing, he could see something moving down there. It pushed at the floor with two hands and rose into a bipedal crouch. He stared, unbelieving, at the green-hued NVG image of what looked like a human physical structure. The creature let out another screech, which grew into a bellowing roar. Then it clambered out of view before he could get a better look.

Whatever it was, it had looked unsettlingly human. But that was impossible. They hadn't found a survivor on the surface in over a century. Nothing could survive the rads, especially here.

X duckwalked to the other side of the platform and scanned the warehouse. He caught a glimpse of the thing darting down one of the aisles. The screeching waned as it vanished with a yowl that sounded like the trailing end of an emergency siren.

Turning back to the exit, he found that he wasn't alone. On the floor beneath the nests, shrouded in darkness, perched a second figure.

Curiosity tugged at X, but he dare not move. He squeezed the rifle stock and the case of cells, afraid that his trembling hands might lose the precious cargo.

The creature dropped onto all fours and skittered to the open doorway. Each flash of lightning outside gave X a fleeting glimpse.

He clicked off his night vision with a bump of his chin and waited for the next strike. A second later, he gasped. Leathery, wrinkled skin the color of eggshells tightened as the creature stretched long limbs laced with ropy lean muscle. Its sinewy body was covered in long scars and bore several glistening abrasions.

Darkness enveloped the room again. When the next strike of lightning lit up the warehouse, the creature was arching its back.

Not a person, not an animal … a monster.

Spiked vertebrae protruded like bony fins from its back. They stopped at its thin neck, where they bottlenecked into scabrous flesh that crested a misshapen head. Thick bristles formed a sort of Mohawk, like the ridge of a feral hog's back, rising over the top of its skull.

X had to consciously slow his shallow, rapid breathing, which had begun to cloud his visor.

Keep it together, X. You have to keep it—

A piercing whine snapped him from his thoughts. He whirled and aimed his rifle at the shelves where the other creature had disappeared. The room was pitch black now. He clicked on his night vision, then clicked it back off when lightning flooded the warehouse through the open door.

Another screech followed, and he spun back to face the monster under the nests. It jerked its head toward him as if sensing his movement. But instead of seeing eyes or a nose, X saw only a wide gash of lips stretching from one side of its face to the other. The lips parted, widening to form a black hole rimmed with gleaming needle-pointed teeth.

"Holy Mother of God," X whispered.

He had seen enough. Cradling the case under one arm, he raised the rifle with the other and bumped his NVG back on. He would need the optics when he got back outside—*if* he got back outside.

That thought prompted a surge of energy. Squeezing the trigger, he charged down the stairs toward the exit. His aim was erratic, and most of the shots pinged off the metal wall behind the monster. Only one of the rounds found a target. The result was an impossibly loud screech of agony. It grew into a whine that seemed to cut right through him, and he had to resist the pointless urge to cup his hands over his helmet.

The other beast, which he still couldn't see, answered with a shriek of its own. The screeching morphed into what sounded almost like the emergency alarm before a dive. X slowed and searched the aisles of shelves to his right for the first monster but saw nothing.

Don't stop. Keep moving …

He pushed forward, through the open door and into the alleyway. The metal case clanked against his armor as he ran.

The high-pitched calls of other monsters he couldn't see joined the chorus. Together, they sounded so like an emergency siren, he had to wonder whether he was dreaming.

He glanced over his shoulder to see two silhouettes skulking in the doorway. One of them burst through the shadows, dropped to all fours, and galloped after him.

Move, X. MOVE!

He had no doubt that these things would tear him apart if they caught up with him. He had to get to the crate and deploy it back to the *Hive*.

He checked his HUD. The beacon was too far

away. These things moved *fast*—he would never make it. That left him with only one option: abandon the crate and get the cells back to the *Hive* on his own. But before he could activate his booster and ride his balloon back to the ship, he needed to find an opening in the clouds. The storm had weakened, but sporadic flashes still lit up the skyline. He pulled his gaze from the sky to glance over his shoulder. Both creatures were trailing him now, and they were gaining. The ganglier of the two broke out in front, using its hind legs to spring forward in great bounds.

X almost dropped the case when he tore around the corner of a tumbledown building. He focused on his breathing and keeping his footing in the darkness. When he was halfway down the next street, he turned to fire, hoping the rounds might at least deter the beasts.

The lead creature leaped through the air. X did his best to steady his aim and squeezed off a burst. The bullets lanced through the humanoid torso, and one clipped the top of its skull. It crashed to the asphalt, shrieking and pawing at multiple wounds that gushed scarlet. The other thing jumped onto a building and clambered up the stone-clad wall. Pulling itself through a broken window, it vanished inside.

The shots had bought X a few precious moments. He clutched the case under his right arm and fumbled for a new magazine, but his hand came up empty. He must have dropped them during his escape from the warehouse.

Muttering a curse, he tossed the now useless assault rifle to the ground and pulled the blaster from his hip holster. He glanced skyward to examine the storm. The optics turned the sky into a swirling sea of green, sparkling with emerald flashes of lightning. He couldn't deploy here. He had to keep running.

A flurry of screeches followed him as he rounded the corner of another building. The gunshots may have bought him time, but it must have attracted more of the monsters.

He caught a flicker of movement across the end of the street. It looked like a tarp or sheet—something very much out of place in the scrap heap of metal, concrete, and glass. The material was wrapped around a light pole and blowing in the wind.

Nausea sank into his gut.

It wasn't a tarp. It was a seven-cell parachute.

"Aaron," he choked.

He sprinted to the lamppost and slumped to his knees, forcing himself to look at his best friend's broken body.

Aaron was lying on his back, his arms and legs telescoped by the fall. Only tiny shards of the mirror-plated visor remained in his helmet. One of his eyes was open, but the other was gone, mashed along with the right side of his face.

A whining shriek sounded in the distance. A second and a third quickly followed. X set the crate and his blaster on the ground and grabbed Aaron's hand. He squeezed it before placing it neatly next to his broken body. X didn't whisper any goodbyes or say any last words to his dead friend. He just closed Aaron's remaining eyelid and stood up to stare at the storm. It was weakening, the flashes much less frequent now. Meanwhile, the electronic-sounding whines grew closer.

X was out of time.

Two of the creatures emerged at the other end of the street. They paced back and forth, as if unsure where he was. But when he reached for the cells and the blaster, their faceless heads shot in his direction. He stood his ground for a moment, studying the monstrosities.

A high-pitched screech broke from a window in the building behind him. His eyes darted upward at two more of the beasts, skidding down the surface. They perched on the curb, swaying their heads to study him.

X didn't hesitate. He raised the blaster, trained the muzzle on one of the creatures, and pulled the trigger.

Crack!

An eyeless face disintegrated in a cloud of bone and flesh. The second shot blew a leg off the other beast.

By the time he turned, the other two were darting up the street toward him. They had already narrowed the gap by half. Three others had joined the chase, their otherworldly wails growing louder as they raced to catch up.

Heart thudding like a trip-hammer, he shoved the blaster into its holster and cradled the case of cells against his chest with his other arm. Then he reached over his shoulder and pressed a button on his booster. A balloon shot upward out of the canister, and helium rushed inside with a loud whoosh.

The abominations barreled toward him, and for the first time he saw them up close: the bristles cresting from their scabby skulls, their thin bodies, the lean, sinewy muscles and the curved talons on their hands and feet. He could even see the even rows of pointed teeth. The scarred and wrinkled flesh blurred together as all three lunged at once.

X closed his eyes and braced himself, but instead of crashing to the ground under a flurry of claws and teeth, he was yanked off his feet and into the air. His eyes snapped open as the beasts collided into one another where he had stood only a moment before. Long limbs reached up, claws slashing at his ankles. Then, as he watched in horror, the pack of five converged on Aaron's body and began to feed. They tore him limb from limb, fighting greedily over his remains and shrieking in their high-pitched wails.

X closed his eyes and forced himself to think of happier times—all the way back to when he and Aaron had been young men, long before Tin was born and long before their wives had died. He wanted to scream, wanted to punch something. But all he could do was hold the precious case to his chest and trust the lighter-than-air buoyancy hauling him upward.

When he opened his eyes again, he was in darkness. The city was gone, lost below the clouds, and he could no longer hear the shrieks of the creatures. Lightning bloomed in the towering clouds, and thunder answered, close enough to rattle his body. He watched the static arc spiderweb across the sky, and hoped for a moment that it would strike him.

But he survived. For some reason, Xavier Rodriguez survived yet again while better men died.

A brilliant strike of lightning sizzled through

the clouds, exposing the oval outline of the *Hive* far above. The ship was already maneuvering into position, the turbofans whirring. Captain Ash had detected his beacon and was adjusting to pick him up. Circular metal doors, looking no larger than his thumb, opened in the bottom of the ship.

X cradled the case in his right arm and reached for a toggle with his left hand. He pulled down on the handle gently, just so, guiding his helium-filled canopy toward the reentry bay. His body swayed as the harnesses redirected the balloon.

A moment later, the ship swallowed him, and the top of his balloon hit the plastic dome of the recovery bay. With nowhere to go, he hung in the air, watching the black clouds churn beneath his feet, and waited for the techs to reseal the bay.

The doors clamped shut, and he reached over his shoulder to punch the button on his booster. The balloon slowly deflated, the helium escaping as he was lowered to the deck.

A cloud of antiseptic mist blasted him as the room repressurized. When it cleared, he saw a team of technicians in yellow suits surrounding the plastic dome. He shuddered at the sight, remembering the monsters twenty thousand feet below. But instead of teeth and talons, only gentle hands awaited him.

Call it luck, mojo, or divine intervention, but X had successfully completed his ninety-sixth jump.

THREE

Captain Ash, with two Militia soldiers flanking her, rushed to the drop bay. Despite her condition, she was still outrunning them both.

"Only one diver made it back?" she asked.

Neither man responded. They were too busy keeping the shouting passengers on both sides of the hallway from getting too close. The corridors were unusually crowded at this late hour. There was only one explanation: someone on her staff had leaked information about the dive.

She would have Jordan deal with that later.

"Move it," the soldier on her left said. He strode ahead and pushed through a knot of teenagers loitering in Ash's path. They were pointing and staring at fresh red paint on the wall that read "*Equal rights for lower-deckers.*"

She didn't slow at the increasingly familiar sight. There was no time right now to deal with the threat of civil unrest from those who lived belowdecks. Her focus was on keeping the damn ship in the air.

With the kids out of the way, Ash picked up speed. It was a five-minute walk or a two-minute run. She ran. The heavy footfalls of boots followed her as the soldiers tried their best to keep up.

The sea of passengers funneling through the hallways reminded her how the *Hive* got its name. Long ago, the ship had been commissioned as the *Persephone,* but as the years passed and the hallways and compartments grew darker, the passengers had started calling it the "Hive." The name had stuck. Most of these people didn't even know the ship's original name.

The launch bay was bustling with activity when she arrived. A medic rushed through the doors just in front of her, and she followed him into the vaulted facility toward a yellow-suited mob. The plastic dome over the reentry bay was surrounded by technicians, watching as the diver inside went through the cleansing process. A grappling hook pulled the dome away a moment later, and violet mist spilled from the sides. Vents sucked it away.

"Out of the way!" came a muffled shout.

The yellow suits parted, and the black matte armor of a diver emerged. The man staggered from the crowd with a case in his hands. He set it on the ground, and his visor homed in on Ash.

"Thank, God," one of the technicians said, bending down to scoop up the case.

God? Ash thought. *God's got fuck-all to do with what happens up here.* Then again, God may have had *everything* to do with what was happening up here. Who could say?

"Captain!" the diver shouted.

Ash froze in her tracks. It was X.

He shoved a technician out of the way and removed his helmet. His forehead glistened with sweat. Those brown eyes that Ash knew all too well narrowed in on her.

"What the fuck happened!" X yelled.

He tossed his helmet and powered through a few outliers who had stopped to gawk. The helmet clanked on the deck and rolled to a stop a few feet from Ash.

"Why the hell didn't you delay the launch!"

"Commander, you're hurt," a medic began to say. "Let me check you for—"

"I'm fine," X growled, waving him away.

"I'm sorry," Ash said, holding up a hand but standing her ground. She felt someone step up on her left. She didn't have to look to know it was Jordan. "There was a faulty sensor," she continued. "We didn't know we were dropping you into a storm until it was too late. You know how fast the weather can blow up. It's unpredictable."

X stopped a few feet away from them, so close she could smell his breath. His chest heaved in and out, and his fierce eyes roved from Jordan to Ash.

"*Unpredictable?*" he snorted. "That's horseshit and you know it. Your ops team should have seen it."

"You think I would send you into a storm on purpose?" Ash said. "You think I would intentionally try to kill my best divers?" She didn't think she sounded condescending, but X continued to glare at her.

"Well you did pretty well—killed all of 'em but one. Will. Rodney. Aaron. Dead. And you expect me to believe it's because of a faulty *sensor*?

How about you tell *Tin* that. Tell him his dad died because of cheap electronics that your people were too goddamn lazy to troubleshoot."

Ash looked at the floor and then back at X. "I'll tell him his dad died for *those.*" She pointed at the metal case at X's feet. "He died to keep us in the air."

X shook his head and stalked off, muttering an oath.

Ignoring Jordan's whispered plea to let the diver go on his way, Ash followed him into the hall.

"Commander!" Ash barked.

X paused, chest still heaving, but kept his back to her.

"I'm sorry, Xavier. Truly sorry. We lost good men today. But they didn't die in vain. Those cells will keep our reactors running for years."

X bowed his head and shoved his hands into his pockets, his face half turned in her direction.

"Aaron told me long ago that if anything should happen to him on a dive, he wanted you to take care of Tin," Ash said.

"I know. Those were his last words. I'm done, Captain. You got that? No more fucking jumps. After what I saw today, I'm through. Between the pointless deaths of my team, and the creatures I saw down there ..." His volume lowered as his words trailed off.

Ash considered letting it go, but if there was another threat on the surface, she needed to know about it. She kept her voice cool and calm. "What did you see down there, X?"

"Done," he said, barely above a whisper.

"Xavier, I need to know what you saw."

"I don't *know* what I saw," he snapped. "But I never want to see it again." He took a step down the hall and stopped. Glancing back at her, he said, "They were monsters. Something I've never seen before." Then he was gone, off to find a bottle of 'shine or maybe something even stronger.

Although she would be well within her rights, Ash wasn't going to reprimand him for insubordination or recall him to his duty, either. Her heart ached for X. Ached for Tin. Ached for everyone on the ship who had lost a loved one. But her rational, efficient mind also knew that X had spoken out of anger. He was addicted to diving as much as he was to the booze. He wasn't going to give either of them up anytime soon.

Ash tugged on the sides of her uniform to straighten it. They had succeeded in their mission today, but the ship was running out of Hell Divers. She couldn't afford to lose X. One way or another, he would be back in the drop tubes the next time the *Hive* needed him.

*   *   *   *   *

It was morning, not that you could tell by the blackness outside the portholes. The airship drifted through the clouds above the eastern edge of the continent once known as North America.

On a normal day, X would have ignored the slight rocking motion and the clank of footsteps from the sea of passengers hurrying through the dimly lit hallways, off to start their shifts at whatever job or task was theirs to do, each of them weighed down with the worries and frustrations and minor indignities that went with life aboard the stifling environment of a broken airship.

On a normal day, X would have just rolled over to sleep off his hangover. Aaron had always said he could sleep through a level-five alarm, but this morning he was awake and dressed before nine, because today wasn't a normal day. Today they would honor the members of Team Raptor who had made the ultimate sacrifice to prolong the miserable lives of those aboard the *Hive*. It was purely cere-monial, of course. When they lost a diver, there was never a body to burn.

X walked to Aaron's apartment to pick up Tin. Snaking along the corridor ceiling were the red pipes carrying helium, and next to them the narrower-gauge white pipes for water and yellow for natural gas, and the wider black sewage lines. He heard the twang of lower-deckers as they complained about tight rations, and the more refined accent of the upper-deckers moaning about the same thing.

The walls, ceiling, and bulkheads had all been covered in murals and graffiti. Some of the artists had a sense of irony, painting fluffy white clouds over the hatches that covered the ship's windows to hide what clouds really looked like. The rusted steel curtains were centuries old. No one but Captain Ash seemed to care anymore what was on the other side.

"Hey, X," said a familiar voice from the crowd. He nodded at Tony, the lead Hell Diver from Team

Angel, who quickly vanished in the sea of passengers. Pausing, X held his ground in the surging mass of people to study the image of an ocean wave painted around one of the red helium pipes. Large gray fins protruded from the faded blue.

The picture brought to mind the creatures he had seen on the surface. He still had no idea what the hell they were, or how he would describe them to Captain Ash and the other Hell Diver teams.

As a boy, he had longed to see what was on the surface. He had heard the stories about a green world with growing things, and a blue sky, and he believed them. Then he had seen what the world was really like. Humans could never return to that poisoned desolate surface. They could never risk landing the airship. It wouldn't last a day in the radioactive wasteland, or survive the monsters lurking there.

X walked on, studying his surroundings as if for the last time. He did the same thing before a jump. His mind, by force of habit, wanted to experience everything it could just in case he didn't make it back. Usually, this involved booze. Today, it meant taking in the sights, sounds, and smells of the *Hive* in all its battered glory.

Pushing through the next corridor intersection, X thought of all the Hell Divers who had been sacrificed to keep the airship in the sky. What bothered him even more than the lingering burn on his skin was his inability to remember their faces. His first diving mentor had warned him that the first thing you forgot about someone was the sound of their voice. That had certainly proved true with Rhonda. He couldn't quite recall the lilt of his wife's voice, but he would never forget the dying screams of his comrades over the years.

At the next junction, he saw something that stopped him again. The single LED overhead illuminated a snaking line of men, women, and children of all races and ages, mostly dressed in rumpled rags, waiting for their daily food ration.

These were the lower-deckers, who did the important but dirty jobs that kept the ship running. Frail and hollow eyed, they were easy to spot. Many of them had cancer—only one floor of shielding separated their two communal living spaces from the nuclear reactors. No matter what engineering did, the radiation seemed to get through to the lower decks.

The sight was never easy to stomach, but it was reality. And it wasn't going to get better anytime soon.

He eyed the Christian crosses some of them wore around their necks. Their belief in God and the hope of something better after death seemed to help them come to terms with their squalid lives. Like a lot of others, X followed no religious doctrine. Pascal's wager posited that a rational person should live as though God existed, and seek to believe in God, but then, X wasn't an entirely rational person. He was a Hell Diver. If God did exist, he had better things to bother with than the fate of the human race. The closest he got to God was at the end of a bottle of 'shine.

The lower-deckers made up the majority of the

Hive's population. They were the citizens he had spent his life trying to save even as he watched their quality of life deteriorate every day. In moments such as this, he wondered what he was saving them *from.* Maybe there really was a heaven after death, and all his efforts did was prolong their suffering and delay their passage to a blissful paradise.

"Hurry up!" a woman at the end of the line yelled, pulling X back to reality. "My son hasn't eaten in two days!" A pale, hairless boy stood next to her, his hand clasped in hers. She saw X staring and glared at him with contempt. "What you looking at, mista?"

X wanted to say something, give some bland and useless words of comfort and hope, but it seemed pointless. He shied away from her gaze as the line surged forward. Two gray-uniformed Militia soldiers stepped closer to the crowd. That small motion quieted all but one of the restless lower-deckers.

A man in a black trench coat emerged from the crowd. He swept a stringy black dreadlock from his face and pointed to the floor. "Do you assholes even know what it's like to live down there?" He shook his head at the ringing silence that followed. A second man, with a scarf pulled up to his nose, joined him. They stood their ground, staring at the sentries, who reached for their batons.

X considered stepping in to help the soldiers, even though it wasn't his duty, but the moment the Militia guards moved forward, the two lower-deckers melted back into the crowd—stupid enough to mouth off, but not stupid enough to get thrown in the brig.

X continued through the next hall, where another sentry stood guard outside a steel door. It led to the farms, one of the most heavily guarded areas on the ship. The crops grown beyond that door were barely enough to keep starvation at bay for the *Hive,* and sometimes a desperate citizen or small group would try to break in and steal food.

Taking a left, X veered off the main corridor. A short, bald man in a maroon robe brushed into him. Their eyes met, and seeing the red coveralls with the white arrow HD insignia, the man threw up his grimy hands.

"Sorry," he mumbled, and hurried away, his sandals squeaking with every step.

X fished into his pocket at once, checking his key card. Feeling it, he relaxed and brushed a grubby handprint off his shoulder. The guy was one of a few Buddhist monks on the ship. That didn't make him a pickpocket, but thieves lurked all over the *Hive.* Normally, they didn't mess with a Hell Diver. After all, without X, the crooks would have nothing to steal.

Tin was waiting. X jogged down the hallway, which curved and narrowed into a corridor lined with hatches on both sides. The apartments were cramped, but it beat the communal spaces beneath his feet, where the lower-deckers lived.

Outside an apartment door stood a short figure holding a bag and wearing a crooked metallic hat.

Seeing Tin, X felt a tug at his heart. The boy was small for his age, and skinny. His blue trousers and black sweatshirt hung loose from his gaunt frame. His tinfoil hat, the source of his nickname, arched into a spike, like some ancient gladiator's helmet. Blond hair spilled over his ears. Tin glanced up with the same bright blue eyes that looked like his fathers, but quickly looked away.

X put a hand on the boy's shoulder. "You got everything you need?"

Tin glanced down at his bag and nodded.

"You ready to go?" X asked.

Tin nodded again and pulled out of X's grasp. He hadn't said a word since Aaron's death. X didn't blame him. He hadn't felt much like talking, either. He followed the boy down the hall to the launch bay where they would honor his dead father.

*   *   *   *   *

The dimmed overhead LEDs spread a carpet of blue light over the *Hive*'s launch bay. Captain Ash stood in the center of the room. She turned away from the dark portholes and took a moment to examine the twelve plastic domes covering the launch tubes in front of her. Each had sent countless Hell Divers to their deaths, and now a small crowd had gathered to mourn the loss of three more.

Ash could not help reflecting on the original purpose for the tubes: to drop not people but bombs—the very bombs that had turned the surface into a wasteland, forcing humans to take to the sky in the very ships that had doomed them.

The *Hive* was never designed to be a life raft. It was a weapon, one of fifty built in the late twenty-first century for the war that did, in fact, end all wars. Flying at an average altitude of twenty thousand feet and impervious to electromagnetic pulses, the *Hive* and her sister ships were the military's response to electronic warfare that rendered even the most advanced drones and jets obsolete.

According to the records that Ash, as captain, was privy to, the world had ended so fast that the airships had become lifeboats for the families of military brass, who had boarded them before the bombs dropped and made the surface uninhabitable. Much of humanity's past was lost in those chaotic days. She didn't even know what had caused the conflict, or which side was in the right. Hell, she didn't even know who the sides had been. She only knew that the darkness and the electrical storms outside the portholes were the result of what her ancestors had done.

The people gathered in front of her didn't care about history. They didn't ask why the sun was hidden behind miles of dark clouds and lightning. Unlike Captain Ash, the poor souls aboard the *Hive* weren't hell-bent on making up for the sins of their great-great-great-grandparents. Most of them didn't even know they were the descendants of the men and women who had brought humanity to the edge of extinction. And most of them, like her own staff, had long since given up on Ash's dream of finding a new home somewhere on the surface. Every captain before her had promised the same thing, but these people no longer seemed to care. They were driven by a far more basic desire: to survive.

In the center of the group stood Aaron's son.

Tears glistened on his pale cheeks. X stood on his right, eyes downcast and three days of stubble covering his face.

Ash wished the ritual weren't so familiar, but she had seen too many orphans and grieving families. The boy deserved to know why his father had died.

Folding her hands together, she launched into the speech she had given so often she knew it cold. "Today we gather to celebrate the lives of three men who made the ultimate sacrifice so that the rest of us might live. They dived so that humankind could survive. For these men, diving was a duty they performed time and time again without complaint, without question."

She pointed at the plastic domes. "For two hundred and fifty years, the Hell Divers have dropped from these tubes to keep us in the air. And on this last mission, they succeeded, once again, in bringing back the fuel cells that keep us in the sky. For their service and their sacrifice, we salute them."

The captain raised a hand into the perfect salute and held it there. She kept her gaze on Tin as the crowd whispered their thanks to the fallen men.

The room fell silent, and Ash dropped her salute. One by one, the crowd filtered out of the double doors.

Jordan squeezed into the launch bay and hurried over to Ash. The moment the last mourner had left, he cleared his throat. "Captain, we have another problem."

She gave her XO a sharp look. "What now?"

"Please follow me," Jordan said.

She hurried after him to the bridge, her mind

racing with every step. The crowded hallways were not the place to have a conversation about another potential issue with the ship. The thought reminded her, she was supposed to visit the lower-deckers later today. It had been weeks since she last showed her face down there.

"Captain," said a sentry posted in front of the bridge. He waved his key card over the security panel, it chirped, and the door whispered open. Ash strode inside and paused at the railing that curved around the topmost deck of the bridge. The two floors below were thrumming with activity.

She followed Jordan to the first deck, past the oak wheel, all the way to the wall-mounted main display. He reached up to flick the screen.

"We just picked up an SOS from *Ares*," Jordan said.

Ash felt a tightness in the pit of her stomach. They hadn't heard from the other airship in weeks. Last she knew, they were on a recon mission to locate a second cache of nuclear fuel cells hundreds of miles to the west, out of range of digital communication.

"We're still trying to hail them, but there's a ton of electrical interference. All we have to go on now is the message we intercepted."

Ash resisted the urge to massage her achy throat. "Play it."

Jordan turned and snapped his fingers. "Ensign Ryan, feed that message to the main screen."

"Aye, Captain," the ensign replied. He shifted his glasses and sat down at his station on the floor above where Ash and Jordan stood.

A moment later, an image of Captain Willis

emerged on the screen. Lines crackled across the display, the feed cutting in and out. But even with the fuzzy video, Willis looked awful. His white hair had receded even further. Deep creases on his forehead overshadowed a scar that ran from his eyebrow to his hairline.

Ash took a seat in her chair.

"Maria. Captain Ash. God, I hope this message gets through. *Ares* was severely damaged in a freak electrical storm a week ago. We lost several generators, and we've been forced to shut down all reactors. We're running on backup power. I'm deploying an HD team to the surface to search for critical parts and cells, but we need your help."

Static crackled from the PA speakers above.

Ash clamped the headset over her ears. A few seconds passed before the audio returned.

"We are hovering above the following coordinates: forty-one degrees, fifty-two minutes, forty-one seconds north; eighty-seven degrees, thirty-seven minutes, forty-seven seconds west."

A second wave of white noise sizzled across the room.

Ash looked up at Jordan. A hint of fear flickered in his eyes. They both knew the coordinates by heart. It was the location of an Old World metropolis, dead in the center of a red zone. The radiation was so high, and the surface temperature so low, that only three missions had ever been attempted to retrieve cells from the area. All three had failed, with all divers lost.

She couldn't remember the city's original name. Everyone on the ship just called the wasteland "Hades."

"Captain, what are your orders?" Jordan asked.

The transmission replayed over and over in her mind. *Damn it,* how could Willis have been such a fool? Sure, every captain knew that Hades was home to Industrial Tech Corporation, the company that had designed and built their airships, and that its headquarters was a gold mine of power cells and repair parts. But as with all great treasure troves, Hades was cursed.

"Cancel my visit to the lower decks, Jordan," she said. "I won't be visiting today."

"Aye, Captain."

As Jordan turned to leave, she added, "Get me Samson and X. I need to see both of them, ASAP."

"Understood."

Ash sank back in her chair as Jordan loped up the stairs. She didn't know what desperation had driven Willis to Hades. But even if Ash could fix the *Hive,* she wasn't sure there was anything she could do to save *Ares.*

FOUR

Commander Rick Weaver shifted in and out of consciousness. The closer he came to reality, the more he wanted to stay asleep. In his fragmented dreams, he was still with his family aboard *Ares*. He could still see his wife, Jennifer, and the freckled faces of his daughters, Kayla and Cassie, standing in the crowd of family members in the launch bay.

"Promise me you're coming back," Jennifer said.

He gazed into those green eyes for a moment. "I promise, baby." He sealed the words with a kiss.

"Bye, Daddy," Kayla said, looking up with the wide, curious eyes of a seven-year-old still innocent of the real world's horrors. Five-year-old Cassie had even less of a clue. And that was fine with him.

"I'll be back in no time," Weaver said. He leaned down and hugged them both, then gave Jennifer a last lingering kiss.

A stab of pain shook him free of the memory. He opened his eyes to find his family gone, replaced by a sky the color of bruises. Lightning flashed overhead, splitting through the clouds like a network of veins.

"No," he choked, reaching toward the storm.

He closed his eyes again in a vain attempt to stay a few more minutes with his wife and daughters.

The rumble of thunder kept him from slipping away. Reality slowly closed in. His family was four miles up there, waiting for him to return with the fuel cells and pressure valves that would save his home and everyone on it.

A voice called out. "Commander, can you hear me?"

Weaver gradually became aware of being on his back, and of someone shaking his armored shoulder. He blinked away the stars floating before his eyes and saw a mirrored visor staring down at him. He recognized the small cross cresting above the visor. It was Ralph Jones, the youngest member of Team Titanium.

"Where's Jay and Sarah?" Weaver mumbled.

Jones shook his head.

Another fragmented memory surfaced: the flash of lightning that hit both divers in free fall. They were dead before they even had a chance to open their chutes.

His eyes lingered on the little white cross. The only thing he really knew about the new guy was that he was a deeply religious man and that this was his fifth jump. Jones had done well in training, but he had almost no surface time. But no matter. He had survived, and Weaver was glad to have another diver at his side.

"Let me help you up, sir," Jones said. He grabbed Weaver under his arm and gently hoisted him into a sitting position. The frozen landscape surrounding them came into focus, and Weaver got his first look at Hades. The skeletal remains of the Old World city stretched to the west. Mounds of snow, like castle walls, bordered the once great metropolis. But these ramparts didn't guard a magical kingdom like those in the books he'd seen. This place was cursed.

"Help me up," Weaver said.

Jones pulled the aluminum capewell covers and popped the capewells free, releasing Weaver from his chute. Then he grabbed him under both armpits and helped him to his feet.

"Shit," Jones said. "Looks like your booster is toast."

Weaver craned his neck and looked at the pack. The helium balloon hung from a crack in the metal booster.

"Great. Just fucking great."

Weaver took another look at their surroundings.

"Sir, I'm not picking up any other beacons," Jones said.

Putting aside the matter of the broken booster, Weaver tapped his wrist computer and waited for the digital telemetry to emerge on his HUD. The data fired and solidified in the subscreen. Besides the beacons of the two supply crates *Ares* had dropped, there was no sign of Jay or Sarah or of Team Gold. Captain Willis had deployed Gold twelve hours earlier. No beacons meant they were dead—whether from the dive or from something else, Weaver wasn't sure. There had been no radio transmission after Gold jumped. The entire team, his brothers and sisters, had joined in death every diver before them who ever tried to jump into Hades.

The weight of this realization squeezed the last

vestiges of grogginess from Weaver, and he snapped alert. Everything was riding on him and Jones. They had forty-eight hours to return to *Ares* with the nuclear cells and pressure valves and save roughly half the humans in existence. The doomsday clock was ticking along in sync with his heartbeat.

He steadied his breathing and took a moment to examine the map on his HUD. The first supply crate that *Ares* had dropped was less than a mile away, but their main target, the ITC headquarters, was six miles from their current location. They would have to trek through the city to reach their objective. *Ares* had dropped a second crate a quarter mile from the HQ.

Weaver's eyes flitted to the radiation readings displayed under the map on his HUD. Whatever luck had saved him from dying in the storm seemed to have vanished when they reached the surface.

"We need to get moving," he said. "Radiation's off the graph here."

Jones nodded his acknowledgment and jogged ahead, his boots crunching over the snow. The greenish-black of his suit's exoskeleton looked alien against the stark white landscape, the blue glow from the circular battery unit the only sign of life in a place where there was only death.

Weaver pulled the duct-taped handle of his revolver from his holster and gripped the gun in his gloved hand. He would have preferred the blaster, but he had lost it on the dive. They would need to keep moving fast if they wanted to reach their objective without attracting the attention of whatever lived in this frozen waste.

No one had ever returned from Hades to describe what was down here, and with the loss of Team Gold, Weaver's mind ran wild with images of mutant creatures prowling the city—monsters he didn't want to encounter without a bigger team and heavy weapons. He imagined the beasts he had seen on other dives: lizards the size of a half-grown child, and one-eyed birds with scaly wings. There were also the massive "stone beasts" he had seen on a salvage dive in the desert city of Las Vegas. The rocky abominations moved like Turtles, but his friend Ned Rico had stumbled into a building where the monsters sat camouflaged, looking like the work of a deranged sculptor. One of them had chomped Rico in half with its massive crocodilian jaws.

The wind howled like a wild animal in the distance. This was Hades—whatever awaited them out there was going to be a lot worse than some mutated little reptile or bird.

"Think we can get across that?" Jones asked, pointing to a bridge over an ice-covered waterway. The structure had partly collapsed, but the right side was intact. Barely four feet wide, but it would have to do; they didn't have time to backtrack or find another way across the ice.

"Follow me," Weaver ordered. He tested the ground with one foot and cautiously made his way across. When they reached the other side, he took off at a brisk trot.

His helmet bobbed up and down as he ran, making it a little harder to scan the windowless buildings that lined both sides of the road as they entered the city's outskirts. Countless decades of accumulating snow had buried much of the Old World, perhaps hiding pitfalls while leaving only the tallest structures visible.

An arctic blast bulldozed into him, making him stagger sideways. Planting his boots against the blustering wind, he couldn't shake the feeling of being watched.

Stay focused, Rick. Pay attention to what's real.

His eyes went to his HUD again. It was hard to believe that anything could survive out here for long. The sensor readings put the temperature at negative twenty-five degrees Fahrenheit, though he was warm enough inside the layered suit. Indeed, his skin felt slimy from the heat. He blinked away a drop of sweat and relaxed into a loping run, keeping Jones' blue silhouette in his peripheral vision. Jones maneuvered around jagged obstacles with a grace that reminded Weaver that he was twice Jones' age. He was having a hard time keeping up with the younger man.

"Stay close," he ordered.

Towers framed his view to the west, blocking his view of the industrial zone. They were in the heart of the city now, surrounded by ruins and tilted or broken skyscrapers. He continued to scan the area for signs of life, but the shifting snow was covering their tracks almost as they made them.

"Hold up," Weaver said. He stopped and crouched. "We gotta get off this road. We're too exposed here."

He spied an off-ramp that led northwest. They were getting close to the first crate. Only a quarter mile now. The thought put an extra spring in his step as they pushed their way down the street.

"Up there," Weaver said, pointing toward a steep snowbank that rose up from the roadside.

He leaped onto the pile and pulled his way up on all fours. At the top, he dropped to his belly, pulled the binos from his tactical vest, and glassed the area, searching for the crate.

Jones dropped down beside him and pulled out his binos.

"Looks like we have to find a way around that," Weaver said, pointing to a massive sinkhole that had swallowed an entire city block to the northwest.

Jones checked his minicomputer, then looked back over the landscape.

"You sure?" he said. "The map shows the crate's beacon somewhere between here and that hole."

Weaver brushed off the layer of snow that had stuck to his visor. Jones was right. They were damn close to the supply box.

"Let's move," Weaver said. He scrambled to his feet and took off in a rolling trot toward the sinkhole. His eyes darted from the nav marker on his HUD to the cavernous pit in front of him. He panted as he worked his way through the thick snow, every stride more exhausting than the last.

"Wait up!" Jones called after him.

"*Keep* up!" Weaver shouted back. He clambered over hunks of icy metal and courses of brick protruding from the ground. Reaching the edge, he dug his boots into the snow and pivoted to brace against the gusting wind. The crate's beacon blinked on his HUD. They were right on top of it. Their supplies, weapons, and extra boosters—it all was supposed to be right there. A blast of ice and grit whistled past him, nudging him closer to the edge.

Jones arrived a second later, gasping for air, his hands on his armor-plated knees. "It's got … It's got to be down there."

"Hold my armor," Weaver said.

Jones slipped his fingers under Weaver's back plate, and Weaver leaned closer to the side for a better look. The pit was too dark for his night-vision optics to penetrate, so he snatched a flare from his vest, tore off the end, and rubbed it against the coarse striking surface. Red flame shot out the end. He held the crackling flare over the edge, and fuzzy outlines of rubble came into view. And there in the center of it all, canted at a steep angle on a pile of concrete and rebar, was the supply crate.

Weaver cursed the technicians. They never managed to drop the crates close to the DZ, and this time, they had dropped it straight into the only sinkhole within a mile of the target zone.

"It's here," Weaver said. "We've gotta find a way down."

He waved the flare left and then right. The red glow spread across the bottom of the hole. There was something else down there. Where there should be only snow, he could see a half-dozen lumps the size of massive pumpkins, covered in some sort of spikes or thorns. Jones held on tighter as another gust of wind slammed into them. Scrambling to keep his balance, Weaver dropped the flare and watched it tumble lazily to the bottom. It hissed, and a halo of red blossomed out to light the enclosed space.

"*Shit,*" Weaver said. He was reaching for his binos, when the floor of the pit came strangely alive. A tremor rippled across the snow, and the thorny bulges dotting the ground began to move.

Weaver stared, dumbfounded. It had to be some sort of illusion.

"Jones, I … I see something," he whispered.

To his astonishment, one of the lumps shook itself and slowly rose up on what looked like two long, gangly legs.

"There's something else down there?" Jones asked.

Weaver took a full step back and tried to say something, but a croak was all he could muster. He didn't need his binos to see that the thing was some sort of humanoid creature. For a fleeting moment, he wondered if it was a Hell Diver who had somehow managed to survive.

He leaned back for a better look, flinching when the beast dropped to all fours and shambled toward the flare. It crouched next to it, tilting a face Weaver couldn't see, and pawed at the fire streaking across the snow. With a shriek of agony, it snapped its hand away from the brilliant glowing heat and darted away, still yowling. In a matter of seconds, similar creatures had arisen from the other strange lumps on the sinkhole floor, and they, too, were shrieking. The wails reverberated out of the hole and morphed into a high-pitched noise that hurt his ears.

Questions, too crazy even to give voice to, bounced and tumbled in his mind.

"What in the hell *is* that!" Jones shouted.

Weaver felt Jones' grip on his armor loosen. "Don't let go!" he snapped. He looked through his binos. The creatures seemed to distort and shift in the glow, but he could see the bizarre wrinkled skin and the jagged vertebrae as they gathered around the flare. The frailest of the group crouched next to another thorny blob in the snow and clawed at it.

Weaver zoomed in and the creature's head came into focus. A bony crest jutted up from its skull.

"What do you see?" Jones asked, his voice trembling over the comm.

The creature suddenly tilted its face in Weaver's direction and stared directly at him. But it wasn't looking at him; it couldn't. The thing had no eyes.

Weaver almost dropped his binos when he saw a meaty red cord hanging from the thing's thin lips. The beast tilted its head back and swallowed it whole. Then it bent down to pluck another piece from the crimson snow and scrambled away, the rope swinging from its mouth. That was when Weaver saw the armored body of a diver in the center of the pit. Jay or Sarah, but the corpse was so mangled, he couldn't tell from here.

Amazement turned to raw fear. "Pull me back!" Weaver said. "Pull me the fuck back and run!"

"Why? What'd you see?"

"Do it!"

Jones yanked him back to safety and took off, his labored breath crackling over the channel as Weaver took another cautious step backward. His slight movements provoked the monsters into a frenzy of motion, and they let out a chorus of whines that intensified until Weaver couldn't stand it anymore. He froze, as if paralyzed by the sounds.

Sirens—they sounded just like emergency sirens.

Motion in the center of the pit snapped him out of his shocked reverie. The creatures scattered in all directions and leaped onto the walls. Some clambered up the near-vertical surface; others, missing a hand- or foothold, slid back down, their claws scrabbling over the rock.

Weaver still wasn't sure whether it was Jay or Sarah down there, but it didn't matter—there was nothing he could do to help them. He eyed the crate one last time and then turned to run.

*   *   *   *   *

Chief Engineer Samson opened the door to Captain Ash's office, stepped inside, and slammed it shut behind him. His cheeks were so covered with grime and sweat, Ash couldn't tell whether he was grinning or grimacing.

She gestured to the chair in front of her desk. "Have a seat."

"I'll stand," he replied, wiping a filthy sleeve across his forehead. "I need to get back to engineering as soon as possible."

Ash grabbed the glass of water she had poured for herself, and handed it to him. He gulped it down.

"I hope you have *something* good to tell me."

Samson gently placed the empty glass on her desk and said, "I've managed to get seven of the eight reactors back online. My crews have also patched

HELL DIVERS   75

four of the internal gas bladders. We're operating at eighty percent power—best we've had in years."

Ash smiled—an expression so unfamiliar, it made her cheeks ache. "Excellent news, and right in the nick of time. We received a distress beacon from *Ares*." The smile disappeared as she remembered the message.

"An SOS?" Samson blurted.

"They lost several generators in a storm and were forced to shut down their reactors. They're running on backup power. Captain Willis sent a team to the surface to retrieve nuclear fuel cells and parts, but they've requested our help."

"And?"

"I was waiting for you to fix the *Hive* before I made a decision."

"It's not exactly fixed." Samson ran a hand back and forth over his smooth scalp. "What kind of help did Captain Willis request?"

"He didn't specify. The transmission cut out. All I know right now is that *Ares* is in trouble and they need our help."

Samson crinkled his nostrils. "We're in the best shape we've been in years. We shouldn't risk—"

"Which is exactly why we're in a position to help," Ash said, cutting him off. She didn't have time to argue with the engineer or anyone else. Besides, she had called him to her office for a report on the *Hive,* not for his opinion on helping *Ares*.

"Anything else?" she asked.

He shook his head and left her office without another word.

A moment later, Jordan entered. "X is on his

way," he said. "Should be here in fifteen minutes."

Ash paced behind her desk as they waited. The dull, tarnished plaque on the wall caught her eye: *Commissioned in 2029. US Army. Model #43.*

"Hard to believe there are only two left," Jordan said.

"Might be only one left if we don't answer Captain Willis' call."

He waited for her orders. She wasn't ready to give them—not until she talked to the most experienced Hell Diver on the ship.

A knock sounded on the other side of the door, and Jordan opened it. X stood outside, with his back turned to them.

"Come in, Commander," Ash said.

X turned away from the bridge and walked into the room. He cracked his neck, on one side and then the other. Unlike Samson, X wasn't covered in workplace grime, but he looked just as bad. His features were hardened into a mask of anger, and even from here she could smell the 'shine on his breath.

"How's Michael?" Ash asked.

"Still an orphan. But with all due respect, Captain, you didn't invite me here to discuss Tin."

Ash sat back down and folded her hands primly on the desktop. "You're right, I didn't. Have a seat, Commander."

X glanced at Jordan, then reluctantly sat.

"*Ares* is in trouble," Ash said. She repeated the same thing she had told Samson a few minutes earlier, then waited, searching X's face for a reaction.

He scratched the stubble on his chin for a few

seconds. "I'm assuming there's something else you haven't told me yet."

X wasn't just a good diver. He was smart. Ash had always appreciated that about him. She told him what she had kept from Samson.

"*Ares* is hovering above Hades. Captain Willis has already dropped a team down there."

X tilted his head, as if he hadn't heard correctly. "*Hades?* What the fuck are they doing there?"

"Good question," Jordan said.

Ash shot her XO a look, then brought her gaze back to X. "We're not exactly sure how they got there, or why, but at this point it doesn't matter. I asked you here for your counsel—to see what you would do if you were in my shoes."

X picked with his thumbnail at something stuck between his front teeth. He had an unusually white smile—a rare feature on the ship. But during Ash's long history with him, he was usually too hungover or angry to crack a grin.

He pulled his thumb away from his teeth and, inspecting the nail, said, "So you're asking if I think we should attempt a rescue?"

"You're the best diver on either ship," Ash said. "You know the skies and the surface better than anyone."

X scowled. "I know as much about Hades as you do. The electrical storms there are the worst on the continent. Even if Captain Willis' divers make it to the surface, they're going to have to deal with off-the-chart radiation, and if they survive the storms and the rads, they still have to survive whatever monsters are down there."

Ash leaned back in her chair, and X fidgeted in his.

"Monsters like the ones you saw on your last dive?"

"Yeah … maybe something even worse." He wrinkled his forehead and squinted as if he had a pounding headache—which, she reflected, he likely did.

"I know it's painful, X, but think back. We need to know what you saw, so we can prepare the other divers before the next jump."

X chuckled. "*Prepare* them?" Tracing phantom quotation marks in the air, he said, "Nothing's going to '*prepare*' them for what I saw."

"And what, exactly, was it that you saw, Commander?" Jordan asked.

X didn't turn to Jordan, but met Ash's stare instead. "Some sort of creature unlike anything I've seen on other dives. They were humanoid, with long arms and legs—bipedal, but to move fast, they went on all fours—like the baboons on the old nature vids. And …" X looked away.

Ash waited patiently.

"And they had no face. No eyes or nose—just a big-ass mouth full of shark's teeth. Their skulls were coated with some scabby-looking shit and bristles. And their backs were covered in spikes, kind of like a dorsal fin or something. Some of them had scrapes on their wrinkled skin. It was leathery and tough, though. Reminded me of dried cowhide. I suspect it protects them from the radiation. I don't know. Shit, it's not like I had time to do a detailed examination. They weren't holding still, and I wasn't waiting for 'em to."

Ash ran a finger over her lips. She had heard all the stories of the creatures the divers encountered on the surface, and she had combed the ships' archives during nights she couldn't sleep. But this? Nothing in the ships' logs was even remotely close to what X described. No one had encountered anything with humanoid anatomy.

"What else can you tell me?" Ash asked.

X straightened in his chair. "I left out the worst part. They make these high-pitched noises like an emergency alarm—a sort of whine so loud it was paralyzing."

"Are you saying these things could be part organic and part technological?"

"No," X replied. "There wasn't anything robotic about 'em."

"You sure the radiation wasn't screwing with your senses?" Jordan asked. "Organic or mechanical—it all sounds pretty far-fetched to me."

X twisted in his chair. "So which is it you're suggesting, sir: that I'm lying, or delusional?"

Ash glared again at her XO. Sometimes, she wondered if he had something against Hell Divers. This wasn't the first time he'd questioned their acuity or their truthfulness.

"I think Jordan meant you were down there for a while and that maybe your eyes and ears were playing tricks on you," Ash said in her calmest tone. "High doses of radiation can do that."

"Was supposed to be a green dive," X said. "There wasn't supposed to *be* significant radiation, remember? Just something else you guys fucked up. Not giving either Ash or Jordan a chance to respond, he turned back to her and said, "I know what I saw."

"I believe you," she replied. "But right now we need to talk about *Ares*."

A moment of quiet fell over the room. X stood and shoved his hands into his pockets. "We're talking about the only other ship in the world, Captain. No one else is going to help them. We're it."

Ash nodded and opened her mouth to speak, but X beat her to it.

"If I were in your shoes, like you said: I'd plot a course and get there as fast as possible. You can reevaluate the situation when we arrive."

"He has a point," Jordan said.

"Indeed, he does," Ash replied. "And I agree with the commander. I won't abandon *Ares*. I won't risk the extinction of the human race if there is something we can do."

"Unfortunately, Captain Willis already put us all at risk when he decided to fly to Hades," X said.

The words lingered as the PA system crackled and played an automated message. Ash used the stolen moment to check the clock. When the static cleared, she stood up. She had made her decision. "Jordan, plot us a course," she ordered.

"Aye, Captain."

Ash looked to X. "Get some sleep tonight, and lay off the 'shine. Tomorrow you start training your new team."

He opened his mouth to protest, but she cut him off. "I know, you said you were done. But *Ares* needs you. An endangered species—yours—needs you. Are you really going to say no?"

He glowered for a moment, then shook his head. "No." He stiffened. "No, Captain. We dive so humanity survives."

FIVE

Commander Weaver ran like a man possessed, his lungs burning with every breath. No matter how fast he sucked in air, he couldn't get enough.

He wasn't running from the monsters in the pit. The beasts had retreated soon after they climbed out of their lair. Something had scared them off. He could still hear their faint wailing in the distance, but now there were other, equally disturbing sounds. A low rumble broke over the horizon, drowning out the cries of the monsters.

Weaver leaped over a rusted tangle of rebar jutting from a piece of broken foundation. A tremor rumbled beneath him, causing the snow on the surface to shimmer.

A dozen yards ahead of him, Jones fell. Scrambling back to his feet, he yelled, "What the hell is happening?"

Weaver turned, shielding his visor from the gusting snow, and scanned the city. Beyond the bare girders of high-rises, he could see only a solid wall of darkness.

"What *is* that?" Jones asked.

Weaver didn't reply. He was frozen in place,

staring in awe at the biggest, most powerful storm he had ever seen or even imagined. Half as tall as the highest skyscraper, the wall of snow stretched for miles across, and it was barreling toward the city at an astounding speed.

"Holy shit," he breathed. Never in his life had he seen such a force of nature.

"Run!" Jones yelled, yanking on Weaver's arm. "Come on, we have to get out of here!"

Weaver ran sideways for a few strides, watching lightning flash over the storm. The eastern edge glowed blue for several seconds before it reached the city and flooded the streets. In minutes, it would be on them. The sounds of cracking ice and groaning metal jolted Weaver to action, and he turned and sprinted after Jones.

The two divers were on the western edge of Hades now, almost to the industrial zone. Weaver could see the ITC warehouses spread out across the landscape. Their concrete walls were built to withstand storms. But *this*? How could anything in Hades still be standing? It was a true testament to human engineering.

Fighting the urge to look over his shoulder, he concentrated on his breathing instead. *Deep and steady, in and out ...* Little dots like swarming bees caromed about at the edges of his vision. He wasn't getting enough oxygen, and his body was paying the price. Every pounding step forward came with a sharp jolt of pain. His calves and quads, at their functioning limit, burned with lactic acid buildup.

They were within a hundred yards of the nearest

structure when a panel of corrugated sheet metal whistled past Jones' head and buried itself edgewise in a snowbank. Weaver ran hunched over, bracing himself as gravel and shrapnel hissed and whined through the air all around them.

In a sudden whiteout, he lost sight of Jones, who then reemerged a moment later at the entrance to a two-story building. The exterior appeared to be metal, not concrete. Jones pulled open the door and waved him forward.

"Come on!" Jones shouted.

Weaver began to yell back when a blast of wind picked him up and cartwheeled him over the snow. The drift broke his fall, but the impact knocked the air out of his lungs.

"Grab my hand, Commander!" Jones shouted from the doorway.

Weaver fought for breath and reached up as waves of red swam across his eyes. A strong grip took his hand and pulled him through the open door.

The steel door banged shut as the screaming storm hit the building. The structure groaned in protest, and the metal walls seemed to sway. A heavy cable detached from the ceiling and whipped the floor next to where Weaver stood. He rolled to his side, shielding his visor, as the warehouse shook violently.

He was going to die. They both were. The storm was going to rip the building from the ground and grind them to paste.

Weaver curled up into a ball, trembling not from fear, but from cold, as the relentless wind pummeled the building. He fought his pounding headache, blinking away the stars, trying to focus.

"Sir! Are you okay?" Jones said. He was shouting, but the words sounded dull in the roar of the storm. There was something else, too: an electronic hum that didn't belong. Jones was dragging him toward a concrete staircase. The noise faded away as the heart of the storm engulfed the building.

*   *   *   *   *

The warehouse trading post was the largest and most frequented room on the *Hive*. X could always hear the chatter of bartering patrons and smell the black-market foods before he rounded the corner and saw the open double doors that led to the dim, cavernous space.

X stepped through the doors, his thoughts as unorganized and chaotic as the flow of commerce going on around him. Days had passed since the dive that he swore would be his last, yet his muscles were still tense, his skin still burned, and his nerves were on edge.

He pushed his way through the throng of haggard faces: a blur of buyers, sellers, and hustlers. Some loitered, hoping to scrounge out a handout from him. He tried his best to ignore the murmured pleas and resentful glares as he walked through the close, sultry air. None of them seemed to care that he had saved their lives countless times. They only saw a member of the privileged elite in front of them, not the parts that X had risked his life scavenging to keep the ship in the air.

Not that he could blame them. Their focus was on one thing: survival. Most of them had never seen the inside of one of the ship's classrooms. Education was reserved for the children of engineers and farmers—people who would grow up to play a vital role in keeping the *Hive* in the air.

X focused on the faded signs and dead light-bulbs that hung from makeshift huts and carts where merchants sold and bartered their wares.

Shouts of vendors echoed through the room. "Moonshine that'll numb your senses!" a man yelled at a group of water technicians passing his booth. One of the men stopped and exchanged a few credits for a bottle of the potent hooch.

An elderly woman with waist-length gray hair waved X toward her stand. She wore a coat stitched together from colorful rags. He recognized her as the woman who had sold them a "cure" for Rhonda's cancer. All Rhonda had gotten from it was a rash. Resisting the urge to rake the bottles of green liquid onto the floor and stomp on them, he contented himself with waving his middle finger at the snake-oil seller.

She turned away without a response. He filed his anger away and walked quickly through the next aisle of merchants, passing tables piled high with soap, candles, and other items that made life below-decks a little more bearable.

Reaching the end of the bazaar, he paused at the cages of guinea pigs, rabbits, and chickens. He could empathize with them. The thing he loved most about diving was slipping out of his own cage for a few hours—something these creatures would never do except at the end, when bound for the stew pot.

"Only two hundred credits!" a child shouted, his hands cupped around his mouth so the words would carry farther.

X raised an eyebrow at the ridiculous price and walked on, to a stand filled with fresh produce. The potatoes and lemons looked small and shriveled compared to those that the farmers grew on the level above. These were the products grown in the two communal living spaces belowdecks, where there was never enough water or light.

Year by year, these small luxuries continued to dwindle. Soon, the last doe rabbit would die, or the grow lights would blink out and not come back on. With the rising prices and disappearing goods, people were growing more desperate. There would be more riots, more bloodshed. In the hallways, he had heard the whispered rumors of rebellion. X had ignored them. He had enough to worry about just keeping the *Hive* in the sky. If the people aboard chose to tear it apart, there was nothing he could do about it.

A cough rang out, and immediately a space cleared in the middle of the crowd as shoppers and browsers backed away in fear. Cancer wasn't the only thing rampant on the ship. A flu could be just as deadly. Several passengers bumped into X while frantically pulling on their white masks.

X just pushed ahead through the crowd, toward his favorite merchant. A sign that read "Dragon" came into view. The lightbulb behind the "N" had burned out since the last time X visited. Looking at it, he ran smack into another passenger.

"Watch it!" the man growled.

X turned to find Ty staring back at him.

"Shit. Sorry, Ty."

The technician flicked the herb stick in his mouth from the left side to the right. "No problem."

X took a step back to let a shopper by, then closed the gap, but couldn't think of anything to say.

Ty broke the awkward silence. Taking the stick out of his mouth, he said, "I didn't have a chance to tell you at the funeral, but I'm real sorry. Shit luck, them sendin' you guys down there in an electrical storm. You doing okay?"

X just nodded. Ty and everyone else wanted to know what had happened down there, what he had seen.

"How's the kid doing?"

"Hasn't said a word since he found out his dad died. He blames me. I can see it in his eyes."

"Sorry to hear that," Ty said. "My boy didn't talk for two weeks after his aunt died of cancer. But he came around." He continued to ramble on, but X was barely listening. He wasn't sure Tin would recover. The kid had lost the sparkle in his eyes; his stare was cold and brittle. He was damaged, like everything and everyone aboard this squalid excuse for a home.

"I'd better get going," X said. "I'll see you tomorrow."

Ty jammed the herb stick back in his mouth. "Oh, right, I almost forgot: tomorrow you get your new team."

"Can't wait," X said, turning to leave. He wasn't

sure who the new divers would be. Angel and Apollo both had extra members, but he didn't know who they'd be willing to give up. He also didn't know where Jordan would find new recruits to replace them. Not many promising candidates remained.

X stopped at the Dragon's stall and sat down on one of the four bar stools at the counter. He rang the little bell.

He heard some clanking behind a partition wall, and a middle-aged man with curly red hair emerged a moment later. Stepping into the dim light, he cracked a toothless grin. "Ah, Xavier! Haven't seen you in a while."

"Hey, Dom, how you doin'?"

Dom looked X up and down, his eyes stopping on the white arrow pattern embroidered on his red uniform. "Today's not so bad. I always like feeding a Hell Diver."

X gave a tired grin. "Good, because I want an order of noodles to go."

"Give me a couple of minutes," Dom said, disappearing back into the booth.

X relaxed, enjoying the moment of solitude. Dom had owned the place for as long as he could remember. As with so many others on the ship, the traditions of his family had been handed down from generation to generation. There was no concept of race on the ship. All were citizens of the *Hive*. But this didn't mean everyone was treated equally. In some ways, it was even worse now than it had been in the Old World. The caste division of lower-deckers and upper-deckers was painfully apparent everywhere.

Dom returned a few minutes later with a steaming carton of the best noodles that remained in the world. The intoxicating scent pulled X back from his thoughts, and for the moment, he forgot about the ship's societal problems.

"How much I owe you?" he asked.

Dom looked up at the broken sign dangling off the canopy. "You get me a new lightbulb, you get free noodles."

X examined the sign. His brow furrowed. "Not many of those left on the surface, but I'll see what I can do."

Dom slid the bag to X, his gummy grin growing even wider.

X took the warm carton, eyed the sign one more time, and left. "See ya, Dom," he shouted over his shoulder.

X walked back to his apartment, wondering what he could say to Tin. He knocked. Twice. It felt odd to be knocking on his own door, but he didn't want to alarm the boy. X wanted him to feel at home.

After two raps, X grabbed the handle and pulled it open. It creaked, revealing the cramped living room. He hated everything about his apartment, from the rattle of the air-handler unit to the cracks in the fake leather couch where his wife used to wait for him every day. He could still picture Rhonda sitting there, legs crossed, judging brown eyes looking him up and down to see if he was drunk.

Tin sat curled up in her spot, tablet in hand, the glow illuminating the innocent face of a ten-year-old boy.

"I got you some noodles," X said, shaking the bag. Tin didn't even look up.

Crossing the room in three strides, X carried the bag into the kitchen. Two backless stools were pushed underneath the simple oval table. Only a dash of the original yellow paint remained.

X put the bag down on the countertop and checked on the tomato plant under the flickering grow bulb. The stem drooped. He scooped up a fallen leaf and put it back into the pot.

Sighing, he squeezed into the bathroom and closed the door. The toilet, or "shit can," as most passengers called them, smelled faintly of something rotten. He held his breath as he relieved himself, then closed the door.

Tin had moved to the floor in the living room. He sat cross-legged on the floor, fumbling through the tool pouch on his belt as he worked on repairing the vacuum cleaner. Unscrewing the front bolts, Tin slid off the cover to expose a skein of wires. He took a small pair of tweezers from his pouch.

"You hungry?" X said from the kitchen.

The boy shook his head.

"Come on, you have to eat. Besides, I got noodles. No one turns down the Dragon's noodles. I figure it's the least I can do to repay you for fixing that vacuum. Also"—he pointed at the sink—"the grow lamp isn't working very well. I'll owe you for fixing that, too, right?"

The savory smell filled the room. Tin's eyes searched the dimly lit space and fell on X for a blink. Leaving the dismantled vacuum cleaner on the floor, he hopped to his feet and went to the kitchen. He checked the lamp, then sat down at the table.

They ate together in silence, X having run out of things to say and Tin doing his best to avoid eye contact.

X had watched Tin grow up, had seen his love for engineering even before he learned to talk. Now the boy spent more time working on projects than playing with kids his own age.

Aaron, Tin, Rhonda, and X had been a family once. X would do anything to have those days back. For the past five years, he had been motivated only by his duty to the *Hive*. With Rhonda gone, his responsibility to the human race had kept him diving. But now he had a new responsibility.

He looked at the boy. "Did you learn anything at school today?"

Tin hesitated before slurping down his next noodle, but said nothing.

X took a different approach. "I spoke with your teacher this morning. She said you guys are going to see the water reclamation plant soon."

The boy pulled his foil hat lower over his ears and continued eating.

"Listen, Tin," X said, his voice deepening. "You've got to help me out here. You have to talk to me eventually. I mean, you're all I got now, and I'm all you got. Like it or not, that's how it is."

This time, Tin looked up, his eyes locking with X's. Swallowing, he jumped off the stool, pushed it neatly under the table, and was gone. A moment later, the door to the bedroom slammed shut.

"Damn," X muttered. He contemplated the full plate of his favorite meal, then pushed it aside. He wasn't hungry; he was thirsty. What he needed right now was a stiff drink.

SIX

Commander Weaver watched the walls around him with a sense of horrified awe. They shook and rattled as if some giant outside were swinging a wrecking ball against them. Bits of acoustic paneling and dust rained down from the ceiling, covering him in white flakes.

He sat on the stairs to the second floor, his head bowed between his legs as if he were praying. Not that he was—he could probably count on one hand the times in his life he had actually prayed. It did seem a miracle, though, that he and Jones had survived the storm even this long.

"Sir, top floor is clear," Jones said from the landing above. "There's nothing here. No sign of life, no cells, and no pressure valves. Nothing."

"I could have sworn I heard something," Weaver said. He shook his head, his senses still rattled from the fall he took before Jones yanked him inside the building.

Jones continued down the stairs and sat down beside Weaver on the step. They sat in silence for several moments, listening to the howl of the storm outside. Jones whispered something that Weaver caught only a piece of.

"What'd you say?"

"A prayer," Jones replied. "A Christian prayer."

"You really believe in that stuff?"

Jones pointed to the cross on his helmet. "If we make it back to *Ares,* I'll tell you about it sometime." He twisted around to face Weaver. "You sure you're okay, sir?" he asked, his dark eyes searching Weaver's in the blue glow of their battery units.

"I'm fine," Weaver lied. He took a sip from the hydration straw in his helmet. The sterilized water tasted like halide tablets, but it would have to do. Half their supplies were sitting in a crate at the bottom of a pit full of monsters.

He hoped the other crate had made it to the surface safely. It was their only chance to save *Ares* and get back home. Without it, they would have no way to get enough power cells or the pressure valves back up to the ship. There was simply no way he and Jones could carry everything on the return trip—their personal helium ascenders would never lift it all. The valves for the eighty-megawatt reactors weighed forty pounds each, and Weaver still had to find another booster. Otherwise, he would be stranded down here forever. Captain Willis could never risk landing to scoop him back up.

Weaver grunted, his stomach churning from the pills he had ingested. They were supposed to turn radioactive snow into safe drinking water, but he had his doubts. His insides were already starting to ache.

"What do you think those things were back

there?" Jones asked. He pulled the blaster from the holster on his leg and brushed off a layer of ice.

"No idea," Weaver said. "But I'm calling them Sirens."

"How's that?"

"Yeah," Weaver replied. "Those noises they made were a dead ringer for a level-five emergency siren on the ship."

Jones looked up at the ceiling, then back to Weaver. "How does anything survive down here in this radiation?"

Weaver shook his head. "I don't know. But they obviously did, okay? Now, stop asking me questions. We need to focus on getting the hell out of here and getting back to *Ares*." He rose to his feet and paced up and down the steps.

"We wouldn't last a minute in that storm," Jones called after him. "We have to wait it out."

"The ship won't wait for us forever," Weaver grumbled.

Jones was staring at the steel door at the bottom of the stairs. "I know, sir. But with all due respect, if we die in that storm, *Ares* is doomed anyway."

"The moment it lets up, we move."

"Understood," Jones replied with a sigh. He unfastened his belt with a click and pulled his waste bags from a pouch in his pants. "Thank God for our helmets," he said as he tossed the bags onto the landing above. "I'd hate to get a whiff of one of those."

On any other mission, the comment would have gotten a laugh from Weaver, but it didn't penetrate the cloud of worry.

"You hear that?" Jones said.

"What?" Weaver jolted alert, half expecting to hear the eerie wailing he had heard before the storm hit. He put a hand against the vibrating wall. The wind had risen to a steady roar.

Weaver took a step backward as a crack spider-webbed up the concrete stairwell. The violent rattle of metal siding pulled his gaze to the ceiling on the second floor. He heard Jones shouting, but his voice was muffled by the sounds of the building coming apart. The concrete stairwell walls around Weaver and Jones were fracturing under the onslaught of tornadic wind.

Weaver nearly stumbled down the steps to avoid a falling chunk of concrete. He braced himself against the opposite wall and watched in horror as a wide crack zigzagged up the stairs, breaking them in half.

"Run!" he shouted. But looking up, he saw there was nowhere to go. The metal roof was rattling so hard, it was only a matter of time before the storm peeled it back and sucked them right out the top.

Jones hesitated on the broken stairs, huddling against a wall and covering his head with his arms. With nowhere to hide, there was only one option.

Weaver pressed his left palm against the wall for balance. With his right hand, he fished in the cargo pocket on his left leg and pulled a coil of 550-pound test paracord. Uncoiling it, he handed one end to Jones.

"Tie it on your belt!" Weaver yelled.

"No," Jones said, waving it away. "We can't go out there!"

"We take our chances out there or we get crushed in here! Pick your poison!"

Above them, a section of roof peeled back like the skin of an orange. They were out of time.

"That's an order!" Weaver shouted.

Jones took the end of rope from his hand and tied it in a figure eight to his belt. Grabbing the door handle, Weaver yelled for Jones to follow. He put his shoulder against it, using all his strength to push it open. The concrete walls of the staircase broke off behind them, the fragments tumbling down the stairs and narrowly missing Jones. The building swayed, throwing them against each other in the concrete stairwell as the structural metal gave out a loud groan.

Weaver gritted his teeth, wishing he could remember the prayer Jones had whispered a few minutes earlier. He tried to plant his boots as he stepped outside, but the wind took him the moment his feet were out the door. The rope on his belt tightened and yanked Jones from the doorway. The next instant, both divers were sucked into the white void, their screams swallowed up by the howling wind.

*   *   *   *   *

X gave up waiting for Tin to come out of his room.

"I'll be back later," he said on his way out. He locked the door behind him and headed down the corridor. His destination wasn't far. The scruffy bar called the Wingman was only a few passages away.

He walked with his hands in his pockets,

eyes downcast. The white flicker of a single light told him he was close. It was like the beacon of a lighthouse, warning ships away from the shore. X ignored the warning every time.

The familiar scratchy mechanical sound of an ancient CD player greeted him at the entrance. Hearing the thumping guitar strains of "All Along the Watchtower," he grinned. The centuries-old Jimi Hendrix tune reflected his mood perfectly.

He nodded at Marv, a middle-aged former Militia soldier who had bought the shit hole of a bar when his term was up.

"Evenin', X. What can I do you out of?" The burly barkeep finished wiping a glass with a rag of dubious cleanliness.

"Usual." X scanned the faces of the other three patrons, recognizing none of them. Fine with him—he wasn't here to talk.

Marv muttered something to a woman at the end of the bar—she was in X's seat. She grabbed her glass, gave X a scowl, and squeezed past him. He took her place and reached for the mug of 'shine that Marv had already set out. Two gulps, and it was gone. He welcomed the burn—welcomed feeling of any kind after the week he'd had.

X hit his chest with a fist and signaled for another. He didn't care that Captain Ash had ordered him to stay away from the 'shine tonight. With the liquid warming his gut, he felt happier than he had in a while. And that, he knew, was a bad sign.

"Not taking it slow tonight?" Marv asked.

"Got things to forget."

He filled the glass to the rim this time. "Don't we all, brother!"

"I'll drink to that," said the man sitting to his right.

X didn't reply. He stared at the only decoration in the bar—a painting of some ancient battle. Men wearing plate armor swung swords at one another, spilling blood on the grassy fields of a place forgotten to time.

"You're a Hell Diver, aren't ya'?" the man asked.

Slamming down the liquid, X tilted his head ever so slightly to catch a glimpse of the talkative patron. He was middle-aged, with a rough face and black dreadlocks down past his shoulders. He looked familiar, but X wasn't here to think about the past. He wasn't here to think at all.

"The red jumpsuit give it away?" X said reluctantly. He tapped his empty glass on the table and anticipated the man's next question.

"I knew some Hell Divers once. They said you guys don't talk about what you see, but come on, man." He nudged X in the side. "I'll buy you a drink."

X didn't like that. His body was the only real estate he truly owned on the cramped airship. Invade, and there were apt to be problems.

"They were right," X said.

The man squinted. "Hey, I've seen you before. You've been around a while. I know you've, you know, *seen* things."

Marv froze, his hand stuck inside another glass with the same dingy rag. He kept an eye on X but didn't say a word.

"Come on, just one story," the drunk wheedled. "I heard you guys found life down there recently."

He wiggled a finger again, back and forth. "But not *human* life."

X didn't like that, either. Rumors annoyed him. His vision began to fade as the 'shine took hold of his senses. Somewhere in the back of his mind, he considered telling the man about the beasts down on the surface, just to see his reaction.

Marv cut in. "Why don't you get going, pal. You've had enough 'shine tonight."

"Wasn't talking to you," the man replied. Shifting his glazed eyes back to X, he reached out as if to touch the scar above his eye. "I know you got some stories in you."

X grabbed his hand, stood, and whipped the arm back around into a hammer lock. Now he remembered where he had seen him. It was the same guy from the hallway earlier, who had mouthed off to the Militia soldiers.

The man resisted, jerking his arm, but X was quick, pushing the trapped hand farther up between the shoulder blades as his other hand bounced the man's head off the table. The smack of bone on wood resounded in the small space.

The man struggled to get free. "Lay off, man! You think you're so goddamn special, don't you? You got any idea how the rest of us live? I think …"

X hiked the arm up a little higher, and the words trailed off into a whimper. The other customers scattered from the bar.

"You weren't thinking all that much," X said. As suddenly as he had grabbed the man, he loosened his grip and let him go.

"*Shit,*" Marv said. Putting the "clean" mug down on the bar, he readied the rag for messier duty.

A beat later, the drunk slid his face off the bar. He staggered backward, murmuring a string of profanities.

Marv mopped up the streak of blood with a quick sweep. "Now, hike your ass out of here!"

The man stumbled away, cupping his mouth with his right hand and flashing the middle finger of his left. He mumbled something, X heard only the tail end of it.

"My dad was never like you."

X shook his head and plopped back down on the stool. "Sorry, Marv," he said, watching the man limp into the hallway.

"Guy had it coming," Marv said, running the rag over the counter one more time. "But you're picking up his tab since you're the reason he didn't pay."

"Yeah. No problem," X replied, downing a final drink. He tossed his credit voucher onto the table and waited for Marv to run it. "Don't happen to know who that guy was, do you?"

"Only been here a few times." Marv slid the voucher back to X, then looked at the ceiling, deep in thought. "Trey? No, Travis. I think his name's Travis. Yeah, that's it."

X had known a Travis once, the son of a former diver on Team Angel. Had that kid really grown up to be such a waste of space? X had never bothered to look in on him after his father died. Was that what he was mumbling about?

His mind was pleasantly clouded from the 'shine. It was time for him to go home. In a few short hours, he would meet his new team—more divers that he would likely be leading to their death.

*   *   *   *   *

Travis Eddie stumbled down the rungs to the lower decks, putting a hand to the goose egg on his forehead. He was drunk and angry—an unstable combination. He felt at the threshold of his self-control, but he couldn't let the gasket blow. He had to stay in control. With two strikes on his record, he was one away from the brig. And if he ended up there, he could never help the lower-deckers or his brother. Rotting away down here was unendurable, but the thought of the dark gallows—now, *that* made him shudder.

No. He was not going out like that. Not before he saw some changes on the ship.

He stopped at the bottom of the stairwell and flicked a dreadlock over his shoulder. The moment he opened the hatch to the first compartment, he heard the sporadic coughing of sick passengers.

Hundreds of bunks lined each wall as far as he could see. Some were surrounded by metal partitions; others were blocked off by nothing more substantial than blankets thrown over makeshift clothing racks. For most, a thin piece of muslin cloth was the only privacy they had from the other bunks.

This was the first of two compartments housing the four hundred lower-deckers. He was lucky to live in the first. The second contained those afflicted with radiation poisoning. He made his way over there only if he had to. The suffering was almost too much to bear. Because of leaking radiation, more and more children were born with deformities. Those who survived early childhood rarely left the second compartment, where they lived like caged animals, confined to their filthy mattresses and forced to rely on their parents.

Captain Ash and her staff rarely ventured down here. Maybe it was easier to live up there and forget about those below. Travis couldn't deny that Ash had made some changes as captain: increased rations, a doctor who made rounds every other day, a crew of engineers who worked to seal off the radiation. But they were hardly enough, and there was more food to go around, but it never seemed to make it down here.

Travis felt a silent scream of rage well up inside him. It wasn't right. No one should have to live like this, and yet, this was how it had been his entire life.

Drawing in a deep breath, he fought the spins from the 'shine. He shouldn't have mouthed off to the Hell Diver. That was a mistake. Next time, he would be smarter.

After the nausea passed, he used the nighttime glow from weak LEDs overhead to navigate his way to his bed. There was just enough light to show him the gaunt faces of those already asleep. Most, like him, were between the ages of twenty and thirty, though they looked twice that. Anyone much older didn't live long—not down here. Flu and cancer were rampant. The average life expectancy was right around thirty-seven years, so he had maybe a decade of this to look forward to.

Travis passed a small candlelight vigil where a dozen monks meditated. He stumbled past them. He had lost his faith a long time ago.

Ahead, Travis saw a line snaking toward the centrally located shit cans. He joined the end of the line. The single metal hatch squeaked open, then shut, as each passenger did what they could to keep the putrid smells mostly isolated by shutting the hatch when done. The trick was to take a deep breath just before entering and hold it as long as you could. Then you could postpone the real suffering until hypoxia forced you to let it out and inhale the stink.

When it was finally his turn, drunk enough to forget this dictum, he staggered inside and almost vomited. With no air circulation, the stench of ammonia and excrement made his eyes water. He squeezed between two men and pissed into one of a dozen wide holes cut into the floor. From there, tubes sucked the waste through the bowels of the ship, to the digester, where it became methane gas for cooking, and compost for the farm. It was best not to think too hard about how they managed the biomass on the *Hive*.

No one inside spoke; they were too busy holding their breath. Travis bore down, voiding his bladder as fast as he could, then zipped up and staggered back out into the relatively clear air of the corridor. He hurried back to his bed and plopped onto his back. He didn't bother pulling the curtain across the railing he had fashioned from salvaged wire.

"That you, Trav?" said a rough voice.

He glanced over to the next bed. Alex was sitting up in his bunk, with his legs thrown over the side. The scarf he normally wore over his face hung loosely over his chest. In the weak light, Travis could see the tight skin on his friend's right cheek and chin, where doctors had removed the melanomal cancer. Ten years ago, Alex had been one of the best-looking kids on the ship, but the cancer had taken part of his face—and, Travis sometimes thought, part of his mind.

"What happened to your head?" Alex asked.

"Ran into a Hell Diver."

"You kiddin' me, man? One that knew your dad?"

Travis shook his head. "Maybe. I don't know."

Alex snorted. "Whatever. They're all the same. And they're all going to pay."

Travis closed his eyes. He didn't want to think about his dad right now, or what he must do to help the lower-deckers. Nor did he want to talk to his crazy-ass friend. He just wanted to sleep off the 'shine so he could visit his brother in the morning.

SEVEN

Tin glanced at X as they walked down the corridor to the school. He wanted to tell him he didn't need an escort, that he could get there just fine on his own, but it didn't matter. The diver wasn't much different from his dad: bullheaded. But at least, his dad had listened to him. X wouldn't listen even if Tin had something to say. He was too selfish for that. X hadn't always been this way. He had changed. Now he was nothing but a barely functioning drunk.

So Tin kept his mouth shut and his head down, especially at school. The other kids teased him and made fun of his hat. But they didn't know his secret. His hat wasn't just a hat. It had a force field that protected him from their comments. They bounced right off. He knew because his dad had told him so when he made it.

"Come on," X said, reaching out for the boy's hand when they came to the next intersection. Dozens of residents were trying to squeeze through the clogged hallway at once.

Tin hesitated, suddenly terrified. Everything

seemed bleaker, darker. Had engineering turned off more lights? Even in the dimness, he caught a glimpse of the purple bags rimming X's eyes. He looked exhausted. Tin had heard him stumble in around nine, but that ruckus hadn't kept him awake—it was the sound of X puking. The sound made him shiver. It reminded him that he was an orphan stuck with a boozer.

"Tin, let's go," X insisted, grabbing him by the hand and pulling him through the crowd.

They kept to the right, hugging the wall. The school was past the medical bay. He hated walking by the glass doors. Each time, it seemed as if more people were there, waiting for a doctor—more people sick with cancer or the cough.

Tin sneaked a look as they passed the clinic. The lobby was already full: young and old, men and women. Cancer didn't discriminate. Neither did the cough.

He looked away and continued toward the sagging yellow sign that read "School." Parents lingered outside the entrance, hugging their children before rushing off to their jobs. Tin looked up at X. The guy would never be a parent to him. He couldn't even take care of himself.

And he hadn't been able to save Tin's dad, either.

"Have a good day, kid," X said.

Tin hiked the backpack farther up on his shoulders and walked past him. He felt in the tool pouch on his belt and pulled out the old coin his father had given him. One side had a bird, the other a man's face. Both were almost worn away. Tin didn't know who it was supposed to be or how much the coin had once been worth, but rubbing its smooth surface always made him feel better.

There's a difference between fighting for what you believe in and killing for what you believe in. Violence is never the answer.

He had never found the right moment to ask his father what he had meant when he spoke those words two years ago, after the riots. But he would never forget the line.

"See ya later, X. Have a great day," X said to his back.

The boy shrugged it off. X meant well, but in a few years Tin would apply for a job in engineering and have his own room assigned to him. He was only ten, but he was good at building things out of spare parts: robots, grow lights, toys, and computers. And they were accepting recruits younger and younger. The ship needed him, just as it had needed his dad.

Tin slipped the coin back in the pouch and zipped it shut. He hustled through the open door, leaving X in the hallway.

The compartment was separated into four classrooms. His was at the end of the passage on the right. A group of kids were gathered outside the door, blocking the entrance. He avoided eye contact and tried to slip between them.

A tall, slender frame stepped in his way. "Hey, Tin!" Andrew said. "Where ya headed?"

Tin wanted to say, *Where do you think I'm going, idiot?* But he just pointed over Andrew's shoulder.

He knew what came next, and didn't even bother trying to stop Andrew's hand. The tinfoil hat fell to the floor. The other kids chuckled. Tin took a step backward and stooped to pick up the hat, but a pair of hands beat him to it.

He glanced up and saw Layla Brower. A curtain of shoulder-length brown hair fell across her face, but it didn't hide her perfect smile.

She straightened and handed Tin his hat.

"Why don't you troglodytes find something else to do?" Layla said. "Maybe make yourselves useful. You know, if you put your heads together, you might be able to fix a broken shit can or something."

"Oh, did your dad teach you how to do that?" Andrew shot back. "He works in the sewers, right?"

Layla's face turned pink, and Tin wondered whether she was going to slug the boy. Her hands shook at her sides, but before she could react, the door swung open.

Professor Lana stepped into the hall, let out a weary sigh, and waved the kids in.

"Class started two minutes ago," she said. Her scowl deepened, accentuating every wrinkle in her face. "Now, come on," she said. "We have things to learn today."

The other kids laughed derisively. Tin had heard them call her a witch and worse in hushed voices. But she wasn't so bad. She had always treated him fairly. She winked at him as he sneaked past Layla and Andrew. Hurrying into the room, he slid into his chair and put his hat back on.

Layla came in a second later. She took a seat

beside him, and Tin spoke for the first time in days.

"Thanks," he whispered.

*   *   *   *   *

Commander Weaver jerked awake in a snowbank that had drifted up against one of the domed concrete warehouses. The densely packed snow had likely saved his life.

He could feel his heartbeat pounding in his temples. When his vision finally cleared, he saw the wall of snow rolling west, crossing into the frozen waste beyond the city.

Then he remembered Jones.

Weaver pulled his arm out of the snow and found the rope end knotted to his belt. He gave it a tug.

"Jones!" Weaver shouted over the comm.

No response. He wriggled free of the snowbank and slid down to the ground, his boots sinking into powder that came up to his ankles.

"Jones! Can you hear me?"

A voice, half drowned out by static, crackled over the channel. The prayer Jones was mumbling into the comm sounded like the same one he had whispered back in the warehouse.

"Where are you?" Weaver shouted.

"I don't know. I can't see anything," Jones finally said. "I'm …" He paused. "I'm stuck."

Weaver checked the minimap on his HUD. The beacon put Jones only a few hundred feet south of the warehouses. He brushed off his suit to check that nothing was broken, then looked at his minicomputer. All systems were functioning, but his battery level was dropping. Without power, he would eventually freeze.

The thought prompted a surge of adrenaline that made him forget his headache. He worked his way through the deep snowdrifts, his boots sinking deeper with every step. Within minutes, he was knee-deep. He pushed ahead until the drifts were almost up to his crotch.

"I can't fucking move!" Jones yelled. "Help me!"

Weaver paused to catch his breath. "I'm coming. Just hold on." Between breaths, he glimpsed motion in the dark sky. For a moment, he thought he saw something with wings, but a lightning flash revealed an empty horizon. He pushed on, plowing ahead into the drifts. Each stride was harder than the last, and the fresh powder seemed denser, hardening around him like concrete.

Frantic now, he used his arms to clear some of the pack in front of him. He could see the tip of Jones' green helmet. Fighting through the last few feet, he finally closed the gap.

Weaver dug around Jones' helmet, then freed his arms and chest. Now with Jones helping clear the pack, they eventually got him standing.

Weaver looked him up and down. "You okay?"

"Yeah, I think so."

Weaver twisted around in the snow to look at the dozens of domed warehouses. Somewhere among those concrete beehives were the fuel cells and pressure valves they needed. He noted the location of the crate on his HUD. It was close—less than a quarter mile away. But with the buildings closer, he decided to abandon the heavy weapons for now and go straight for the goods.

"Let's go," Weaver said. Working his way back the way he had come, he stopped at the first dome. "We need to split up," he said. "Keep radio contact and let me know if you find anything."

Jones nodded and shook off a layer of snow. "Good luck, sir."

As Weaver turned to run, a faint sound caught his ear. The distant high-pitched screech was unmistakable. But this wasn't coming from the ground. It was coming from the sky.

"Wait," Weaver said.

Both men scanned the clouds.

"You think someone's really listening to all those prayers?" Weaver asked.

Jones nodded. "Absolutely, sir."

"Good. Do me a favor and say one for us and the ship."

* * * * *

X stood in the training bay, directly over the white arrow symbol of the Hell Divers. He had a notepad in his hand. He had seen each of the three divers standing in front of him, but he knew little about them. The teams trained independently from one another. They all shared the same facility, but there wasn't a lot of mingling—not during training, anyway.

Jordan had plucked members from Team Apollo

and Team Angel, just as X had expected. He looked them over without saying a word. On the left was Magnolia Katib. She wore a black jumpsuit and, over that, a gray coat held together by chains. Half his age, probably only twenty-one or twenty-two, she had shoulder-length black hair streaked with blue highlights. Her thin lips were coated in purple lipstick, and her electric-blue eyes were rimmed in heavy dark liner. The makeup was black market— expensive and hard to get hold of. Her vibe gave him the creeps.

Reaching into her coat, she pulled out a metallic pin and twirled it between her fingers. "You're freaking me out mister. You gonna say something, or what?"

"Shit, and here I was sorta thinking the same thing about you," X said. He glanced down at his notepad and skimmed the file that he had already memorized. "Says you're a thief. You can sneak in and out of places. And you're good with electronics."

She cracked a grin. "Yeah, that's right. Why— got a blown diode?"

"Let me guess: it was either this or the inside of a prison cell."

X didn't wait for her response. As the woman's cocky grin withered, he moved on to Clint Murphy. The engineer was a head shorter than she, but his outfit was every bit as striking. A pair of crimson goggles hugged his receding hairline. His eyes darted back and forth, scanning the room, reminding X of a jonesing stim addict. *Nice.* Command had given him a thief and an anxiety case.

"You're an engineer, Clint?"

"Y-yes sir. That's r-right." He repositioned his goggles and scratched his thin, curly hair. "People call me Murph."

X turned to Sam Barker. The third diver, at least, held some promise. Dark-skinned and muscular, he stood ramrod straight even at parade rest. He had rolled up the sleeves of his skintight gray shirt to show the Militia shield tattoos on both biceps.

Sam stared ahead, his gaze unwavering. He was a soldier, through and through.

"Says in your file you were instrumental in quelling the riots a few years back."

Sam dipped his chin. "I was in the first wave into the farms."

X knew what that meant. The man had seen people die. He would fit right in on Team Raptor. The others were going to take some work. X had his task cut out for him.

"Welcome to Raptor," X said in the sincerest tone he could muster. Tucking his notepad back in a cargo pocket, he waved the group toward the wind cylinders in the center of the room. When he got there, he propped his shoulder against the glass. He looked at his new team in turn and said, "How many dives you got under your belts?"

"Seventeen," Magnolia said in a proud voice.

She had attitude to spare ... like Rhonda. For a moment, he saw her superimposed there, staring defiantly back at him the way she had done so many times after one of their arguments. He blinked away the memories and looked to the engineer.

"Fourteen," Murph said.

"Ten, sir," said Sam.

X had more than twice as many dives as the three of them combined. He had to remind himself that this wasn't unusual. Will and Rodney had been in the same position as the divers standing in front of him. Indeed, Aaron was the only diver on the *Hive* who had even come close to the number of jumps X had completed.

Murph took a half step forward. "Commander?"

X glanced up from his notepad. "What?"

"I just wanted to say I'm sorry to hear about your team. I want you to know I'm glad to be here."

X nodded and glanced at Magnolia, catching her in a smirk. She flicked her hair out of her face and started spinning her toy again.

"What the fuck is that?" X asked. He snatched it from her hand.

"It's a lock pick, man." She held out her hand. "And it's *mine*."

He clenched his jaw. "Magnolia, you have three choices. You can call me 'X,' 'Commander X,' or 'sir.' I don't much give a shit which one, but that's it. Got it?"

She nodded, and he dropped the instrument back in her palm.

"How many dives have you made, sir?" Sam asked.

"Ninety-six. Now, do you suppose that's all luck?"

Murph raised a hand.

"It was a rhetorical question," X said. "I have survived because I learned from my mistakes and the mistakes of others. Hell Divers are rarely afforded that luxury. You all have an advantage: you get to learn what *not* to do before you saddle up in the launch bay again. I don't know what you learned on your other teams, and again, I don't much care. Because you're going to learn *my* way of doing things."

X gave this a moment to sink in and then said, "Diving requires more than courage. You have to bury your fear and realize there is more to life than your own survival. We dive for humanity. So get those selfish thoughts out of your mind," he said, holding Magnolia's gaze an extra beat.

She rolled her eyes.

X almost rose to the bait, then stopped himself. "Listen up, everyone. I'm here to train you and keep you alive when the time comes."

"Like you did your old team?" Magnolia muttered.

"Excuse me," X said. "What did you say?"

Magnolia tipped her head back, uncertainty in her wide eyes. "I said you couldn't keep your old team alive."

"Captain Ash dropped us into a fucking electrical storm," X said. "My team was dead before they ever got to the surface."

Magnolia nodded and took a step backward. "I'm sorry."

X doubted it. But at least, he knew where he stood with his new team. They had about as much confidence in him as he had in them. And why should they feel any differently? They were replacing men *he* couldn't save.

"I don't expect you to trust me," X said. "But I do expect you to listen—"

A voice over his shoulder cut him off. "Commander X!"

He turned to see Lieutenant Jordan, flanked by two Militia soldiers, coming across the room.

"Commander X," Jordan repeated, stopping a few feet from him. He seemed uncharacteristically agitated. "Captain Ash would like to see you."

X reached for his earpiece and realized he had left it in his locker. "I'm almost done here," he replied.

"She needs to see you *now*," Jordan insisted.

X could read the urgency in Jordan's eyes, and he doubted it was some half-assed rumor of civil unrest. The captain didn't want to talk about a food shortage or a problem with the ship. This was about Hades.

*   *   *   *   *

Captain Ash stood with her back to the wall, studying the two Hell Diver team leads seated at the command table. Cruise, of Team Apollo, sat tapping his finger on the white table. He had big shoulders, a shaved head, and the air of a man you didn't want to keep waiting.

To his right sat Tony, Team Angel's lead.

At the knock on the door, the captain stopped massaging her neck as X and Jordan entered.

"Sorry we're late," Jordan said. "Commander X wasn't wearing his headset."

X nodded. "I was too busy figuring out what to do with the sorry excuses for divers you guys assigned to my team."

"Sam and Murph are okay," Tony said.

"Magnolia can be a pain, no doubt about it," Cruise added. "She is a criminal, after all. But she ain't all bad."

Ash stepped to the table and gestured for the two new arrivals to take a seat. She could feel all eyes follow her as she sat at the head of the table. She had earned their respect over the years, but with it came responsibility.

"A day ago, we received a distress call from *Ares*. Captain Willis sent coordinates from a location directly over Hades."

She saw the sudden tautness on the faces before her. Cruise shifted nervously in his chair. It was the first time Ash had ever seen him show any sign of apprehension.

"What the hell are they doing *there*?" Cruise asked.

Ash reached forward and activated the table's built-in console. The SOS video from *Ares* emerged on the individual screens in front of the divers. She waited for them to digest the information.

"Willis is a bigger fool than I thought," Cruise said. "He would've been better off trying to make it to another location than attempting a dive over Hades."

Ash took a deep breath and said, "Whatever desperation drove him to attempt a dive at Hades doesn't matter right now. All that matters is that we help them."

Cruise muttered something profane. "You have got to be kidding me. We can't risk our ship for theirs. They made their decision, they have to live with it."

"Team Raptor has just provided us with enough

nuclear fuel cells to keep us in the air for years," Ash said. "We have the juice to get to Hades—"

Cruise cut her off. "And X's men paid the full price to make sure we don't end up in the same position as *Ares*. I can't believe you would risk that!"

Before Ash could respond, X rose from his seat and loomed over Cruise. "Excuse me, *Commander*, but your superior officer was speaking. I'm with Captain Ash on this. If we have the ability to aid *Ares*, then why not do it? If we get to Hades and can't provide support, then we pull back."

Cruise snorted. "Am I the only one that thinks this is a crazy idea? Tony? Jordan?"

No one spoke, and X sat back down. Ash let Cruise fidget for a moment. It was the best way to defuse the situation. Dressing him down in front of the other team leaders would only infuriate him more.

"God only knows what's down there," Cruise said under his breath.

"God isn't the only one," Ash replied. She punched in another command. "We received another transmission about an hour ago. Only a chunk came through."

After entering in her credentials, she pulled up the confidential file. Static crackled from the PA system. Ash crossed her arms across her chest and listened to the message for the fourth time.

"Commander, I just reached the second warehouse. Shit, this place is a fucking gold mine, sir! There's got to be hundreds of cases of fuel cells!"

"What about the pressure valves?"

"Still searching."

"Stand by, Jones. I'm on my way."

The audio cut in and out, only to return a few seconds later.

"Our father in heaven, hallowed be your name ..." [Static.] *"Forgive us our debts ..."* [Static.] *"And lead us not into temptation, but deliver us from evil."*

"What the hell is he yammering about?" Cruise asked.

"Lord's Prayer," Tony replied. "My mom used to recite it when I was a kid." He flinched at the sound of gunfire that followed the words.

"Commander ..." Hiss of static. *"The Sirens— they're inside!"*

"Get out of there, Jones!"

There was a flurry of gunshots, followed by a piercing screech. The sound sent a chill through Ash. She recalled her conversation with X. Were these the same creatures he had stumbled onto?

"Jones, come in. Jones, where are you?"

White noise.

"Oh, Jesus! They're coming!"

Labored breathing broke over the channel, then the crack of more gunshots.

"Jones, do you copy? Where are you? Where the hell are you?"

A throaty gurgle came next, then a barely decipherable answer. Ash could make out only three syllables. It sounded like *"God help me."*

A high-pitched screech—a sound that could not have come from human vocal cords—ended the transmission.

For several minutes, the three divers sat in

silence. Ash studied them one by one and stopped on X. His features were tight, his jaw clenched, as if he was trying to forget a nightmare.

"Those sounds were familiar, weren't they?" she asked.

X nodded. "Yes, Captain. The things they are calling 'Sirens' sound exactly like the creatures I encountered on my last dive."

Cruise twisted in his chair to glare at X. "You saw something down there and didn't tell us?"

Ash intervened. "He told me, and now we're telling you."

"Excellent," Cruise replied. He put his hands behind his shaved head and leaned back in his chair. "Am I always the last one to hear about stuff that could get us killed?"

Ash resisted the urge to take Cruise down a peg in front of his peers.

"We don't know the status of *Ares,* but we're going to find out in ..." She looked down at her wristwatch. "In five hours. Oh, and, gentleman, you'd better get your teams ready just in case we have to mount a rescue operation."

Cruise stood, and his eyes flitted from X to Captain Ash. "You're going to get us all killed."

"Dismissed," Jordan said sternly.

Cruise stalked out of the room. Tony and X followed him out, but X paused in the doorway. "Wait for me to tell my new divers," he shouted after Cruise and Tony. Then he turned and met Ash's gaze.

"Captain," he said, "I hope you got a plan when

we get to Hades, because after seeing what I saw down there—those things, the Sirens—chances are, Captain Willis' divers are already dead."

EIGHT

The beam from Commander Weaver's headlamp cut through the inky darkness of the warehouse. He clambered up the stairs and raced over the skeletal platform, the light bouncing across his path.

"Jones, do you copy?" Weaver repeated for the hundredth time.

The maddening crackle of static was the only response. He ran up another staircase and across a second mezzanine, which ended at a steel door connecting the two warehouses. Weaver approached cautiously, pistol up.

Snippets of Jones' last words repeated in his mind: *The Sirens. They're everywhere!*

Weaver cursed himself for not making the arduous trek to the crate and loading up on weapons. The allure of the buildings, close by and full of supplies for the taking, had clouded his judgment. He would trade the rest of his water for a blaster or an assault rifle.

It was too late now. There was no turning back to the crate unless he had the cells and valves. His eyes flitted to his minimap. He had set a nav marker on

Jones' last known location. If the computer was correct, Jones—and the Sirens—were in the next building.

He eased into a cautious trot across the catwalk. The ancient metal shook and groaned. He grabbed on to a railing with one hand and glanced over the other side. It was farther down than he had thought. Even with the armor shielding his vital parts, he would likely break something if the catwalk gave out. The sturdy warehouses had been built to last, but two and a half centuries was a long time.

Walking across the final stretch to the door, he crouched down and shined the headlamp over the rusted frame. Long gashes ran down the length of the metal. He crab-walked closer, examining the door under the glow. The abrasions were deep and looked recent. Rust hadn't worked its way into the deep crevices yet, but something else had. A jagged piece of what looked almost like bone stuck out of one of the incisions. He pulled it and held it under the light. It looked like the broken-off end of a long, curved talon from something big—something the size of a Siren.

He rotated it under the light. The jagged, yellow claw was rough, but when he tried to bend it, it wouldn't budge. It had the strength of steel and the coarseness of sandpaper.

The wind outside beat the sides of the building, rising into a howl that sounded alive. Weaver swallowed and looked at the crevices again. He forced himself to think of his wife, his kids, and the mission. The nuclear fuel cells were on the other side, and the pressure valves could be there, too.

He shut off his lamp and activated the night-vision optics. *You can do this,* he told himself. *You have to. Jones could still be alive.* The words sounded hollow and unconvincing.

Holding the pistol in one hand, he grabbed the knob and rotated it. The loud click of the latch made him cringe, and he braced himself for the high, keening wail that was sure to follow.

Nothing.

He inched the door open and peered into the darkness. He could see the outline of another mezzanine, and the top rows of shelves. Curiosity won out over fear, and he sneaked through the opening.

He was on the third level of the massive ware-house, standing over hundreds of shelves. Some had come crashing down, perhaps decades ago; others leaned against each other like some giant's house of cards. The catwalks stretching over the maze sagged or listed in places, but the one in front looked study enough.

Weaver stepped out onto the nonskid metal grate. It creaked under his boot, and a shriek answered. He froze like a child caught stealing cookies.

The noise came again, echoing through the space. He whipped his head around, searching for the source, but nothing moved in the NVG's green-hued field of vision.

The otherworldly shrieking died away until he could hear only the echo of his breath inside his helmet. He had to find Jones and the salvage they had come for, and get back to the ship.

He took three silent steps without attracting any audible response.

Jones, where the hell are you?

At the end of the walkway, he stopped and grabbed the railing to look over the side. A shelf had collapsed below, spilling its contents across a floor he could hardly see.

He continued, searching the darkness for any sign of Jones, when a distant screech stopped him in mid stride. Another came from the east, and a third from the west corner of the room. They rose and fell in a whine that made him shiver in his warm suit.

Weaver trained his pistol in each direction, but he couldn't see much of anything. His night-vision optics simply couldn't penetrate the darkness of the warehouse. The battery unit under his vest glowed weakly, giving off barely enough light to see a foot ahead.

The gun shook in his hands as the eerie wailing started up again, coming from all three directions. With a bump of his chin, he deactivated his night vision and let the darkness swallow him.

You're fine. Everything is fine …

Weaver listened to the alien vocalizations. Everything was *not* fucking fine. He took another long, calming breath and reached up to click on his headlamp.

The slight motion cued a symphony of the strange cries. He moved the light over the floor below, seeing nothing. Then he swept it over the catwalks, stopping on something bulky. Lying in the center of one of the walkways, a body. Jones' right arm dangled over the side, his hand open.

The whines sounded louder and closer, but Weaver felt stuck, frozen in place. His light had captured a naked, leathery creature kneeling next to Jones. The shape looked almost human, but of course, that wasn't possible.

He moved the beam over the spikes jutting from the wrinkled skin of the creature's back.

The thing suddenly tipped its head in his direction. The beam of light caught it where its eyes should have been, and Weaver saw lips, stretched into what looked like a wide grin, flecked with blood.

Weaver's beam stopped on Jones' limp hand, dangling over the edge of the catwalk. Leaning over the railing, he saw a case on the ground below.

The sound of scrabbling claws pulled his gaze upward. Three of the creatures scampered effortlessly across the ceiling. The sight shocked him into motion, and experience took over. Taking a step backward, he raised his revolver and aimed it at the shrieking things.

He fired off a shot that went wide and ricocheted off the wall. The long-limbed monsters darted away, nails sparking against the metal.

Steady, Weaver. Steady.

Closing one eye, he squeezed off two more shots. Both pinged off the wall. The creatures were so damn fast, he had to lead them more. By pure luck, he hit one in the back, and it dropped from the ceiling, arms flailing as it caromed off a catwalk and went cartwheeling to the floor. The sound of the squishy impact sent the Sirens into a frenzy. They fanned out in all directions. Motion below revealed more of the eyeless monsters scuttling across the floor of the warehouse.

He lined up a shot and hesitated.

How many bullets did he have left in the cylinder? Two? Three? He could hardly think. He was operating on instinct and adrenaline. The beam of his light rolled over a half-dozen bulb-shaped nests on the eastern wall. The area was alive with movement. One of the Sirens landed on the platform in front of him and dropped to all fours. It lunged, and a hollow-point bullet blew out the back of its skull. The beast slumped to the floor and slid to a stop inches from his boots.

He heard the clank of another Siren dropping to the platform behind him. He whirled and shot it in the neck as it charged. It flopped to the walkway, choking on its own blood.

Weaver fired until his revolver clicked, then kept squeezing the trigger, hoping for a bullet that wasn't there. Talons scraped across the metal platform as more of the beasts closed in. Their screeching reverberated from every corner of the warehouse.

He looked at Jones' inert body once more, glanced back down at the case of cells, and ran.

*   *   *   *   *

Ash felt the *Hive* slow as they reached airspace above the edge of Hades. She stared at the surprisingly crisp feed from the bow of the ship. Flashes of electricity streaked across the main display and danced across the horizon, illuminating a shelf of storm clouds that stretched across the entire skyline.

"I hope to God *Ares* isn't in there," she whispered.

Every officer on the bridge had stopped to stare at the monitor. Jordan stood at Ash's side as they waited anxiously for any sign of their sister ship.

"Have we heard anything?" she asked.

Jordan shook his head. "The last transmission we received came over seven hours ago."

"What about radar? Have we detected *anything*?"

"Negative, Captain. The interference is too strong. If they're out there, they're blind, deaf, and mute."

Ash sighed. "Willis, where the hell are you, you old bastard?"

"Captain?" Jordan asked.

"Nothing." She changed the subject. "What's our current power situation?"

Jordan held up a clipboard. "Samson reported that we're running at ninety-two percent of power. That was three hours ago."

"A bit better than yesterday."

"Aye, Captain."

Ash took a moment, painfully aware that whatever decision came next could put the entire human race in jeopardy. She had hoped *Ares* would be waiting on the outskirts of the storm. Then she could have sent Hell Divers with fuel cells and whatever parts Willis needed.

Now she didn't have many options—at least, not many good ones. Ash couldn't leave the ship to die, but she couldn't risk navigating the storm to find it, either. An impossible choice, but she already knew what she had to do.

Flashes of lightning bloomed across the screen

in brilliant arcs, and in that fleeting glow, she saw an outline. Could it be … ?

"Did you see that?" Ash stepped closer to the screen.

Another bright net lit up the sky, but this time she saw only churning clouds. Perhaps that was all she had seen: a dark pile of cumulus in the form of a ship.

Jordan came and stood by her side. "What madness do you think drove Captain Willis inside there?"

"Desperation," Ash said.

"*Ares* is a strong ship. They could still be afloat."

"Aye," Ash replied. "But for how long?" Still peering into the storm, she said, "What did Samson say?"

"I haven't asked."

"Don't bother." She already knew the answer. The airships were built to survive storms, but only for a limited time. It didn't take many direct lightning strikes to rupture a gas bladder. Worse, the lightning could fry the extensive electrical network snaking through the bowels of the ships. Either event would be catastrophic.

Ash felt the eyes of her crew on her. Everyone was looking to her for orders. The moment she saw the storm, she had made her decision. Now it was time to give the hardest order of her command. She hated to say it, but Cruise was right: she couldn't risk the *Hive* to save *Ares*.

"The captains before me didn't keep the *Hive* in the sky by taking unnecessary risks," Ash said. Turning from the monitor, she looked toward her navigation officers. "Ryan, Hunt, keep us on the edge of the storm. Do not—I repeat, do *not*—enter without my command. I don't care if the *Ares* is ten feet on the other side."

Both ensigns acknowledged with short nods.

"Jordan, tell our comm team to keep hailing *Ares*. I want to know the minute we hear anything."

"Aye, Captain," he replied.

Ash spied a hint of a frown forming on Jordan's face. Like the phantom ship outline, it disappeared in the blink of an eye.

*   *   *   *   *

Travis stopped at a row of tomato plants in Compartment 1 and spat into the first pot. The dirt was moist with the saliva of other lower-deckers. They all worked together down here, using every resource they could to survive. Manure from the livestock that still remained became fertilizer for the plants growing under the lights. Hides and fur from slaughtered animals became clothing. He had a blanket made of rabbit furs, and his leather shoelaces were from a hog killed years ago. Nothing went to waste. Everything was used and reused.

He passed hundreds of cages of squawking chickens and chirping guinea pigs, and the platoons of workers tending the precious livestock. Captain Ash had apportioned these animals to the lower-deckers after the food riots nearly two years ago. It was a measure to prevent future rebellions, but only a Band-Aid on a bigger problem. Extra rations of eggs and guinea pig meat wouldn't begin to get at the real needs belowdecks.

Travis followed a line of passengers toward the two Militia soldiers standing guard at the stairs leading up. Some lower-deckers were going to work, others to the trading post to barter their produce. He wasn't doing either. He was on his way to the brig, to visit his brother.

The line surged forward, and Travis pulled out his ID. His head pounded from a migraine that he couldn't shake. The stench was starting to get to him again. Passing a pen of hogs, he coughed into the sleeve of his trench coat.

When he finally got to the front of the line, he thought he was going to puke. He handed his ID to the guard on his right.

"What's your business?"

Travis pulled a piece of paper authorizing access to the brig and gave it to the man. "I'm visiting someone."

The sentry held the ID under the bank of lights overhead and glanced at Travis, then studied the piece of paper. He gave both back to Travis and jerked his head toward the stairs. "Get moving."

Travis climbed the steps and negotiated the maze of corridors to get across the ship. He could have done it blindfolded if he wanted. He knew each passage, nook, and cul-de-sac by heart.

Passing the Wingman Tavern, he felt his anger rise. He hadn't realized it in his state of intoxication, but the HD who had smashed his head into the bar was Xavier Rodriguez, the most infamous diver on the ship. Travis' father, Ron, had dived with Xavier almost fifteen years ago, but Xavier probably wouldn't have remembered him, since he died ten jumps in. Just enough dives to earn Travis and his mother quarters abovedecks. But when the cough killed her, Travis joined Alex and his other friends down here. He had lived in Compartment 1 ever since, working as an electrician whenever there was work to be had.

He took a right at the junction. The corridor was empty except for a few soldiers coming from Militia Headquarters. The brig was the second door past the entrance to the HQ. Stopping outside, he brushed his dreadlocks over his shoulder. He entered the dimly lit room, furnished only with two chairs, and approached the front window.

A female guard, her blonde hair in a bun, glanced up at him from the other side, brushed the breadcrumbs off her gray uniform, and got up.

"Travis Eddie to see inmate Raphael Eddie." He held his authorization slip and ID against the window, and she took a look.

"Wait here," she said.

Travis watched her open the door to her booth and step into a narrow passageway. A few minutes later, the door opened again, and a man wearing a black hoodie walked into the guard booth. Hands shackled in front of him, eyes roving, he shuffled forward. He seemed oddly disoriented.

"You got ten minutes," the guard said, shutting the door with a thud that made the hooded man flinch. He looked at the door, then back at the glass window. His face was shadowed, but Travis could see the bony outline of his cheeks.

"That you, Trav?" the man whispered in a voice that sounded too weak to be Raphael. He stepped forward, raised his bound hands, and pulled the hoodie back. Thin black hair fell over his shoulders, and dark bags rimmed his eyes. He squinted into the light and blinked rapidly.

Only six months had passed since he last saw Raphael, but Travis hardly recognized the man standing before him. He wanted to cry out at the sight.

"Yeah, bro, it's me," Travis said. "Guess they aren't treating you all that well in there."

Raphael coughed, and a pained grin formed on his dry lips. "That's what happens when you help lead a riot. They don't waste rations on us, you know?"

Travis hardly noticed himself nodding. He was still shocked to see the frail man in front of him. The brother he remembered was strong, with broad shoulders and thick black hair like his.

"How are things out there, little brother?" Raphael asked. His right eye twitched as he sat down in the chair.

For months now, Travis had considered what he would say to Raphael, repeating the words over and over in his head before he went to bed each night. Now he couldn't remember them.

"Things are bad," Travis finally said. The Militia would be listening, but he wasn't going to lie. "Rations are still too low, and the one doctor Captain Ash assigned to the lower decks can't keep up. People are suffering worse than ever before."

Raphael stared ahead vacantly. His right eye twitched every few seconds, and he shivered in his chair. Travis wasn't sure he was even listening.

"You only got two more years in here," he said.

"That's nothing, man. When you get out, I'll have a jar of 'shine and a chicken for you—a *whole* chicken! I've been saving credits."

"Remember what Mom used to tell us?" Raphael blurted. "About the fall of Babylon and the end of the world?"

Travis thought back, the pained memories ricocheting through his mind. He could hardly remember her dark-brown eyes, let alone her stories.

"She was right, little brother," Raphael said, rocking a little in his chair now. "We brought this on ourselves. The human race was never supposed to live in the sky. We were supposed to die down there." He pointed a curled, yellowed fingernail at the floor.

A heavyset male guard opened the door and stepped inside the room. He crossed his arms over his chest and said, "You got one minute left."

Travis glared at him. "That wasn't ten minutes!"

Raphael shied away from the guard, scooting to the edge of his chair. He glanced back at Travis with sunken eyes bereft of hope, and Travis knew in that moment that he had lost his brother.

"You hang in there," Travis said. "You're gonna be fine. I'll see you in a few months."

Raphael mouthed something that Travis couldn't make out. At first, he thought it was "Help," but no, that was wrong. Before he could say anything else, the guard hoisted Raphael to his feet.

"Time to go," the guard said.

Raphael looked back at Travis once more and said, "Goodbye, Trav."

"Goodbye, Raphael," he whispered. He put a

hand on the glass and watched through a blur of tears as the guard whisked his brother away. It would have taken three guards to haul away the Raphael he remembered, but that man was gone now. It was up to Travis to fight and to prove that their mother had been wrong about humanity.

*　　*　　*　　*　　*

A Hell Diver hovered in the upward blast of air in one of the wind tunnels. X shut the door to the training facility and watched from the entrance. He could tell by the diver's graceful movements that it was Katrina DaVita. Arms and legs spread and head tilted upward, she rode the column of wind effortlessly. Ripples rolled across the slack in her suit as she moved precisely backward, forward, and sideways.

"Perfect," X whispered.

Katrina's moves prompted a few whistles and cheers from the other divers. X put a stop to that with a clap of his hands.

"Listen up!" he said, crossing the room in a hurry.

Tony gave a thumbs-up to Katrina. She flipped into a cross-legged sitting position, and he deactivated the wind tunnel with the flip of a switch. Settling gently to the floor, she flipped her visor and smiled at X. The joy in her grin told him Cruise and Tony hadn't disobeyed the order to keep quiet. The other teams still didn't know about *Ares*.

The divers circled around X, Tony, and Cruise. Katrina shucked off her helmet and brushed her cropped brown hair from her face. Her lips slowly relaxed into a thin line.

X waited till he had everyone's attention. When all eyes were on him, he said, "A few minutes ago, I was informed that we have arrived over the eastern outskirts of Hades."

At the news, all trace of civility disappeared in an instant, and the room erupted into chaos. Magnolia shouted the loudest.

"What the hell are we doing there?"

This got X a smirk from Cruise.

"Calm down," X said. "Everyone just calm the fuck down." The shouts dwindled into chatter and, eventually, silence.

"Captain Ash received an SOS from *Ares*. Details are still sketchy, but what we do know is, their ship was damaged in an electrical storm. Captain Willis came here to attempt a salvage op. He deployed a team to the surface—"

"They sent a team down *there*?" Murph gasped.

Several other divers shouted more questions while Katrina just bowed her head at the news. Murph scratched at his cheek, and even Sam couldn't hide the fear behind his stoic silence. Magnolia gaped, but when she saw X looking at her, she closed her mouth and started picking at a black-lacquered fingernail.

X unfolded his arms and rubbed his eyelids as the divers continued their rapid-fire shouting. He was tired and would rather be doing just about anything than field questions he didn't know the answers to.

"So what's this mean for us?" a diver from Team Angel said.

"Are we diving, too?" someone else asked.

"Let Commander Rodriguez finish," Tony said.

"There is *no* reason to believe we are going to dive," X added. "Captain Ash has only ordered us to prepare for a *possible* rescue operation. That's all."

"Wow, what a relief," Magnolia muttered. "Can't tell you how much better that makes me feel."

"A rescue op?" Sam asked.

"Yeah," X replied. "If we can locate their ship, then a team of divers will link up with *Ares* and provide whatever support they need. Could be parts, could be cells, or it could be something else. I simply don't know at this point."

Cruise shook his head. "We haven't done one of those for years. Half of us aren't even trained for it."

"All the more reason to stop talking and start prepping," X said.

"You heard him," Tony said. "Let's start the rescue-op drills."

"You're not going to tell everyone about the Sirens?" Cruise said. "About what you saw on your last dive?"

"Sirens?" Magnolia asked.

The words hung in the air for an uncomfortable moment. He shot Cruise a glare, holding back the dressing-down he wanted so badly to give.

"Well?" Magnolia said. "You gonna talk, or what?"

X hesitated, his gaze still burning into Cruise. They needed to train, not discuss man-eating monsters, but there was no way he could let this go now. He had to address it before fearful speculation spiraled out of control.

He turned to Magnolia and said, "I saw several creatures on my last dive. Some sort of mutants. Apparently, the divers from *Ares* saw them, too." He waited for the inevitable barrage of questions, but no one spoke—not even Magnolia, who stood twisting a strand of blue hair around her finger.

"I'm not sure what they are—or were—but they communicate in …" X grimaced at the memory of those paralyzing sounds. "They communicate through these high-pitched shrieks that sound exactly like an emergency siren."

"*That's* what killed your team?" Magnolia prodded in a voice just above a whisper.

"No," X said. "I told you. The storms killed them. But those things did try to hunt me. The Sirens, or whatever the hell you want to call them, must use some sort of sonar, because they don't have eyes."

His words met with silence, which only added to the tension he could feel swelling in the room. He thought of Aaron and the swarm of monsters that had torn him apart after the balloon yanked X out of their reach.

Tony clapped his hands. "Okay, people. Enough questions for now. Time to get started on the rescue drills."

Several divers groaned and started toward the operations room. Tony stopped to pat X on the shoulder, then followed the others. Katrina was the only one to stay behind. She walked over to X and stood by his side.

He gave her a sidelong glance. She was beautiful, but it wasn't just her looks. She was as strong as any of the men, both physically and mentally. She held her own in training and on dives, and every diver respected her.

Katrina smiled, seeing she had caught his attention.

X looked away. He had carried on an affair with Katrina behind his wife's back for almost six months, but then Rhonda got sick, and the day she was diagnosed with cancer, he broke things off with Katrina. He had stood by his wife in those agonizing last months, but even now, over a year later, just looking at Katrina felt like an insult to Rhonda's memory.

"You think this is a good idea?" Katrina asked.

It took a second for X to realize she was talking about *Ares*. "Hard to say," he replied. "Guess we will find out soon."

"Guess so," Katrina said. She brushed against him as she left.

Magnolia was waiting for her halfway across the room. They spoke in whispers, but X still heard every word Magnolia said.

"Hades is cursed after all … I've got a feeling we're about to find out why."

NINE

Weaver exploded out of the open warehouse doorway with such force that he tripped and crashed to the ground. He landed helmet first in the snow and bit his tongue. Ignoring the pain, he pushed himself back up and spun around to see shadowed shapes darting like lizards across the interior walls of the building.

Pounding through calf-deep snow, he reached into his vest pocket, fingering through the extra bullets until he had one between gloved fingers. A loud thunderclap overhead startled him, and he dropped the bullet in the snow.

Lighting rippled across the skyline—a brief display of blue against a bleak, dark horizon. The cries of the creatures followed Weaver through the maze of buildings. He had to find a place to hide before they found him.

He tried the door of the closest warehouse. *Locked.* The next was the same. As he bolted from building to building, the shrieks of the Sirens grew steadily louder behind him. The final structure had caved in like a crushed can. It was the same one he and Jones had escaped from earlier.

With nowhere to go, Weaver dashed out into the open industrial zone, searching frantically for shelter. In the distance, he could see a snow-covered road and the rounded bulky shapes of vehicles buried by the snow. Not the ideal place to hide, but he was out of options.

Panting hard, he pushed on, the coppery-salty taste of blood on his tongue. Every dozen yards, he would turn and scan for his pursuers which hadn't yet come into view, then pound ahead toward the oblique white mounds that hid Old World cars beneath them. Tripping over some hidden obstacle beneath the snow, he lost his balance and tumbled. He leaped back up to his feet and made a final dash toward the vehicles and away from the horrifying shrieks.

His only wisp of a chance was to lure the Sirens away from the buildings, find a vehicle to hide in, and then double back to grab some heavy weapons. That would give him a chance to fight his way into the warehouses and get the cells and pressure valves. If he survived that, he could deploy them—and himself—back to *Ares* in the crate.

It was a plan—admittedly, a crazy one, but it was the best he could come up with. A half-baked plan, adrenaline, and the desperation of a father trying to get home to his family were all he had, in this moment, to keep him moving.

Hazy lightning bloomed through the clouds, and the roar of thunder gave a brief reprieve from the shrieks behind him. He darted another glance over his shoulder, and this time he saw them. They came bounding over the snow on all fours, heads tucked down between bony shoulders, dorsal fins waving back and forth as they hurtled forward.

They were fast, and they were gaining. He had to get away from those awful teeth and talons.

Swiping away the grit that had collected on his visor, he pounded toward the snow-covered vehicles. Most of them were completely buried, but the wind had eaten away the drifts on a few, exposing doors and broken windows.

In the fifty yards, the boom of thunder seemed to come from all directions, as if the storm itself, swirling above Hades, were alive. He flinched at the raucous boom and the horrible squalls that followed.

Reaching the road, he found firmer footing, then slid on both knees to a half-buried vehicle. He pawed through an open window framed with crusted snow, climbed inside, and flattened out on the seat.

A barrage of thunder rang out over Hades. The reverberations shook the rusted vehicle, and flakes of snow rained down from the roof. But meanwhile, the sounds of the monsters grew strangely fainter. At first, Weaver thought it was the storm masking their cries, but when he slowly raised his helmet to peek out the window, he saw them galloping away from the road, kicking up a plume of snow in their wake.

Another thunderbolt cracked overhead, drawing Weaver's attention to the sky. A brilliant web of lightning, with a dozen arms, flashed across the horizon. Two blue tendrils licked the top of the highest tower in the distance, and sparks showered down on the frozen streets. The storm was intensifying. The Sirens, as if sensing it, vanished in the maze of domed ITC buildings a moment later.

Weaver lowered his helmet, breathing a sigh of relief. He could deal with the storm now that he was safe from the Sirens.

A sudden tremor shook the ground, causing the rusted metal to rattle around him. He poked his head back up and checked again to make sure the creatures were really gone. Seeing no sign of them, he climbed through the window and dropped to the snow. He had been given a reprieve, and he wasn't going to waste it hiding.

As soon as he pushed himself to his feet, another explosion shook him. He surveyed the storm clouds roiling above the abandoned city to the east. It was hard to believe that this had once been a thriving metropolis, with more people than Weaver had ever seen in one place. Now only Sirens occupied this cursed ground.

Another resounding crash of thunder exploded somewhere deep in the clouds. The roar rattled his senses, forcing every thought from his mind but one: he couldn't stay here any longer. If he did, he risked being hit by lightning. And so he ran until he thought he would vomit.

The compact snow shook under his feet as the thunder amplified, but something didn't add up: the sky was dark. There was no lightning.

He was halfway back to the ITC warehouses when he finally stopped and stared up into the storm. Explosions continued to boom, but without one trace of lightning.

Weaver's chest thumped with the concussion of

each blast. The sky suddenly blossomed with a blast of red so bright, he had to shut off his night vision. As he blinked away the light blindness, a deafening whistle shrilled louder and louder.

Up in the clouds, a glowing shape split through the storm. Weaver froze and watched as red tendrils streaked away from the flaming hulk that arced toward Hades at a forty-five-degree angle.

"No," he whispered. "Please, God, no."

Part of him still didn't believe it was possible, until he saw the curved outline of *Ares* break through the clouds. Flames trailed the airship as it screamed toward the city. The sound morphed into a screech louder than all the Sirens combined. Weaver watched in shock.

He was too late. He had failed his family—failed every soul aboard *Ares*. For one deluded moment, he held on to the hope that Captain Willis could land her still—that maybe they could salvage the ship and find a way to launch her back into the air.

Then the ship smashed into one of the skyscrapers, shearing off the spire with a hollow crack. It hit another and another, taking the tops off cleanly.

Fire exploded out of the sides of the damaged craft as it came crashing to earth. The shattered bow of *Ares* collided with the ground, sending up a cloud of dirt and dust into the sky. A crimson bubble expanded and popped, bathing the dead city in fire. The explosion engulfed the entire ship, leaving no question that every soul on board had perished.

With a whimper, Weaver fell to both knees and

watched as a thousand-foot fireball consumed his family and the only home he had ever known.

*   *   *   *   *

Tin studied the flickering bank of LEDs, rocking gently with the motion of the ship, above Professor Lana's desk. He counted the seconds between blinks: three this time. Something was wrong. Last time, they had flickered for two seconds.

He leaned over to Layla and tapped her desk. Her elbow slipped, and the palm holding up her head up fell away.

"Hey!" she whispered. "I was trying to work." Her sleepy eyes said otherwise.

"Right," Tin whispered, grinning as he settled back in his seat. He concentrated on the lights again. The panel hanging in the front of the room was no more interesting than Professor Lana's lecture on how the *Hive*'s massive internal gas bladders worked, but he had already finished reading the training manual. He knew how to patch one if it failed.

"Why do you think we changed course?" Layla whispered.

He shrugged. "Probably to avoid an electrical storm."

"Aren't the engineers still fixing the wires that got fried in the last power surge?"

"Yup. They're probably in the crawl space below us right now. That'll be me someday, you know."

"The gas bladders are the most fragile part of the *Hive*," Professor Lana said. "Like a living creature losing too much blood, if the ship loses too much helium, it will die." She looked at the red oval clock behind her desk and stood. "Looks like it's time for our next class, everyone. Finish your lessons and pack up. Oh, and don't forget to read lesson three-point-one tonight on helium and how we keep a steady supply. It's very important."

Tin shot out of his chair. His next class wasn't a class. It was a field trip! He stuffed his books into his bag and followed the other kids into the hallway, where two senior engineers in light-blue coveralls were waiting.

Professor Lana approached them and murmured softly, "Is it safe to leave the classroom right now? The ship's been rocking a lot lately."

The older of the two said, "Safe as safe can be. I'll keep 'em close. Nothing to worry about, I'm sure." He was probably too thick in the middle to maneuver in the crawl spaces anymore.

The other engineer was short and wiry—the ideal body type for someone who had to spend most of his time in cramped spaces. He had a thick silver beard with a mustache that curled at the ends. The bent bill of a ball cap covered his eyes.

Professor Lana smiled and said, "Kids, this is Eli, and this is …" She looked to the larger engineer.

"Ned." He grinned and took it from there. "So you kids want to be engineers?"

"That *is* why we're here," Andrew quipped.

Lana shot him a disapproving look. "Yes, everyone here has enrolled in the engineering program. I was teaching them how to fix the internal gas bladders just today."

"Is that right?" Eli said, scratching at his beard. "Gas bladders are very important, but today, we're showing you something else. Who's ready to see the water treatment plant? Some of you might end up working there someday."

Tin raised his hand. He looked around him. It appeared that the others kids didn't seem to share his enthusiasm for water reclamation technology. They all wore the same bored look. For them, this was just an opportunity to get out of class, nothing more. Andrew smirked at Tin's obvious eagerness and whispered something. Several of the other boys chuckled.

But Tin wasn't going to let them ruin his mood. Not today. He snugged the tinfoil hat down on his head as the two engineers led the class through the passages, to a three-way intersection. A sentry holding a big rifle stood at a door across the hallway. It led to the second and third floors—off limits to most residents, except today. Touring the water reclamation plant was a rite of passage for students in the engineering program.

Eli pulled a key card and his identification from his pocket. The soldier gave a brusque nod, pulled out his own key card, and waved it over the security panel. The door clicked open.

"Stay in single file," said the soldier. "And don't touch anything."

"Did everybody hear that?" Professor Lana asked.

Tin fell in behind the other ten kids. Unable to see over the heads in front of him, he edged his way around to the side and waited impatiently as the other students slowly filed into the stairwell. As he was about to enter, he spied a man with long black hair and a trench coat across the hall. He seemed to be watching them. Another man, wearing a scarf pulled up to his nose, ambled by and nodded at the lower-decker in the black coat. Tin hovered outside the doorway, scrutinizing the two men from a distance. It wasn't all that cold in the passage, so why would anyone wear a scarf?

"Let's go, kid," the soldier said.

Tin continued into the stairwell and glanced over his shoulder as the guard was closing the door. Then it occurred to him that the two men were interested in the security checkpoint, not in Tin's class.

This was strange, and it gave Tin an uneasy feeling, but he wasn't going to let anything distract him from the tour. He looked back up at the other kids. The glow of a single red light spilled over the group as they shuffled noisily up the rungs.

Halfway up the stairs, they stopped. Tin stood on his tiptoes and put his hand on Layla's back. The two engineers were standing on the second-floor landing, outside the farms, where Eli was talking to another soldier.

"What's going on?" Tin whispered.

Layla shook her head.

Eli stepped away from the soldier and looked down the stairs. "Today, we have a special treat for you," he said. "Today, you also get to see the farms. You all can thank Hell Diver Xavier Rodriguez for that. He managed to convince Command to let you sneak a peek."

Tin couldn't believe his ears. X had done that?

For *him*? Tin removed his hand from Layla's back and saw that Andrew was staring down at him. He had an odd look on his face, as if he was sorting something out. He flashed Tin a smile. A *real* smile, not a cocky I'm-going-to-kick-your-ass-later smile.

The soldier pulled the rusted door open and waved the group forward. The brilliant white glow of the grow lights blasted Tin's eyes, and he shielded his face. Grow lights were ten times brighter than any other lights on the ship.

He followed the kids in front of him into a plastic bubble room, where his eyes adjusted to the most beautiful sight he had ever seen.

"You're standing inside the vestibule to the clean room," Ned said. "All farmers are required to go through a rigorous cleansing process before entering the farm." He turned and looked through the translucent sides of the bubble. "For two hundred and fifty years, this massive space has provided the *Hive* with the nutrients to keep our species alive, as it will for the next two hundred and fifty."

"Feel free to take a look around," Eli said.

"But remember, don't touch anything," Professor Lana added.

The translucent plastic box was the size of their classroom, with sinks set up in the east corner. Tin walked to the northern wall, where the other kids had gathered to look out over the fields.

Ned crowded behind them, and Tin could feel his hot breath on his neck. It stank of 'shine and coffee.

"Pretty great, isn't it?" Ned said.

Tin nodded and worked his way up to the front

of the group, squeezing next to Layla. His eyes swept over the farm. Rows of mature corn, taller than he was, ran from stern to bow. A plot of green beans and spinach grew in the field to the east. The different shades of green practically glowed under the full-spectrum light.

For the first time in his life, he felt the tightness lifting around him, as if he had shed a garment that was too tight. He no longer felt so trapped or isolated.

"The farms are six hundred feet at their longest point and two hundred and twenty feet wide," Eli said. "We cultivate twenty different vegetables and ten different fruits, all genetically modified to grow in the conditions here. The lights are attached to the ceiling with steel wires that can be lowered and retracted. Somewhere in the central control center, a technician is monitoring exactly how much light the crops have received over the past twenty-four hours. A program will indicate whether they need to be dimmed, brightened, or shut off."

He pointed to the other end of the room. "Over there is where we raise our livestock."

Tin followed the man's finger toward dozens of pens and several long sheds with low roofs. They shifted to the other side of the room, which put him in the back once again. He stood on his toes, trying to see over the other kids' heads.

"We have chickens, cows, sheep, pigs, rabbits, guinea pigs, dogs, and turkeys," Eli continued.

"How do you keep healthy populations?" Lana asked.

"The livestock are also genetically engineered.

We've lost quite a few populations over the years. Needless to say, every single animal in this room is on the endangered-species list."

Layla nudged Tin in the side. "Makes you wonder what other animals used to live down there, huh?"

Tin nodded and looked into the animal pens, where a dog stared back at them. It had a silver coat, with a dash of chocolate brown circling one of its blue eyes.

The animal stood at the gate, looking directly at the plastic room. A smaller dog with a mane of black fur strolled up beside it, tilting its head and studying their observers.

"That's Silver and Lilly," Eli said. "They're both huskies."

"But why dogs?" Andrew asked. "It's not like we eat 'em."

"Good question," Eli replied. "Ever heard the saying 'a dog is man's best friend'?"

Most of the kids around Tin shook their head or just gave him a blank look.

Eli frowned and said, "Someone must have really loved them back in the day. They come from a long line of huskies that have lived on the ship. Those are the last two, though. And the male is sterile—another example of where genetic engineering failed."

"Why continue to feed them?" Lana asked. "That's food that could be used for more productive purposes."

Silver gave a low, throaty growl, as if he understood her. A farmer inside the pen knelt to calm him, but the dog took off running. He circled the enclosed area, barking as he ran. In the blink of an eye, Lilly started barking excitedly and went chasing after Silver.

"What the hell?" Ned muttered.

Tin saw flashes of motion in the other fenced-in areas. The turkeys were squawking, the cows were pawing and bawling, and the hogs were slamming into their metal barriers. Everywhere he looked, the animals were frantic.

The ship suddenly shook violently, knocking Tin and several of the other kids to the deck. Screams filled the plastic room. Tin reached for something to hold on to as the floor tilted. Sliding across the cold floor, he felt a sharp pain in his forehead as it whacked against the exposed pipe underneath a sink.

A strong tremor rippled through the ship as it leveled back out. Tin sat up and touched the drip of blood from his forehead. The sound of crunching plastic pulled his attention to the entrance of the room. Two farmers unzipped the front door and hurried inside. The woman on the left ripped a white mask away from her mouth and yelled, "Everyone out! Get to the emergency shelters!"

Tin could see the others scrambling to their feet around him, but he couldn't get up. The sweet scent of the harvested fruit lingered. The majesty of the dogs, and the breathtaking feat of engineering, mingled somehow with the terror he felt from the lurching ship. It was as if his brain couldn't separate the beauty from the horror.

Tin closed his eyes and felt powerful hands pulling him to his feet. Someone carried him into a stairwell. When he opened his eyes again the lights were flickering. His blurred vision cleared enough that he could distinguish Eli's silver beard in front of him.

"Hold on tight, kid," he said. "I'm taking you to the med ward."

Over the discord of the groaning ship and emergency sirens, Tin heard Silver and Lilly barking. A moment later, a hollow thud reverberated through the *Hive*, and he was shrouded in darkness.

*   *   *   *   *

Red light flooded the bridge, and the wail of an emergency siren echoed through the room. Captain Ash cupped her throbbing forehead and pulled away from the medic trying to assist her. There were more important things to worry about than a minor bang on the head.

"What the hell happened?" Ash yelled, making her way down the aisle of monitors to navigation. Jordan was already at Ensign Hunt's station.

Ryan, the skinny nav ensign, hovered behind them. He met Ash's searching gaze with a rueful look.

"Captain, the storm—it grew before we could react," Hunt said. "We were on the border when it swallowed us, like *that*. He shook his head and looked at his screen.

"How bad's the damage?" Ash said.

"Not sure, Captain," Jordan replied. "Engineering hasn't given me a Sitrep yet."

"Hunt, how far are we from the storm?"

"Three miles, ma'am."

"Double that margin," she ordered.

"Aye, Captain."

Ash could hardly hear the ensign's reply over the wail of the sirens, but she could see his strained face in the red glow of the emergency lights.

"Someone get me a goddamn Sitrep from engineering!" Ash shouted. She was furious at herself and everyone else on her team. The storms were unpredictable, but Ryan and Hunt should have seen this coming. And she should never have left the bridge. It was the second disastrous mistake in a week.

"I'm getting a report from Medical," Jordan said, cupping his palm over his earpiece to listen. "So far, we have four dead, from engineering. They must have been killed belowdecks."

Ash shuddered at the thought. She had seen only images of the dark, hot, cramped passages, but Mark had been inside them during his training when they were newlyweds. He had said the tunnels were barely large enough to squirm through—and he was not a big man.

What an awful place to die.

"Medical's reporting multiple injuries, too," Jordan added.

"How many?"

"I don't know, Captain. They don't have an accurate count yet."

"Video coming back online," Ryan said.

Ash glanced at the screen. The cams on the *Hive's* stern flickered back to life, capturing a live feed of the horizon. Lightning flashes split the darkness, lighting up the billowing cumulus from within. The purple edges of the storm swelled, reaching out as if it were giving chase, and Ash finally saw why it had caught her nav team by surprise. The men hadn't been asleep at the helm; the storm was expanding faster than any they had ever seen.

"Captain, I'm picking up beacon," Hunt said. "I think it's ... Wait, that can't be right."

"What?" Ash's hoarse voice barked.

Hunt squinted at his screen and then glanced up at Ash, his eyes wide. "I think it's *Ares'* beacon," he said.

"Where?" said Ash. "How far?" She hurried down the ramp to the bottom floor, hoping to catch a glimpse of the airship onscreen.

Hunt's response sounded distant. "From the surface, Captain. The ship is ..." His voice trailed off, drowned out by the wailing sirens.

Ash closed her eyes. Her entire body went numb, as if it no longer belonged to her. Her worst fear had finally come true. They were Earth's last ship.

The *Hive* was alone.

TEN

X pushed his way through the frantic hubbub outside the med ward. Most people made way when they saw his uniform. One man, however, eyed him with blatant resentment. As if X's ninety-six jumps didn't count for dirt. As if X was gaming the system.

Well, he was. But he didn't care.

Tin was somewhere inside the overcrowded clinic, and X was desperate to find him. He scanned the beds of burned or wounded patients, hesitating every time he saw a kid. Some were almost unrecognizable under the bloody rags covering their wounds.

X grimaced and kept moving.

"Tin!" he yelled, his voice hardening. "Tin, where are you?"

A weak tug on his sleeve pulled him toward a shadowy hallway. Tin's friend Layla was standing there, her cheeks shiny with tears. "Over here," she whimpered.

X hurried after her, passing more injured patients. His gut tightened when he saw Tin with a bandage wrapped around his head. He was hunched over an old man's bedside, hands clamped down over the patient's thigh.

"Are you hurt?" X said, rushing over.

Tin shook his head and glanced back down at the man. He pushed harder, eliciting a groan of agony.

"Shit," X said. "Let me." Brushing Tin's hands aside, he saw the deep gash and quickly applied pressure. Blood seeped around his palms, staining everything red.

"He's bleeding out," X said. "Where the hell are the nurses and docs?"

His words fell on deaf ears. The few medical workers were doing triage—busy saving people they could actually save, and leaving the old, weak, and mortally wounded to die. He knew because in their shoes he would do the same thing. It was the reality of working with limited resources. Life-and-death decisions were made on the fly, and efficient triage meant that some people just weren't going to make it.

Realizing now that his efforts were futile, X let up on the gushing wound. The man stared at the ceiling with blank eyes. His chest moved up and down twice more before his gasps for air weakened to nothing.

X wiped his blood-soaked hands on his red uniform, looked at Tin, and frowned. "Sorry, kid."

The boy didn't reply. He bent over and grabbed something from below the bed that X couldn't see.

"Commander!" a voice boomed above the confusion.

He turned to see a Militia soldier in gray fatigues, running down the hallway. The mirrored visor on his riot helmet was flipped up, and X saw the urgency in his eyes.

"Commander, Captain Ash has requested all Hell Divers meet on the bridge immediately."

"I'll be there in a few minutes."

"Sir, my orders are to escort you to—"

"I said I'll be there," X snarled.

The soldier nodded and hurried away. Looking down at Tin, X missed his best friend more than ever. The boy had removed his bandage and replaced it with the tinfoil hat.

"You sure you're okay?" X asked, looking into his eyes, checking the pupils.

Tin nodded and straightened his hat. But his eyes couldn't hide the truth: that he had just seen someone die and that he wasn't okay. After everything the kid had been through, X wasn't sure he would ever be okay again.

"You stay with Layla and her family until I get back, okay?"

Tin nodded again.

X imagined Rhonda's disapproving frown as he patted the boy on the shoulder and turned to double-time it back to the bridge. She never did understand the oath he had sworn to the *Hive*. Or, perhaps selfishly, she didn't want to. Aaron would have understood, though. For a Hell Diver, duty to the ship came before everything else.

*   *   *   *   *

If not for the mission clock on his HUD, Weaver

wouldn't have known that night had fallen. He sat with his legs hanging off a pile of rubble, watching *Ares* burn in the distance. Tendrils of flames reached toward the sky.

His body felt numb—whether from the fatigue, the cold, or the emotions swirling through him, he couldn't say. He remembered wondering what it would be like to be the last man on earth. Now he knew. Even if the *Hive* was still out there, he was the only man on the surface.

The cries of the Sirens reverberated through the city, but he paid them little attention. If they came now, he wouldn't run. There was no reason to carry on. Everything had changed when *Ares* came crashing down to earth. His wife and kids were gone, along with every human he had ever known.

Before this dive, he had been thinking about asking for a transfer to the Militia so he could spend more time with his family. Usually, Hell Divers kept jumping until their luck finally ran out. But if Weaver were to die, his experience would die with him. He had done this his entire life. He had put his time in, fulfilled his duty. That would have been his pitch to Captain Willis.

An explosion ripped through the burning debris—a painful reminder that none of that mattered now. The glare dazzled him momentarily, and he closed his eyes to block out the nightmare for a few seconds—only to have a memory of his family reassemble in his mind.

He could see Kayla and Cassie vividly. Both girls sat on the living room floor of his cramped apartment, their freckled faces bright in the glow of candles from Jennifer's birthday cake.

Another blast roared in the distance, but Weaver kept his eyes closed, trying to stay back in the sky with his family as long as he could. After a few minutes, he was only vaguely aware of the burning ship.

"Happy birthday, beautiful." Weaver heard his own voice in his head and saw his wife turn and smile that same perfect smile he had fallen in love with twenty years ago.

"Come over and help me blow out these candles!" he remembered her saying.

In the memory, Weaver walked to the table and put his arms around his daughters. Jennifer blew out a weak breath and frowned, looking to Kayla and Cassie.

"Can you girls help me?" she said.

His daughters leaned in and blew with every bit of breath in their lungs. Weaver recalled his own smile, and how odd it had felt at the time.

Kayla and Cassie had laughed and looked up at him. But something was different now. There was something wrong with the cake in his memory. The candles were burning out of control, the wax leaking onto the vanilla frosting. He could see Jennifer's smile relax with the rest of her features, and then her cheeks contorted, her skin melting and falling away from her jaw.

The once-happy memory now a nightmare, Weaver wanted to open his eyes, wanted to make it stop. But if he did, he would open them to the real nightmare of his home and family gone. There was no escaping it.

Tears rolled down his dry skin, and he watched in horror as his daughters' faces softened and peeled away from their bones. Their clothes caught fire, and they slumped to the ground. The shriek of a Siren ripped their burning bodies away from his mind, and his eyes finally snapped open.

"No!" Weaver shouted. "No!"

He gasped for air, clutching at the armor over his chest with one hand and pushing at the ground with the other. Rising to his feet, he looked out over the bluff. Pinpricks of red light surrounded the charred remnants of the airship.

"I'm sorry," Weaver whispered. "God, I'm so sorry for …" He choked on his words, distracted by a blur of motion in the sky. Something swooped from the clouds and soared over the field of embers, vanishing in the plumes of smoke.

Weaver fumbled for his binos, wondering if he was really losing his mind. He pulled them from his vest and zoomed in on the debris for the first time. Scattered coals glowed everywhere he looked. Pieces of shrapnel, hunks of metal … His breath caught at the sight of smoldering bodies.

"My girls," he murmured. "My beautiful baby girls." He felt like tossing the binos and screaming at the top of his lungs, but another flash of movement streaked over the embers. He followed a dark outline to the edge of the field, where it dropped to the ground. Another brilliant explosion ripped through *Ares,* spreading a curtain of light over the wreckage.

Weaver shielded his helmet with one hand and waited a moment for the brilliance to pass. When the light began to recede, he brought the binos to his visor and searched the field. A Siren stood over one of the embers, but this one was different. Leathery wings hung at its sides. It dropped to all fours and hunched its back, and the spiked vertebrae split in half, swallowing the wings like a mouthful of teeth closing over some morsel. The monster let out a screech, and a cacophony of wails answered from the sky.

Within seconds, a squadron of Sirens was soaring through the smoke and wheeling over the smoking bodies. He staggered closer to the edge of the bluff.

The realization hit him harder than a crosswind on a dive. The creatures were here to scavenge. Waiting for the fires to die down so they could feed on the burned bodies of his family and the other dead passengers of *Ares*. He started to feel his body for the first time since the crash.

When the numbness had finally passed, and the anger of a man who had lost everything took hold, he swung open the cylinder of his revolver and, with cold, stiff fingers, loaded the last of his bullets. Then he tapped his minicomputer to run a diagnostic on his suit. The cracked screen was frozen solid.

It didn't matter. All he needed was enough battery to get to the wreckage and search it for his family so he could give them a proper burial. He would rather the Sirens ripped him apart than let them feed on his girls' remains.

Weaver pushed the final bullet into the cylinder of his revolver and closed it. Trekking toward the wreckage, he tried to remember the words from

Jones' prayer, but after a few minutes he gave up. "I'm coming home, girls," he whispered. "I'm finally coming home."

*   *   *   *   *

Captain Ash ran through the hallways on her way to engineering. She couldn't remember the last time she had visited Samson in the filthy compartment tucked just inside the hull of the *Hive,* but she couldn't wait for him to report in. She needed to know their situation *now.*

The closest entrance was a two-minute walk from the bridge. Her presence drew the gaze of every resident flowing through the halls. Most were gazes of resentment and anger. They wanted someone to blame for the power shortages, the radiation poisoning, the meager rations. Naturally, that blame rested with her, even though she had done everything in her power to keep the lower-deckers alive. She had given them a third of the livestock from the farm, given them their own doctor—even given them extra rations. None of that seemed to matter to anyone. Most of them didn't have any real grasp of how the ship operated. In the past, they had reverted to riots, and there were rumors of another rebellion brewing. She turned a blind eye to the black-market goods they sold, but violence was the one thing she absolutely would not tolerate on her ship.

Ash walked with her head held high because in the end, it didn't matter what they thought, so long as she kept them alive. It was the burden many leaders had carried before her, and she shouldered it without complaining. One day, they would thank her when she led them to a new home, one with real ground beneath their feet and the sun overhead. But that dream seemed far away now.

A soldier standing guard outside engineering threw a quick salute as Ash and her armed escort approached. The entrance was tucked away in a dimly lit hallway off the main corridor.

"Captain," the man said. He raised a clipboard. "I wasn't expecting anyone from command this morning."

"Samson doesn't know I'm coming."

"No problem, ma'am," the guard said. He waved his key card over the security panel and hoisted the door open.

"Stay here," Ash said to the two soldiers. The door sealed behind her with a metallic snick, and she could hear the hum and clank of the engine compartment. The noise reminded her that she was about to enter a world of grease and smoke—a world much different from the spotless white bridge.

Samson waited at the bottom of the staircase with his hands on his wide hips.

He scowled and raised his brows as if to say, *I told you so*. Ash didn't have time to argue with him. She needed to know their situation, and she needed the information ten minutes ago.

"Talk to me," she said. "How bad is it?"

Samson grunted. "Bad, Captain. Really bad. We're running on battery power. I was forced to shut down *all* the reactors. There are several leaks."

He paused and massaged his forehead. "They're contained—for now. But I lost four men. They sacrificed themselves so the radiation wouldn't kill everyone aboard."

Ash felt the anger threaten to take hold again. "I'm sorry, Samson ..."

He held up a hand. "I don't think you understand, Captain. The damage to the ship is critical. I'm not sure I can fix her this time. Six of our gas bladders ruptured from a power surge. We lost a thousand cubic feet of helium, and as you know, it takes time to produce more through our usual collection method."

Ash could hardly believe what she was hearing. How could the ship go from being in its best in years, to worst?

Hades, that's how.

Burying her misgivings over the ill-fated rescue attempt, she said, "How much longer until the gas bladders are fixed and refilled?"

Samson rubbed his eye, leaving a streak of grease. "I ... I don't know. Harvesting helium isn't easy, Captain."

"Then show me the damage."

"With all due respect, I don't have time for a tour," Samson said. "I need to fix our ship!"

"And I need to see the damage so I know what I'm dealing with."

"Suit yourself," he huffed. He led her across the small lobby and into the offices. Row after row of faded metal desks filled the room, but only two engineers were working there.

Samson stopped at a door on the opposite end of the room and lifted a breathing apparatus from a cabinet on the wall. He handed it to the captain. "There was a fire earlier. Might still be smoke."

Ash slid the mask over her face and tightened the band around her ponytail. Samson waved at the security camera and gave a thumbs-up. The door chirped and swung open.

A wave of heat rolled over them as they stepped onto the catwalk extending over the machinery. The hiss of steam and clack of parts that needed grease filled the room.

Engineers in light-blue coveralls clustered around the generators, checking displays and gauges to make sure the turbines were working properly, oblivious of the observers above them. They each had a task that, combined with the others, kept the *Hive* flying.

Samson moved to the other side of the mezzanine and pointed to a metal block, covered in white foam, on the aft starboard corner of the room. "One of the generators was destroyed," he said. "There's no fixing it. But it's the reactors I'm most worried about."

As they continued down the walkway, Ash imagined the thermal energy flowing from the reactors belowdecks to the generators. The steam produced by the heat turned a turbine inside as it passed, and the rotary motion created the electricity. The electric power then traveled through miles of conduit that stretched throughout the bowels of the ship, to all the places it was needed. That energy fed everything from the ship's motors to the lights above her head. The nuclear reactors were the heart of the ship, powering all its systems.

"All but one of our reactors has been damaged," Samson said. "The pressure valves on reactors two through eight are stuck. Even if I can unstick them, they still have to be replaced." He pointed toward the west wall. "I have a team belowdecks now, and I've already diverted power from every source I can, but it's not going to be enough."

Ash followed Samson's pudgy finger, which pointed to an open hatch. An engineer in a space suit crawled out of the opening and dropped to the deck. Even from a distance, she could see the grease and ash that covered him. The worker removed his helmet and broke into a coughing fit. A medic wearing a red cross on his arm rushed over, pulled an oxygen mask out, and helped the injured man slide it over his face.

Ash blinked, taking it all in. The damage was beyond comprehension. Her effort to save *Ares* may well have doomed her own ship.

"My God," she murmured.

"No," Samson muttered. "Not even God can save us if we don't get the reactors back online. Until then, I'm requesting we shut down every noncritical system on the ship and divert that power to the turbofans, the farm, and the water treatment plant. It's time to get out the candles."

"Are you sure that's the only way? There's been increasing unrest lately. A blackout will only make things worse. We could face another—"

"Damn it, Captain, we need to shut down the

power to the lower decks. Every dwelling, every store—*everything* that's nonessential. The mechanical threats are worse than any human threat on board."

Ash took a few seconds to consider the ramifications of Samson's request, then nodded. "I'll have Jordan put out the order to increase security on the ship. Every Militia soldier will be put on patrol and sentry duty."

"Good," Samson said. He pulled a folded piece of paper from his coveralls. "I've put together a list of what I need to get the reactors back online. In the meantime, the remaining gas bladders will keep us in the air—as long as we don't lose another one. We can only run on backup power for about forty-eight hours."

Ash took the list and turned away from the railing. "I'll tell Jordan to plot us a course to the closest location for the items on your list."

He held up his hand. "We won't make it far. The turbofans and rudders will drain the backup power faster if we try." He paused and gave her a meaningful look. "I can't believe I'm saying this, but I'm afraid our only option is a dive into Hades."

The lesion in Ash's throat burned, and her gut ached. Resisting the urge to put her hand to her stomach, she clenched her jaw and looked out over the compartment. Everything had changed in the blink of an eye. *Ares* was gone. The *Hive* was dying, and she was going to have to do exactly what Captain Willis had been forced to do. She finally understood. Willis hadn't been crazy, or even foolhardy—just desperate. They had all just been trying to survive—like her, trying to save their people.

"How long can you hold off on diverting energy from the noncritical functions?" Ash asked.

"I'd like to do it ASAP," Samson said. "But if you need time …" He glanced down at his watch. "I'd say you have nine hours, tops."

"I'll make an announcement tomorrow morning, first thing. You stay close to the damn radio, Samson. We may be forced to turn those reactors back on. You got it?"

The engineer nodded again, his dewlaps jiggling. "I'll keep things running the best I can until then." He pushed off the railing. "Now, if you'll excuse me, I need to get down there with my crew."

Taking his place at the railing, she gripped the warm metal and stared at the hatch that led down to the reactors. The injured engineer was slipping his helmet back on and preparing to reenter the tunnel. They all had jobs to do, and like the engineers below, Captain Maria Ash had to get on with hers. She had a ship to command, a riot to forestall, and over five hundred souls to protect.

ELEVEN

X breathed hard on his way to the bridge. The slow flow of foot traffic was giving him ample time to regret the advice he had given Captain Ash about the journey to Hades. Regret was something he had lived with his entire life, but this time he feared he had helped drive the final nail into *Homo sapiens'* coffin.

That was the thing about extinction: every move became a life-or-death decision, with the fate of entire species on the line.

Emergency sirens blared from the wall-mounted speakers. Ignoring the sounds was impossible, and X didn't want to look like some milquetoast by cupping his hands over his ears. So he worked his way stoically through the crowd.

Red light bathed the frightened faces around him. He pushed through a knot of lower-deckers who had gathered outside the bridge. They yelled in their twangy accent at a pair of Militia soldiers wearing riot gear and shoving the swelling crowd back.

"Ya can't do this!" an emaciated man yelled. "We got a right to eat!"

Jordan, standing behind the soldiers, raised a

hand and shouted, "Rations will be handed out in a few hours!"

No sooner had the words left the lieutenant's mouth than the furious crowd surged forward. Angry screams broke out over the sirens.

X waited for the guards to push the lower-deckers back. He scanned the faces, stopping on a man who hung back in the shadows. Even in the muted red glow, he could see the bruised face. It was Travis, the man he'd had the run-in with at the Wingman three nights ago. He had three others with him, each with a hard and hungry look on his face. A man wearing a scarf pulled up to his nose stared back at X with crazed eyes. He remembered that one, too, from the encounter in the hallway yesterday. These were the same two who had mouthed off to the Militia soldiers.

"Xavier, let's go!" Jordan shouted.

X looked Travis up and down one last time before pushing his way through the crowd. That hothead was trouble. He'd have to warn Ash to keep an eye out.

Even with the emergency lights, it was dark inside the bridge—darker still when one of the guards sealed the doors behind X. He hurried across the top landing and followed Jordan to the conference room.

The other Hell Diver team leads were already waiting inside. Ash sat at the head of the table with a disconcerting look on her face. All eyes gravitated to X as he entered. He had forgotten about the blood-stains on his uniform.

"Listen up, everyone," Ash said. She waited for silence, then said, "*Ares* is gone and the *Hive* is in critical shape." Her voice had a mournful tone. X imagined he would have sounded about the same.

No one replied for several seconds.

Jordan was first to speak. "Samson has shut down all the reactors, and we're running on backup power. We also lost six of the gas bladders. He's got his crews working on everything, but it's not looking good."

"What?" Tony asked. "How the hell … ?"

Ash silenced him with a raised hand. "Doesn't matter right now. All that matters is that we get more fuel cells and pressure valves."

"Or what?" Cruise asked.

"Or we join *Ares* on the surface," Ash replied. "Lieutenant, fill everyone in on our current location."

Jordan activated the console in front of him. A holographic map stretched over the table. "There are several known locations of fuel cells in the zone to the east. Unfortunately, they're all too far away. It would take us too long to get there, expending power we don't have. As I said, we're running on battery power. A journey to any of these possible locations would drain the system."

"We're out of options," Ash said. "We have to send you to the surface."

Cruise slammed the table with his fist. "I told you this was a bad fucking idea! Now you expect us to give our lives for your mistake?"

X understood Cruise's anger. What he couldn't excuse, though, was his utter lack of empathy. He gave him a hard look that did little to change his tone.

"Since when did you start forgetting your duty, Commander?" Ash replied.

"Excuse me?" Cruise said. "I've *never* forgotten my duty to the *Hive*."

"I'm talking about your duty to humankind," Ash said.

Cruise stared at her with the resentful eyes of a man who had argued himself into a corner. "Last I checked, we're all that's left of humanity *now*."

Ash's face hardened. "Look, I'm not going to apologize for my decision to attempt a rescue mission. I had the future of the human race in mind."

"And you fucked humanity in the process," Cruise grumbled.

"You forget yourself, Commander," Ash said. "Now, the past is behind us. I suggest you leave it there. We have to look at the future. If you can't deal with it, get out. Now. We'll manage without you." She was breathing heavily.

He looked at the ceiling, then back at her. "I don't have any other choice. If I don't go, we're all dead anyway, right?"

"Without your team, probably." After letting her reply hang in the air for a moment, she said, "Lieutenant, show us Hades."

The map flickered, and the red zone appeared over the table. Jordan leaned closer to examine a nav flag in the middle of the transparent layers.

"The fuel cells and other parts Samson has requested will be in one of the buildings outside the HQ."

Tony tapped a finger on the table. "We don't know which one?"

Jordan shook his head.

Ash took over. "As you already know, Hades has the most severe conditions on the planet. The radiation and freezing temperatures make it, for lack of a better word, hell on earth. But this is it, gentlemen. Either we dive to Hades and bring back fuel cells and pressure valves, or we die. Pretty simple."

All the HDs nodded, even Cruise.

"All right. What's the plan, Captain?" X asked.

"I'm breaking protocol. Instead of sending in one team, I'm sending in our remaining three. It'll give us the best chance."

"When?" Cruise asked.

"Tomorrow."

"I'd better get busy drinking and screwing, then," Cruise replied. "Because it'll be my last chance."

X started to get up and give Cruise the ass-chewing he had been saving all day, but Jordan spoke first.

"There may be one other option," he said. "I discovered another facility outside the borders of Hades. I checked right before the meeting, and it's outside the electrical storm, too."

X sat forward.

"I'm sorry I didn't have time to tell you yet, Captain, but you were in engineering," Jordan added.

"Show me," Ash said.

Jordan keyed in a string of commands on the monitor in front of him, and the topographic map expanded over the table. He punched in another command that zoomed in on a hexagonal building.

"This is an ITC factory on the outskirts of Hades. The *Hive*'s computers show they produced nuclear fuel cells and parts for the ship's generators. The problem is, we don't know if it still exists."

Ash leaned closer to the table, studying the building. "Do you think Captain Willis knew about this?"

"I'm not sure," Jordan replied. "It took some digging to find it. Even if he knew about it, he may have abandoned the idea. As I said, I'm not sure it's even still there."

Ash unbuttoned the top of her uniform and massaged her neck. She glanced over at X. He knew what was coming. She was about to ask him a question he couldn't answer.

"X, do you think it's worth the risk of exploring?"

"Hard to say, Captain. I've made plenty of dives to facilities that turned out to be piles of rubble or craters in the ground."

"But this is an ITC facility," Jordan said. "They were built to last. I think it's worth checking out. We have forty-eight hours of backup power. We can attempt this dive with one team. If they fail, we still have time to dive into Hades with the other two."

Ash looked deep in thought. "There might end up being nothing down there, but it's worth a shot. I'd rather risk one team outside the storm than send you all down to Hades."

"Agreed," Cruise said. "Who you going to send?"

He was testing the waters, but X already knew who Ash was going to send. He was the best diver she had, and Murph, Sam, and Magnolia were all still fresh. They were expendable. If he were in her shoes, he would do the same thing.

"Raptor," Ash said, staring at X. "They dive first thing tomorrow morning, once Samson stabilizes the ship."

X immediately thought of Tin. Any chance of sitting this one out and staying with the boy vanished with the critical news. He had promised Aaron to look after Tin, but Cruise was right about one thing: if the Hell Divers didn't jump, the kid and everyone else was dead anyway.

*   *   *   *   *

Candlelight flickered through the open doors of the private mess hall. The light beckoned X and his team toward the sound of raised voices. Words and laughter blended together, tinged with both excitement and fear. The same as before every dive.

X paused outside the entrance, studying the assault rifles the two Militia soldiers held. With the *Hive* on lockdown, Ash must have ordered the big guns out. The warm light glimmered off their mirrored visors as the faceless men acknowledged Team Raptor with slight nods.

"Sounds like we're late to dinner," Murph said. He pulled his goggles down over his forehead and ran a hand through his fiery-red hair.

"What the hell are they celebrating inside?" Magnolia asked. "Our impending deaths?"

X sighed. "It's tradition. You know that. The

night before a dive, all of us get together. Drink. Eat. Some of us fu ... "

Magnolia chuckled at his slip as the team walked into the mess hall together. The soldiers sealed the doors behind them. Large candles burned on the two rows of tables, which were littered with empty mugs and plates. Teams Apollo and Angel had gotten a head start. The divers sat intermingled on the benches. They weren't separate teams tonight. Tonight, they were the same.

Tony and Cruise both stood unsteadily to greet X. They had a head start on him in more than just the food. Well beyond buzzed, they were fast moving toward falling-down drunk. And from the looks of it, so were half the other divers.

"Glad you finally made it," Cruise said. He stumbled slightly, beer sloshing out of his mug.

Tony called out to Katrina, who was getting refills for her team. "A round for everyone on Raptor!"

She grabbed three full mugs and a glass of 'shine. X watched her move across the room. A smile dimpled her flushed cheeks as she handed him the 'shine.

"Thanks," he said.

Katrina winked and returned to her seat.

When everyone had a drink, Tony said, "Well, what the hell is everybody waiting for? The fat lady's already sung nekkid. So let's toast."

"To what?" Magnolia asked.

"To life," Tony said.

"And all those who lost theirs," X said, raising his glass. He thought of Aaron, Will, Rodney, and all of the others as the 'shine burned a path from his throat to his belly.

He found an empty seat and motioned for his team to join him. A feast awaited them. Bowls of steaming noodles. Plates packed high with squash, spinach, and tomatoes. There were even apples. For a moment, X recalled the hungry, pinched faces of the lower-deckers. None of them had ever eaten this well, not once in all their lives. Meanwhile, he and the other divers were treated to a feast like this one before every dive. It didn't seem fair.

"This seat taken?" Murph asked.

X bit off the end of a carrot, relishing the sweetish crunch, and scooted over. Sam took a seat across the table, next to Magnolia. Her jaw moved as if she was holding back words; then her shoulders sagged.

After a swig of 'shine, X told her, "Just say it."

Spreading both hands on the table before her, Magnolia said, "Okay. You all know I was sentenced to prison. Stealing, mostly. When Lieutenant Jordan gave me the choice, I thought *anything* would be better than rotting in a cell not much bigger than this table."

"This goin' somewhere, kid?" X asked.

"At first, it did occur to me that I had traded a prison sentence for a death sentence. Bad trade …" She paused to down the rest of her mug, then wiped her mouth on her sleeve. "Look, what I'm sayin' is, I know I've been a real bitch. But the truth is, we all gotta die sooner or later. And if it's gotta be sooner, well, I'll be proud to have done one worthwhile thing with my life first."

X sat back in his chair, studying Magnolia thoughtfully.

"I guess I just want to say sorry for the way I've acted," she said. "I hope you don't hate me."

X caught a glimpse of Katrina, watching from her seat at the other table.

"No need to apologize," he said. "Just don't fuck it up tomorrow, and we're good."

Magnolia smiled and took another drink. "Shit, this is really good beer. Where they been hidin' it? Makes me wonder what else we've missed out on."

"I often wonder that, too," Murph said, banging his empty mug down on the table.

Magnolia played nervously with a lock of purple hair. "Sometimes, I think about all the things we'll never know about. Foods we'll never taste, places we'll never see. Things from the books, like waterfalls and forests."

"And Sirens," Cruise called out from the other table, laughing.

Magnolia scowled at him, then winked as she reached for another beer.

"That's why Captain Ash is looking for a new home," Sam added, his face serious and stern. "So that someday, our children, and *their* children, will grow up with all the things Magnolia mentioned."

X set his empty glass down on the table and scratched his chin, considering his next words carefully. As a younger man, he, too, had longed to see the things Magnolia described. He knew better now, of course, and he also knew that grasping on to false hope was worse than facing reality head-on.

"Every captain in the history of the ship has been looking for a new home," X said. "But like I said yesterday, that shit doesn't exist. Ninety-six dives, and I've never seen anything remotely habitable. Forests are dust and a few fallen snags. Waterfalls are cliffs of polished rock. The only life is mutant monstrosities like the Sirens."

"Nice buzz kill, boss," said a musical feminine voice. He didn't need to look up to see Katrina standing behind Sam.

"Pull up a chair," Magnolia said, patting the bench beside her.

"Thanks," Katrina replied. "You'll have to forgive X. He can be a bit morbid—just one of his many charms."

"Doesn't everyone deserve to know the truth?" X said, slurping down a forkful of noodles.

"Right, because you're the master of telling the truth," said Katrina, a tinge of bitterness in her voice.

X's team looked from their leader to Katrina. After a moment, Magnolia broke the tension.

"Most people don't give all that much of a shit," she said. "They only care about surviving. Another day, another handful of credits. They don't worry about anything 'cept their next meal."

"You're right," Katrina said. "Anyway, it doesn't matter. We do what we do, so the rest of those poor bastards keep flying—and breathing—for another day."

Sam looked over at Murph. "Alright, I know why Magnolia became a diver, but how about you?"

The engineer folded his hands. "I lost my wife to cancer, and my son to the flu, a little over four years ago." He bowed his head. "I miss them every goddamn day. But I always wanted to see the surface—imagine how it must have been once. Figured I have nothing to lose."

X realized how little he still knew about the divers from the other teams.

"Sorry to hear about your family, Murph," he said. "I lost my wife about a year back." He turned to Sam. "How about you? Why'd you saddle up to jump?"

Sam didn't look entirely sure he wanted to talk. After a moment, he said, "I joined the Militia a few years back, thinking it was the best way to protect the ship. After the food riots, I realized maybe I could make a difference some other way than cracking heads."

"I'm glad you picked diving," X said. "And I'm glad all of you are on Raptor."

"Thanks," Sam said. "Good to be here, sir."

X looked at his watch. It was after eight in the evening. He had lost track of time, and Tin was still with Layla's family.

"Sorry I got to duck out early," he said, "but I got a kid to get home to."

Katrina's eyes pleaded with him to reconsider. She arched her back ever so slightly, the swell of her breasts beneath the red jumpsuit reminding X of what he could have.

Part of him wanted to take her up on the tacit offer. But the rest of him knew it was a bad idea. He had other responsibilities now. He hadn't been much of a husband, and he never had the chance to be a father, but he'd be damned if he didn't do right by Tin tonight.

"I'll see you all in the morning," he said. "Get some rest. Tomorrow's a big day." He patted Murph on the shoulder and nodded at the rest of his team, smiling like a benevolent patriarch.

Then he grabbed an apple and, cradling a bowl of noodles under his arm, left.

He felt the stares from every diver burning his back. Two months ago, he would have stayed and drunk them all under the table. Now he was hurrying home to make sure his dead best friend's kid ate a decent dinner.

When he had the sudden, overwhelming gut feeling that this could be the last chance he ever had to take care of Tin, he started walking faster.

*   *   *   *   *

Commander Weaver tracked the high-pitched cries through the city street. They had dwindled into a lonely sound, cold and melancholy. As a kid in history class, he had once heard a recording of whales communicating. The sounds were similar, but those extinct giants of the former oceans were far different from the leathery horrors now hunting him on the ground.

He stopped and rested, leaning against an ice-crusted streetlamp. A long screech, sounding as if an electronic oscillator had been possessed by demons, echoed through the city. Two more of the voices answered, but their lonesome cries died in the howling wind.

Weaver holstered his revolver and unsheathed

the tactical knife strapped to his thigh. He took a moment to get his bearings. Two skyscrapers leaned together overhead, their pointed tips creating a skewed arch. He felt unsafe just looking at it. It should have crashed down long ago.

His stomach gurgled as he stood there. He hadn't eaten in over a day. He took a sip from the straw inside his helmet and sucked mostly air. Idly he wondered which would kill him first: the Sirens or dehydration. He raised the tip of his knife to his visor and considered the ways he could use the weapon to end it all right now.

But instead of opening an artery in his throat or wrist, he carefully chipped away the ice on his visor.

The clear view of the world made everything seem bigger, the streets wider. He continued into the next intersection and took a right. The end of the street had collapsed and sloped down, disappearing into what looked like a tunnel. He checked his minimap and saw that the passage was supposed to lead under the next city block. If he was correct, it would come out somewhere near the *Ares* wreckage.

Trotting over to the edge of the decline, he crouched and pulled out the binos.

Perhaps he jounced down too suddenly, because the snowy crust beneath him broke away and sent him sliding on his back down the icy slope.

He rolled left to avoid impaling himself on a black claw of rebar that jutted from a shattered concrete buttress. The binos flew from his hands as he hit a ramp of snow and went airborne before crashing down on a patch of icy concrete a moment later. His armor saved him from any broken bones, though the impact knocked the breath from his lungs. Sharp pain shot up his spine, and he flailed for something to grab on to as he continued his downward slide.

At the bottom of the slope, icicles as tall as he was hung from the lip of the tunnel. Beyond that, he could see only the pitch blackness of the underground passage. He shot underneath the icicles and finally skidded to a halt.

Groaning, he sat up and reached for his back. The armor had likely saved him from a broken tailbone or worse. After the pain subsided, he checked his suit for visible tears. It would be hard to find one in the darkness, but the digital telemetry in the HUD subscreen showed no punctures.

He sat there for several minutes, listening to the whispering wind and taking in his surroundings. He was in the mouth of the dark tunnel, whose frozen walls continued—on the map, at least—for another two hundred yards.

He drew the revolver and took a few tentative steps into the darkness. The voice in his head told him to turn and find an alternative route to the *Ares* wreckage, but climbing back up the icy incline behind him was also a risk. By some miracle, he hadn't ripped his suit, but it could happen easily enough if he slipped again.

Weaver continued for several minutes until he reached the edge of the hole. He stomped the ground a few feet from the edge. It was solid—a concrete surface under the snow. Across the pit, the tunnel continued. He dropped to his belly and peered over the side. Listening, he heard only the faint sound of the wind hissing across the street above the incline.

He shut off his night vision and reached for his headlamp to search for a way across. The beam revealed ancient pipework jutting from the walls. He trained the light around the hole but saw no path to the other side.

Weaver cursed and pushed himself to his knees, knocking loose a chunk of rock. It skittered over the side and clanked to the bottom a few seconds later.

The noise reverberated through the tunnel, where the only sound for centuries had been the howling wind outside. He stepped back from the hole and started retracing his steps. He would have to risk climbing back to the street after all.

A screech froze him in midstride. Gun in hand, he worked his way back to the pit and trained the headlamp beam downward, steeling himself for what he might find.

Deep below, Sirens were slowly crawling out of their bulb-shaped nests. Dozens of the monsters writhed and stretched, as if waking from a long slumber. They seemed oblivious to the beam of light playing over them, but when his boot scuffed the surface ever so softly, they began a frenzied squawking.

The beasts darted for the walls, where they leaped and began scrambling up the sides. Weaver aimed his revolver at one of the leathery abominations and took a cautious step backward as the shrieks grew louder. He thought he was ready to fight and die, but seeing all those open maws, he felt a familiar sensation: primal fear. Shutting off his headlamp, he backed away from the hole, then turned to run.

TWELVE

X knocked on his apartment door and prepared for another night of awkward, resentful silence. So when Tin opened the door, he stumbled backward in surprise. The boy had never done this before.

"Hey," X mumbled. "How you doing?"

Tin shrugged and continued through the living room and into the kitchen. X hurried after him, cradling the bowl of fruit and noodles under his arm. He hesitated when he saw two plates of left-overs sitting on the kitchen table. Tin took a seat and started wolfing down the food.

X put his cargo down in the middle of the table and glanced down at the day-old noodles Tin had set out.

"For me?" X asked.

Tin nodded.

"Thanks," X said. "You must be feeling a little better."

Another nod.

X had hoped the tour of the farms would improve the boy's mood, but given all that had happened afterward, he expected Tin to be traumatized. Hell, what he'd seen in the medical ward this afternoon had rattled *him,* and he was not a man easily rattled.

"How's your head?"

"It's fine," Tin said.

X dropped his chopsticks in surprise. Tin had actually spoken to him, and not just with a monosyllabic grunt. Real words!

Tin took another bite, then said, "I saw the farms this morning ... but you probably already knew that." A smile tugged at the corners of his mouth.

"I thought you'd get a kick out of it."

"We saw two dogs. They were magnificent. Eli said they're called huskies. Silver and Lilly ..." Tin's eyes drifted with his voice. "I hope they're okay after the storm."

"I'm sure they're fine," X said.

"Did you know they're the last two dogs on the planet?"

X shook his head. "Nope. I've actually seen the farm only a few times, would you believe it?"

"I think I want to apprentice there," Tin said.

X felt his own smile. It was the first time in years that he felt ... What was it called? Oh, right: *happy.*

Tin scratched under his hat. "I've never seen anything like it. I can't imagine all the things that keep the farm running. I mean, I can, but ..."

"Only a few more years until you're eligible to apprentice, right?"

Tin clutched his plate and stood. "They're taking younger recruits now. Maybe they'll take me early. That would be great. I'd even have my own room assigned to me!"

X's heart ached. The boy was only ten years old. *Ten* goddamn years old and talking like an adult. As with most kids these days, he hadn't had a childhood.

X folded his hands on the table. "Tin, I want you to know something. Will you please sit back down?"

The boy placed his bowl on the table and readjusted his hat. He eyed X skeptically, then sat.

"Your mom and dad would be very proud of you. *I'm* proud of you. You're going to keep this place going. Kids like … Young men like you will keep the *Hive* flying."

Tin rewarded him with a half smile. "Thanks."

X put a hand on the boy's shoulder. "No, thank *you,* for finally talking to me!"

"I'm sorry …"

"Don't be," X said. "You're a good, smart kid. Strong, too. Just like your dad and mom. Someday, long after I'm gone, you'll probably be running this heap of metal and helium."

X realized that he was talking as if the ship had a future when, in reality, its continued existence had never been more uncertain. But Tin knew what was what. He had grown up knowing that every day might be the last—not just for him, but for all humankind.

"Tomorrow I have to do something to see that you have a future," X said.

"A dive?" Tin said. His jaw continued moving, but no other words came out. "I was hoping you'd be around for a while."

"Me, too," X said. "But I'll be back." He didn't have the heart to tell the kid how bad things really were.

Not now, not after they had just started talking again.

"Okay," Tin said. He got up again, grabbed both their plates, and took them to the sink.

X could see the wheels turning in the boy's head. After losing his parents, the kid had built up walls. He had just lowered them for X, and the last thing X wanted was to see them go back up.

"Hey, why don't you show me what you've been working on," X said. He took a seat in the cramped living room and patted the faded place beside him on the couch.

"The vacuum cleaner?" Tin asked. He knelt on the floor, pulled a multitool from his tool belt, then grabbed the dismantled vacuum cleaner on the floor.

"Yeah, that thing's a heap of junk," X said. "Hasn't worked in years." He hardly remembered the feeble groan the thing had made when Rhonda pushed it back and forth over the thin carpet.

"I'll get it to work," Tin said as he twisted off a screw and pulled off a panel.

X watched with interest as the boy worked on the machine. Memories coalesced into images in his mind, and he remembered a time just like this when Aaron had sat by his side, watching Tin work on one of his projects. Rhonda was there, too, knitting X a new pair of socks.

There was something absolute about it all—something final. A lump of anxiety formed in X's stomach at the thought. Normally, he suppressed such feelings by numbing his senses. It hurt to be sober.

But no matter how badly he wanted a drink, X decided to enjoy the moment with Tin, even if his gut ended up being right and it proved to be one of the last they ever shared.

A few minutes later, and the vacuum cleaner whirred to life. Tin glanced up with a broad grin on his face.

"See? Told you I could fix it."

*   *   *   *   *

Maria Ash's alarm clock went off at five a.m. Somewhere ten thousand feet above the *Hive*, the rising sun was setting ablaze the tops of the clouds that covered Earth.

She kissed Mark on the cheek, put her feet on the floor, and got up. Their schedules had conflicted since their last conversation on the bridge, and in the chaos of the past several days, she hadn't had much chance to talk to her husband. She hadn't even told him about the dive yet.

"What time is it?" he mumbled.

"Early. Go back to sleep for a bit."

"I never even heard you come in last night." Mark sat up and rubbed his eyes. "Did you think about our conversation again?"

Maria threw on her uniform and pulled her hair back into a ponytail. "My mind hasn't changed, love. Besides, we have more important things to think about right now. In a few hours, I'm sending Team Raptor to the surface."

"What!" He stared at her with wide eyes. "The ship was damaged *that bad*?"

She nodded.

Mark rested his head back on a pillow decorated with cats. "Just promise me one thing."

Maria straightened her cuffs, waiting patiently.

"If Raptor returns and Samson fixes the ship, and, by some miracle, you do find a place to put the ship down …" He paused to search her eyes. "Promise me you'll resign and accept treatment."

"Raptor will return and Samson will fix the ship," Maria replied. She leaned over the bed and kissed Mark on the lips. "And I will find a place. *Then* I promise to accept treatment. I'll see you tonight," she said with a smile.

"See ya," he whispered.

Maria drew in a breath and opened the door to the corridor, where two soldiers stood guard. Tucking the promise she had just made into the back of her mind, she walked with them to the bridge. Though she had slept only a few hours, she was filled with energy.

Jordan was already waiting for her in the command center.

"What's our status?" Ash asked. She strode to the communication station and stared at the comm link button. With a push of her finger, her voice would feed to every intercom in the *Hive*. Every one of the 513 citizens would hear her voice. The new number had been confirmed after the storm. When the final tally had reached her desk, the ship had suffered thirty-three deaths.

Now she was about to share with the survivors the most difficult message she had ever relayed in her command. Her throat burned at the thought.

"Captain, we have another problem," Jordan said.

"Enlighten me."

"Ty said there's a problem with the launch tubes. The reentry bay is working, but the launch tubes aren't. Something about an open circuit or something. We're going to have to delay Team Raptor's drop."

"No, we won't," came a voice at the top of the bridge.

Ash knew that cold tone. It was X. She turned to see him leaning on the railing.

"Captain, give me access to the roof," he said. "We'll jump from the top of the ship. I've done it before."

Jordan joined Ash at her side. "I've already got a team of engineers working on the launch tubes," he said. "We can delay the drop for—"

"We don't have time to delay the launch for a single minute!" X said, his raised voice drawing the stares of several officers. "The clock is ticking. We have to jump now."

"He's right, Jordan; we don't have time," Ash said. She prayed X knew what he was doing.

X moved away from the railing and hurried down the stairs. "I want to see the storm for myself."

Ash joined him at the nav station. She nodded at Ensigns Hunt and Ryan.

"You heard the commander," she said.

Ryan put on a pair of glasses and took a seat. "Tapping into the cameras on our stern."

While they waited together, it dawned on Ash that X didn't reek of booze from last night's celebrating. Unusual for him, but she wasn't going to ask questions.

The main display at the front of the bridge flickered to life, and a striking image of the electrical storm over Hades came into view.

"We're six miles east of the storm, Captain," Ryan said. "And all sensors show the skies are clear below."

"Looks clear," Hunt added.

X nodded, satisfied. "Ah'ight, I'll have my team back in a couple hours." He turned to walk back up the stairs. "Hopefully, with everything Samson needs to keep us in the sky."

"X," Ash said.

He paused and turned halfway.

"Be careful."

"Roger that, Cap," X said, throwing a haphazard salute. His lips formed what could almost be considered a grin, his pearly white teeth showing for a fleeting instant. Then he was gone, bolting up the stairs and racing out into the hallway. She wasn't sure how to take his change in mood. She hadn't seen him like this for years.

"Jordan, give Ty access to the roof," she finally said.

Ash imagined what the new members of Raptor were feeling. She could picture the black clouds swirling around the *Hive,* and the deep fear that the vast emptiness evoked. The thought made her bow her head in shame—only minutes ago, she had indulged in self-pity at having to deliver a difficult message.

A message, nothing more.

She shook her head. She had bigger worries, and X and his team were about to risk their lives.

Ash cleared her throat and punched the comm button. The ancient speakers chirped. She repositioned the microphone and said, "Citizens of the *Hive,* this is Captain Maria Ash. This morning I am tasked with sharing dire news. Yesterday, we reached the edge of Hades after receiving a distress call from *Ares.* I don't know how to say this easily, so I'm just going to tell you. *Ares* has been destroyed." She paused, herself still shocked that it was true. "Our ship," she continued, "our *home,* was severely damaged in the electrical storms."

Ash scanned the bridge. Officers she had worked with for years stared back at her, their eyes pleading for some reassurance.

"We still have hope," Ash said. "I'm deploying Team Raptor to the surface, to search for the parts that we need to keep our home in the sky."

The comm crackled, and Ash waited for the interference to clear. "In the meantime, engineering will divert all power from noncritical areas of the ship, including the living quarters in both upper and lower decks."

Ash looked down at her watch and added, "In two hours, those circuits will go offline. I ask everyone to remain calm during this time, and for all nonessential personnel to stay in their quarters. In addition to your cooperation, I also ask that you think of our divers. To those of you who pray, these brave men and women could use some. The future of the *Hive* now rests in their hands. Thank you."

A strong hand gently squeezed Ash's shoulder. It was the first time in her career that Jordan had tried to comfort her—or touched her at all, for that matter.

"X will come back," he said. "He always does."

Ash sighed. "I hope you're right."

*   *   *   *   *

X was first to arrive at the HD facility. He stood in the darkness, savoring the solitary moment and listening to the ship speak through its creaks and groans. It helped him relax before a dive.

After a few minutes, he flicked the lights and walked over to the wall of lockers. The rusted metal was decorated with the faded graffiti of previous owners. Skulls, bullets, extinct animals no living person had ever seen—each symbol had once held meaning for its user. X had drawn the head of a raptor on his locker: yellow eyes and hooked beak, a black head crested with white feathers. The bird was more than the icon for his Hell Diver team. It also symbolized the essence of what diving embodied. He, too, was a predator, but like the memories of the divers before him, the raptor's image was already starting to fade.

One hundred and five, he thought. That was how many divers had perished. X was the most senior diver aboard the *Hive*—and, he now realized, in the whole world. The idea was numbing. So many lives lost over the years. He closed his eyes for a moment to acknowledge the men and women who had dived and died before him. Then he opened his locker and started pulling out his gear.

Ty's voice boomed across the room as he came in. "You sure this is a good idea?"

X nodded. "I've dived off the roof before."

"Your team hasn't."

"We don't have any other choice. And you don't have to remind me."

Ty took a half-chewed herb stick out of his mouth. "You're right. Sorry, Commander."

Before X could reply, he heard the footsteps of his team approaching. Watching Magnolia, Murph, and Sam walk across the room, he realized that beyond what he had read in their files, he knew only what they had told him over dinner last night. He was about to dive—and possibly die—with people he didn't know and, therefore, couldn't fully trust.

The three new Raptor members joined X and Ty in the center of the room. "Launch tubes aren't functioning, so we're going with plan B," X said. He pointed up to an aluminum ladder. "That gets us to the roof."

"The *roof*?" Magnolia said. "Please tell me plan B doesn't mean—"

"Means we're jumpin' from the top of the ship," Murph said.

Sam looked up at the ladder. "That'll be a new one for me."

"Come on," X said, motioning to the lockers. "We're wasting time. Let's suit up."

Team Raptor spent the next fifteen minutes checking and double-checking equipment. Ty had chutes laid out neatly on the deck. He crouched next to them and went over each one slowly and deliberately.

When gear malfunctioned, it was easy to blame a technician, but X never blamed Ty. He was a perfectionist, and when things broke, they broke because they were fossils, like everything else on this dinosaur.

X pulled his armor from the locker. It was the only piece of his gear he always trusted. Time after time, the tough black matte polymer had saved him during dives.

He sucked in his gut, zipped up the front of his suit, and donned the armor. All around him, his team was doing the same thing. Sam, the first to finish, came and stood beside X. They turned to watch Murph struggle with the clasps on Magnolia's armor, grunting as he finally snapped them into place.

"You guys good?" X asked.

Magnolia turned stiffly. "This damn stuff has never fit me."

Ty walked over to her and said, "Breathe in." She did, and he worked his finger under the right side of her ceramic plate. "If you can breathe, you can dive."

The squeal of metal drew their attention to the front of the room. Jordan walked in with two guards, each carrying a metal case.

"All set?" Jordan asked.

"Just waiting on those," X said.

The soldiers set the cases down, and X bent down to open them up. He pulled out a pistol, extra magazines, and a vest stuffed with flares and shotgun shells. Then he grabbed a blaster and holstered it.

"Eyes and ears," X said. He waited a few moments for his team to finish with their gear. "Once we get on the surface, we'll have approximately two hours to search for the building Lieutenant Jordan has identified as a potential location for the cells and valves. Check and double-check your weapons. I don't want any self inflicted malfunctions on the surface, especially if we do encounter Sirens down there."

Magnolia's blue eyes widened, but she didn't say a word.

The other divers loaded their blasters with shotgun shells and flares. X slapped a magazine into his pistol and pulled back the slide to chamber a round, then pushed the safety lever up. The chorus of final preparations filled the room as the other teams arrived.

Tony, Cruise, and the other divers gathered inside the facility to say their goodbyes. They sized the members of Raptor up from across the room.

X twisted in his extra-snug suit and cracked his neck from side to side, then slipped on his helmet and inserted the battery unit into the chest slot. His HUD powered on. All systems were green.

"Let's go," X said, impatient to get started. He didn't like waiting, and he really hated being watched. He guided his team across the room to the ladder.

"Good luck, Raptor!" a voice shouted from the entrance.

X grabbed the first rung and turned to see Captain Ash hurrying across the room. A few of the other divers echoed Ash's words as X climbed, but he wasn't listening. His mind was focused on the mission. Not on the other teams, not on the threat of a riot, or of *Ares* itself—not even of Tin. All that mattered was what he had to do to keep the *Hive* aloft.

The light from a single red LED guided him up the ladder. When he reached the top, he turned the wheel handle on the hatch. It clicked and unlocked, and he heaved it open. Wind screamed into the tunnel, rushing past him. He fought the gust and stared into darkness so thick, it seemed to wrap around the ship and squeeze it.

When his eyes adjusted, he saw that there was also light above. It was faint—just a trace of gold bleeding through. The sun was up there, hiding behind the dark clouds.

*　　*　　*　　*　　*

Weaver ran through the darkness, his chest heaving in jagged, painful breaths. Slowing only to scoop up the dropped binos, he pounded upward on the slope that led back to the street above. But after only two strides on the collapsed road, he hit a patch of black ice and slid back down in a flurry of ice spicules.

"No-o-o-o!" he moaned, jumping to his feet. Excited shrieks reverberated from the tunnel behind him. Turning, he saw the first creatures climbing from the pit. Pulling themselves up with talons the length of his tactical knife blade, they raced toward him on all fours, their dorsal spikes swinging from side to side. He scrambled onto the road again, clawing frantically at the ice with his fingers. And again he slid back to the bottom.

The squalling and the scrabble of talons made him want to curl up and hide, just as he had as a kid when the emergency sirens on *Ares* started to wail.

But now there was no bed to crawl under, no closet to hide in. He was in the open, exposed and vulnerable.

As they drew nearer, he grabbed his revolver, but it wouldn't budge from the holster. The tip of the barrel seemed to be frozen to his battery unit.

His eyes shot back to the eyeless faces and grinning mouths. He worked the grip of the revolver back and forth.

The Sirens would be on him in seconds. He could see the scabby crests on their skulls—could even see the tiny bristles on their heads.

Weaver pulled again at the gun with both hands, and it finally freed with an audible crack. The sudden release sent him stumbling backward, and he felt the battery unit come loose. The ring-shaped device flew through the air and landed in the snow between him and the Sirens.

His suit quickly powered down, and the HUD flickered off. He tried the headlamp, but it, too, was dead.

He was blind and surrounded by predators.

A lump of terror congealed in the pit of his stomach. As a Hell Diver, he had given a lot of thought to how he would die. He had always assumed it would be out in the open air, falling through an electrical storm or cratering into the cold, hard ground. Never had he expected to be trapped in darkness, surrounded by sightless monsters.

Straining to see in the pitch blackness, he pointed the pistol toward the sounds of claws skittering on ice. The creatures were searching for him, too, but their eerie screeching had stopped abruptly the moment his HUD deactivated.

Their claws scraped through the snow. Closer now. He heard a clatter of plastic and metal. They had found his battery unit. But why would flesh-eating monsters be interested in *that*?

Weaver resisted the urge to blindly fire off shots in the direction of popping joints and skittering claws. Not daring to move, he listened to the noise of talons fumbling with his battery unit. There was a sudden grunt that sounded like the snort of a frustrated animal.

The scratching ceased a moment later, replaced by the sound of the creatures retreating back to their lair.

Weaver stood there for perhaps fifteen minutes, shaking in his suit, still not budging for fear the monsters would return. He couldn't see his visor fogging up, but he knew his cold breath was clouding the plate. Without the battery, it wouldn't take long for the frigid cold to work through the layers of his suit. The battery didn't power just the HUD; it also powered the tiny heat pads inside his suit.

Finding it was his only hope. Like a blind dog in unfamiliar surroundings, he moved tentatively across the ground on all fours. After a few moments of searching, he bumped something with his knee, and it rattled over the ice. He fumbled about some more and finally wrapped a finger around the familiar toroidal shape. Feeling a wash of relief, he carefully inserted it back into his armor.

His HUD activated with a warm glow.

He had never in his life been so happy to see the artificial green of the NVG optics.

The sight sparked an epiphany, a theory forming in his mind. *Energy. They're drawn to energy.*

He had always assumed that the Sirens were drawn to movement, but now he finally understood. The beasts must be attracted to the energy that his battery unit produced. Perhaps they could see after all, with some sort of infrared vision that homed in on his suit.

The display suddenly flickered. He checked the stream of data in the subscreen. It flashed a second time, then a third.

"No," he muttered. "Useless piece of crap." He tapped the side of his helmet.

The Sirens must have damaged the unit. He raised his wrist and cleared the screen on his mini-computer. Then he deactivated the heaters inside his suit and rerouted all power to his HUD. That would buy him some time to survive long enough to find the wreckage of *Ares.* He wouldn't let the monsters feed on the corpses of his family and friends.

Glancing up from his wrist computer, he scanned the darkness. The tunnel was still clear. The creatures had returned to their lair. He pulled his knife and studied the collapsed road for footholds. Grabbing a jutting piece of rebar with one hand, he jammed his blade into the ice with the other hand, then looked for any rough, ice-free surface that his boot would stick on.

As he climbed up the slope, he concentrated on a new mission—one he had to complete before returning to *Ares:* find one of his dead divers and salvage their battery unit. If he was really lucky, maybe he would even get a blaster and some water, too.

THIRTEEN

Tin found Layla waiting for him in the hallway, chewing on a fingernail.

"Looks like we have some time before the lights go out," she said. "Let's stop by the trading post. My mom gave me a few credits to buy a cookie. I'll split it with you." She seemed to scan his face for a reaction.

"Aren't you scared?" Tin asked.

Layla's eyebrows scrunched together. "About what?"

"The ship's in trouble."

"Wake up, Tin. The ship's *always* in trouble."

Looking up and down the hallway, he saw life going on as it always did. People ambled to their workstations or apartments at the same casual speed. He caught snippets of conversations about a dive and *Ares,* but for the most part, people went about their day as if shutting off the lights were just another inconvenience to take in stride. And indeed, Tin couldn't remember a time when the *Hive* hadn't been in some sort of danger. Most of the other passengers probably weren't any more frightened now than they had been a month ago, during the last electrical storm.

But Tin knew better. This time, the threat to the ship scared him more than it ever had before. And with *Ares* gone, he felt an emptiness that he didn't quite understand.

They walked along in silence until Tin saw Andrew in the crowd ahead.

"Don't worry," Layla said. "I think he's going to leave you alone now."

"Why's that?"

"Because of X. They know he was the reason we got to see the farms, and …"

He halted in the middle of the corridor. "And what?"

"I kinda kicked Andrew in the marbles the other day. The other boys saw him cry."

Tin laughed. The sound was so unfamiliar to his ears, it almost made him stop.

Layla's smile broadened. "Yeah, I don't think he's going to be bothering anyone for a while."

Tin's amusement turned to confusion. He scratched his forehead and squinted. "Layla?"

"Yes," she replied as they started walking ahead.

"Why are you my friend?"

She smiled and shrugged. "Because you're my person. You're smart. Funny, too—when you actually talk, that is. And … I don't know, I always wanted a little brother."

Tin chuckled again. "Thanks. I guess I always wanted a sister, too."

"Cool. Then I guess that makes us stepbrother and stepsister by default. Now, come on," she said. "I want one of those cookies before they flip the switches."

They stopped in the middle of the hallway. The corridor was a tide of variously colored coveralls. Layla slipped ahead in the crowd, and Tin tried his best to keep up. She was slender and fast. She would make a great Hell Diver.

"Look at that," Layla said. She stopped in a three-way intersection and pointed to the citizens waiting for their food rations. Four Militia soldiers in gray riot gear hovered around the crowd. Their faces were hidden behind mirrored visors, and they gripped the handles of their batons and waved them whenever one of the lower-deckers got too rowdy.

"I'm lucky my mom works in engineering," she whispered. "I'd hate to wait like those people."

A woman in faded brown coveralls at the front of the crowd caught Tin's attention. She clutched an empty bag under her arm. The duty officer handing out rations eyed her and the two girls she had in tow. Both looked like four or five years old. The younger one scratched at her nose. Tin's heart sank when he saw the cherry-size red lump that hung over her right eyelid. Deformities were common in children belowdecks, but every time he saw them his heart ached.

The duty officer looked at his clipboard and marked it with his pen. Then he turned to a second worker at the bins of fresh produce and said, "Two potatoes, three tomatoes, and three measures of spinach."

"That's it?" the woman protested. She held out her bag. "That won't last us a day!"

The young girl caught Tin staring, and he turned away. He was ashamed. Like Layla, he had grown up privileged. Neither of them knew what it was like to be truly hungry or to live with deformities or pain. He always went to bed with a full stomach. These people fought over scraps, and scraps couldn't keep them alive forever. Everywhere he looked, he saw sunken faces and desperate eyes. It wasn't right.

"Let's go," Tin said.

She grabbed his hand and worked her way back into the flow of traffic. They walked that way all the way to trading post.

"Which merchant?" he asked.

Layla shook her head. "I don't know. My mom said some noodle vendor made cookies and was selling them for three credits apiece."

"I bet I know who it is."

Vendors touted their wares as they walked by. Some customers stopped to barter, handing over soap or homemade goods. Tin blocked them out until he saw the woman from the food ration line and her little girls again.

The girl with the lump over her eye tugged on her mom's sleeve, whining, "Mama, I'm hungry."

Her mother didn't respond. Instead, she pulled her kids toward a booth. Reaching into her bag, she handed one of the merchants a potato in exchange for a tiny bag. Tin stopped, and Layla's hand slipped from his. It wasn't the first time he had seen someone trade their rations for drugs, but he had never seen a mother do it.

"What's wrong?" Layla asked.

Tin didn't reply. He spied the painted dragon on the booth, walked over, and tapped the countertop.

The shop owner turned and looked out over the crowd.

"Down here," Tin said, tapping again on the counter.

Dom glanced down and smiled. "Ah, Tin. Good to see you, my little friend. I was just about to close for the curfew. Shouldn't you kids be in your bunks?"

"We were on our way," Tin said. He put his hands on the counter and whispered, "But we heard you might have some cookies."

"Ah, you heard that, did you?"

Tin nodded.

"I did have cookies," Dom finally replied. "But they went fast."

Tin sighed. "Oh, well, maybe next time."

"Wait," Dom said, holding up a hand. He disappeared inside his shack and returned, holding out both fists. "Maybe I have some left, but you have to play the game."

Layla stepped up to the counter. She studied both hands, eyes shifting left to right.

"I pick …"

"Choose wisely," Dom said with a grin.

"Left." She paused as he began to open his left hand. "Wait," she said, shaking her head. "Right."

Dom opened his right hand to reveal two triangular cookies.

"How much?" she asked.

He looked over his shoulder, then quickly handed her the cookies. "Free, but don't tell my wife."

Tin cocked an eyebrow and looked up at Dom.

Nothing was ever free. The word had almost lost its meaning over the years.

"Are you *sure*?" Layla asked.

"Yes. Now, please, take 'em before my wife comes back."

"Thanks!" She took the cookies and handed one to Tin.

"You're the best, Dom," Tin said. Smiling, he closed his fingers around the warm cookie.

"Be safe!" Dom shouted as they left.

Tin looked over his shoulder and nodded as Layla pulled him to a small common area with a dozen tables.

"How about here?" she said. She took a seat several chairs away from a mother and her small boy.

Tin examined them from a distance. They both wore the same threadbare brown clothes as other lower-deckers. An empty bowl sat in front of them. The boy's face was grimy, and his wild hair spiked out in all directions. Tin could smell them from where he stood.

"Come on," Layla said, "I'm hungry!"

"Shouldn't we get to our bunks?"

She rolled her eyes. "We have plenty of time. Look around. There's still a lot of people in here."

Tin reluctantly sat down beside her. He eyed the mother and child a second time. This time, she caught his gaze and quickly shied away.

"These aren't normal cookies," Tin said. "They're fortune cookies. Go on, crack it open."

Layla looked confused, but she broke the cookie in half. The little boy at the other table watched curiously, his eyes locked onto the two pieces she had laid on the table.

Tin broke his open over the table and pulled out the sliver of yellow paper. The last time X had brought the cookies home, Tin could hardly read Dom's handwriting, but this fortune was surprisingly legible.

Accept your past without regrets. Handle your present with confidence. Face your future without fear.

"What's yours say?" Layla asked.

"I can't tell you, or it won't come true."

Layla held her paper in front of her and said, "Oh." Then she scooped up the pieces of the cookie and popped them in her mouth.

Tin tucked the fortune into his shirt pocket and cupped the cookie parts in his hand. He thought about the words. They made a lot of sense. He had treated X like crap since the day his dad died. And he had let his fear of the future rule him. Well, all that was about to change.

"Ready?" he asked.

Layla was still chewing her cookie. She smiled, revealing small chunks stuck in her teeth. Tin led the way this time, stopping at the end of the table. "Here," he said, offering the two halves of broken cookie to the boy. The child's eyes brightened, and he let out a coo of excitement as his grubby little fingers reached out.

"Go ahead, Jed," his mother said. She looked up at Tin and said, "Thank you *so* much."

The young boy took the pieces and stuffed them into his mouth, his eyes never leaving Tin.

"You're most welcome," Tin said.

He grabbed Layla's hand and led her out of the warehouse. At the exit, he looked back to see the boy waving at them. Tin waved back, wishing he could also have given cookies to the two girls he'd seen earlier. Layla stopped him with a hand on his shoulder. Her smile was gone. "I should have given him mine, too, huh?"

Before Tin could reply, someone plowed into him, knocking him to the floor, where he banged his elbow.

"Hey!" Tin shouted. He looked up to see four men. The one who had run into him had long black dreadlocks hanging over his shoulders. Tin recognized him instantly. He had seen him loitering outside the farm, with the same men. He wore the shabby clothes of a lower-decker but had the build of someone from the upper decks.

A bearded bald man with him said, "Why don't you watch where you're goin', little man." He chuckled and said, "Let's go, Trav."

Travis glanced down at Tin and Layla. "You kids better get to your shelter, where it's safe."

*   *   *   *   *

Travis had felt something inside him break when he left his brother in the brig. Seeing Raphael like that was unbearable, and then when Captain Ash announced the new power shortage, it was the last straw. All the pain and heartbreak over the years had stewed inside him and was about to boil over.

It was finally time to act—finally time to force some changes.

He waited with his back to the wall, outside the trading post entrance, and watched the boy with the funny hat and his friend with cookie crumbs on her shirt walk down the hallway. Both were upper-deckers. He could tell by their skin. It wasn't filthy and pallid like most of the kids living below his feet. One day long ago, he had walked in their shoes, oblivious to the plight of those belowdecks. He hardly remembered those days now.

When he looked back at the trading post, Alex, Brad, and Ren had vanished into the thinning crowd. They were headed to the booth that Ren's family ran. For years, they had sold odds and ends to both lower- and upper-deckers. Nuts and bolts, scrap metal, and glass—stuff that was always in short supply. It was the perfect place to hide the weapon that would change the fortunes of those suffering in the lower reaches of the *Hive*.

The Militia never searched the shops. In one of her failed attempts to keep the lower-deckers happy, Captain Ash had doomed her command. She just didn't know it yet.

A few minutes later, Alex strode out of the crowd with his right hand pressed against the side of his long coat. He hurried out of the trading post and joined Travis at the wall. Ren and Brad hung back, ready to provide a distraction if any Militia gave them trouble.

"You got it?" Travis asked.

Alex nodded, patting the side of his coat.

Travis exchanged a look with Ren and Brad, and the four men walked together toward their assigned shelter.

*   *   *   *   *

X climbed to the top of the ship and grabbed a rope attached to the roof. He steadied himself against the crosswind. He planted his boots and battled the gust until it passed. Then he bent down and helped the other divers onto the shell.

"Hold on to the rope until we dive!" X shouted. Even with the helmets' comm system, it was hard to hear over the buffeting wind.

He allowed them a few moments to take in their surroundings. The clouds up here were thin and translucent, unlike the dense cover a couple of miles below. X raised a hand, and his fingers slashed through the haze, which bent around his body like water flowing.

"Is it safe up here?" Magnolia shouted over the comm.

"As long as you don't let go of that rope," X yelled back.

"It's so dark," she said, her voice melting into a whisper over the channel.

X tilted his helmet and scanned the sky again for any sign of the sun. Being out here, beyond the confines of the *Hive,* made him tingle all over. It was wild and dangerous and free, and X loved every second of it. Even now, with the sun shrouded by clouds, it was still breathtaking.

He turned to check on his team and saw something that dialed his enthusiasm down a notch. The sky to the west looked like a mountain range with jagged peaks reaching toward the heavens. Lightning flashed through the towering cumulus, illuminating the darkness with shades of sapphire and purple.

"It's beautiful," Murph said.

Sam grunted. "Wait till you get to the surface. 'Beautiful' won't even be in your vocabulary."

"That's Hades?" Magnolia asked.

X nodded and waved everyone forward. Every second they wasted was one less they had to complete the mission. He led the team down the back of the ship. The wind whipped over his suit, pushing and tugging him by turns. He worked his way forward, holding the rope. They were far enough from the sides that the wind wasn't a serious problem, but he wasn't going to take any chances. What concerned him more was the monster storm. He couldn't keep his eyes off it.

Three minutes later, they were standing on the stern of the ship, peering over the side. X faced his team and said, "I'll lead the formation. Stay three hundred feet apart. Keep your eyes on your HUDs, and follow me. Got it?"

Everyone nodded.

"Then let's move." X took three steps backward, let go of the rope, and broke into a run. Reaching the edge of the ship, he took a final bound, leaped, and was gone. In an eyeblink, the void had swallowed him.

The wind took him, and he embraced it.

After he had maneuvered into stable position, he glanced around to check on his team. Sam's and Murph's blue battery units pulsated to the right, but Magnolia was nowhere in sight.

His eyes flitted to his HUD. Her beacon was still idle. She hadn't jumped off the ship yet.

"Magnolia, what the hell are you doing?" he yelled.

It was hard to hear anything over the roaring wind, but her faint response came through the comm.

"Don't get all worked up. Just admiring the view."

A second later, her beacon was moving.

"You stay with the team," X growled. "That's how this works."

He relaxed on the mattress of air and watched his HUD. Magnolia's beacon was moving fast, gaining speed, closing in on the others. Was she in a nosedive?

X risked a backward glance. Sure enough, she was blasting through the sky like a falling arrow. When she was a few hundred feet away, she maneuvered into stable position, arms and legs spread out gracefully with her back to the *Hive*.

Relieved, he checked his HUD again. Ice crystals grew around the edge of his visor. At fifteen thousand feet, it was negative forty degrees Fahrenheit.

X was first to sail through the ten thousand mark. The scalloped black floor of the clouds was rising fast toward them. They were halfway down. He could see the slight change in the darkness where the clouds began to thin.

When he craned his neck to check on the others, a crosswind sent him tumbling out of control. Experience took over, and he threw his limbs out straight and went into a hard arch, which set him belly down again. From there, he pulled arms and legs loosely in and was back in stable position.

"Crosswinds coming!" he shouted.

A sidelong glance gave him a view of the other three divers just as they hit the turbulence. Sam and Magnolia held steady, but Murph tumbled like a leaf in a whirlwind.

"Shit," X muttered. "Murph, hard arch!"

"I can't!" Murph shouted. "Can't get control …" His voice was lost in the crackle of static.

X looked up to see him spinning like a boomerang.

"Stretch your arms and legs out!" Magnolia said. "Arch your back as far as you can!"

With the surface racing up toward them, Murph needed to stabilize. He tumbled through the darkness, his screams muffled by the wind. X cursed and watched helplessly. Losing their engineer now wouldn't be just bad luck; it could doom their mission before it really started.

Come on damn it, Murph …

At five thousand feet, Murph finally stopped screaming. He flipped several more times before leveling out. Arching his back and spreading his arms and legs, he did another lazy somersault before settling back into a stable position. His labored breathing swelled over the channel.

X thanked all the gods he didn't believe in. He just might get his team safely to the ground.

"Prepare to activate your night vision and pull your pilot chutes," he said. "The moment we're through the cloud cover, do it."

The clouds vanished at four thousand feet, and the ground rushed into view. He bumped on his optics and scanned for a landing zone. The surface came into focus, but the ground wasn't exactly level. They were falling over the biggest sinkhole he had ever seen.

At first, he had figured it was just another place where the earth had eroded from below and caved in on itself, but this was different. This wasn't the work of nature; this was man's doing. They were falling toward a crater produced by one of the mega bombs dropped hundreds of years ago.

X pulled his pilot chute, held it a moment, and let it go. Feeling the rig inflate, he reached up and grabbed the toggles and steered away from the hole, gliding west toward whatever was left of the city.

The frozen landscape was flattened for miles around the blast zone. Nothing but rubble with a crust of snow. At least, he didn't have to worry about crashing into a tower.

"What the hell is that?" Magnolia asked.

"What it looks like," X replied. "A big-ass hole in the ground. Follow me to a new DZ."

Murph's voice crackled over the comm. "Sir!"

"Hold on, I'm looking for a place to put down."

"But, sir!" Murph insisted.

"What? What's wrong?" X asked.

When he checked his subscreen for his altitude, he saw the radiation level. The readings were off the charts. The entire drop zone was one massive radioactive night-light.

X looked up just in time to see Murph ghosting toward him.

"Watch out!" X shouted, toggling hard way from the encroaching canopy.

"Sorry, sir!" Murph yelled back.

X swooped toward the drop zone, his heart pounding. A collision with another diver, collapsing both their chutes, was a nightmare he could do without.

Bending his knees, X performed his usual two-stage flare. When his boots hit the ground, he ran out the momentum across the compact snow, ground to a stop a few minutes later, and pulled one capewell, collapsing his chute. It rippled in the wind as he pawed through it to look for the other divers. Murph was sprawled on the ground a hundred feet away. Sam and Magnolia glided down to the east, both of them landing gracefully in the snow a few seconds later.

As soon as their feet touched down, X was running toward them. Every second in this radio-active pit was borrowed time.

FOURTEEN

Weaver couldn't feel his hands or feet. Even so, his body seemed heavy, as if his bones were made of lead. He slogged through the snowy streets. The shrieks of the Sirens and the roar of the wind had ceased—either that, or his helmet speakers had frozen.

He was so cold, he could hardly think, hardly move. His legs moved by instinct, and his thoughts seemed to float disconnected from his body. A gust of snow beat him several steps backward. A second blast hit him in the back, knocking him to his knees. Pushing at the ground with hands that felt like bricks, he rose to his feet.

For the past several days, he had thought a lot about death. He had long since given up on the idea of a hereafter, knowing there was nothing but the rot that followed. But when he perished in this icy wasteland, he would be stuck here for eternity, his body a frozen fossil—unless those screaming beasts got to it first.

His mind drifted as he trudged ahead. The haunting images of Jennifer's, Cassie's, and Kayla's burning bodies tormented his flagging awareness.

The memories of better times were gone now. He saw only their melting faces.

Weaver tripped over a chunk of stone and went facedown in the snow. He caught the metallic taste of blood.

For a moment, he lay there, eyes searching the desolate landscape for the *Ares* wreckage. He didn't want to give up, but he was so cold. An intense wave of despair took hold. In that moment, everything came clear. He felt vividly what it meant to be the last human on the planet. And he understood, perhaps for the first time, what the word "*forever*" meant.

The word prompted a fear unlike any he had ever experienced.

Defeated and alone, he rested his helmet in the snow. He needed to close his eyes and rest. Just for a few minutes …

He sobbed at the thought of his wife and his daughters and all the other passengers aboard *Ares*. Tears cascaded down his frozen face, growing cold on their way down his chin. "God, oh God," Weaver whispered, drowsy now. "I have to get to my girls."

He crawled a few feet, blinked away the tears, and squinted. Something was moving at the far end of the street, where the snow had drifted to form a low barricade. An apparition danced across the snow. A green cape flapped in the wind.

He clawed toward it, dragging his heavy legs. He made it four feet before collapsing onto his stomach. The fierce pain of his frozen body paralyzed him, and he contorted into a fetal position, shaking violently. He sucked in frozen shards of air that cut his lungs. Tilting his ice-crazed visor, he stared at the sky—the vast empty space where he had spent most of his life. He watched the lightning in awe.

Get up, a voice boomed in his mind. *You have to get up.*

The words were so distant, yet he recognized the voice at once. It was Jennifer's.

You still have a mission to complete, she said. *You promised us you'd come home, Rick.*

His body was shutting down. He was dying. His brain would be the last to go, but reality was already slipping from his grasp.

Using every ounce of energy, he rolled on his side and saw the flapping apparition. No, a parachute. It wasn't far, and with any luck, the body of a diver would be attached to it. A diver with a battery.

He struggled upward, balanced for a moment, and dragged one foot forward … then the other, toward the canopy. His feet were frozen anchors, but somehow, he willed them forward. He was light-headed, and his vision was fading, but he continued because he had no choice—he couldn't break his promise.

After a struggle, he reached the chute and pulled it out of his way, following the cords to a hump in the snow. He dropped to his knees and wiped off a layer of drifted powder with his arm. He heard the faint sound of metal on metal. A second swipe exposed a helmet with a tiny red heart painted just above the visor.

"Sarah," he murmured. He rotated her helmet carefully until it unlocked. Then he slowly pulled it away, grimacing as her frozen head slid out onto the snow. Her brown eyes were still open, the eyelashes covered in ice.

"I'm sorry," he said.

He set the helmet down with shaking hands and took her water bottle from inside the lip of her armor. Then he pulled out her food pouch. Both were frozen solid. He laid them on the snow and cleared the snow from her chest armor. His fingers shook as he dislodged his battery and exchanged it for hers.

He punched his minicomputer with wooden fingers and turned his heaters back on. The small devices bit his freezing skin, like bees stinging all across his body. He gradually felt the prickle of blood flowing to his extremities. The burn started at his feet and hands and worked its way up his legs and arms. His skin itched and tingled, and he sobbed again from the excruciating pain of his body slowly warming. He had been so cold. Now he was on fire.

When the pain subsided, he unlatched the locks on his armor, pulled the front plate up, and inserted Sarah's water bottle and food pouch.

He secured the armor with a click, then searched Sarah's corpse. A blaster was frozen against her leg. He grabbed it and yanked the grip, and the weapon broke free, sending him sprawling on his backside. He gripped the stock and gazed up at the sky, wondering what, as the last human being on Earth, he ought to do now. He heard his wife's voice again. It sounded clearer now.

Live, Rick.

*   *   *   *   *

X reached down and offered his hand to Murph, who lay on his back, his mirrored visor looking up at the sky.

"How many dives did you say you've done?" X asked.

Murph grabbed his hand and groaned as he pulled himself upright. "Not enough."

"Holy shit," Magnolia said. She stood beside Sam, facing west. "Is that … ?"

"Hades," Sam said.

"Regroup," X said. "We don't have time for sightseeing."

The team circled around him. Flakes of toxic snow fluttered from the sky. Magnolia held out her hand and caught a flake on her palm. X shook his head. She had no idea of the danger they were in.

"Sam, you're our eyes. Take point. Murph, plot us a course to the target and the supply crate the *Hive* dropped. Magnolia … just stay close to me."

"I've never seen rads this high," Murph said.

X checked his monitor for the third time since landing. "Me, neither. We need to double-time it to get to this facility." The Hell Divers lived by the law of the clock, and they were running out of time. They had an hour and fifty-seven minutes to return to the *Hive* with cells and valves.

Looking past the data, X scanned the wasteland to the west. For miles, nothing stood as high as a man. The landscape to the east was much the same. Foundations of buildings peppered the terrain, but only a few structures rose even to one story. X pulled his binos and dialed in on a bridge that stuck out of the snow like the dorsal fin of some monstrous fish. Beneath the snow, a network of highways and roads had connected the Old World. X had traveled on many of them on other dives.

He zoomed in on a cluster of towers beyond the bridge. Even from a distance, he could see that the skeletal buildings were badly damaged. Some were nothing more than husks. He had his doubts that anything inside could remain intact, especially after the blasts. But they had to try.

"I've mapped us a route to the supply crate," Murph said. "Uploading to your minicomputers … now."

X tapped his computer and looked at the map on his HUD. The crosswind had knocked them off course. They were a mile from the supply crate, and two miles from the main objective. He set his nav markers on both targets.

"All right, Raptor, let's move out," he said.

Sam pulled his blaster and took off at a lope. The wind had cleared the snow ahead, exposing a road that X hadn't seen earlier. A network of fissures, where the earth had opened and swallowed portions of the road, stretched across their path. Sam leaped over the cracks, stopping at each one to make sure X and the others got across.

X turned to watch Magnolia. She nodded back at him and jumped over a crevasse. A few minutes later, they reached the edge of a parking lot littered with rows of rusted vehicles.

"Keep sharp," X said, pulling his blaster and working his way forward. The metal graveyard was the perfect place for an ambush, although he doubted that even the Sirens would frequent this place.

"Bombs did this?" Magnolia whispered.

X pointed at the crater to the north. "Bombs dropped from airships just like the *Hive*."

"No way."

"You didn't know that?" Sam asked.

"The bombs that poisoned the world also caused the electrical storms," X said. He wasn't terribly shocked that Magnolia didn't know. Most people didn't talk much about why things were the way they were now.

"Wh-why?" she said. "Why would anyone do that?"

"Doesn't matter," X said. "Keep moving."

When they reached the edge of the parking lot, he scoped the buildings in the distance. There were three—two, really, and a pile of rubble. The sight of the debris sent another wave of doubt through him. Their chances of finding fuel cells and pressure valves out here were looking more unlikely by the second.

Thunder growled to the west as they continued into the wastelands. Sam stopped a few feet ahead to stare at the swirling storm over Hades. Lightning streaked across the muddy clouds. "Looks like it's growing," he said.

"More reason to move our asses," X said. "Come on."

They worked their way through knee-deep snowdrifts for the next few minutes. They were getting close to the crate.

"On me," X said. He broke into a trot, passing Sam and waving the team forward. To the east, he could see where the snow dropped steeply away. They worked their way to the ridgeline overlooking the stark landscape. X halted at the edge and tested the snow with his boot before peering over the other side. He didn't need his binos to see the supply crate at the bottom. It was jammed between oblique concrete walls that jutted like headstones from the snow.

"Think we need a rope?" Murph asked.

X shook his head. "No time. Follow me, and be careful on your way down."

Sitting down, he tucked his hands against his sides and slid over the embankment, glissading over the slick surface. When his boots hit the bottom, he used his momentum to roll up onto his feet and trotted over to the crate.

Magnolia and Sam came sliding down a few seconds later. Murph came down a little less elegantly, kicking up a cloud of snow.

X opened the crate and tossed Sam an assault rifle.

"Load up and move out," X said. He waited a few moments for Magnolia and Murph, then started off with Sam. They trekked side by side over a half-covered highway, just as Aaron and X had done so many times before. The trust felt good. He was beginning to like Sam.

"Keep up!" X shouted. "Our suits won't protect us from this radiation forever." The words were the perfect motivation. He could hear Murph's and Magnolia's labored breaths as they struggled to catch up.

A harsh wind beat against the team as they worked their way through the blast zone. They loped along for another ten minutes—long enough for X to work up a sweat inside his layered suit. When they reached the outskirts of the wasteland, he swore. The road ended at a mountain of snow that had drifted around the two buildings and the pile of rubble between them. The wall of white rose several stories high.

Neither building bore any marking—nothing to indicate where they should be looking.

Thunder clapped in the distance, and X glanced at the storm rising over Hades. They were running out of time.

"You got any idea what we're looking at, Murph?" X asked.

"The *Hive*'s database puts the location right here. But it's not accurate enough to tell us which building."

"Ah, shit," X said. "We need to split up. Sam, you and Murph check the building to the left. Magnolia, you're with me. Stay in radio contact."

"Copy that," Sam said. Slinging his rifle over his back, he began climbing the wall of snow around the first building.

X scrambled up the mound to the right. The snow was compact and hard under his boots, and by kicking steps into it, he could move at a good clip. When he got to the top, he unstrapped his rifle and pointed it through an open window. The hallway beyond was covered in a layer of snow. He checked it for tracks before climbing through.

"Stay close," he said. "Eyes up."

"Right behind you, Commander."

X hurried down the frozen corridor to the first room. The door was gone, probably buried under the snow. He shouldered his rifle and eased into a room furnished with rusted chairs and a boxy metal desk.

"It's an office," X muttered. "A fucking *office.*"

"What's that mean?" Magnolia said.

"It means no fuel cells or pressure valves."

She lowered her rifle. "So what do we do?"

X looked around, thinking. For the first time on the mission, he felt a helpless dread growing inside him. He had doubted that they would find the needed parts here, but he had hoped for *something.*

"Follow me," he said, anger replacing the dread. He aimed his rifle down the hall and continued to a stairwell. The frame of the door lay on the landing below, blown off its hinges long ago. A cracked picture frame still hung on the wall.

He flicked off his night vision and clicked the headlamp on, angling the beam up and down the stairs.

"What's this?" Magnolia asked.

X centered the beam on the next floor. A network of cracks had splintered the walls, but somehow they had held over all these years.

"X," Magnolia entreated.

"What?"

"This looks like some sort of map."

He turned to find her looking at the picture frame he had passed earlier.

"Looks like we're in an ITC building," she added.

X hurried to her side and brushed off the dust. He was scanning the map when his helmet speaker crackled.

"X, this is Sam. Looks like a dead end here."

X kicked the wall. "There's nothing here, either." The building they were looking for was likely buried under a pile of rubble and snow. He stared at the map again, scrutinizing it for something he had missed. He rubbed off a layer of dust covering the upper corner. The fourth floor was labeled "Operations Center."

An idea seeded in his mind. Jordan had said they didn't know the exact locations of the cells or valves in Hades. Maybe, just maybe, there was something inside the ops center that would tell X where to find them. If the *Hive* was forced by circumstances to send all three teams into Hades, he could at least tell them where to go.

"Sam! Murph!" he yelled. "Get over here. I may have something."

*   *   *   *   *

Captain Ash sat impatiently in the command center on the bridge. Over an hour had passed since Team Raptor jumped off the ship. Desperate for news, she picked at a crack in the chair arm's leather. The wait during a dive was always excruciating, but this time it was even worse. The human species' very existence rested with the luck of a few brave men and women twenty thousand feet below.

An alarm chirped on the top floor of the bridge. She craned her neck up to see Ryan rush to his station. "What you got, Ensign?"

Ryan stared at his monitor, then swiveled his chair to a second display. "I'm … not really sure, Captain."

Ash jumped up from her chair and rushed to the second floor. "Jordan, get over here."

Moments later, she and her XO were crowded around Ryan's monitors.

"Captain, the storm appears to be growing again," Ryan said. "It's moving. Fast."

"Bring it onscreen," Ash replied.

The main display on the floor of the room activated. The edges of the electrical storm were surging outward like a loaf of bread expanding in an oven. And the *Hive* was right in its path.

The lesion in Ash's throat burned at the sight. She turned away from the view toward her XO. "Do we know where Raptor is?"

"No. We haven't had any sign of their beacons for an hour now."

"Ensign, how much time do we have before the storm hits us?" Ash asked.

Ryan shook his head and typed several commands. Lines of text scrolled across the screen.

"This can't be right," he said, looking up. "According to the data, if the storm continues moving at its current rate, we have about forty-five minutes. And that's just an estimate. It could be here faster."

"Jordan, direct power to the rudders and hold position for further orders. I want to be ready to move the moment they get back."

"But, Captain, that's going to drain the backup power."

"Jordan!" Ash barked.

He snapped to attention. "Yes, Captain."

"See if you can get X online. Tell him to get his ass back here," she said. "A private comm link, Jordan. I don't want his team to panic."

Jordan hesitated. His features hardened, and he said, "We can't afford to wait for them to get back."

She watched a streak of lightning zip across the display. It arced to the top of the storm clouds and vanished into inky darkness. It was hard to imagine a sun still shining somewhere above that blackness.

The thought blossomed into an idea. The ships were built for limited high-altitude flying. If she could fly them above the storm …

"Maybe there's another way," Ash said. "Jordan, divert all available power to the turbofans. I have an idea."

FIFTEEN

Weaver looked up. The high-rise across the street was gone, its top four stories sheared off by the impact with *Ares*. The embers of his home, his family, and all that he held dear smoldered just a city block away. The flames from a recent explosion in the hulking wreckage continued to lick the sky, warding away the scavengers that swooped and wheeled overhead.

The debris was spread as far as he could see: hunks of smoldering metal, the twisted blades of turbofans, a piece of an engine, parts of bodies.

He had assumed that he would feel rage when he got here. He was *supposed* to feel it. But as he looked over the destruction, all he felt was hollowness. His emotions had evaporated like the helium from a ruptured gas bladder.

Holding Sarah's blaster out in front, Weaver continued toward the crash site. The battery unit, food, and water he had retrieved from her corpse had prolonged his life, but he wasn't sure for how long. The sky was filled with ravening monsters. Their unearthly cries reverberated through the city as they searched for an opening in the flames below.

The screeches flowed together in a rhythm that surely meant something to them.

There were dozens of the creatures, maybe more. He still couldn't quite get his mind around the idea that they had survived down here. Somehow, they had adapted to the brutal life on the surface. Maybe it was their leathery skin, or something else he couldn't see. He didn't give a shit either way. All that mattered was keeping the abominations away from his family.

Weaver holstered the blaster, pulled out his binos, and focused them on the ship. The bow was buried under a mound of dirt, and the hull was split down the middle, exposing aluminum beams like the rib cage of some prehistoric behemoth. He flinched as another explosion rocked the ship. A yellow plume of fire billowed up in his scope. The tendrils reached into the sky and engulfed one of the winged creatures. Screeching, it managed a few more wing beats before spiraling down into the flames.

Seeing it, Weaver felt some hint of emotion at last: a tingle of satisfaction. He stuffed his binos back into his vest, scrambled up a mound of snow, slid down the other side, and bolted toward the nearest building. Reaching it, he slowed to a walk, hugging the walls, his blaster trained on the sky. The winged Sirens didn't seem to notice his presence. They were more interested in the ship.

The distraction allowed him to get closer. He ran down the final stretch of street, slipped around the corner, and took shelter in the lobby of a building lit by the glow of the burning debris field.

He watched for an hour from the safety of the doorway. Falling snow slowly drowned the raging fire, and thick plumes of smoke rose into the sky. The lowering flames allowed the creatures to get closer to the wreckage. Weaver watched one of them swoop down between the exposed ribs of the hull. It flapped out of the swirling smoke a moment later, fighting for altitude. Something was weighing it down.

Weaver pulled his binos again and zoomed in on the monster's legs and the charred body gripped in its talons. His rage forced him out of the safety of the building.

"No," he whispered. "I won't let you take my family."

Another Siren sailed over the debris field and grabbed a tiny corpse and flapped away into the darkness. Several others soared after it, screeching in their strange, dissonant language.

"NO!" Weaver shouted, his voice edging on hysteria. He strode out onto the street and aimed his blaster into the sky. The fierce anger of a father who had lost everything returned. Blinking away tears, he ran toward the wreckage of his home. Beyond his blurred vision, he saw something that brought a pain worse than what he had felt when *Ares* came crashing down.

Corpses and body parts were strewn across the snow-covered dirt. His friends and family sizzled as the snow hit their scorched bodies. Their faces surfaced in his memory, but he buried them. He wouldn't let their memories weaken him right now. He needed his strength for what was about to happen.

"Hey! Hey, you flying fucks!" Weaver shouted in a voice that sounded deranged even to him.

The shriek of a Siren answered his call. It pivoted in the sky, flapping toward him now. Two more of the creatures flanked the beast, cutting through the air and diving at him. Weaver centered the iron sights of his blaster on the approaching monsters. When all three were within range, he squeezed the trigger.

The gun made a strange popping sound, and sparks shot out the left barrel. The creatures whistled through the air, the wind over their backswept wings rustling like the suit of a diver in free fall.

Heart pounding, Weaver hit the selector switch and pulled the trigger a second time. This time, the gun fired two Magnum loads of double-aught shotgun pellets. The projectiles spread, punching through delicate wings, and tearing into lean muscle. The Sirens let out a cacophony of pained wails and crashed to the ground ten feet away in an explosion of dirt and ash. Weaver snapped open the breech, ejected the two spent shells, and dropped two fresh ones in.

Weaver stared at the field of the dead. The dying embers scattered across the dirt shimmered under a flash of lightning. Pulling his gaze away, he raised his blaster and fired at another formation of monsters swooping toward him.

*   *   *   *   *

The beams from Team Raptor's headlights cut through the darkness, dancing across the concrete walls of the narrow stairwell. Sam was on point, with X on his six. They moved up the stairs quickly, with Magnolia's and Murph's footfalls close behind.

"Should be the next floor," X said. "Check it out."

Sam moved with a soldier's precision, sweeping his weapon across alternating fields of fire. He continued up the stairs to the next landing and disappeared from view. X used the moment to check the radiation. It was lower here but still high. They had to move quickly.

"All clear," Sam said a moment later.

X glanced at Magnolia and Murph, in the shadows below. He didn't need to see their faces to know they were terrified.

"Stay here," he said to them, and he was darting up the stairs before they had a chance to protest. Sam waited outside a heavy door on the next landing. He grabbed the handle and twisted it, but it clicked: locked.

"See if you can hack in," X said.

Sam searched the wall and brushed off a layer of dust to reveal a rectangular security panel. Pulling a cable from his vest, he uncoiled it and plugged one end into his wrist computer, the other end into the panel.

X was impressed. Sam operated as if he had done this a hundred times before. Hacking into Old World facilities wasn't all that hard if you had the right gear. The minicomputers the divers carried had codes to most of the ITC facilities, and enough juice to jump-start the old tech. It was just a matter of time before they cracked this one.

The wait was shorter than X expected. The panel chirped, and the door creaked open.

"On me," X said. Rifle up, he swung the door open.

Inside was a space frozen in time. Row after row of dusty tables filled the room. The floor was littered with shattered computer monitors. In the center of it all, a single desiccated corpse stared with empty eye sockets up at the ceiling.

X worked his way down the aisle toward the body and motioned for Sam to take the adjacent row.

"Think any of these computers work?" X asked.

"Probably not, sir."

X stopped to examine the corpse. There was little left. The clothes had mostly disintegrated, revealing a membrane of dried skin stretched over bones. It was hard to tell whether it had been a man or a woman.

"Murph, Magnolia, get up here," X said over the comm. He flung his assault rifle over his back and continued toward a rack of file cabinets at the front of the room.

"Murph, see if you can get one of these computers working. Might be a long shot, but it's worth a try." X checked his mission clock. They were down to the bone: thirty minutes remained.

He pulled open a cabinet and thumbed through the contents. "Magnolia, get over here and help me," he said. "Sam, you watch the door."

Magnolia said, "What am I looking for?"

"A map, I don't know. Something that tells us the location of the manufacturing buildings in Hades."

He pulled out a piece of paper that flaked apart in his hands. The next piece was so faded, he couldn't make out the text.

"God damn it," X said.

They spent the next fifteen minutes digging through the contents, looking for anything that might give them a lead to the location of the ITC factory in Hades. X tried to think, but it was impossible to concentrate when they were so close to the wire. The *Hive* was waiting, and without anything substantial, he considered telling the team to abandon the search. With the ship running on backup power, Ash still needed time to maneuver into position over Hades and drop all three teams. On top of that, they needed time to actually find the parts and then get back to the *Hive*. He hated the idea of returning with nothing concrete, but they had run out of time.

"Nothing works," Murph said ruefully.

X scanned the room. It was a dead end. They had gambled and lost, and there was nothing to do but suck it up and return to the *Hive*.

"Fuck it, we're out of time," he said. "Let's get the hell out of here." He waved the divers toward the exit, but Magnolia hung back. X could hear her rifling through the file cabinet.

"Wait," she said. "Maybe I got something." She pulled a laminated paper from a drawer and held it under her beam. He brushed off the surface.

"Looks like a map," she said, handing it to X.

X snatched it from her hands and gave it a quick glance. She was right. It was a map of someplace called Chicago, Illinois—and it showed the location of the ITC headquarters. "Chicago" must have been the original name of Hades.

Magnolia reached back inside and pulled a second map. This one gave the location for the factories around the HQ. There were dozens of the domed buildings, and each was labeled. They would tell Samson exactly which structure they were looking for.

"Jackpot," X said. "Any more?"

Magnolia peered into the open drawer and shook her head.

X stuffed one of the maps into his vest pocket and handed the other to Sam. "Just in case one of us doesn't make it back."

Sam took it reluctantly.

"Let's get back to ship," X said. He led the team back toward the building at double time, twice nearly stumbling down the stairs.

The speaker in his helmet crackled to life when he got back to the hallway. The faint sound of an emergency alarm filled the channel, and he could hardly hear the message over the noise.

"Commander X, do you copy? Over."

X halted and said, "Roger that."

A flurry of white noise crackled in his ear. He clenched his jaw, waiting anxiously for it to pass.

"Commander, we've been trying to reach you for thirty minutes!"

It was Jordan, and his normally calm voice held an edge of panic.

"You need to get back to the ship ASAP! The storm above Hades is heading your way. You have fifteen minutes to get home. I repeat, fifteen minutes!"

"On our way," X said. Flicking off his headlamp, he switched on his night vision and peered out the window they had entered through. He could see in green the surging clouds and the lightning that webbed across the horizon. There was something else, too—something in the air that looked like bats, moving away from the storm. It wouldn't be the first time his eyes played tricks on him.

"Got to move!" X shouted, waving his team forward. The static in his earpiece had faded, but the electronic whine of the emergency siren aboard the *Hive* continued as he raced toward the window. When he got there, he slid to a stop. The noise wasn't coming from his comm channel. It was coming from the tiny dots flapping across the skyline.

X stared at the formations of winged creatures sailing toward him. There was no doubt in his mind they were the same creatures that had torn Aaron's body to pieces, but somehow, these had evolved to fly.

"What the hell *are* those things?" Magnolia shouted, pushing past him and staring at the sky. Then, speechless, she slowly backed away until she hit the wall.

"Sirens," X said, barely comprehending what he was saying. He watched the beasts and the storm beyond in terrible slow motion. For the past few days, he had promised himself he would be strong if he encountered the monsters again, but he never imagined seeing them in the air. Even the sky wasn't safe from the monsters.

The shouts of the team sounded faint in the background. Magnolia had cowered away from the window and was sitting on the floor with her knees to her chest. Murph had crouched right behind her, his visor roving from side to side as he scanned the horizon.

The Sirens worked their way into a solid V formation, turning slightly as the lead creature fixated on Raptor's location. There were a dozen of the pale creatures, flapping their leathery, frayed wings like demons in some fevered nightmare.

X felt a hand on his shoulder and heard Sam's robust voice.

"Commander!" he shouted. "Commander, we have to move!"

"We're too far away from the ship," Murph shouted back.

Sam shook X again, harder this time.

"We have to get into the sky," X finally said. "It's our only chance. Captain Ash will pick up our beacons and maneuver the *Hive* accordingly." He faced his team. "Everyone get outside and deploy boosters. Now!"

"No," Magnolia said, her entire body shaking. She stood and turned to run. "We have to hide!"

"There's no time" X yelled. "We have to get back to the ship!" He grabbed her by the wrist and yanked her back to the window, then climbed out onto the mound of snow and pulled her with him. Before she could react, he spun her around, punched her booster, and yelled, "Shoot 'em if they get close!"

Magnolia launched into the sky, screaming her lungs out. X went next. Reaching over his shoulder, he punched his booster. He gripped his rifle tightly as the balloon exploded out of the pack, inflated with helium, and hauled him up into the sky.

The moment he was off his feet, he shouldered his rifle and took aim at the Sirens. Several of them had broken off from the right side of their formation and were already swooping toward Magnolia. Behind them stretched a wall of clouds as far as he could see. Lightning streaked across the swollen edges of the storm.

He lined up the sights and fired a volley of shots at the creatures. The bullets found targets, tearing through wings and torsos and sending the Sirens spiraling or tumbling back down to the surface. But the kick from the gun also jolted him backward in his harness, so that his feet rocked up in front of him.

Swinging back upright, he aimed again, this time squeezing off single shots. The rounds ripped through the torso of one of the creatures, and it flapped spastically away, losing altitude with every wing beat.

Gunfire cracked below, and three more of the Sirens fell from the sky. But others were quickly closing in, and bullets didn't seem to deter them much.

X looked to his HUD. Five minutes had already passed since the message from command, and they were only seven thousand feet in the air. Even if they could hold back the Sirens, he wasn't sure they would make it back to the ship in time. He twisted his body around for a better view of the storm expanding to the west. The clouds churned, the electrical flashes providing a snapshot inside the belly of the storm.

A voice broke over the flurry of static. "X! This is Captain Ash, do you copy?"

"We're on our way back!" X quickly replied.

"Do you have the cells and valves?"

X hesitated, knowing his response could lead Ash to abandon them. "Negative. But we have something else: a map that shows where the cells and valves are."

There was a terrible pause.

"You've got ten minutes to get up top before we have to get the hell out of here," Ash said. "Make it work."

"Understood."

The distant sound of thunder boomed over the whine of the Sirens. Two were sailing toward Magnolia, and three swooped down on Murph and Sam. X twisted in his harness to focus on the two making a run at Magnolia. Aiming at the leader's wings, he fired off a short burst. A gust of wind threw off his aim in the last second, and the rounds went wide, narrowly missing Magnolia.

Cursing, X grabbed a toggle to steer his balloon with his right hand. He raised the rifle with his left and, leading the Sirens with the muzzle, squeezed off another volley. This time, one of the monsters' skulls exploded.

There was no time to celebrate. A scream erupted over the comm channel, and X glanced down just as a Siren crashed into Sam. The creature wrapped its wings and legs around him, then began slashing at his helmet with the talons on its hands.

"Sam!" X shouted. He trained his gun on the blur of armor and flesh but knew he couldn't risk firing. Helpless, he watched predator and prey tumble away through the clouds.

Another Siren came whistling through the sky as Sam vanished from sight. X raised his rifle and fired two shots. The first took off the creature's jaw, and it spun out of control, its wings narrowly missing the suspension lines to X's balloon.

Magnolia, firing wildly, held off the other Siren above. Then, at fifteen thousand feet, the last few of them wheeled away, returning to a surface that X could no longer see.

"Sam," X said over the comm. "Sam, do you copy!" He searched the clouds for any sign. Sam's beacon was still active on X's HUD, but he wasn't responding.

"Where's Sam?" Magnolia said, the trepidation in her voice weakened by static.

"They got him," X replied. "The bastards fucking got him." He continued to scan below his feet. Murph looked up at him, his mirrored visor hiding his eyes.

The team continued their ascent in silence. Hope for Sam faded as the beetle shape of the *Hive* came into focus. The edge of the storm was closing in.

Above, the oval doors in the belly of the ship separated, revealing the small recovery room. Magnolia tugged on her toggles and steered her balloon inside. Her feet disappeared as her balloon pulled her to safety. X used his toggles to adjust his own ascent. With one eye on his HUD and the other on the recovery bay, he followed Magnolia.

A blip on X's HUD pulled his attention to his visor. His heart skipped a beat when he saw Sam's beacon rising a few thousand feet below. X glanced down as he was pulled into the ship. Magnolia dangled a few feet away, where her balloon rested against the translucent domed ceiling. As soon as Murph joined them, the ship began moving.

X bumped his chin pad. "Captain, Sam is still down there!"

The metal walls of the recovery space groaned as the ship's turbofans flared to life. He blinked, realizing that Captain Ash wasn't abandoning Sam; she was maneuvering into position to pick him up.

"Where is he?" Magnolia said.

"We're picking him up," X replied.

The three divers probed the clouds below. As the ship moved, a tiny blue dot rose into the sky.

"Sam, you're almost here. Just hang on!" X shouted.

The diver didn't reply, and as he got closer, X saw that his head was bowed to his chest. His balloon pulled him into the reentry bay right in front of X. Blood flowed from Sam's cracked visor, spreading over his vest and armor. Steam rose off it. There was too much blood—an impossible amount that left no question: Sam was dead. The doors clamped shut, and X reached forward to pull Sam's right hand outside his vest. Even in death, he was protecting the map, clutching it so tight, X had to pry it from his bloody fingers.

SIXTEEN

"All clear," Ensign Ryan shouted. "The storm is below us."

But not a soul on the bridge was listening. Everyone, including Captain Ash, was huddled at the porthole windows before the bridge. Where they had known only darkness, they saw light.

With no time to outrun the storm, Ash had used the turbofans to rise above it. Silence washed over the room as the ship ascended higher into the sky. Ash squinted and shielded her face from the dazzling glow. They were looking at a sight that none of them had seen in years: the sun.

The ball of fire hung suspended in an ocean of blue. The clearest, most beautiful blue that Ash had ever seen in her life. High above the dark morass below, thin yellow clouds drifted, their translucent outlines fired with golden light.

But overshadowing the beauty was the failure of Raptor's mission. Still without the cells and parts, she would be forced to send all three teams down to Hades.

Jordan cupped his headset and pivoted away from

the view. "Captain, I just got a message from Ty ..." He paused and caught her gaze. "We have a casualty."

"I thought all four divers made it back," Ash said, keeping her voice low. Ryan and Hunt looked in their direction but didn't speak.

Jordan shook his head. "I'm afraid Sam Baker was killed, but we did manage to recover his body."

Ash allowed herself one final look at the sun before turning away. "I'm going down to the HD facility."

"Wait, Captain," Jordan said. "Samson also sent a message. His team managed to get one of the reactors up and running. It buys us a bit more time."

"How much time?"

"Not much, but enough to give Raptor a breather."

Ash looked at her watch. It was almost noon. Raptor had been gone only a few hours. She considered sending Apollo and Angel to Hades now but didn't want to risk maneuvering into the storm twice. "Send out the message. All three teams dive at four o'clock p.m."

Ash was already moving up the stairs before Jordan could reply. Her escorts waited outside the bridge, though she wasn't sure she needed them, considering how empty the corridors were on the way to the HD facility.

The other teams were already at the launch bay when Ash arrived. Word of Sam's death had traveled fast. The divers had crowded around the plastic dome of the recovery room, eager for any tidbit of news.

A heavy cloud filled the dome as the surviving members of Team Raptor held out their arms and turned slowly under the cleansing misters. Below them, a body lay on the floor, as inert as the deflated balloons around it.

Ash moved past Cruise and his team and stood on the redline border surrounding the dome.

A remotely operated chain with a grappling hook dropped from the ceiling and latched on to the top of the dome. Sharp clicks rang out as the locking mechanisms unlatched.

"Back up!" Ty shouted, waving the crowd of divers and technicians away.

Ash followed them back to a safe distance. For a moment, she didn't feel much like a ship's captain, because there wasn't much she could do right now to help.

A subtle shift in the *Hive*'s course rumbled through the launch bay. Ty waited for the turbulence to pass before giving the all clear. The grappling hook lifted the dome into the air, spilling mist from beneath it, which the floor vents sucked away.

X was first to stumble out. His dented black armor, spotless from the rigorous reentry cleanse, sparkled under the bright LEDs. He took a moment to scan the room, found Ash. He pulled off his helmet, set it gently on the floor, and came over to her.

"We didn't find any fuel cells or valves," X said. "But we did find this." From his vest, he pulled out two laminated pieces of paper—maps, by the look of them. One was covered in drying blood. He handed her both of them. "At least we'll know where we're heading when you send us to Hades."

"Thank you," Ash said. "I'll get these to Samson immediately for review." X ran a hand through his sweaty salt-and-pepper hair. He muttered something under his breath, then said, "When do we dive again?"

"Samson was able to get one of the reactors back online," Ash said. "Bought us some time, but not much." She turned to face the divers who had huddled around. "Go and rest; spend some time with your families. Meet back here at three o'clock. You all dive at four."

Teams Apollo and Angel left the launch bay in relative silence, but Ash could hear their silent protests in her mind. She was about to send them to an almost certain death. Cruise stopped in the doorway to stare at Sam's body, glared at Ash, and stalked out of the launch bay.

"Promise me something, Captain," X said.

Ash turned back to X and the remaining members of Raptor. Heartsick already at having lost a diver, now she was about to lose many more. Under the glow of the LEDs, X looked twenty years older. He had wrinkles she never noticed before, and a streak of gray that the light seemed to accentuate.

"Sure, Commander," she said. "What is it?"

"Promise me someone will look after Tin when I'm gone."

"I promise. I'll send someone to your room as soon as you dive."

X shook his head. "No, Captain. I mean when I'm gone for good. Promise me Tin will be taken care of if anything happens to me."

She put her hand on his shoulder. He seemed to sink under the weight of her touch. "I promise you, Tin will be taken care of."

X turned to look at Sam's broken body. Magnolia was sobbing, and Murph put an arm around her. No others words needed to be spoken. Like Cruise, everyone on Team Raptor knew they were likely to join their comrade soon enough.

*   *   *   *   *

X wandered the halls on his way back to his apartment. The ship was on lockdown and eerily quiet. He walked with his flashlight shining down the dark, empty corridors. An odd feeling that he couldn't place came over him. He breathed in the cold air and studied the paintings on the next bulkhead. The longer he looked at them, the stronger the feeling grew. Sam was dead, but X had never felt more alive.

And he hadn't even had a drink.

Seeing the newfound strength in Tin had inspired something inside him that he hadn't even known still existed. For the longest time, the guilt over not being able to save those he loved most had haunted him, leaving a scar that only he could see. So he had poisoned his body with 'shine, wishing deep down that his luck would finally run out on a dive. Now he had a chance to redeem himself. If he could save the *Hive,* he could save Tin and fulfill his promise to Aaron.

When X arrived at his apartment, he knocked hard and twisted the knob. The door creaked open to the flickering of a candle near the end of its wick. His eyes gravitated to the curled-up silhouette of Tin on the living room floor.

"Hey," Tin whispered. He rubbed his face and took a seat on the couch. A mess of mechanical parts from some new project littered the floor.

"Are you okay?" Tin asked, looking him up and down.

"Yeah," X lied as cheerfully as he knew how. "You hungry?"

"Kinda."

"Should still be leftovers," X said, grabbing a bowl of apples and a bottle of water from the kitchen and returning to the living room. He set the bowl on the table in front of Tin. The boy's eyes searched the fruit, but instead of grabbing an apple, he stood and wrapped his arms around X.

"Thanks," Tin said. "For looking after me."

Not knowing what to say, X patted the boy's back. In that second, time seemed to slow. His senses picked up every detail around him: the sounds of the rattling ceiling fan and the cough of the wall heater. He saw the wax crawling down the stump of gray candle as it hardened into a puddle on the table. He caught the sour whiff of his own sweat, and the sweetness of the apples. He wanted to remember it all exactly this way. It was the moment that he realized he loved the boy as he would love his own son. He had always known that he would gladly give his life to keep Tin safe, but now he felt it in his bones.

Instead of filling him with despair, it made him smile. He flicked the tip of Tin's foil hat, and they both grinned.

They ate in silence for several minutes. X felt

every second, each one bringing him closer to the dive that would take him to Hades. He hadn't even told Tin he was going yet. On his walk from the launch bay, he had reflected on the things he would tell Tin, knowing that whatever he said would likely stick with the boy for the rest of his life. But now, with the shadows closing in around the faltering candlelight, X didn't know what to say.

"X?" Tin whispered. "What's wrong?"

"Sorry. Just ..." He shook his head and sat forward on the edge of his seat. It was time to tell the boy the truth.

"I have to dive again in a few hours—this time to Hades."

Tin tilted his head ever so slightly. Studying, scrutinizing.

"I won't lie to you. Hades is a very dangerous place. That's why Captain Ash is sending in all three teams instead of just one: we'll have better odds of success."

"You don't think you're coming back, do you?"

X's heart sank. "I'm not sure anyone will make it back, but as long as we send the crate up with the parts ..."

Tears welled in Tin's eyes.

X reached out and said, "I've already made arrangements with Captain Ash. You'll be looked after. You'll be fine."

Tin stood up, pulling away from X's fingertips. "Who else is going to look after me? Huh? Who?"

"I'm not sure," X replied. "But Captain Ash reassured me—"

"I don't want someone else to look after me!"

X rose to his feet. "Tin, I will do everything I can to come back. *Everything.* I promise."

"That's what my dad always said. But he didn't come back, and you couldn't save him."

The words stung, but X didn't blame the boy for saying them. "Tin, please. I'm doing this for you and everyone else on the ship. Just like your father did."

Tin tightened the string of his hat around his chin. "Why do the people I love always have to be the ones to die? Why can't someone else dive?" He wiped a tear away and sucked in a long breath.

"Because there aren't many people left who can do what your father did or what I do," X said. He kept his voice as calm as he could, hoping the boy would understand.

Tin shook his head. "There are plenty of people on this ship, but it's always the ones I care about that die."

X reached out, but Tin ducked and stormed away to the bedroom. He stopped outside the door and said, "I'll be better off on my own. Better off looking after myself. *Everyone* I ever cared about has died anyway. And now you're going to die, too."

X slowly walked over to him, but Tin slammed the door between them. X pressed against the door with both hands and lowered his head. "Tin, please. Please don't make me leave this way. I'm doing this for you. For the *Hive!*"

The only response was the faint sound of sobbing. X backed away, his mind racing. Only a few hours remained before the dive, and everything he had begun to rebuild with the boy was wrecked. He was tempted to go find a drink to take his mind off things, but instead he wrapped himself in a blanket and lay down on the couch, hoping Tin would someday forgive him for what he had to do.

*   *   *   *   *

X slept fitfully for the next hour. His thoughts were scattered and chaotic. He finally gave up trying to rest and relit the candle on the table. Then he padded over to the bedroom and gently pushed the door open. The glimmering golden light illuminated Tin's still body through the open door.

X slipped inside and knelt beside the bed. The boy's eyes flicked and quivered beneath the lids. He was in deep sleep. The events of the past few days had worn him out.

"I'll save the *Hive,* Tin," X whispered. "I'll make sure you get to grow up. And someday, you'll be an engineer, or maybe a farmer. You'll do great things. I know it. You'll build things and help people. And maybe someday you'll understand why your dad and I had to keep diving until it killed us."

He put his hand gently on Tin's shoulder for a moment. For the past year, X had done his duty and dived without much thought beyond a hangover and a death wish. But feeling the boy's back move up and down reminded him that there was something in this world still worth living for and protecting.

*   *   *   *   *

An hour later, X was suiting up in the HD facility.

Tony and Cruise were already there, checking their gear and loading two plastic crates in the center of the room. Both team leads were freshly groomed, their shaved heads glistening under the bright LEDs. It was a ritual for them. Pretty silly in X's opinion, but if it helped psych them up for the dive, it was fine with him.

"You guys ready?" X asked.

Cruise ran a finger back and forth over his jaw. "What do you think?"

X looked Cruise up and down. "I think you better down some electrolyte tablets. You look like you had a few too many last night."

Tony let out a snicker. "I told you not to get so stupid, man."

"I'm fine," Cruise said. "You pick your poison, X; I'll pick mine."

"Last I checked, I'm not hungover for this dive."

Cruise tilted his head at X as if trying to get a read, but X turned his back, bending over the boxes to examine the contents. They were filled with assault rifles, magazines, flares, medicine, food, water, climbing gear, and extra boosters.

Cruise hovered over him. "You think we really have a chance down there?"

"If we make it through the storms, yeah, maybe," X said, double-checking the gear.

"At least we got some real firepower for this dive," Cruise said. He crossed his forearms, which made his biceps bulge. "We run into any of your Sirens, I'll blow 'em to itty bits."

"A word of advice," X said, glancing up. "If

you make it to the surface and you see anything down there, run."

Cruise clenched his jaw.

"You hear me, Cruise? No time to kill the local wildlife on this dive. Your priority is the mission objective. No cowboyin'."

"I heard you the first time," Cruise growled.

The other divers and team technicians drifted into the room. X scanned each of them. Murph and Magnolia were the last two inside.

"Atten-*shun*!" came a stern voice at the entrance. "Captain on deck!"

Captain Ash and Lieutenant Jordan strode inside with two soldiers on each flank.

"Briefing in fifteen," Jordan said.

"You heard the lieutenant," X yelled. "Suit up and meet in the briefing room in fifteen."

The launch bay came alive with the sound and motion of predive rituals. Plates of armor were fastened and boosters clicked into place. Chutes were checked, double-checked, and checked again. Mirrored visors were polished with spit and rags.

Ty gnawed on his herb stick and waited with his tablet to run diagnostics on Team Raptor's gear. X held up a finger—almost ready—then checked on Magnolia and Murph, who were helping each other with their armor.

"You guys get some rest?" he asked, kneeling to pull the laces tight on his boots. He grimaced as he stood up.

"I did," Murph replied.

"Some," Magnolia said.

"Good, because you're going to need it." He turned instinctively to look for Team Raptor's fourth diver, then remembered. He still couldn't believe Sam was gone. If only they had left a minute sooner. A goddamn minute could have saved his life.

X slammed his battery unit into the slot in his chest armor harder than he needed to. In less than an hour, he would see the cursed heart of Hades, and more Hell Divers would join the ranks of those who had perished there.

* * * * *

Captain Ash's fingers gripped the ancient wooden lectern. Every man and woman sitting in front of her knew what was at stake. She would make this quick.

Ash nodded at Jordan. He flipped the lights, and a map of Hades emerged on the wall behind him. Stepping to one side, Ash said, "This, as you all know, is Hades. Industrial Tech Corporation had a campus on the eastern edge of the city. This is where they manufactured the parts of airships like the *Hive*. Chief Engineer Samson has studied and analyzed the maps Team Raptor retrieved." She paused to nod at X and his team.

"We've authorized the use of heavy weapons and extra flares for this mission. You are to deploy the flares when you jump, to help guide you through the storms," Jordan said. "Once you make it through, your DZ is on the outskirts of the industrial zone. To give you the best chance of survival, we've plotted three separate courses for the teams:

here, here, and here." He pointed to dots marked "Raptor," "Angel," and "Apollo."

"After you land, you're to rendezvous at the ITC HQ and campus. There are multiple buildings and warehouses in the area, but Samson has identified this building as your target." Jordan pointed to a single structure. "We've preloaded the coordinates to your minicomputers. Once you acquire the fuel cells and pressure valves, you'll return to the crates and send them back to the *Hive*."

Ash cut in. "After you drop, we'll move out of the storm and wait at a safe distance for you to return." She loosened her grip and bent over the podium. "You have twenty-four hours to complete the mission, at which point we will move back into the storm. If we detect the beacons from the crates sooner than that, we'll swoop in and retrieve them. Make sure you're with them. Any questions?"

In the silence, Ash scanned the faces, stopping on X. If anyone could inspire the others, it was him.

"You want to say anything, Commander Rodriguez?" she asked.

The veteran diver stood and pushed in his chair, then walked to the front of the room and stood beside Ash. He ran his hand over the scar above his eye. She had seen him do it before when he was nervous.

"If we fail today, the human race is gone forever," X said. "But we're not going to let that happen, are we?" He brushed off his dented armor, using the time to command the gaze of everyone in the room. X had a presence about him—something Ash felt whenever he walked into a room. The thought of losing him made her throat constrict.

"Today we dive to a place no Hell Diver has ever returned from—a place that many of you have been told is cursed. I'm not going to lie to you and tell you Hades isn't as bad as they say. Magnolia, Murph, and I have seen what's down there. It's nothing pretty. But like the rest of the surface, Hades isn't cursed. And those things, the Sirens—they can be killed. You stay focused and alert, and you *will* survive. Those things may control the surface, but we still control the skies. Today, we're going to make sure life continues up here."

"Damn right," Tony muttered.

"We aren't going to let the *Hive* go crashing down to earth without a fight, are we?" X said, his voice louder now.

"Hell no, we aren't!" Cruise shouted.

"We aren't joining *Ares*!" another diver yelled.

"No," X said. "We aren't. Because today we're going to dive faster, smarter, and stronger than we ever have before. Today we dive ..."

The other divers roared in unison, "So humanity survives!"

SEVENTEEN

The launch bay was teeming with activity. Technicians performed last-minute diagnostics on the drop tubes as divers hugged their family members goodbye behind an area cordoned off with rope.

X skimmed over the faces and sighed. Tin wasn't coming, no matter how badly X wanted him here. Maybe it was for the best. Maybe it would only hurt worse to see the boy before the dive.

X looked away and tapped the minicomputer on his wrist. The operating system that controlled his suit emerged behind the cracked surface. Everything looked good to go. The routine he had gone through ninety-seven times before had started, and the final count was ticking down.

Captain Ash walked through the launch bay, stopping to shake hands with each diver and wish them well. She stopped when she got to X, and pulled him aside.

"There's something I need to tell you before you dive," Ash said. "Let's take a walk."

X checked the crowd one more time, then followed Ash away from the other divers. He wasn't feeling up for any more bad news, especially after Tin's reaction to learning of the dive.

Ash put her hands on her hips and stared toward the portholes on the starboard side. "My throat cancer has returned," she said.

He didn't have any good reply to that. "I'm ... I'm sorry to hear that, Captain."

Ash continued looking at the windows for a few more seconds before returning her eyes to X. "I've had a good life. And I still have a few good months left. Maybe more. I'm not going to just roll over and die. I'll use what time I have left to continue searching for a new home. Assuming you complete today's mission."

"We will, Captain," X replied.

"I trust you," she said, "and I want you to know that you can trust me, too. Whatever happens, Tin will be taken care of."

"Thank you, Captain. I just wish he were here to say goodbye."

Ash smiled and looked toward the crowd. X followed her eyes to a familiar shiny, peaked hat. Tin pushed through to the rope cordon and waved.

"He had a change of heart," Ash said with a wink. "I may or may not have enticed him by telling him he could see the farm again. I'll have an engineer take him to the emergency shelter there after he says goodbye. He can wait there until we maneuver back out of the storm. Figured another tour of the farm would help take his mind off things."

"I appreciate that, Captain," X said. "More than you know." He felt a smile start on the edges of his mouth as he walked over to the rope. Tin, wearing a sheepish grin, reached out from the crowd.

X grabbed him and hoisted him over the ropes.

"I'm sorry, Tin," he said. "I'm so sorry your life has been so tough and—"

Tin let out a groan. "Too tight. Too tight."

"Sorry," X said, putting him back on his feet and readjusting the foil hat he had knocked askew.

"I'm sorry about last night," Tin said. "I'm just scared you won't come back."

X crouched down in front of him. "Even if I don't, you won't be alone. You can still talk to me. You can talk to your parents, too. We might not talk back, but that doesn't mean we're not listening."

Tin looked at the ground and reached into his pocket. He pulled out a small crumpled piece of paper and handed it to X. "Maybe this'll bring you luck."

X read the paper aloud. *"Accept your past without regrets. Handle your present with confidence. Face your future without fear."*

A siren wailed in the distance. The first warning. They were almost out of time. "Thanks, Tin. This is perfect."

Tin gave X a look that held a mix of fear and sadness. He hesitated as if unsure what to do next, then wrapped his arms around X again. He pressed his head against the hard chest armor. His curved hat scraped the stubble on X's cheek, but X didn't dare move. He patted Tin's back and said softly, "It's okay, buddy. Everything's going to be okay."

"Please come back," Tin murmured. Sniffling, he tilted his head back to search X's eyes.

"I will do *everything* I can to make sure I do." He knew in his heart this was true, even if it meant fighting the Sirens with a rusted blade and his bare hands.

Tin brushed a tear from his eye, sniffled again, and drew in a deep breath. "Promise?"

"I promise," X said. He wrapped his arms around Tin once more and exchanged a nod with Captain Ash.

X winced at the second warning siren. The sound reminded him of what he was about to face on the surface below. He tightened his grip around Tin and let go a moment later.

"I have to go now," X said.

Captain Ash grabbed Tin's hand and led him back to the edge of the crowd. "Good luck," she said, her gaze on X as she walked away.

X waved two fingers at Tin, then tucked the paper into his vest pocket. The other divers were already climbing into their launch tubes by the time he walked to his.

Ty helped X into his tube and closed the dome over the top. This time, X didn't feel any of his normal predive jitters or the side effects of a hangover. His body was energized, his mind at peace, and he was focused on the mission. He had never been readier to do his duty.

*   *   *   *   *

"All right, people," Captain Ash said. "Let's make this as smooth as possible." She turned the oak wheel and looked to the front of the room as the electrical storm above Hades emerged on the main display. They were heading into the beast—the same maneuver that she had condemned Captain Willis for two days ago.

"Jordan, how far to the coordinates?" Ash said.

"Three minutes, Captain."

Every officer on the bridge watched the display. The swirling purple vortex expanded to fill the entire monitor. Branches of electric blue snaked away from the center like blood vessels from a pounding heart. The storm looked alive. The sight of it filled her with foreboding.

"Coordinates in T minus thirty seconds," Jordan said in a cool, crisp voice.

Lightning flashed across the bow as the ship pushed into the edges of the storm. The hull rattled and groaned, and Ash eyed the flickering banks of LEDs on the ceiling.

"Steady," she whispered. "Steady as she goes …"

A second tremor, this one deeper, shook the ship, and from the bridge they could hear the sound of a distant crack. The vibration rippled through the walls.

"Almost there, Captain," Jordan replied.

An emergency siren wailed, the red light splashing over the deck. The *Hive* shook fiercely, the bulkheads creaking and groaning. Ash realized she was holding her breath, and let it out just as Jordan confirmed they were in position.

She cleared her throat before speaking into her headset. "Raptor, Angel, and Apollo, you have a green light for launch. Good luck and Godspeed."

As the words left her mouth, the ship lurched forward, through the outer wall of the surging storm. Lightning streaked in all directions across the main display. The storm engulfed the *Hive* like a whale swallowing a shrimp. The ship quaked under the onslaught of electrical strikes.

Ash pulled the wheel a few degrees left, doing her best to keep a steady course despite the violent rocking. Two decks beneath her, under the guts of the ship, humanity's last hope was about to dive into the abyss, and there was nothing she could do to help them.

*   *   *   *   *

X fidgeted in his metal cocoon and waited for the glass doors of his launch tube to split open. An emergency light bathed his pod in red. He braced himself against the metal walls as a tremor shook the *Hive*. His earpiece crackled, but he couldn't make out the transmission. The storm had already knocked out the comm and the minimap in his HUD subscreen.

The launch tube rattled as if they had suddenly entered a pocket of extreme turbulence. He watched the flashes of lightning beneath the glass floor. A few minutes ago, he hadn't felt any of the messy, addictive fear that the sight normally prompted, but now the rush had his heart thumping at almost double time.

"Come on, God damn it, let's *go*!" he said, knowing that no one could hear him. Flexing his hands and chewing on his mouth guard, he buried the rising fear in his gut.

The walls of his tube rattled again, knocking him against the side. He crossed his arms over his chest and cursed.

"Come on!"

The sirens clicked off, their whine still lingering in his ears. X blinked just as the panels split beneath his boots. In the same fraction of a second, he heard the unmistakable crack of gunfire above. And the next moment, he was falling into darkness.

*   *   *   *   *

"Hold on, kid," Eli said. The silver-bearded engineer looked over at Tin and narrowed his eyes beneath the bill of his baseball cap.

Tin stood with his back to the wall in the small shelter, gripping the belts that secured his body to the wall. They were alone in here. X had already jumped, and Tin felt like a bean being shaken in a can. But that was not the reason his heart was thumping out of control.

"Wha ... what's that popping sound?" Tin stammered, although he thought knew the answer. He had never heard gunshots before, but the sharp *Pop! Pop!* reminded him of a video that Professor Lana had shown their class a few months ago.

Eli looked just as unsure. They both stared at the small window over the hatch. Red light filled the hallway outside, but Tin didn't see anything in the glow.

He tightened his grip on the belts crossing his chest, when the popping sounded again. This time it was closer, and he could hear it clearly over the emergency alarms and groaning metal bulkheads around him.

"Stay put, kid," Eli said. "I need to check this out." He unbuckled his harness and went to check the window. "What in the hell … ?"

Tin wanted to tell him not to leave, but Eli opened the hatch and stepped into the hallway.

"Hey! What are you doing!" Eli shouted at someone Tin couldn't see.

The ship rumbled, knocking Eli to his knees. Before he could move, something exploded out of his back and punched the bulkhead behind Tin.

Screaming, Tin unbuckled the belts and dropped onto all fours. He crawled across the floor, keeping as low as possible. He could feel his fingers sliding through warm liquid. He glanced up, straining to see in the dim red light.

At the end of the hallway, a single emergency light churned. The rotating light crossed the paths of four approaching men.

"Mister … mister, are you okay?" Tin whispered, nudging the limp body. The man's throat made an awful gurgling sound. A few feet away, a Militia soldier lay in a widening pool of blood.

Tin's eyes flitted back to the four men as they stepped into the red glow. The leader wore a trench coat and had hair that hung like thick vines over his shoulders. Tin recognized him instantly. It was the same guy he had seen lurking outside the farm before the tour, and the same man who had bashed into him at the trading post. When he saw Tin, he pointed and yelled, "Don't let that kid get away!"

The ship hit a pocket of turbulence and tilted to starboard, sending the four men sliding across the floor. Tin scrambled over the dead guard and bolted into the open stairwell that led to the farm. Grunting, he struggled to close the heavy steel hatch behind him. Pushing with all his strength, he slammed it shut just as a volley of bullets pelted the other side.

*   *   *   *   *

X's mind spun as he fell. One second, his thoughts had been focused and clear; the next, they were agonizingly slow and confused, unable to process what had happened. Someone had done the unthinkable: fired a gun aboard the *Hive*. Whether it was sabotage or a horrible accident, it didn't matter. All that mattered now was the mission. He had to trust that Captain Ash would keep Tin safe and deal with the situation. Letting himself get distracted now would doom everyone on the ship, including Tin.

Focus, X.

He got one last glimpse of the *Hive* and half expected to see it come blazing through the clouds. But the smooth beetlelike hull looked still intact. The ship appeared suspended in motion in the dead center of the storm as lightning danced around the ship. An eyeblink later, his home was gone, swallowed by the clouds.

After relaxing into stable position, he pulled his left hand in as if saluting, while his right fished a flare from his vest. Then, bringing both hands in front of him to maintain equilibrium, he twisted off the plastic striker cap, taking great care not to lose it in the blasting wind. He struck the flare's tip against the striker surface once ... twice ... The moment he saw bright red flame spurt from the struck end, he tossed the flare away into the black. He did this twice more, then looked at his HUD.

The data flickered in and out, and X realized that it was going to be mostly useless the entire dive. They had to be at around eighteen thousand feet. He put his velocity at a hundred miles per hour, give or take. Intermittent strikes of electricity curved across his flight path. The storm wasn't as bad as it looked from above, but it would only get worse.

The divers from all three teams were working into a wedge formation. He counted the glowing battery units cutting through the clouds, and the flares that left streaking, tumbling red tracers behind them. He had never seen anything like it on a dive, but the flares would give the others something visual to key on in a sea of darkness.

His HUD suddenly winked back on. Before the data vanished again, he caught the altitude reading: five thousand feet down, fifteen thousand to go.

A thunderclap reminded him of the gunfire he had heard. Was Tin okay? Was the *Hive* in trouble? He blinked away the thought and focused on the clouds. A web of lightning arced across his field of view. The dark floor gave way to a roiling purple maelstrom, and their entire flight path lit up as if floodlights had turned on. They were about to pass into the heart of the storm.

Teams Angel and Apollo broke from their positions, and X watched as their blue battery units fanned out, flickering like stars across the darkness. He scanned for Magnolia and Murph. They were spreading out, too, but he couldn't spot Magnolia's battery.

At thirteen thousand feet, the sky transformed into a colossal static generator. Arcs slashed through the clouds all around the teams. How could anyone survive that?

X brought his arms back to pull himself into a nosedive. Tucking his chin against his chest, he pulled his arms all the way into his sides, palms forward at his thighs. The other divers would be doing the same thing: streamlining themselves so they would fall as fast as possible.

Thunder cracked as X tried to calculate his speed and altitude. His body shook from the wind shears pulling at him. Somewhere in the distance, he thought he heard a scream, but that was impossible, of course, when in free fall.

He punched through the clouds like a bullet, his armor whistling in the wind. His eyes roved back to his HUD. Ice crystals were already forming around the edges of his visor, narrowing his view by half. The internal display was a mess of numbers flickering out of control.

The minimap flashed, revealing that two of the beacons had already disappeared. He blinked and checked again, but the map had already cut out. Only a few moments had passed since they entered the storm. That couldn't be right.

His eyes confirmed what he already knew. Two

divers, both from Team Angel, were gone—the first casualties of the colossal storm.

He waited several tense seconds before the map flickered back to life. Tony's and Katrina's beacons were still there.

X breathed out just as three separate strikes flashed across his path. He torpedoed through the light-blue visual residue with his eyes wide open, fully expecting to feel his insides cooking. But seconds later, he felt nothing but the force and push of the wind.

He did a slow 360-degree turn to check on the other divers. The glow of their battery units glimmered on the eastern horizon. Then, without warning, one tumbled away, whisked off by a freak crosswind—directly into a lightning strike. The arc shot through one of the flares trailing the diver, exploding it in a dazzling splash of red.

"No … !" X howled. He had shifted his gaze back to the clouds below when a flash of blue cut through a second diver in his peripheral vision. His eyes flitted to his HUD. Cruise's beacon went offline a beat later.

"*Fu-u-u-uck you, Hades!*" X shouted into the void.

Ten thousand feet, and a third of them were already gone, including the lead for Apollo—the most experienced diver besides Katrina and X.

The hair on his neck prickled, and he braced for a shock. The ice crystals continued to spread across his visor. Jerked to his left by a crosswind, he watched a strike angle through the trajectory he had been on only moments before. Saved by the selfsame phenomenon that had killed Cruise's teammate.

The howling wind and periodic thunderclaps drowned all other sounds. Sweat dripped into his eyes, and the sting suddenly enraged him.

"God damn it!" he roared into the mute comm.

Another beacon vanished from his flickering HUD. Then, not three seconds later, another.

Apollo was gone—the entire team killed while still in free fall.

X bit down on his mouth guard and glanced skyward. The red streaks from the flares of the dead continued to fall. Six thousand feet to go and only six divers left. He scanned the data on his display. His velocity now, falling head down, was around 180 miles per hour.

He risked another sidelong glance. Lightning, inexorable and immense, rippled across the sky in all directions. There was no pattern to the strikes, no way to predict where—or who—the next flash would hit. Avoiding the earlier strike had been sheer luck. It occurred to him that one reason no one had ever returned from Hades could be that very few divers had even made it to the surface alive.

His hair stood up again as he watched a bolt bend through his trajectory. He closed his eyes, then snapped them back open, heart pounding. Was he hit?

A wave of gray and white exploded into view.

He wasn't dead, but he was about to enter hell all the same.

Gutted skyscrapers lined the horizon as far as he could see, their frosted tips leaning this way and that. Hades was buried in snow and ice.

X fought his way into stable position, punched his minicomputer, activated his night vision, and whipped out his pilot chute.

The opening shock yanked him upward. He tilted his helmet toward the sky to see a single diver burst through the clouds.

Surely, that couldn't be it ... could it? Just one survivor?

A beat later, three more divers emerged from the storm.

"Pull!" X shouted over the comm. He scanned his HUD. The storm had thrown them over a mile off course. Descending under canopy now, he searched the frozen landscape. Right below him, a sinkhole the size of the *Hive* had swallowed most of a city block. Rubble surrounded the lip of the crater, and skeletal strips of metal bristled over the side. The north side looked clear—all the buildings there had toppled into the hole. Brick and concrete foundations still remained, making for a risky drop zone, but it was the only potential DZ in sight.

"On me," X said into the comm.

The other divers acknowledged with shaky replies, the fear in their monosyllabic responses evident even on the staticky comm channel.

X glided past a windowless building. Snow had filled the rooms, burying the frozen artifacts from the Old World. Pulling his left toggle, he steered his canopy to the left and passed over the sinkhole.

The ground rose closer and closer. He shifted once more to avoid a foundation, flared, and stepped out of the sky. A halo of powder poofed up into the air. He popped one capewell to deflate his chute, shucked his harness, and checked his HUD for the nav marker. They were a mile south of the first supply crate. The second crate was somewhere in the industrial zone.

A blur shot past his peripheral vision. It was Magnolia. She flared too early, swung forward and then rocked back, and rolled in the snow.

Tony landed across the snowy field. Next came Katrina and Murph.

X hurried over to Magnolia, who was getting dragged by the breeze. He pawed his way through her flapping chute and popped a capewell, and the billowing mass deflated. "You okay, kid?"

A moan sounded in his helmet's speakers. She lay on her back, her visor angled at the sky. A reflected lightning bolt streaked across the mirrored surface.

"Did we make it?" she choked.

X reached down to help her up. "Yeah. We made it."

"Where are the others?"

X shook his head. He looked at Tony, Katrina, and Murph. "We're it."

"Cruise?" Magnolia asked, her voice wobbly.

He shook his head.

Magnolia dropped to a half crouch, her breathing labored, raspy. "He's … gone?" She clutched her stomach.

Katrina rushed over and put a hand on her shoulder. "Don't puke in your helmet.

Magnolia nodded and waved Katrina away. "It's okay. It's back down."

"We'd better move, X," Tony said.

He noted the mission clock. Three minutes into the mission, and over half of them were dead.

"Get it together, kid," X said. "We got to start moving, okay? We have twenty-four hours to save the *Hive*."

She managed a weak nod. X stared up into the swirling clouds, hoping another live diver would emerge from the darkness, but knowing it wouldn't happen. The other divers were dead, and if anyone came falling from the sky, there would be no graceful landing under a chute. They would frap in the snow, breaking every bone in their lifeless bodies and turning the rest to mush.

X pulled his binos and swept them across the landscape, stopping on the towers to the northwest. The tops of three buildings had been stripped away. Odd, since the rest were still standing. He moved the scope to a flattened area to the west and saw the stern of an airship jutting up from the snow. There wasn't much left: just aluminum struts and debris strewn across half a square mile of the dead city.

He didn't need to zoom in to see that it was *Ares*.

EIGHTEEN

Captain Ash swung the wheel right, steering them toward the western edge of the storm, where the lightning flashes were less intense. All she had to do was keep them away from a fatal strike for a few more minutes.

"We've lost the divers' signals," Jordan yelled.

"We have a rupture in gas bladder twenty-one," Ryan said.

Jordan rushed to the ops station. "Divert helium from bladder twenty-one."

Ash heard each voice, but she was busy trying to steer the ship out of the raging sea of static electricity.

A jolt hit the stern, setting off a chorus of sensors and alarms. She blinked away a drop of sweat and continued staring at the main display. The *Hive*'s bow pushed ahead toward the wall of glowing blue.

"That's the edge of the storm," Hunt shouted from navigation. "We're almost out."

Ash kept the wheel steady as they glided through the final stretch of lightning. She couldn't see the invisible barrier between the storm and clear skies, but she felt it the moment the bow split through to the other side. Every wall and beam seemed to groan and creak, as if in relief.

Warning sensors continued to chirp, but she ignored them all. They were safely out of the storm now, but they had other problems. Someone had fired a gun at the very moment the Hell Diver teams had dropped from their tubes. Her throat ached, and she reached up to massage it. Her mind was trying to grasp everything that had happened during the past fifteen minutes.

Before she could make much sense of it, she heard Jordan's voice in her ear. "Captain, we have a strike team on standby and ready to go."

"Do we know how many assailants there are, or *who* they are?"

"Negative, but Eli and Cecil are dead, and Tin is missing."

Ash rubbed at her throat. "No," she choked. "I promised X ..."

"We'll find him, Captain."

"We'd better," Ash said. Her eyes flitted from station to station, checking each worried face. "Do we have a damage report from the storm?"

"Samson's working on it."

"What about the HDs? Do we know how many made it to the surface?"

Jordan shook his head. "I'm sorry, but we lost contact with them shortly after they dropped."

Ash wiped the sweat from her brow. "Lieutenant, is there *anything* you can tell me?"

"That's all I know ... Hold on. I'm getting a transmission." He cupped a hand over his earpiece and listened for several moments.

When he looked up, his anxious gaze told Ash she was going to have to make another decision.

"The strike team is asking for orders. Should I give them the green light?"

"No!" Ash yelled. Several officers looked in her direction. "We can't risk it, especially if Tin is in there."

A few seconds of silence passed before Ash spoke. "How the hell did they get hold of an automatic rifle?"

"Some of the weapons were never recovered after the riots two years ago," Jordan said. "They must have had one stashed away."

"Tell the strike team to stand down for now. I want to know who these people are and what they want. Don't they know we don't have time for this shit?"

"They certainly knew when to strike," Jordan said.

Ash had to temper her fury with the knowledge that her own leniency with the lower-deckers was partly to blame. "Whoever it is, they don't give a shit about the *Hive*'s current predicament. Do they realize they could kill us all? Do they even *care*? We need some answers."

A chirp pulled her gaze to the main display at the front of the room. Samson's strained face emerged on the screen.

"Captain," he said, "I just finished running a diagnostic report. I have bad news and good news."

"Good news first."

The engineer nodded, his pink cheeks jiggling. "The reactor is still online. We didn't suffer any damage there."

"That *is* good n—" Ash began.

Samson raised his hand. "But we did lose another internal gas bladder during the attack. That was the last straw. We're losing altitude—slowly, but the ship is dropping. My crews still haven't been able to fix the other six bladders we lost two days ago."

"Can they fix this one?" Ash asked.

"Yes, if they could get there. But the access hatch down here was destroyed when the storm ate us two days ago, and the only other entry is through a passage on the farm."

"How the hell did this even happen?"

"I'd guess a stray bullet's to blame—not a lot of safe places on an airship to go shooting off a rifle. If that's the case, we can patch it. The other gas bladders were ruptured by the storm. Those'll take more time."

Ash turned back to Jordan. "If we send in the strike team, we risk more damage to the ship, not to mention more casualties if those men decide to fire again. They've already proved they don't mind killing people."

"But if we don't, we won't be able to fix the bladder," Jordan argued.

"He's right, Captain," Samson said. "The *Hive* is struggling to stay in the air. I've routed all the power I can to the turbofans, but we're sinking. We need that bladder!"

"Can you keep us in the air for twenty-four hours? Long enough for the HDs to get back here?"

"You aren't giving me any other option, are you?"

Ash took one hand off the wheel. "Jordan, take the helm. Samson, prepare an engineering team."

Samson frowned. "What are you going to do?"

"I'm going to negotiate."

*   *   *   *   *

Powerful gusts of wind showered the five-person team with ice and grit as they trekked through the derelict city. The intermittent lightning flashes allowed the divers to go without their night-vision optics. X stared out over the ash-colored landscape of Hades. Mother Nature was gradually finishing what the bombs hadn't quite been able to do. Most of the buildings were gone, buried by God only knew how many feet of snow.

The remains of *Ares* rested in a shallow grave in the center of the city. X kept looking in amazement at the three topless buildings. The ship must have sheared them off as it came crashing down. That would have dealt the final blows. He wondered what had gone through Captain Willis' mind in those final moments.

"That was *Ares*?" Magnolia asked, as if reading his thoughts.

X checked his mission clock. The blue numbers were steadily ticking down. "Yep," he said. "And if we don't hurry, the *Hive* is going to look just like that."

Magnolia picked up her pace, her boots crunching in the snow behind him. "Think anyone else made it?"

"Everyone else is dead. If they had survived, we would see their beacons. Keep moving."

They didn't have the luxury of time to mourn their dead. He waved the team forward, breaking into a trot toward a stretch of snow that sloped into a valley. That was where most of the buildings were—and, according to the nav flag on his HUD, also the location of the first crate.

At the edge of the downslope, he signaled to stop. Tony joined him, crouching by his side. Both pulled out their binos to scan the city.

"Looks like that bridge leads into the city and the industrial zone," X said. "The crates should be on the other side."

"They never can get them close, can they?" said Katrina, behind them.

"Looks like there's a way down over here," Tony said. He trained his binos on a stretch of highway that curved down into the valley. The wind had cleared the ancient roads, exposing a strange-looking vehicle. X had never seen the like. He zoomed in on the turret that topped the boxy machine. Mounted on it was what appeared to be a cannon of some sort.

Moving his scope to the left, he saw a half-dozen of the strange machines of war.

"Let's go," X said. He led the team along the edge of the bluff and down a slick, icy hillside to the highway. With his blaster leveled over the street, he ran toward the armored trucks, or whatever they were.

He slowed as he drew near the massive machines. Icy pieces of the armored shell were scattered around the vehicles. The one good thing about this place, he reflected, was that the freezing temperatures had preserved much of the Old World. He couldn't even begin to imagine what lay beneath the mounds of snow burying the rest of the city.

A quick scan of the road showed no immediate threats. X lowered his blaster and brushed the snow off the back of the closest vehicle.

The comm flared to life. "We should keep moving," Tony said.

"Hold up," X replied. "I just need a second." Squinting, he read the lettering aloud. "M-three Abrams … built in 2029, in Lima, Ohio."

He brushed away more snow.

"United States Army."

X took a step back, remembering the bulkhead on the *Hive*'s bridge. The same name was engraved in a plaque above the entrance to the room. Like the M3, the *Hive* had been commissioned for war. He had known it before, but seeing the armored vehicles, and the monster crater a few days before, reminded him that *people* had done this. Humans had destroyed this world.

"You good, X?" A hand shook his shoulder gently. It was Katrina, and he could tell by her soft voice she was ready to get moving.

X nodded, then froze. A new dot was blinking on his HUD—something that should be impossible in this lifeless place.

"We got a contact," Tony said.

"I see it," X replied. The dot was some sort of beacon, but the signal didn't match anything from the *Hive*. Whatever it was, it was moving.

"What do you make of this, Murph?" X asked.

The engineer trotted up to his location. "It's not one of ours."

"I know that," X said. "So what do you think it is?"

Tony stepped forward. "I could give you a theory."

"I'm listening."

"One of the Sirens took the beacon off a dead *Ares* diver. Hell, maybe it *swallowed* it."

"Or maybe somebody from *Ares* survived the dive," Magnolia said.

X furrowed his brow. "No way in hell they could last out here this long, though, right? And no way anyone survived that crash."

"Right," Katrina said. "Couldn't be a survivor."

"Has to be something else," X said. "Let's find a path around." He flashed an advance signal, but Katrina grabbed his shoulder a second time.

"Wait," she said. "If it's a Siren, then why does it look like it's on a direct route to one of our supply crates?"

X checked the map. She was right. The beacon was moving toward their supplies.

"I don't know," X replied. "But we're going to find out."

*   *   *   *   *

The animal pen stank of manure, but Tin didn't dare move. He kept his eye up against the fence, peering through an inch-wide gap at the armed men in the distance, trying meanwhile not to breathe in the awful smell.

The chickens were crowding the enclosure around him, pecking at morsels in the dirt and generally doing whatever chickens did. Gently, to avoid causing a ruckus among the hens, Tin scooted away from them and caught a glimpse of Silver, in the next pen. Watching the men outside the plastic clean room, the dog let out a low growl. Lilly went over to him, her ears perked. Heartened that the dogs were keeping watch, too, Tim squirmed back to the fence for a better look.

The two men walked away from the plastic vestibule—the same room Tin had visited two days ago. The man with the black dreadlocks turned to another guy, who wore a scarf over his face.

"I told you not to shoot anyone, Alex!"

"Sorry, Trav, but the guard aimed his gun at—"

The one named Travis snatched the rifle from Alex and backhanded him. The blow knocked away Alex's scarf, exposing tight, scarred flesh on his right cheek. A fresh bandage covered his chin. He didn't bother pulling the scarf back up.

The two men glared at each other, and the intense silent moment lingered between them until the door to the clean room unzipped. A big, thickset man shuffled out. Tin had seen him before, too. He recognized the bald head and full red beard from the trading post.

"The Militia's surrounded the first-deck entrance," he said. "We're trapped in here."

"How many, Brad?" Travis asked.

Brad ran a nervous hand over his shiny pate. "A dozen at least, all armed to the teeth."

"This changes nothing," Travis said. "Our demands are still the same." He cupped his hands around his mouth and said, "Ren, get those farmers over here." His deep voice carried the length of the huge enclosed field.

Tin wiggled flat against the dirt for a better view through the mesh wire fence, keeping his head low to the ground, careful not to be seen. The fourth man, Ren, had a group of six farmers herded together. He wielded a long, rusted blade that looked like a butcher's knife. Ren pushed the hostages along a path between a plot of green beans and another of tall corn.

"You need to think about what you're doing," one of the farmers was saying. "The Militia will kill all of you, and for what?"

Ren pushed the man to the dirt and kicked him in the ribs.

"Leave him alone!" a woman cried. She dropped to the injured farmer's side.

"That's enough, Ren," Travis said.

Together, Alex and Ren corralled the group and ordered them to sit in the dirt in front of the clean room, where Brad cuffed their hands behind them with plastic ties.

"Anyone see where that kid went?" Travis asked, scanning the room.

Tin scooted lower, pressing his face into the dirt and chicken droppings. Realizing he had lost his hat, he felt a wave of anxiety. Without the hat, he felt exposed, naked.

"See if you can find him," Travis said.

Tin listened to boots squelching over the moist ground, coming closer. He closed his eyes and imagined he was back in his old apartment with his dad and X. The squishy footsteps continued toward him, then were suddenly drowned out by the crackle of static over the PA system.

"To whoever has taken over the farm, this is Captain Maria Ash. I would like to speak to the man who decided to fire a gun inside my ship."

Tin peeked through the fence as Travis hurried over to a control panel on the port side of the plastic room and punched the comm button. "This is Travis Eddie. Son of dead Hell Diver Ron Eddie and brother of prisoner Raphael Eddie."

White noise hissed through the speakers. The captain didn't immediately respond.

Tin wiggled away from a chicken that pecked at his sleeve.

"Travis," Captain Ash said. She hesitated for a brief second before continuing. "I'm truly sorry for your suffering. You have experienced much hardship, like most of us on the *Hive*—"

Travis punched the comm link again. "You don't know anything about hardship, *Captain*. Or what it's like to live on the lower decks. The cancer. The starvation. The disease. When's the last time you were down there?"

There was another pause. "I was supposed to visit very recently," Ash replied. "But obviously, something came up. For what it's worth, I can relate to your suffering. I have cancer myself."

Tin watched Travis glance over at his men.

"Travis, if you truly care about the well-being of everyone on this ship, then you will let one of my engineers into the farm. That gun you fired tore a hole in gas bladder twenty-one. We're losing altitude. If we don't fix it, then *everyone* is going to die."

"She's bluffing," Alex said. "I bet she's lying about having cancer, too."

"Yeah," Ren added. "And that 'engineer' she wants to send is more likely a soldier in coveralls."

Turning back to the panel, Travis said, "Why can't you fix the bladder through engineering? I know there's access hatches down there."

"Because the access tunnel was destroyed in the electrical storm two weeks ago," Ash replied.

Tin couldn't believe his ears. If what the captain said was true, the only way to reach the bladder was through the farm. He rolled to his side and looked around for the hatches. A metal ladder led up to a catwalk that ran along the starboard side of the ship, where several elliptical hatches lined the wall.

Without considering the repercussions, Tin stood up and shouted, "You have to let them in!"

Ten faces turned in his direction. Travis quickly nodded at Alex, who ran toward Tin.

"Come on, kid," he said. "Get over here with the others."

Tin backed away. "No, the captain isn't lying! Those are access points." He pointed to the hatches along the catwalk on the starboard side.

Alex didn't bother to look.

"Please, Travis, just let one of my engineers in," Ash pleaded over the comms. "We'll figure this all out after he's done fixing the bladder."

Travis punched the button. "That's not going to happen until you meet our demands. First, you're going to turn the lights and the heat back on in the so-called noncritical facilities. Then you'll double food rations for everyone belowdecks. I want equal health care provided to everyone on this ship. And finally, I want my brother released from jail."

"You and I both know that I can't meet all those demands," said Ash. "We're in no position to turn any lights or heat back on right now. We need that power for the turbofans and generators. For God's sake, Travis, think about what you're doing!"

"I'm not sure you understand, Captain, but this isn't up for negotiation. You either meet our demands or you don't get anything. No access to the farm, no hostages released, nothing. When you change your mind, I'll be right here." He shut off the system and faced his men.

"Ship's always in trouble, Trav," Brad said. "This is just another one of Captain Ash's lies. I wouldn't trust her for a second."

Travis' eyes flitted to Tin. There was a fleeting moment where Tin thought that maybe the man was going to listen to him. But then Travis raised the muzzle of the gun from the ground and pointed it at the farmers.

"I don't believe her, either, and I'm not letting an engineer inside," Travis said. "Now, get that kid over here."

"No!" Tin shouted. "You have to listen to the captain. She's not lying."

Grinning, Alex jumped over the fence, grabbed Tin, and yanked him across the dirt.

Struggling to free himself from Alex's grip, Tin pulled away and kicked him in the shin as hard as he could.

"You shouldn't have done that," Alex snarled. Before Tin could move, a fist caught him in the side of the head, knocking him to the dirt. Silver and Lilly growled and threw themselves at the gate.

Tears welled in Tin's eyes. He blinked and tried to get up but fell back to his stomach. Silver snarled as Alex bent down.

Tin tried to scoot away, but his body felt weak and disconnected from his mind. He could hardly move his arms—hardly move anything at all. He blinked several times, but a dark red shadow encroached around the edges of his vision. The last thing Tin saw was Lilly and Silver, barking and snarling at Alex and jumping at the fence.

NINETEEN

A dark sky churned above Hades, and lightning slanted down through one of the skeletal high-rises ahead. Battling fierce winds, the divers had crossed the highway to the edge of the city. X stood on the roof of a half-buried vehicle, with his blaster leveled at the closest building.

He shielded his visor from the relentless blasts of windblown grit. He was anxious to be out of the open, but the city streets could harbor worse threats than the wind. The road led through the heart of the ancient metropolis, to the industrial zone where the *Ares* team had encountered Sirens.

X jumped down off the vehicle and checked his HUD. The rogue beacon was now on top of their supplies. Whatever it was, it had found their gear, and until he had heavy weapons, he didn't want to risk a confrontation with a potential hostile.

The second supply crate was in the industrial zone, over three miles away. Two hours had elapsed. They should have been at the crates and on their way to their main objective, but a quarter mile of knee-deep snow had cost them time and energy.

"These radiation readings are getting higher," Murph said. "We're slowly cooking standing here."

"We aren't going to be down here long enough for it to make a difference," Katrina said, pushing her way through the powder to where X stood. "Whatcha thinkin'?"

"Something doesn't smell right," X said. He was fixated on his HUD. The beacon had stopped at their crate for several minutes now. "The way I see it, we have two options. We could abandon the first crate and risk crossing the rest of the city and the industrial zone without automatic weapons, or we could check this one out."

Tony said, "We still have twenty-two hours. I say we find a way around the first crate. If one of those things is there, I don't want to face it with a blaster and this dinky pistol."

"Yeah, well, I'm not sure I want to cross the industrial zone with these dinky pistols and blasters, either," said X. "If we run into Sirens, we're fucked."

"We gotta think about the weather, too," Murph added. "If it gets worse, we don't want to get stranded without supplies."

"He's right," X said. "We need the gear from the first crate."

"Okay," Tony said.

X waited for a "but" to follow. When it didn't, he said to Katrina, "You good with that?"

She nodded.

"Me, too," Magnolia said. "Not that anybody's asking."

X turned back to the street. "Stay close, and

keep sharp. The first crate is four blocks from here. We move fast but cautiously. Got it?"

Getting four nods, he broke into a jog across the snow, and the others followed. A light powder began to fall as they ran.

At the next intersection, he signaled for all to stop. The divers crouched and stared at a green apparition flapping in the wind on the right side of the road. Finally realizing that it was a parachute, X lowered his blaster. The chute was green, but divers from the *Hive* always flew black chutes.

"Diver at six o'clock," X whispered. "Doesn't look like one of ours. I'll check it out."

Hugging the banked snow against the buildings, he warily approached the canopy. Beyond the chute, he saw armor half covered by snow. He pulled the canopy away and bent next to the body. The head was buried in snow, and he dug for several seconds to uncover a female face he didn't recognize, staring back at him with frozen, dead eyes.

He waved his team over without shifting his gaze away from the woman. She must have been part of the *Ares* team. Brushing the snow off her chest plate to search for a weapon, he saw the empty battery housing. Indeed, she had been stripped of much of her gear.

"What the fuck?" X said.

His team hovered over him and stared at the corpse.

"Where's her gear?" Tony asked.

"I don't know. Makes no sense."

He wiped the toxic flakes that had collected

on his visor. The beacon on his HUD was finally moving away from their crate. He didn't have time to ponder what it all meant. Now was their chance to get to the crate and arm themselves before they ran into the Sirens.

"Time to move," X said. He motioned his team on, and they left the dead diver where they had found her, just as he had left Aaron and so many others before her.

*　　*　　*　　*　　*

Travis leaned down and put a hand on the kid's shoulder. He was still unconscious. Alex had hit him hard—way too hard.

He glared at Alex, wanting to slap the crooked grin off that scarred face. Killing a Militia guard for their cause was one thing, but shooting an unarmed engineer and hitting a kid?

"What the hell is the matter with you?" Travis snapped.

Alex took a step back. "Little fucker deserved it for kicking me, Trav. He's one of them spoiled upper-decker brats."

"Doesn't give you the right …" Travis took a breath. Arguing with Alex wasn't going to get Raphael out of jail or get them any closer to justice for those belowdecks. He had to keep a tighter rein on the others—especially Alex.

He checked the boy once more. He looked to be not much older than ten—about the same age Travis had been when his father lost his life on a routine dive. He respected the boy for standing up to Alex. It reminded him of himself at that age.

"Don't touch him again," Travis said. He rose to his feet and looked at the overhead and the curved bulkheads.

The ship wasn't shaking anymore, but something was still wrong. Every few minutes, the *Hive* would shiver as if it was fighting for altitude. Maybe Captain Ash wasn't lying after all. Maybe the ship was in trouble.

No, Brad was right: the ship was always in trouble. Nothing had changed, and he wasn't about to back down now. His brother was still rotting in jail, and the lower-deckers were still suffering.

Travis slung the rifle over his back. Alex, too, was right about something: the kid was an upper-decker, and that made him valuable.

"When the kid comes around, let me know. I have an idea."

*   *   *   *   *

Captain Ash hammered the wall with her fist, drawing several stares. She was beyond frustrated. The Militia should have seen this coming. They should have had someone keeping an eye on Travis since his brother landed in prison after the riots years ago. Somehow, amid the chaos of life aboard the ship, Travis had fallen through the cracks. She blamed herself, too. She had been too lenient with the lower-deckers when she put an end to the random Militia searches for contraband and weapons. She had required the Militia to have probable cause before searching the trading post and belowdecks. Her decision was an effort at appeasement, but in the end, it had helped doom them all.

But pointing fingers or dwelling on her mistakes wouldn't fix the ship. She had to move on. She had to continue to lead.

Jordan's voice pulled her from her thoughts.

"Captain, we have no other choice. We can't meet their demands, and Travis doesn't sound like he's going to budge. We have to raid the farm."

Ash looked at her second. His features were stern and strict. He was the most loyal officer she'd ever had under her command, but his overeagerness to raid the farms proved he still had a lot to learn about leading.

"There has to be another way," Ash said.

She walked over to the top of the ramp. The main display on the bottom floor showed the Hell Divers' mission clock. Below that, another number was counting down: the *Hive*'s altitude.

"Nineteen thousand feet," Ash said.

"And dropping," Jordan replied. "Which is why we need to get control of the farm. We need one of Samson's men in there."

Ash continued down the ramp to her chair.

As she passed navigation, Ensign Ryan stood. "Captain, I'm getting odd readings from the electrical storm over Hades."

Ash paused on the stairs. "What kind of readings?"

"Something seems to be happening inside the storm."

"Is it growing?"

"Slightly, but our sensors are picking up activity on the surface. Looks like a surface storm of some sort is moving across Hades."

"What's our distance?" Ash asked.

"We're two miles away."

"I doubt we can go above it this time," Jordan added. "And there's no way we can outrun it if it grows bigger."

"We can't abandon the divers, either," Ash said. "They're our only chance of staying in the air."

"I know, but I would suggest putting some distance between us and that wall of cumulus," Jordan said, staring at the screen.

"Agreed," Ash said. "Tell Samson to direct some power to the rudders. Take us off autopilot. You've got the wheel. Remember, if the divers send up those crates, we have to be in range to pick them up."

She watched lightning break across the skyline on the front display. X was down there, doing his part to save the ship. He had never asked for anything back until this last jump, and she had already broken her promise to him. Tin was now a hostage, or worse.

"On second thought, I'll take the wheel," Ash said. "Jordan, radio the strike team. Tell them I want a plan that doesn't involve shooting up the ship and getting everyone on the farm killed."

*   *   *   *   *

Icicles like spears hung from the metal awning of a building at the end of the street. The lower floors were buried in snow, and X couldn't see a way into the frozen structure.

They were four hours into the mission, and he wasn't going to risk another step until he had a look at that crate. It had landed in the street beyond this building. If they could get inside, he could scope the area before committing them to the open ground surrounding the crate. The rogue beacon had vanished off the minimap, but he wasn't going to take any chances.

"Looks like there's a way in over here," Magnolia said. "Come on."

X trailed the divers through the gusting wind to a snowbank that rose to a third-floor window. He had missed it on his first pass.

"I'll go first," Magnolia offered.

"No, kid, you won't," X replied, pushing past her as he unsheathed his tactical knife. "I'll check it out. You guys hold here."

Magnolia protested, but X scrambled up the wall without her. Sure, she was fast, and she was good at sneaking into places, but Hades wasn't some guarded pantry on the *Hive*. She wasn't ready for what likely awaited them at the ITC building. X wasn't sure *he* was ready.

He lost his footing before he reached the window, and only a quick two-handed thrust of the knife into the hardened snow saved him from sliding back down to the street. Punching knees and toes and elbows into the snow, he carefully worked his way up, jammed the blade in with each incremental gain. At the top, he grabbed the twisted window frame and peered inside. The hallway was a foot deep in wind-blown snow, but he could see all the way through to the other side. He stood there for a moment, listening to the building's whispers and creaks.

"See anything?" Katrina asked over the channel.

"Negative. I'm going in." X pulled himself through the window frame and crouched on the other side. The only sound was the hiss of the wind and the soft breathing of his team over the comm.

With his blaster out, he moved cautiously down the hallway. Pausing at every doorway, he peered into each room. In the final room, the top of a boxy machine rose above a deep drift of snow. The faded round red, white, and blue logo bore the letters "PEPSI"—an acronym for some ancient make of 'shine, judging by the image of a bottle below the logo.

X pushed on, working his way down the passage. The rusted legs of several office chairs formed a barrier a few feet from the window at the far end of the hall. Careful not to disturb anything, he navigated his way around them.

Reaching the window, he set the blaster down on the snow-covered floor and pulled out his binos. The street below was still except for the white flurry carried by a gust of wind. Drifting snow was already covering the crate, but whoever or whatever had been there earlier was gone now.

"All clear," X said. "Get up here. I've got eyes on the supplies."

Magnolia was first through the window at the opposite end of the hallway. He could hear her crunching over the snow at a brisk pace.

"Slow down," he whispered over the comm.

She kept coming fast until she reached the end of the hallway, where she tripped over the first chair leg, snapping it free and crashing into the wall.

The loud clatter reverberated through the building.

X muttered an oath and scrambled over to her. "God damn it, Magnolia, tell the Sirens where we are, why don't you!"

She stood up and brushed off her armor. "I'm fine. And ... I'm sorry. I wasn't paying—"

A distant high wail cut her off. A second call answered, echoing through the frozen ghost city. X plucked the blaster off the floor and hissed, "Quiet, everyone!"

Tony, Murph, and Katrina stopped at the other end of the hallway.

"What is that?" Katrina whispered.

"Trouble," X said. "You have better eyes than mine. Check it out."

She continued down the hall, stepped around the upended chair, and took his binos. She raked them back and forth over the street. "I don't see anythi ... Wait, did you see that the crate's open?"

X nudged closer to the window and took the binos back. Sure enough, the crate's lid was popped open. Whatever had beaten them to the supply box had also found a way inside.

"Kid, you still want a chance to show how fast you are?" X asked.

Magnolia started to nod, then froze as another wail came on the wind.

"Don't worry," he said. "I'll be right behind

you." He examined his blaster, hoping it wasn't too frozen and praying he wouldn't have to use it.

*   *   *   *   *

Tin awoke to the worst headache of his life, and the overwhelming stench of chicken manure. He tried to open his eyes but couldn't manage to crack them more than a sliver. He tried to move his hands, but they were bound behind his back.

He could hear human voices—faint but close. There were animal noises, too. Barking dogs and … Then he remembered the ruptured gas bladder.

His heavy eyelids popped open to the sight of dirt. Using his head to push against the ground, he got his knees under him. He gagged and spat out a mouthful of dirt and manure.

"Kid's awake!" shouted the man who had hit him. He sauntered over.

Tin wiped his mouth against his chest and looked around. The hostage farmers were sitting to his right. They were all just outside the entrance to the plastic clean room.

Alex stopped in front of him. "You left a nice bruise on my ankle, kid. Looks like I left you with a bigger one, though." He chuckled and made a fist. "Want a matching set?"

"Hitting a kid," one of the farmers said. "That's makes you a real sack of shit in my book."

Alex walked over to the farmer and kicked him in the gut. The man rolled on his side. Between gasps, he yelled, "You son of a bitch!"

"You don't know when to shut your mouth," Alex said.

"Enough!" Travis shouted. He and the other two men emerged from the plastic door of the clean room. Alex kicked the farmer a second time, then walked away.

"I'm sorry," Tin whispered.

The man groaned. "It's okay, kid. Better me than you."

Tin struggled with the bindings, working his wrists back and forth until he felt them tighten into his flesh.

"What's your name?" the farmer asked.

"Tin."

"I'm Angelo. Do me a favor, okay?"

Tin nodded.

"Don't do anything stupid."

The squeak of the plastic door pulled Tin's attention back to the four men. They were talking in hushed voices by the entrance, but he could hear most of the conversation.

"Trav already told you we aren't killing hostages," said Ren.

"Ash isn't going to take us seriously until we put a bullet in someone," Alex said.

Travis spat in the dirt near Alex's boots as another warning. "You already did that."

"I'm talking about hostages," Alex replied, his tone more reserved.

Travis shook his head. "Get the captain back on the comm one more time," he said. "Now that the kid's awake, I have a new offer to make."

Alex shook his head. "Kill the little shit. Then she'll listen."

Travis glared at Alex. "Don't make me ask twice."

Scowling, Alex followed Ren to the comm while Travis and Brad remained at the door to the clean room.

Tin clicked his tongue to get Angelo's attention. When the men weren't looking, he whispered, "I have to get to that gas bladder."

Angelo gave him a stern look. "No," he whispered. "Didn't I just say not to do anything stupid?"

"I have to," Tin said. "The ship's going to crash if I don't."

Angelo seemed to consider Tin's words. After a pause, he whispered, "You're going to get killed."

Tin wiggled his wrists again, wincing as the plastic ties cut into his flesh. "Maybe, but if I don't do it, *everybody's* going to die."

TWENTY

X hugged the snow barriers around the buildings, with Magnolia close on his heels. Flurries swept across the road, blurring his line of sight. According to his sensors, it was negative thirty degrees Fahrenheit.

"Stick right behind me," he said. "When we get to the end of the street, you're going to work." He didn't know that he was making the right call, but she was faster than he.

"Roger that," she replied.

Halfway to the crate, he paused and listened. There it was, faint and blending in with the whistling wind: the distant keening of the Sirens. The creatures were out there, prowling the city for their next meal, and it was only a matter of time before they found X and the other divers.

He waved Magnolia forward and broke into a hunched-over trot, keeping as low as he could. At the intersection, he dropped to one knee and waited, eyes scanning. Searching.

"Okay, you're up, kid. Get to the box and check it for weapons. I'll cover you from here."

X watched the glow of Magnolia's battery unit as

she darted across the street. A few seconds later, her staticky voice crackled over the comm.

"There's a few assault rifles, but it looks like a couple of things are missing ... Didn't Command say they were sending us some food and water? Because I'm not seein' any."

The missing provisions troubled him, but at least they had heavy weapons. They were still in business.

"Do Sirens eat energy bars, X?" Magnolia asked.

"How would I know that?" he replied. "Hold your position, Magnolia. Katrina, Murph, Tony, get down here."

"On our way," Tony replied.

X sprinted across the street. Above the noise of the wind whipping his suit, he caught another sound, closer now: the piercing wail of a Siren. As usual, it seemed to come from no particular direction.

"You hear that?" Katrina said over the comm.

"Yeah. Now, hurry up. We need to gear up and get gone." He swept his blaster over the surrounding terrain. "You see anything, kid?"

She brushed up next to him, her voice barely more than a whisper, "Wh-what are those?"

Magnolia pointed toward a snow flurry drifting across the far end of the street. Within the swirling flakes, wrinkled, leathery shapes swayed from side to side as they approached.

X holstered his blaster and pulled an assault rifle from the crate. Then he grabbed four loaded magazines, stuffing three into his vest pockets and slapping the fourth into the weapon.

"Pick a rifle and load up on ammo!" X shouted.

He aimed at the pack of Sirens, trying to count them in the gusting flurry. A half-dozen approached on all fours, moving slowly through the fierce wind.

"Magnolia!" X shouted. She wasn't moving.

"I'm not good with guns!" she yelled back, panic rising in her voice.

Looking down the rifle sights, X followed the monsters as they clambered across the road and up the sides of the buildings. Some perched on ledges or sills, watching the divers. Others moved in the partial concealment of the swirling snow, waiting for an opportunity to strike. The creatures had always attacked right away in the past, but now they seemed more cautious, as if sizing up their quarry.

"Katrina, Murph, Tony!" X shouted. "Where the hell are you?"

"Here. We're at your five o'clock," Katrina said. He glanced over his shoulder and saw a flash of movement behind the approaching divers.

"More contacts!" X yelled. "Tony, Murph, Katrina, you got the three o'clock position. Magnolia and I got nine o'clock. Hold your fire until I give the order."

As the Sirens continued to prowl, X said to Magnolia, "Kid, you need to listen close. I want you to hold the gun snug to your shoulder, but don't grip it super tight. Aim it dead center at one of those things and squeeze the trigger for a short burst. But whatever you do, do *not* shoot one of us. You got it?"

"Okay," she mumbled. The rifle shook in her hands, and X considered taking it away. Her file said she had failed combat training, but she had done okay on the last dive, and he needed every weapon in this fight.

X took aim. The Sirens were creeping in from all directions, like a vise slowly closing. A snow flurry clouded his vision for a moment. He blinked, refocused, and trained his rifle on a thick-bodied Siren leading a pack of four.

The beast let out a piercing shriek and charged.

"Fire at will!" X shouted. Deactivating his night vision, he used the light from the sky to guide his shots. The first went wide, kicking up a puff of snow. His second hit one of the creatures at the base of its thick neck. It reared its head back, and the painful croak from its wide mouth sounded like an emergency alarm coming through a broken speaker on the *Hive*.

The pack fanned out in all directions as the creature collapsed to its knees. A brilliant arc of lightning streaked overhead, and he could see open maws, spiky backs, and taloned hands and feet. Another flash lit the exterior of a building across the street. The structural steel was alive with Sirens.

Mindful of the limited ammunition and the sheer numbers of the enemy, X fired a controlled burst at the pack in front of him. He cut down a second beast with two shots to the chest. It slumped to the ground with one last agonizing shriek.

He took out the other three with single shots. The monsters flopped in the snow, unable to continue their advance. X got the next pack in his sights and knocked down two more.

Over the crack of gunfire, the unearthly wails formed a chorus, and over this came the heavy clap of thunder. A brilliant web of lightning streaked overhead, the tips branching out and licking the tips of skyscrapers. Sparks rained down on the streets as the Sirens continued their assault.

"On me!" X yelled. The other divers came together to form a perimeter, but the five of them wouldn't be able to hold the monsters off for long. Worse, the gunfire seemed to attract even more of them.

He scanned the battlefield as he fired. A spray of blood erupted from a wrinkled neck. A bony head crest puffed into scarlet mist. Three more of the abominations crashed to the ground before his ammunition ran out.

In one continuous motion, X ejected the spent magazine, slapped in a new one, and knelt. He was firing as soon as his knee hit the snow. His next shot punched through a Siren's chest, and it fell dead, tripping the one behind it. As the second beast bounded over the carcass, X shot it in the mouth. He twisted to the right and squeezed the trigger, counting the bullets and watching the bodies pile up. Steam rose from the spilled blood.

Over the cacophony of firing and shrieking, X heard someone yelling.

"Power down!"

X ignored the voice, acquired a new target, and fired again, cursing a blue streak all the while. The voice on the wind wasn't familiar. Was he really hearing it?

The same voice shouted again, "Power your suits down and don't move!"

A bleep on X's minimap pulled his eyes away from the monsters. He turned to see an armored diver running toward them from the north.

Waving frantically, he was still screaming, "Power down!"

X watched the creatures closing in all around them. There was no possibility of holding them all back.

"Power down and don't move!" the man yelled again. "Trust me!"

X pulled the empty magazine and reached for another as the new diver sprinted to them. He pulled the battery unit from his own armor, still yelling, "Power the fuck down!"

X saw no other option. They were dead anyway.

"Do it!" he shouted to his team.

Lowering his rifle, he yanked out his battery. His HUD went dark instantly. A moment later, a brilliant red light streaked across the street. One of the monsters, which had stopped behind the barrier of bodies, burst into flames and lay thrashing in the snow.

A second flare hissed in the opposite direction.

The screeches started to grow fainter. X couldn't believe his ears. They were retreating.

The mysterious newcomer was busy reloading his blaster, and X couldn't see his face behind his visor. With the Sirens on the move, the new diver spoke only one more word: "Run!"

*   *   *   *   *

Captain Ash wiped the film of sweat off her forehead. It was a reminder that the bridge, unlike the noncritical areas of the ship, still had heat. Some of the shelters were heated, but there weren't enough for everyone on the ship, so most of the *Hive*'s passengers would be huddled together under blankets in their designated safe areas belowdecks. No safety belts to buckle into, and no heat to keep them warm.

At the sound of footsteps, she turned to see Jordan taking the stairs two at a time.

"Does the Militia have a plan that won't result in my entire ship being shot up?" she asked.

"Yes, Captain," Jordan said. "Sergeant Jenkins radioed in a few minutes ago."

Ash followed Jordan to his station, where he pulled up a map of the *Hive* on his monitor.

"This is an old access point to the farm," he said, pointing to a blue line. "Jenkins has equipped a six-man fire team with crossbows. They plan on infiltrating the farm through this vent while the current strike team, positioned in the hallway, approaches the front entrance to the farm. That will keep Travis and his men distracted long enough for Jenkins to take them out."

Ash leaned closer to the monitor. The old vents were unknown to most of the passengers. Travis would likely never see them coming, but if he did, the entire plan could backfire.

"I don't like it," she said.

"Captain, with all due respect, you can't let your promise to X about Tin cloud your vision. There are over five hundred other souls counting on us."

"Five hundred and ten, Lieutenant," she said. "If you don't count the divers—who, we both know, might die today." Her voice softened. "Get me Samson."

Jordan gave a low whistle. Hunt nodded from his station.

Samson emerged onscreen an instant later. His face was camouflaged with grime and grease. "Got any good news for me?"

Ash shook her head. "I was hoping you had some for me."

"I'm doing all I can, Captain, but the turbofans and existing gas bladders simply can't hold the mass of the ship. Not to mention, I had to divert some power to the rudders. We need that gas bladder. I'm working on two others that I *might* be able to fix, but I don't think we have time." Samson turned away from the screen as one of his engineers leaned in and whispered in his ear. "You have to be fucking kidding me."

Ash wasn't sure she could take any more bad news right now. A thought she had stuffed down many times before began to emerge from the depths of her mind: that maybe there was nothing she could do to keep the human race from extinction. No matter how hard she tried to believe that humans could change from their violent past, a man such as Travis would come along and shatter that illusion. She had fought her whole life, first in the Militia and then as captain, to save the people aboard her ship. She had given up everything for them, and now she had chosen to die from cancer rather than leave her post.

And for what?

In the end, it hadn't been a storm that finally brought down the *Hive*. It had been a bullet.

Ash was tired. Tired of fighting gravity, tired of fighting the lower-deckers, tired of fighting the cancer.

Samson turned to face the screen and stood up. "I have another fire to put out. I'll update you when I know more about the gas bladders. Good luck keeping us in the air, Captain."

Before Ash could reply, the feed sizzled off. She felt Jordan's intense stare as he waited. All the options crossed her mind. In the end, only one made sense, but she would not leave anything to chance. She unbuttoned the top of her collar.

"Tell Jenkins to stand by and wait for me."

Jordan tilted his head to the side. "Captain?"

"Nope. That's you now, Jordan, until I get back."

"But—" Jordan began to say, when she cut him off.

"You didn't think I'd sit here and *watch* our fire team raid the farms, did you?"

"Sometimes, I forget you were in the Militia," he said. The hint of a grin formed on his face, and he threw a salute. "Good luck, Captain."

Ash returned the salute and ran up the ramp. She burst into her office and hurried over to her armor hanging from the wall. She had kept her gear polished and ready all these years, just in case.

Three minutes later, she was running down the hallway with a two-man armed escort. Her armor didn't fit as it had ten years ago when she was a lieutenant in the Militia. The cancer had cost her several pounds of muscle. It rattled as she moved, but she didn't let it slow her down. Indeed, she picked up the pace when she saw the six-man fire team waiting two corridors away from the farm. Sergeant Jenkins greeted her with a salute. He had been just a kid when she was in the military; now he was one of the highest-ranking soldiers on the ship.

"Captain," Jenkins said. "You coming in with us?"

She nodded grimly. "If that bastard wants to make demands, he can make them to my face."

Jenkins handed her a crossbow and a quiver of bolts. The stock felt good in her hands. She had forgotten how powerful it made her feel—one more reason she had done everything she could to keep the crossbows and rifles from ever falling into the wrong hands.

In this, she had failed.

Buckling the quiver at her waist, Ash said, "What are you waiting for? Let's go."

*   *   *   *   *

Weaver stopped at a concrete wall to listen. The faint shrieking was not the lonely cries from the night before—these were sounds of hungry, enraged creatures. The Sirens were searching. Hunting for the divers.

"Who the fuck *are* you?" someone behind him said.

Weaver straightened and offered his hand.

"Commander Rick Weaver, from *Ares*. If you want to survive down here, you'll keep quiet and follow me." He could see the man's eyes narrow behind the visor.

"I'm X, and this is Murph, Magnolia, Katrina, and Tony. Let's get going, then."

Weaver nodded to the other divers who had crouched against the wall. He knew their names now, but part of him still wasn't convinced they were real and not just figments of his imagination. After days of trekking on the surface, he was running on vapors and instinct. His bones, eyelids, even his lips felt heavy. And it wasn't from a lack of nutrition. He'd found plenty, first on Sarah and then in the supply crate. His body was suffering from exhaustion. Sleeping for only a few minutes at a time had taken a toll. If the other divers suddenly turned into snow flurries in the wind, he wouldn't be surprised.

Besides, what kind of a name was "X"? It sounded like something a disordered mind would dream up.

"Stay close to me and keep one eye on the sky," Weaver said as the noises waned and faded to nothing.

"Where the hell are you taking us?" X said.

"Somewhere safe. Just remember, if those things find us, we power down." He checked to see that the others heard him. They weren't on the same frequency, and he almost had to yell to be heard over the wind. It was dangerous, but he had no choice.

"Let's go," X said. He waved his team forward.

Weaver slowly guided them through the dead city. He looked to the skyline as they crossed an intersection. Floor after floor of steel frameworks towered above, with here and there a section of granite-clad wall. Hundreds of years ago, any one of them had housed many times the planet's current population. Now they were home to the Sirens.

Beyond the next high-rise, he saw the gap that his falling home had punched in the skyline. They were close now. In a few minutes, he would explain everything and try to make a plan to get off this cursed hell world. The idea of leaving Hades hadn't entirely sunk in till now. Brushing with death for days had taught him to suppress any glimmer of hope.

That glow faded as one of the divers yelled, "Contact!"

One minute, the snow-covered street was lifeless and dead; the next, it was crawling with the creatures. Weaver didn't even have a chance to tell the others to power down. In an eyeblink, Tony had swung up his assault rifle and fired a burst.

"No!" Weaver screamed. But his words were drowned out by the crack of gunfire. Shots pinged off the buildings, and bullet casings rained down with the snowflakes.

Weaver contemplated taking out his battery unit and hiding. He had survived too long by himself to let some rookies get him killed.

He turned to run, then stopped. Something in him, even more powerful than the adrenaline, stopped him. If he left these people here, he would be alone because they would surely die. He couldn't bear the thought of being down here by himself for another second. It would be even worse than dying.

Weaver twisted, aimed, and fired his rifle. The burst found a Siren, spattering gore across the concrete wall behind it. He swung to his right, taking out two more. Then a third.

More Sirens streamed out of the empty windows and slid down to the street, screeching as they came.

Weaver finished off his magazine and yelled,

"We have to get out of here. We're attracting every one of these things in Hades!"

But again gunfire drowned his words. Taking another magazine from a cargo pocket, he caught a glimpse of motion on their right. Two Sirens had crept up behind Tony, who was busy firing in the opposite direction.

"Watch out! They're flanking us!" Weaver shouted.

Everyone seemed too busy dealing with immediate threats to hear him. The other divers were firing on their own targets. Weaver aimed and squeezed off a shot. The bullet hit the skull of the first creature, and brains exploded into the air.

He tracked the second with his sights and pulled the trigger. The Siren shuddered from the impacts as a jagged chunk of its spinal column blew out behind it. Somehow, it kept moving, pulling itself along by its hands at alarming speed. A moment later, it was lunging at Tony.

Weaver centered the sights on the abomination's skull and squeezed the trigger.

Click.

"Shit!" he shouted. He slapped the bottom of the magazine, then worked the bolt to free the jammed round. But he wasn't fast enough. The thing grabbed Tony, spun him around, and ripped at his suit. A scream of agony rang out as talons found human flesh.

Weaver continued working the bolt on his weapon, knowing that every second was time Tony didn't have to spare. The jammed round finally popped out, and Weaver unloaded a three-round burst into the creature.

Tony had dropped to his knees, catching something that fell from his suit. Weaver laid down covering fire and backed over to where Tony knelt. Only then did he see the rising steam and realize that the ropy cords in Tony's hands were his intestines.

"What the fuck happened!" X yelled.

"Oh, my God, oh, my God!" Magnolia cried out.

"I have the medical kit," Murph said. He lowered his weapon and pulled the small box out of a cargo pocket.

Weaver grabbed it, knowing that nothing inside the box would patch up these wounds. Tony stared up at them from behind a cracked visor.

The other divers formed a perimeter around the fallen man and kept firing. Weaver wanted to cover his ears against the ghastly screams of the dying Sirens and the crack of gunfire, amplified and echoed by the buildings' walls. But instead, he held Tony in his arms, helpless to do any more than keep his guts from spilling onto the snow. He lost track of time as the battle raged around him.

At some point, the guns went silent, and he looked up at the retreating Sirens. Their intermittent squawks faded as they shambled away, trailing blood into the darkness.

"We need to get out of here," Weaver said. "They'll be back."

X bent down and grabbed Tony under his armpit. He screamed in agony and pulled away.

"I'm hurt, X," he said. "Hurt bad." He tilted his visor toward his stomach and let out another strangled cry. "I'm done. Ya gotta leave me."

"No," X said, shaking his head.

Weaver saw a flash of movement behind them. "We have to go. NOW!" He pointed to a dozen Sirens, perched like gargoyles, on a ruined parapet.

"It's okay," Tony said, wincing. "I'll hold 'em off. Help me sit up." He grabbed Katrina's hands, and she hoisted him to a sitting position. Tony looked over at X and said, "Please …" He coughed, spraying blood inside his visor. "X, you gotta save the *Hive*."

"I will," X said. He placed a hand on Tony's shoulder.

Weaver knew what they were thinking, because he was thinking it, too. Life was precious, and it could end quickly and violently. X lingered there for a moment— perhaps to console Tony, or maybe just from the shock of seeing another friend mortally wounded. Weaver wasn't sure, but they had run out of time.

"We have to go," Weaver urged.

X stood up, looking unsure what to do. "Come on," he finally said.

Magnolia, whimpering, staggered after the others, her eyes still on Tony as they left him to die.

Weaver felt a strange mix of emotions: sadness at the death of a fellow diver, and elation that he wasn't the one dying. "I'm sorry," he muttered, repeating it like a mantra as he began to run, unsure whether he was apologizing for his thoughts or for leaving Tony behind. Maybe it was a little of both.

Eventually, the burning in his muscles made him forget his mantra. They rounded the next block and made it to the end of the street before the report of Tony's rifle echoed behind them.

Weaver didn't slow until he cleared the next corner. He skidded on his knees across an icy stretch of concrete. When he came to a stop, he was staring at the sagging remains of *Ares*. Panting, he cocked his chin toward the ship and said, "We're here. That's … that's my home."

TWENTY-ONE

The *Hive* rocked gently. Tin could barely feel the sporadic shudders, but he knew what they meant: the ship was struggling to stay in the air. That realization made up his mind for him. He was going to patch the gas bladder. All he had to do was wait for the right opportunity to escape.

He looked for the armed men. Travis waited at the comm link with Ren. Alex patrolled on a catwalk above, but Brad was out of sight. He had gone inside the stairwell minutes earlier and hadn't come back. Silver and Lilly were quiet now. They lay in the dirt, only their eyes active, roving and watching.

"Don't get any ideas," Angelo whispered.

"What's your name, kid?" Travis said.

Tin glanced up. "Me?"

"No, the other kid," Alex sneered.

"My name's Tin."

Travis walked over to the wall and punched the comm button. "Captain Ash, have you had time to reconsider my offer?"

A youthful male voice answered him. "This is Lieutenant Jordan, interim captain. Captain Ash is currently in engineering with Chief Engineer Samson, trying to keep us in the air."

Travis glanced over at Ren, who stabbed the dirt with his rusty blade. "Told you, Trav. The bitch didn't take us seriously."

Travis punched the comm button a second time. "I'd like to make a new offer. A trade: Tin for my brother, Raphael."

White noise crackled from the speakers for several seconds.

Tin's heart was pounding now. He couldn't let them trade him. He had to stay here, had to fix the gas bladder.

Jordan's reply came a few seconds later. "I'll need to speak with Capt—"

The transmission was interrupted by a violent tremor that vibrated through the room. The walls groaned, and the chickens behind Tin squawked and scurried.

Travis looked at the ceiling. "What the hell was that?"

Ren pulled his blade from the dirt and sheathed it. "I don't know. Haven't felt one of those in a long time. Maybe something really is wrong."

Tin wanted to scream, to tell Ren that yes, he was right, and that he needed to let an engineer inside. But his throbbing head reminded him what had happened the last time he tried that.

"No!" Alex shouted over the roar of the ship. "Captain Ash and her henchman Jordan are lying. She's probably planning to break down that door and kill all of us."

"Will you shut your yap for once, Alex," Travis snapped. "You've done enough harm. She's not lying. The *Hive*'s in deep shit."

Brad emerged from the clean room, his face a shade paler than before. "Travis, that team outside is moving."

"Shit!" Alex said. "I told you!" He climbed down a ladder and dropped to the dirt. He unsheathed his blade and rushed over to Brad.

Travis punched the comm again and got only static. The connection had been severed.

Tin worked his hands back and forth, trying not to make a sound as the plastic dug into his wrists. It hurt, but at last he felt the left thumb knuckle slip through. With that hand free, he soon had both restraints off and tucked in his hip pocket. He kept his eyes on the men.

"Don't, kid," Angelo whispered.

"I have to do this," Tin replied. With his hands still behind his back, he squirmed away from the farmers. X and the other divers were on the surface of Hades, risking their lives to save the ship. But if someone didn't fix the gas bladder, the ship was going to crash. He couldn't let that happen. He wasn't just going to sit by when he knew he could fix it.

"Ren, follow me," Travis said. "And, Alex, don't touch the hostages." He grabbed Alex's vest. "You do hear me, right?"

Alex nodded, smirking.

"Let's go!" Ren said.

Travis loosened his grip but held Alex's gaze for a tense moment. The ship groaned again, and an emergency siren blared in the corner of the room. Travis shoved Alex aside and followed Ren into the clean room.

Now was Tin's chance. He took off running toward the cornfield, ignoring Angelo's pleas.

By the time his captors realized he had slipped away, he was already batting his way through cornstalks that rose above his head. Silver and Lilly went wild, their guttural barks echoing through the vaulted room.

Tin spotted the ladder on the starboard wall. That was his target—how he would get to the gas bladder. He took a look back over his shoulder, tripped, and tumbled.

"Hey, where'd the kid go?" Alex shouted.

Tin jumped to his feet and raced through the field to the ladder, hoping the corn would conceal him.

"Get back here, you little shit!" Alex yelled.

Tin leaped onto the bottom rung of the ladder. Hearing noise at the other end of the catwalk, he looked across. Alex was climbing, too, trying to cut him off before he got to the hatch.

Tin climbed faster and pulled himself onto the mezzanine. He searched the hatches. There, halfway between him and Alex, he found the one marked "Gas Bladder twenty-one."

Sprinting to the hatch, he grabbed the wheel handle, twisted it, and pulled. The cover groaned open, revealing a dark tunnel.

"Don't go in there!" Alex yelled.

The clank of footsteps grew closer, and Tin climbed inside. An emergency supply cabinet was mounted on the bulkhead, and next to it a speaker system. For a fleeting moment, he thought about calling for help over the intercom. But no, there wasn't enough time. He had to do this himself.

When he turned to close the hatch, Alex was almost there. The scarf had fallen away from his mouth, and blood trickled from the bandage on his chin where Travis had smacked him. His eyes were wild and determined—the look of a killer.

Tin slammed the hatch shut in the scarred, enraged face. The world went dark, and he threw the lock bar down just as he heard Alex grab the wheel on the other side. He paused to catch his breath and get his bearings. Each gasp burned his lungs. It had to be over a hundred degrees in here. He fumbled for the supply cabinet as Alex pounded on the hatch.

"Open up, kid! Open the damn hatch!

Tin's fingertips slid across the warm metal and the speakers as he searched for the box. He punched the comm link first but heard only the crackle of static. The radio probably hadn't been serviced in years. He was on his own.

He found the cabinet on his second pass and popped the lid while, outside, Alex pounded on the hatch. The man couldn't hurt him anymore. Tin sucked in a warm breath of relief and rummaged through the supplies.

His fingers brushed a long metal cylinder, which proved to be a flashlight. He felt for the off-on switch, not wanting to rejoice until he was sure the thing worked.

Please work, Tin thought. He pushed the soft

rubber button with his thumb, and a white beam shot out of the flashlight—weak, but a beam nonetheless.

"Yes!" he said, though he knew that his luck could be short-lived. Even if the light worked now, it wouldn't likely last very long.

He shined the ray at the box and pulled out two patch kits, sealed in envelopes. Then he grabbed a breathing mask with a tiny oxygen tube and slipped it on. That left the tube of sealant. *There.* He grabbed it and stuffed it in his pocket.

Tin shined the light over the tunnel. A second hatch separated him from the gas bladder. He crawled toward it, away from the sound of Alex's pounding.

He spun the wheel left, and the hatch creaked open. He played the beam over the curved bulkheads and then climbed inside, astonished at the bladder's sheer size.

His heart fluttered as he stood in the dark, hot emptiness. He had escaped from Alex, found a flashlight, and made his way into the gas bladder. But the space didn't look much like they had in the books, and Tin suddenly wasn't so sure he could find the leak, let alone patch it.

*   *   *   *   *

The wind whistled through the remains of *Ares*. Somewhere above, a lone Siren soared through the clouds, its alien cries drawing X's attention upward.

Weaver had stopped at the edge of the debris field and knelt beside a row of sooty aluminum ribs protruding from the snow.

"We need to keep ..." X stopped talking when he saw that the metal wasn't just random debris. It was too neat for that, too organized. Weaver must have placed them there.

Grave markers, X thought. It was an Old World tradition that he had read about in history books. Modern humans, living on airships, didn't have the luxury of burying their dead, but Weaver had clearly been busy over the past few days, using his time to bury them down here. Snow gusted across the graves, covering them with fresh powder.

"Let's go," Weaver said, motioning them toward the skeleton of *Ares.* X and the other divers followed him under the aluminum struts. There wasn't much left in the hulking wreckage.

Rumbling thunder echoed overhead, and X looked up, half expecting to see the *Hive* come crashing down through the clouds. They were running out of time to save her.

"Help me," Weaver said. He stopped at a warped hatch and grabbed the side.

X resisted the urge to ask questions. The guy obviously had some screws loose, but they had to trust that he was taking them somewhere safer than out here in the open. And after Tony's death, the divers needed a chance to regroup and make a plan to get to the industrial zone. X could only hope that Weaver wasn't too crazy to help.

Weaver gripped the edge of the hatch, and X helped him pull it away.

The makeshift hideout wasn't much—just a burned-out hull of what had been an apartment. A few boxes of salvaged supplies sat in one corner.

"Hurry up," Weaver said. He crawled inside and crouched beside the boxes.

X exchanged a look with Katrina. "What do you think?" he asked over the private comm channel.

"I think the guy's wacked," she replied. "What about you?"

"We have no choice but to trust him," X replied.

Magnolia shrugged. "Not like we got a lot of options here, right?"

"Right," Murph said.

X motioned them inside, hoping he hadn't made a terrible decision. They all had been rattled by the dive, the Sirens, and Tony's death, but they had only a few minutes to get it together.

Magnolia and Katrina crowded around the supply boxes with Weaver while X and Murph sealed the door.

Weaver took a seat on the cracked rim of a shit can. "Sorry about your friend," he said, "but I told you to power down. I told you to run."

X rested his assault rifle against a wall and sat on the ground, facing the others. He sucked down some water from his straw. There was nothing to say that would bring Tony back.

Weaver flipped his visor, and X saw his face clearly for the first time. Thinning, sweaty fair hair clung to his forehead; dark circles lined wild green eyes that darted back and forth on hypervigilant high alert.

"Radiation's minimal here," Weaver said. "You should all take in some extra nutrition and refill your water bottles. I'd add some chems to it if I were you. Never know when you're going to need the extra kick."

He lit an emergency candle, dripped some wax, and stuck it on the floor. "The shield protecting the reactors is still intact. I haven't detected any major leaks."

X checked his minicomputer. The reading wasn't exactly minimal, but it was lower than he had seen in this godforsaken place. It wouldn't hurt to have their visors popped for a few minutes. He nodded at his team.

"You sure?" Murph asked.

"Your call," X said, flipping up his visor and sucking in his first unfiltered breath of Hades. The sharp, cold air burned inside his nostrils. He picked up a variety of smells—the vapors of spilled chemicals and the strong scent of smoke. There was another smell, too, vague but unmistakable: the stink of charred flesh.

"Here," Weaver said, holding out a handful of chem pills.

X took the chems, twisted the cap off his water bottle, and dropped two of the pills into the water. Then he shook the bottle and took a big gulp. He closed his eyes and waited for the stimulants to work into his system. He opened his eyes with a sudden burst of energy, scanning the room as his pupils dilated.

Weaver pointed at the boxes in the corner. "I recovered some food from your supply crate. Help yourself." He brought a shaking hand to his mouth and bit the end off a stick of jerky.

Maybe it was partly from the chemicals, but somehow, Weaver offering them their own food rankled X. "We don't have time to eat," he snapped, his breath fogging as he spoke. "The *Hive* is up there, and they're counting on us to come back with cells and pressure valves."

Weaver glanced up sheepishly, like a child being scolded, then looked at the floor. X couldn't begin to understand the horror Weaver had been through, but they didn't have time for niceties. He had questions that needed answering. He went over and crouched in front of Weaver, snapping his fingers to get his attention.

"Weaver," X said. "You with me?"

The shortest of nods told X he was listening. "Don't get me wrong," he said. "I appreciate you saving our bacon back there, and I'm sorry about your ship—I really am. But our mission clock is ticking. We have less than nineteen hours to get back to the *Hive*."

"I understand," Weaver murmured. "I'll help you if I can."

X pulled the map from his vest and held it in front of Weaver. "We need to get to this location ... right here."

Weaver swallowed a chunk of jerky and squinted. The low glow from the candlelight lit up his pale face, but he didn't say anything.

"Have you been there?" X asked.

Weaver muttered as if he didn't know what X was talking about. He took a sip from a straw in his helmet, then nodded. "Jones and I raided one of those buildings, but he didn't make it back outside. They ate him."

"I need you to show us the safest path there."

Weaver let out a sad laugh and looked up from the map. "Safe? No such thing. And even if you do make it there, the Sirens *nest* in those buildings. You won't get close to what you're looking for."

An electronic-sounding wail broke over the howling wind. *A warning.*

Weaver dropped his finger and continued chewing with his mouth open. "Sirens are out hunting again."

X snapped his fingers a second time. "Forget the creatures for a goddamn second. We need your help. We're only here because of *Ares*—because of Captain Willis' SOS."

A moment of clarity washed over Weaver's face. The words meant something to him. He glanced up and said, "I'm sorry." Then he hugged his knees and went back to his nervous shaking.

X closed his eyes and sucked in a breath. His thoughts drifted to the *Hive* and Tin. He had managed to clear his mind for the entire dive, burying his worries about the gunfire he heard as the tube opened. But those worries were beginning to resurface.

He pushed the map back at Weaver. "Please. Just take a look."

Weaver snatched it from his hands and held it close to the candlelight. "This building?"

"Yes. That's the one we're looking for."

"I never made it inside that one. Couldn't crack the access codes."

X jerked his chin toward Murph and Magnolia. "That's why I brought *them.*"

"If I couldn't hack the system, I doubt they can."

Murph patted his vest. "I brought something along that can hack anything."

Weaver shrugged and continued rocking.

"If you couldn't get in, then maybe the Sirens couldn't, either," Katrina said.

"Yeah," X said. "That's our best shot." He stood and put a hand on Weaver's shoulder. "Will you take us there?"

Weaver tore off another bite of jerky and chewed furiously. "I suppose I could sit around here and wait to die. But I've been trying to die for days now. Not exactly working out the way I thought it would."

X couldn't help but grin. In many ways, the man reminded him of himself: too stubborn to die, try though he might. He had to like the guy, even if he was a bit crazy.

"All right," X said. "Gather round and relax for a few minutes. Weaver's going to show us where we're going. Then we move out."

The divers crowded around the candle as Weaver and X planned. Murph, Katrina, and Magnolia waited in silence, their frightened eyes tracking the shadows and flickering light inside the small room.

It wasn't long before the lonely, maddening wails of the Sirens began again, drawing closer. And somewhere four miles above, the *Hive* waited for X and his team to pull off a mission that seemed more and more in need of a miracle.

*   *   *   *   *

Captain Ash kept her hand on the armor of the Militia soldier in front of her as they inched through the tight passage. They moved at a frustratingly slow rate, but it was the only way into the farm besides the front entrance. The corridor opened up behind the livestock pen. If they could get in undetected, they could take out Travis or whoever else had the assault rifle.

The second strike team would still be waiting outside the first-floor entrance to the farm. The distraction might give her sharpshooter a chance—and without the risk of firing a bullet. Each of the soldiers carried a crossbow. The arrows would slice through flesh but would never make it through the wall to the gas bladders. Her main concern was the danger, to both the ship and the hostages, posed by return fire.

"In position, Captain," Jenkins said.

Despite her confidence in the soldier, Ash's heart was racing out of control. She craned her neck around the soldier in front of her. Light seeped under the warped hatch cover at the opposite end of the tunnel. The team awaited her final orders.

"One shot, one kill," Ash said. "The target is whoever has the gun."

"Roger," Jenkins replied. "Montoya is the best sniper we got."

Ash nodded. "You're clear to fire as soon as you have a clean shot."

Jordan's voice suddenly crackled over a private channel. "Captain … Captain, do you copy?"

"Copy," Ash responded.

"Captain, stand down. I repeat, stand down."

"What? *Why?*"

"The hatch to gas bladder twenty-one has opened. Someone's gone inside!"

Ash squirmed to get a better view of the hatch leading into the farm. Jenkins clutched the wheel handle, preparing to twist it.

"Captain, I think someone's trying to patch the bladder," Jordan said.

Tin, Ash thought. It had to be him.

"Jenkins, stand down," she said, almost shouting.

TWENTY-TWO

Tin thought he heard a scream. He stopped to listen, but the noise didn't repeat. A drip of perspiration ran down his face, and he mopped his forehead with his sleeve. He had examined most of the gas bladder with his flashlight but found nothing. No hole, no puncture.

"Where the hell is it!" Tin yelled, finally venting his frustration.

He scrambled to the other side of the large, cylindrical room and wondered if Captain Ash had been lying after all. Maybe the bladder had been offline for some time. Maybe there wasn't a hole at all.

No, Tin thought. *You can't think like that.* Ash was a good person, and she had always been straight with him in the past. He wouldn't let her down.

He played the beam over the smooth surface of the bulkheads, then stood on tiptoes and examined the overhead. Another hatch covered the pipe that delivered helium to the compartment. Engineering would have drained it as soon as the leak showed up in the system. Helium was precious and difficult to acquire on the surface. The *Hive* had several tanks in reserve, but they couldn't afford to waste it on an unchecked leak.

After a quick scan, he dropped back to the floor. The hatch that led to the engineering compartment a few decks below was sealed. He had tried it just to be sure.

He wasn't even sure how long he had been in here, but his body was starting to feel weird. His actions were growing sluggish. He licked his dry lips, cringing at the salty taste.

The curved bulkhead was hot to the touch, and he had avoided contact after burning his forearm earlier. Now he had no choice—he had to find the leak. He reached out and ran his fingers along the metal. His skin sizzled, and he jumped back, dropping the flashlight. It bounced on the floor with a loud click and was suddenly much dimmer.

"*No!*" Tin whispered. He fell to both knees and scooped the light up, tapping the end as the beam weakened.

He waved the fading light over the bulkhead and then overhead. "Come on," he said. "Where are you?" His voice trailed off with the last of the glow from his flashlight. The darkness pressed in on him, and with it came a wave of fear. The same helplessness he had felt when his father died returned. He was alone now, and terrified. Worse, he had failed the *Hive*.

*   *   *   *   *

The suffocating darkness closed in. Even with night-vision optics, X was beginning to feel smothered.

He watched a snow whirlwind scudding across the landscape. The snowflakes fluttering down to earth were beautiful. One could almost forget they were radioactive.

The divers fought against the full brunt of the wind. Sporadic lightning flashes lit up the industrial area. They were close now. X could see the quarries where people had once excavated the sand, stone, and gravel to build the networks of roads that connected their megacities—roads like the one they traveled now.

The area seemed empty of Sirens. So far, he hadn't heard a single screech. Maybe they knew something he didn't. The only sound was the low rumble of thunder, and then a voice that X had avoided far too long.

"Xavier," Katrina said over a private comm channel. He could tell by her tone that this wasn't about the mission.

"Yeah?"

"Can I ask you something?"

"I guess so."

"What went wrong between us?"

The question stung, but it wasn't unexpected. When the prospect of death loomed large, such questions became important. He had heard it a dozen times from other divers when things went badly on the surface. In those moments, the answers mattered, and X owed her one.

"When Rhonda got sick …" X reconsidered his words and started again. "The *Hive*. Life. *This,*" he said, gesturing at the blasted landscape. "It's all broken. Every loss has taught me, getting that close to people results in one thing."

"Heartbreak," she said, looking over at him. "We all know what it feels like. You're not the only one, you know."

She was right. But it had taken a child to teach him that lesson. Tin had shown him what true resiliency and vulnerability meant, and that opening your heart to someone was worth the risk.

Even if you lost them. *Especially* if you lost them.

"What's the point of living if you push everyone away?" she asked.

"I've been working on that."

"Tin?"

X nodded but didn't speak for a moment. He stopped in the middle of the empty street to wait for Magnolia and Murph to pass, then held out a hand to Katrina. "I'm sorry," he said.

"I know."

Her armored fingers curled around his for a moment, and he imagined the warmth of her skin. She smiled behind her visor. "You owe me dinner when we get home."

"Deal," X said, as if he believed it was actually possible.

"Almost there," Weaver shouted. "Keep up. What are you two doing back there?"

X and Katrina shared a chuckle, like two teens caught smooching, and trotted to catch up with the others. He was glad to have something pleasant to think about in this flat, featureless maze of ruined foundations and half-buried vehicles. The constant snowfall and eerie light from the electrical storms made the whole place look like a black-and-white photograph. They used up another half hour trekking to the outer edge of the zone.

"Radiation here's insane," Murph said. "I'm not sure our suits can protect us at this level."

"Don't worry," Weaver said. "We're going around the worst of it. This way."

X examined his HUD. The nav system displayed a route that went directly through the radioactive zone. He was glad they had found Weaver to guide them.

A single gray structure stood alone on the bleak landscape ahead. It was missing its roof and every single window, but the walls were still intact.

As they ran the quarter mile to the shelter, the wind beat against them every step of the way, threatening to push them into the craters to the west. The outlines of the other divers disappeared as they entered the building. X was the last one in. He paused in the entrance and scanned the snowy plain behind them. Though nothing appeared to be following them, he heard a weak scratching that didn't sound like the wind.

"You good, X?" Murph asked. He was waiting inside with the other divers.

"Yeah. Thought I heard something, is all."

By the time X joined them, Weaver was already moving up the stairs. He tested a step halfway up with his boot, then motioned the divers to follow. The metal groaned under the team's weight, and lightning surged above the missing roof. The light guided them to a second-floor hallway. Weaver continued into a room overlooking a scarred, barren field.

"What the hell is that?" Magnolia said over the comm as she approached one of the windows.

X slung his rifle over his shoulder and looked through the binos. The earth was pockmarked with craters, some as much as a thousand feet in diameter, and inside each dark hole moved a sea of flesh.

"Holy shit!" Murph breathed. "Are those … ?"

"Sirens," Katrina said. "But what are they doing?"

X scoped the nearest hole. Hundreds of the creatures were digging in the dirt. "I don't give a shit what they're doing," he said. "We need to keep moving."

He zoomed in on a cluster of towers beyond the pits. A few stood much taller than the others. The buildings had withstood the years of relentless wind and snow. He didn't need a sign to tell him this was the ITC campus.

"There are so many of them," Katrina said.

X twisted to face Weaver. "Why the hell did you bring us *here*?"

"I thought you should see," Weaver said. "Thought you should understand."

"You wasted ten minutes," X snapped. He unslung the rifle and grabbed it by the stock. "We don't have time for sightseeing."

Weaver shrugged. "So you don't want to know what they're digging for?"

X shook his head. "Not really."

Katrina tapped him on the shoulder. "Maybe you should listen."

"Fine. What, Weaver? *What* are those mutant fucks digging for?"

Weaver pointed to the nearest hole. "Same thing we're here for."

X walked back to the window and took a closer look with his binos. What he saw didn't make any sense. The creatures were eating the dirt and then spitting it back out.

"Power," Weaver said. "Not the same we're after, but I think they feed off radioactive material."

"And us," Magnolia added.

"All the more reason to keep moving," X said. He didn't know what the Sirens were or where they had come from, but one thing was clear: the bombs dropped by his ancestors hadn't just destroyed the Old World—they had created a new one and populated it with monsters.

*   *   *   *   *

The image of Tin crawling through the tunnel in gas bladder twenty-one was etched on Captain Ash's brain. She ran back to the bridge as fast as her bulky armor would let her. If the boy really was inside, perhaps they wouldn't need to raid the farm at all. She just needed to give him a chance to fix the bladder. Maybe no one else had to die.

She hurried past the two guards standing outside the bridge. The place was buzzing with activity when she arrived. Jordan stepped away from the oak wheel at the bottom of the room and saluted.

"Welcome back, Captain," he said. "That was quick. I think I just had the shortest command as captain in the history of the ship."

Ash grinned. She couldn't recall Jordan ever cracking a joke before. Unclasping her body armor as she walked down the stairs to her chair, she set the pieces neatly on the floor.

"Have we confirmed that it's Tin inside the bladder?" she asked.

"*Tin?*"

"Who else would it be?"

Jordan shook his head, "I don't know."

"We need to figure it out. Right now! Gonzalez said he was a second away from putting an arrow in someone's chest. Both strike teams are still on standby, but before we make our move, I need to know who's in that maintenance tunnel. If there's a chance Tin can fix the bladder ..."

"You're leaving this up to a *kid*?" Jordan asked. He bit the inside of his lip and looked away. "I'm sorry, ma'am."

"Tin's not just any random kid. He's brilliant."

"Captain, even if he's been through the technical training, actually patching a bladder is a far cry from memorizing the instructions in the technical manual. The bladders are hot inside. And they're *huge*."

"I've made my decision. We give Tin—or whoever's inside the gas bladder—a chance before I risk a battle inside the farm. Tell Jenkins to stand down and fire only if the hostages are in danger."

Before Jordan could reply, Ash changed the subject.

"Have we heard anything from X or the other divers?"

"Nothing yet."

She checked the mission clock. They still had

seventeen hours, assuming the *Hive* lasted that long.

Ash ran up to navigation. "Ensign, what's the status of the storm?"

Ryan's fingers pecked at the keyboard. "She's holding steady, Captain."

"What's our altitude?"

"Sixteen thousand feet and dropping," Hunt replied.

"Jordan," Ash said. "Get over here."

He hurried over with his hands on his earpiece, talking as he moved. The red glow from the rotating emergency lights swirled across his path. He paused on the first step of the ramp. "Samson's on his way here, Captain."

"Good," Ash said. "I'll meet you at your station."

Jordan nodded and hurried off.

Ash glanced at the main display. "You let me know the moment that storm starts to grow."

"Aye, Captain. I'm keeping an eye on it."

Samson arrived a few minutes later and stopped on the stairway, hands on his knees, panting. His chubby face was covered in grime and sweat. The glow from the emergency lights made his glistening skin look drenched with blood.

Ash gave him a few seconds to catch his breath before waving him over to Operations. Jordan was already pulling up the *Hive*'s blueprints on his monitor. Hundreds of different-colored lines, depicting tunnels and pipes weaving through the compartments of the ship, emerged on the screen.

"Show me the gas bladders," Ash said.

Jordan punched a button and drilled down a

layer. The other tunnels and pipes vanished, replaced by a blue overlay of passages that connected to the twenty-four lozenge-shaped helium bladders. Each had two entrances: one angling from the lower engineering deck, the other crossing straight over from the farm.

Samson pointed at the screen. "I have teams inside bladders nineteen and three. They're working on fixing those now." He scratched his shiny scalp. "What's our altitude?"

"Sixteen thousand feet and dropping," Jordan replied.

"How about that storm?" Samson asked. "We still at a safe distance?"

"For now," Ash said.

Samson leaned over Jordan's shoulder. "Bladder twenty-one is sealed off. Whoever went inside locked the entrance to the farm. We have no way of knowing whether it's been patched unless we fill the bladder with helium. But if someone's still inside ..."

"Have you tried contacting them?" Ash interrupted.

Samson put his hands on his hips and sighed. "Those speakers are two centuries old. They haven't even been serviced since before I was born."

"Try to get a message through, Jordan," Ash ordered.

He pulled up the control panel for bladder twenty-one.

"Let me," Samson insisted. "I know this system a lot better than you do."

Ash nodded, and the two men exchanged places. Samson's stubby fingers typed quickly, tapping into the system. Then he scooted the mike closer to the monitor and said, "Does anyone in bladder twenty-one copy?"

Ash twirled her wedding ring absently. She hadn't had a chance to check in with Mark for hours. He had responsibilities just as she did, and was busy working in the water reclamation plant. If the worst happened and the ship went down, she'd be duty bound to stay here on the bridge, while Mark would be trapped belowdecks—they would never see each other again.

A crackle of static interrupted her morbid thoughts. Samson dialed down the volume while Jordan glanced over at Ash.

"Try again, Samson," Ash said.

A moment later, the crackle of static broke into a voice that was soft and high—a kid's voice.

"Tin," Ash said.

"Can anyone hear me?" the boy asked.

Ash took the mic from Samson and pulled the cord with her. "Yes, Tin, this is Maria. Are you okay?"

"It's really hot in here, and I can't find the leak. It's too dark."

"Do you have a flashlight?"

"It's not working."

She looked to Samson. "Is there any way to guide him through the bladder?"

Samson scratched his head again. "Yes, but to locate the leak, we would have to fill the bladder with helium."

"Tin, do you have breathing equipment?" Ash asked.

"Yes."

"Listen to me very carefully, son. Samson says that the only way to find the puncture is to flood the bladder with helium. You should be able to hear the leak." Ash bowed her head, then brought the mic to her lips. "Are you sure you can do this?"

"Yes, I think so."

A smile spread across her face. The boy was just like his father. And like X, too: stubborn and determined. He would make a good Hell Diver.

"Hold on, Tin," Ash said.

"It'll take a few minutes to flood the passage," Samson said.

"Tin, you still there?" Ash asked.

"Yes."

"Is your breathing mask on?"

"Yes, but I'm not sure how to work it."

"Just twist the top of the tube that's connected to the mask part. You should be able to breathe in the filtered air."

"Hold on, I'll try."

They waited a minute before Tin came back online.

His voice was weakened by static. "Okay, it's working."

"The tank's got a thirty-minute supply," Samson said. "Assuming it's not broken like every other damn thing on this ship. Tell him that in order to hear anything, he'll have to close the hatch to the tunnel and seal off the bladder."

Ash nodded. "Tin, you're going to have to close the—"

"Got it," the boy replied.

"Be careful, Tin," Ash said.

"I will." There was a pause. "Okay. I'm ready. Go ahead."

Ash nodded at Samson. He gave the boy a few minutes to get the second hatch closed.

When Jordan's monitor showed it was sealed off, Samson said, "Hope this works."

He punched the button, and Ash closed her eyes, picturing Tin inside the dark, hot gas bladder.

"Captain!" Ryan yelled. "We have a problem ..."

The words faded away, lost in the chirp and wail of emergency sirens. Ash didn't need to hear Ryan finish his sentence, anyway. She could see the storm on the main display. It was growing again, and the *Hive* was right in its path.

TWENTY-THREE

Weaver had guided the divers along the border of the industrial zone for over an hour. X's thoughts drifted like the swirling wind. He followed Weaver toward the tunnels that Weaver claimed would take them to the ITC towers on the other side of the craters—under the pits where the Sirens dug madly for radiation or whatever it was they were digging for. X still wasn't sure he could trust Weaver, but he didn't see any other option. The man had been down here for days, and he seemed to know his way around. He was likely their best chance of reaching their objective in one piece.

Ahead, Magnolia suddenly stopped. Snow flurries rose around her armor, caking the matte black with a layer of white.

"Something's wrong," she said. The static and whistling wind broke her voice, but X could still hear the trepidation there. Something had her spooked.

X halted. "What you got, kid?"

"I don't know," she said. "What do you make of *that*?" She pointed to the skyline to their east.

"All I see are buildings."

"Beyond the towers, in the sky. It looks like a cloud, but it's too low."

He zoomed in on the electrical storm stirring above the city. The skyline was the color of a bruise, with smatterings of scarlet. A network of blue electricity zigzagged across the swollen clouds, and thunder rumbled in the distance, the low, dull explosions following the flashes. Beneath the storm, a shadow crept across the horizon.

"See anything?" Magnolia asked.

"Why are we stopping?" Weaver shouted. "We need to keep moving."

X held up his hand for silence. He centered the binos on the shadows hurtling toward the eastern edge of the city. A web of lightning illuminated a carpet of white beneath the black clouds.

"My God," X said, taking a moment to comprehend what he was looking at. He panned from north to south. A solid wall of snow stretched for miles, farther than he could see with the binos. And it was heading straight for the frozen metropolis.

Years ago, he had seen a sandstorm roll through another city, but it didn't compare. This storm dwarfed anything he had ever seen.

The street shook again as the wave of snow reached the eastern edge of the city. A moment later, snow, like an avalanche from the heavens, exploded through the desolate streets.

"Run!" X shouted. "We have to get out of here!"

Weaver was already on the move. "We're almost to the tunnel. Come on!"

The divers darted across the buckled street. X

squinted through the blizzard. Ahead, he could vaguely make out a smooth embankment and what looked like grated steel gates, sealing off passages that led under the industrial zone.

A chorus of screeching arose from the pits as the Sirens heard the storm barreling toward them. X ignored the sounds and ran faster.

"We're not going to make it!" Magnolia screamed, glancing over her shoulder and tripping in the process. She crashed to the ground and slid over a patch of ice.

Barely breaking stride, X bent down and hauled her to her feet.

"Hurry it up!" Katrina yelled.

The groaning of metal from the city they had left behind sounded in the distance. A hollow crack followed as one of the buildings met its long overdue fate. A hundred stories of twisted metal and glass came crashing to the ground. The ground under X's feet shuddered, and the concrete fractured into a network of cracks. He leaped over a newly formed chasm in the dirt. Magnolia hurdled it after him. The tsunami of snow was gaining. If it caught them …

No, X thought. *We're going to make it. We didn't come this far to get taken out by a snowstorm.*

"Hurry!" he yelled. "We're almost there!" The blaster strapped to his leg dug into his layered suit, and the assault rifle clattered against the back of his armor. The weapons pulled him off balance, making it difficult to run.

There was another raucous crack, and a second building crumbled behind them, the structural steel snapping like frozen bones. He ran faster, harder than he even thought possible. His muscles ached, and each breath burned as if he were sucking in icy air.

Murph and Katrina were right behind Weaver now. Magnolia was falling behind, but X could still see her black armor in his peripheral vision. The dark tunnel entrances were less than three hundred feet away, but the roar behind them was growing louder. In seconds, they would be engulfed.

A blast of wind knocked X to the ground. He tumbled, then fought his way back to his feet as Magnolia ran past him.

"Let's go!" she shouted.

Weaver was first to reach the embankment. Running to the tunnel in the middle of the hill, he grabbed the gate. He tugged for several seconds and then turned, waving frantically, screaming something X couldn't make out. Katrina and Murph arrived a second later, gripping the bars and pulling so hard, their boots slid over the ground. The realization hit X hard enough to prompt another shot of adrenaline through his veins.

The gate was frozen shut.

They were trapped with their back to a wall. If the storm caught them, it would eat them alive.

X tried to slow as he approached, but slipped and fell against the upslope. He grasped the metal bars and heaved with every ounce of energy he had left. The gate inched open to the left, but the gap was too narrow even for Magnolia to squeeze through.

"Pull!" he yelled.

Together, the team wrenched the door open another foot.

"Go!" X grunted. He held the gate open as Katrina slipped through. Magnolia followed, then Weaver.

The outer edge of the snowstorm hit before X could pull himself inside. A torrent of snow blinded him, and Murph vanished in the cloud of white.

"Murph!" X yelled.

A muffled reply over the comm drowned out the next second in the roar of the wind. There was nothing he could do for the engineer right now.

X pulled himself to the left, bar by bar. The gate was closing from the force of the storm, blowing against the sheet metal that was welded onto the gate's upper half, above the grate.

He wrapped his left foot around the edge of the gate and pulled himself into the opening. When he had wriggled halfway through, the bars pinned him against the concrete with the next gust. He squirmed as the metal pressed against his chest armor, crushing him against the tunnel wall. With the right half of his body stuck outside, he watched helplessly as the wave of snow came at him. He had only seconds before the storm's full fury hit. It would crush him like an ant under a boot.

"Come on, God damn it!"

In a sudden fit of rage, he arched his spine against the concrete behind him and pushed the metal bars with both arms. After a few seconds, he let out a defeated groan. The force of the storm was too powerful. He was going to die right here, pinned with his back against the wall of a storm drain, and popped like a ripe tomato.

A wave of helplessness and anger washed over him.

He gritted his teeth and pushed again. The armor that had saved his life countless times cracked, and his chest plate pushed in on his ribs. He couldn't breathe ...

The compression on his armor slowly let up. Before he knew what was happening, someone yanked so hard on his arm, he thought his layered suit was going to tear. He fell to the ground as strong hands dragged him over the concrete and around a bend in the tunnel.

X lay there, sucking in deep breaths. He could hear voices over the comm but couldn't make out what they were saying.

As his vision slowly cleared, the outlines of three divers came into focus. But where was ...

"Murph," X mumbled.

He sat up and scrambled toward the snow streaming around the corner of the tunnel. A hand pulled him back, knocking him to the floor.

"No, X! You can't go out there!" Weaver shouted.

"We have to save Murph!" X yelled. He crawled across the floor, but the hand tightened around his ankle and pulled him back again. X dragged his fingers over the concrete, struggling for leverage.

"Let ... me ... *go!*"

"He's gone!" Weaver yelled. "And you're lucky as hell you weren't crushed. If Katrina and I hadn't pushed on those bars, you'd be dead, too."

X fell back to his stomach and probed the tunnel, praying that Murph would suddenly emerge. The passage was quickly filling with snow behind them.

"We have to do something," X said, more to himself than to anyone else. Murph was their best chance of hacking into the ITC security system. They needed him, and X wasn't about to give up now. He pushed himself to his feet, and before anyone could stop him, he bolted toward the river of snow spilling into the passage.

"X, don't!" Katrina yelled.

Ignoring her, he ran around the corner, into a gust of wind. The blast sent him flying backward before he could react. The fraction of a second was enough for him to see the barren landscape covered in a rolling wave of white outside the tunnel. A beat later, he smacked into a concrete wall. Air exploded from his lungs, and he slumped to the ground. He slowly raised a battered hand to shield his visor from the storm. The muddled shouts of the other divers calling him were lost in the screeching wind, and in that moment, X didn't even care.

Hades had taken another diver—this time, the man who was supposed to get them inside the ITC building.

*   *   *   *   *

Captain Ash stood behind Jordan's station. Her eyes shifted from the storm on the main display to the status of bladder twenty-one on her XO's monitor. She massaged her throat and longed for a cup of tea—anything to soothe the burning ache.

"Captain," Ensign Ryan yelled from nav. "The disturbance on the surface appears to be a massive storm. Sensors indicate it's about ten miles in diameter."

"How the hell is that possible?" Ash asked,

glaring at the ensign. He was just doing his job, but every time he spoke, it was to deliver more bad news.

Ryan shook his head. "My guess is, the electrical storm must have caused it."

"*Must have?*" Ash shouted.

"Captain, with all due respect, it doesn't matter anymore," Jordan said. "That electrical storm is headed right for us. At its current speed, it'll hit us in about thirty minutes if we don't maneuver out of its path."

There was no time to think. Ash had to make a decision immediately.

"There's something else, Captain," Jordan said. "The surface storm has already moved through the city and is passing over the industrial zone right now."

Ash met his eyes. "The divers ..."

"I'm sure they would have seen it coming in time to take shelter. Right now we have to focus on the ship. The *Hive* just sank to fourteen thousand feet. Even if we get those bladders fixed, it's going to take us a while to regain altitude."

Ash clasped the back of her chair. "Has Tin found the leak?"

"He's been in there for ten minutes. So far, nothing ..." Jordan cupped his hands over his headset. A beat later, his eyes brightened. "Samson just reported they got bladder three online. He's filling it with helium right now!"

Ash felt a wave of relief, as if the helium were buoying her spirits along with the ship. "Finally, some good news. Tell him to direct all power to the turbofans and rudders. If Tin patches bladder twenty-one, we should have a good shot at getting above that storm before it can hit us. Without it, I don't know if we can make it."

Ash gripped the spokes of the oaken wheel and stared at the monster storm raging toward them on the main display.

"Jordan, take us off autopilot," she said. "I'm taking the helm."

*   *   *   *   *

Travis stood with his back to the wall, by the comm speaker. Besides the humming of air handler units above, there were only random grunts and clucks from the livestock. No one spoke, not even Alex.

Brad had just informed Travis of the strike team's retreat from just outside the farm entrance. That meant Captain Ash had more important things to deal with than the farm. He suspected now that she wasn't lying about the gas bladder or the danger the *Hive* was in. The ship continued to shudder and shake every few minutes. Turbulence was common, but this felt different, as if the ship was fighting to stay in the air.

Alex broke the silence by shouting from his sentry post on the platform above. "We just going to sit here all day and wait for the Militia to make a move, or what?" He climbed down the ladder and jumped onto the dirt.

Travis thought of Raphael and wondered what he would do in this situation. His big brother hadn't always been a violent man, but over the years, the *Hive* had broken him as it had so many others.

Sometimes, you have to sacrifice the innocent for the greater good.

Raphael's words echoed in his mind. The dark-skinned farmer whom Alex had kicked in the gut glared at Travis before looking back down at the dirt.

"Trav, you hear me, man?" Alex said.

Travis scarcely heard Alex. He loved Raphael, but they had always been different. He couldn't bring himself to kill one of the hostages. That was never the plan, and he wasn't going to change it now. Ash had either called his bluff or was too busy trying to save the ship from whatever was happening with those dark clouds outside.

"Trav!" Alex shouted. He stopped a few feet away and pulled his knife. "Only way the bitch is going to take us seriously is if we stick one of them hostages."

There was a rumble from a close lightning strike, coupled with the creaking of the bulkheads around them. Travis held out his hands to steady himself as the deck beneath him shook violently. The panicked sounds of the livestock and the frightened screams of the farmers added to the general din.

Alex fell to his knees. "What the hell's happening?"

"Everyone grab on to something!" Travis yelled. He looked up at the hatch to gas bladder twenty-one and hoped the kid inside knew what the hell he was doing.

*   *   *   *   *

The lump on Tin's forehead throbbed as if it had a heart of its own. He was light-headed and exhausted, but he continued through suffocating heat and darkness, toward the faint hissing sound. His sweaty clothes clung to his body. He stopped to wipe the stinging sweat from his eyes, then crawled ahead.

Working his way toward the noise, he took shallow, conservative breaths from his finite air supply. The leak was close now and sounded as though it was coming from the bulkhead. He waved his hand over the hot surface of the bulkhead.

The ship lurched again, and the entire room seemed to shift to his right, sending him sliding across the floor. A moment later, it had leveled back out, and Tin pushed himself to his knees. Captain Ash was probably trying to maneuver away from an electrical storm. The realization filled him with dread.

He continued, crawling blind on his hands and knees, back toward the faint hiss. Even with the air tank, his breathing was jagged and raspy. And he was dizzy. Really dizzy.

Come on, he thought. *Just show me where you are.*

His fingers scraped across a small fragment of metal. He picked it up between three fingers. Even in the darkness, he knew that it was a piece of a bullet. He dropped it and kept searching for the puncture. Working methodically, he gridded the surface out in his mind, running his hands over each section. A few minutes later, his right hand slid over the hole. Weak suction pulled on his skin.

Tin let out a yell muffled by his breathing apparatus. "Yes!" Keeping his right hand on the leak, he pulled out one of the patch kits he had tucked in his pants, and placed it on the deck. Then he grabbed the tube of sealant and put it between his knees.

Unzipping the patch kit, he pulled out a flexible metal sheet, peeled off the backing, and laid the patch, adhesive side down, over the leak. Next, he traced a finger around the edges, applying the sealant along the seam. He thought he had done it right, but the true test would be whether it held. Luckily, the hole was small. He just hoped it was the only one.

Digging into his pouch, he felt for the Old World coin his father had given him. He rubbed its smooth contours and thought of his dad.

Listening again, he no longer heard the hiss of escaping helium. It would hold—for now, at least. With luck, he had bought Captain Ash enough time to send in a real engineer.

Tin pushed himself to his feet. Feeling a sudden rush of dizziness, he stretched his arms out for balance. After the feeling passed, he walked slowly across the bladder, hands out in front, and felt for the hatch. Finding the handle, he twisted it open and pulled himself into the tunnel, squirming on his belly across the floor. He closed it behind him and latched it, then crawled through the passage to the hatch that opened onto the farm.

Tracing his way back through the tunnel, he felt a huge grin. He had done it—he'd really done it! The pride of knowing he had patched the bladder slowly drained from him when he reached the other end. He hadn't thought about what came *after*. What would Travis and his men do to him? He was so hot and exhausted, he didn't have the strength to care.

Tin opened the hatch and scrambled out onto the catwalk. He stripped away the mask, squinting in the radiance of the grow lights. Then he sucked in the longest, freshest, most delicious breath of fruit-scented air he had ever known.

"The kid's back!" someone yelled across the room.

Tin shielded his eyes with his hand and scanned the field to find the voice, but his gaze stopped on his tin hat, winking like a star in the dirt below. Smiling, he collapsed onto the catwalk, his vision fading to black.

TWENTY-FOUR

The concrete shelter rattled as the blizzard raged outside. After the first fifteen minutes, fatigue began to set in as X felt the draining effect of seven and a half hours' surface time. Snowflakes laced with nuclear fallout fluttered from the ceiling as he waited for the storm to pass. The rest of the team sat in silence with their backs to the wall.

Bumping his comm pad, X said for the tenth time, "Murph, do you copy?"

The howling storm was his only reply.

"As soon as this passes, we need to get moving," Weaver said. He stood looking at the knee-deep snow around the bend in the tunnel. "He's gone. You have to accept that."

"I'm not leaving until we know for certain Murph is dead," X said.

Weaver kicked the concrete wall. "We're wasting time just sitting here!"

"Want to talk about wasting time?" X snarled. "How about that little sightseeing tour you took us on!" He stood up. "You may know where we're going, but I'm calling the shots. You got that?"

"And you're going to get us killed," Weaver said. He looked away. "Wouldn't be the first time you tried."

Katrina held up her hands. "Guys! Please stop!"

"I'm with X," said Magnolia, still sitting cross-legged on the floor. "We're not leaving Murph until we at least have a look. He could be unconscious, and that's why he's not answering."

"Or he could be dead and buried under five feet of snow," Weaver said. "Dead is the more plausible—"

"Stop it!" Katrina yelled. "Calm down, sit down, and stop acting like children. We need to work together if we're going to get through this."

X was still glaring at Weaver when a sudden flash of gray, wrinkled flesh appeared from the darkness behind Katrina. The Siren lunged through the air faster than X could move. The beast, covered in snow, landed on Katrina, pinning her against the floor.

"Help!" she shouted, arms flailing.

X cursed himself for not paying more attention. He pulled his blaster and fired at the creature's back as it reared up straight, giving him a clear shot. A high-pitched screech louder than the gunshot bounced off the concrete walls. The monster grasped at a fist-size hole in its torso before slumping on top of Katrina. She pushed at the body and slid out from under its dead weight.

The beast hadn't come alone. A pack of snow-covered Sirens flooded into the tunnel. Katrina scrambled away. Weaver saw them at the same moment, shouldered his rifle, and fired. The muzzle flashes illuminated a passage crawling with the creatures, their lean, sinewy bodies shifting in the glow.

X stepped in front of Katrina and fired off his last shell. The blast took the leg off of one of the creatures. It tumbled and thrashed across the floor.

Others leaped to the walls and ceiling while X dropped his blaster and unstrapped his rifle. "Get behind me, Magnolia!"

"I can shoot!" She raised her gun, but X pushed her back, not wanting her to kill Weaver or him in the process.

"Get the fuck behind me!" X yelled. He squeezed off several shots as soon as Magnolia was out of the way. A beast that had been darting across the ceiling fell to the floor on its back, gurgling one last breath through its strangely wide mouth. The next volley of bullets ripped through more leathery bodies, spattering the concrete wall with steaming blood.

Now he understood: the first pack were just stragglers trying to escape the storm. Six more came scrabbling down the passage, their spiked vertebrae cutting through the darkness.

"Katrina! Help! Now!" X yelled.

Katrina stepped up between Weaver and X and joined them, taking single shots as Sirens crashed into one another, trampling the fallen to get at the divers.

"Changing," Weaver said.

"I still can't get my gun to work!" Magnolia cried.

X yelled to her, "Just retreat back to the gate!"

Lean, stringy bodies thumped to the floor, tripping those surging into the passage. But on they came. When one fell, two more appeared, some of them taking to the walls and ceiling.

"Get out of here!" X shouted at Magnolia. He

squeezed the trigger again and again, watching more creatures fall shrieking to the ground as their blood spattered the concrete.

"Hold the line!" X shouted, pulling a spent magazine out of the rifle and reaching for another. He didn't need to look down to see that he had only two left. In seconds, he was firing again.

With each beat of his heart, the Sirens moved closer. In almost slow motion, X saw scabby crested heads hurtling forward. He saw the abrasions criss-crossing their wrinkled skin, and their ropy muscles stretching as they moved. Gaping mouths opened and unleashed the screeches that made him want to drop his weapon and cover his ears. Undeterred, he kept shooting. The oscillating discord seemed impossibly loud, even overwhelming the racket of gunfire in an enclosed space. It continued to shock him no matter how many times he heard it.

Katrina backpedaled as the monsters advanced.

"Hold the line!" X yelled again. But Weaver was falling back with her, too.

"We can't hold them!" Weaver shouted.

X fired quick bursts as he, too, retreated. The ammunition wasn't going to do him any good if he was already dead. He flipped the selector to full auto, sweeping the passage, no longer bothering to pick his shots. It was a final, desperate attempt to hold back the leathery horde. If they died here in this concrete tomb, the *Hive* was doomed.

X knew they had run out of time when his left boot sank into the knee-deep powder that marked the curve of the tunnel.

"Get out of the way!" someone shouted over the comm. X was shoved to the side as a hunched figure, covered in snow, limped past him.

X stared, uncomprehending, at Murph. He didn't know how it was possible, and he didn't care. The sight energized him. Righting himself, he raised his rifle at three advancing Sirens and squeezed off a shot to the left, then the right, then the center of the pack. The monsters toppled and skidded across the floor.

Murph lobbed a black ball the size of a really big apple into the darkness behind the dying beasts.

"Run!" he yelled.

The ball plopped in the snow amid the front-runners of the next pack. Katrina and Weaver were already running for the gate, but X held back and grabbed the man that was supposed to be dead. Murph grunted as X helped him around the bend in the tunnel. The guy was short but dense, and heavy as hell.

Magnolia was already at the gate, crouching with her hands cupped over her helmet.

A thunderous explosion rocked the tunnel behind them. The blast wave propelled X and Murph into the air. X lost his rifle and braced himself with his arms folded across his head as he landed in the snow. Fragments of concrete rained down on him, one piece hitting his helmet so hard he bit his tongue.

He tried to raise a hand to protect his visor, but the arm wouldn't respond. Another chunk of rock hit his back, but this time he only heard the impact. Everything below his waist was numb. The trailing rush of adrenaline amplified his heart rate. Blood rushed in his ears, and behind the ringing were voices over the comm channel—faint and muddied, but he could hear them.

Desperate to see if his team was okay, X tried again to move his extremities. A toe twitched. Then his entire foot. Good. It meant his spine wasn't broken. He fought the stars in his vision, blinking until he could see dimly outlined shapes.

The walls seemed closer now, as if the tunnel were shrinking around him. Suffocating, he struggled to draw air.

Three figures moved at the opposite end of the hallway, near the gate. And another sat, back to the wall, a few feet away.

As X finally managed to move his entire body, a rising melancholy screech echoed down the passage behind him.

The Sirens!

He crawled across the dense powder, fingers searching for his lost rifle, knees sinking with every lurch forward. His vision slowly cleared, and he checked over his shoulder. Smoke swirled through the tunnel, but nothing stirred amid the destruction.

X turned and clambered toward the armored figure a few feet away. It was Murph, gripping his gut.

"Did I do good?" he murmured.

"Yeah, Murph. You did great."

The engineer gave a feeble grin. "Homemade grenade. I knew Ty would never let me bring it into the launch bay if I told him. Was saving it …" He broke into a coughing fit and brought his hands to his helmet, revealing a wide gash beneath his chest armor. Blood had frozen around the wound.

"They're all dead!" Weaver called out from the bend in the passage. "You killed every last one of those things!" His laugh carried an edge of hysteria.

"You're hurt," Magnolia said to Murph.

"I'll be okay," he choked. "Somebody help me up."

Katrina reached down to help X to his feet, and Magnolia helped Murph up.

"You okay, X?" Katrina asked.

He put a hand on his helmet and nodded, his vision still clearing. "Yeah, I'm good."

"We need to get going," Weaver said. "Come on, before those things find us again."

Murph leaned on X, an arm over his shoulder, as they followed the other three divers into the tunnel.

"This yours, X?" Magnolia asked.

She picked a rifle up from the snow and handed it to him. He threw the strap over his shoulder and continued around the curve, where they found dozens of mangled, smoldering bodies. Steam rose off puddles of cooling blood. One of the Sirens was still twitching.

X pulled his knife and said, "Hold on, Murph."

The engineer winced as X pulled away and knelt beside the monster. It tilted its misshapen head in X's direction. A bloody froth gurgled out of its mouth, and its lips stretched in what looked like a grin. Long, pointed teeth protruded from its swollen gums.

"Come on, X!" Weaver hissed.

"Hold up," X said. He had never seen one up close like this. He took a moment to examine the small bristles dotting the mangy scalp, and the fresh abrasions on its pallid skin. Looking closer, he saw scars crisscrossing the creature's body. It had been a fighter, a predator, and even in its final moments it remained so, snapping at X's hand before he brought the blade down in the center of its skull.

The metal punched through bone with a satisfying crunch. A muffled sigh burbled out of the Siren's gaping mouth. X twisted the blade and then yanked it free, wiping the blood off on the leathery skin before sheathing the knife.

A few feet away, he spied the handle to the blaster he had dropped earlier. The barrel was blackened from the blast, but it was still intact. He scooped it up and holstered it.

"We're not far," Weaver said. "Follow me."

The green-hued darkness brightened around the next passage, and X could see another gate, this one wide open. The divers weren't the only ones trying to escape the storm. Now the attack made sense: not an ambush, but an inconvenient meeting between two species just trying to survive.

As he helped Murph down the final stretch, X checked the blue numbers ticking down on his mission clock. Sixteen hours and ten minutes remained.

"I know we don't have time to sightsee, but check this out," Weaver said from a few paces ahead.

He stopped and bent down next to two bodies on the floor. "I found these guys before but didn't have time for a closer look."

Both wore some sort of spacesuit, not so different from those the Hell Divers wore. The face inside the first helmet was completely decomposed, with only thin strands of hair and patches of skin clinging to its skull.

These divers had been dead for years, maybe decades, and if not for Murph, X and his team would have joined them in their concrete tomb.

*   *   *   *   *

The *Hive* breached the clouds, rising at a forty-five degree angle. Warning sirens blared over the bridge, and from speakers throughout the ship, a pleasant female voice reminded all aboard to please stay calm and report to their assigned shelters.

Turbulence rattled the airship as it fought for altitude. Captain Ash put Tin, Mark, the Hell Divers, and every other concern out of her mind. All that mattered in this moment was getting the ship above the storm. She felt every rattle, heard every groan, as if it were her own body, and not the ship, in extremis. Beneath her feet, the last survivors of the human race waited in their shelters, their fate pinned to her success.

She held the wooden spokes, feeling the burden but trusting her own aviation skills over the autopilot system. Drowning out every voice and sensor around her, she kept her eyes on the main display, analyzing, calculating, and responding to the data. She spun the wheel to compensate for a change in the storm's speed and continued to steer the *Hive* higher, farther from the storm. With only one reactor online, she had limited power, and running it at full capacity, she risked a surge that could knock out the turbofans. If that happened, they would suffer *Ares'* fate.

Samson had warned her "not to push the old tub," but the storm was closing in. If it swallowed them, they wouldn't survive long. She had no choice. If the turbofans blew, they blew.

"Eighteen thousand feet, Captain," Jordan said.

"We're two miles from the storm's edge," Ryan added.

"We're going to make it," she said. She imagined Captain Willis offering the same reassuring words to his crew, right before he lost control of *Ares*.

"Nineteen thousand feet," Ryan called out.

Ash glanced at the data. She had put some room between them and the storm. It would buy them time—maybe just enough for the divers on the surface to complete their mission. She leveled the ship out and took a long, relieved breath, even though the real battle was likely occurring nineteen thousand feet below. She could only imagine what X and the other divers were facing down there.

*　　*　　*　　*　　*

Tin woke up screaming. He sat up and clawed at the icy water streaming over his head. An emergency alarm whined, and a calm female voice repeated the same message over and over again.

He opened his eyes to find Travis towering over him. Tin scrambled across the dirt and searched for an escape. Alex, Ren, and Brad had formed a perimeter around him and the other hostages. There was nowhere to run.

"Calm down," Travis said. "I'm not going to

hurt you." He tossed the bucket on the ground and crouched down next to Tin. "You're one hell of a brave kid; I'll give you that."

Tin wrapped his arms around himself, his soaked sleeves providing little warmth. He shivered, and his teeth chattered. "I patched the bladder," he said defiantly.

"Yeah," Travis replied. "You sure as hell did." The *Hive* rocked slightly, and he looked up at the ceiling. "So Captain Ash was telling the truth the entire time."

"You're really going to let the kid *go*?" Alex asked. "Without even trying to negotiate again?"

The coldness in Travis' eyes thawed a little. "Yeah," he said. "He saved us, and he needs a doctor."

Alex snorted. "We lose him and we lose a prime bargaining chip."

Travis stared at him as if at some strange life form. "After all this, you still don't get it, do you? We lost all our fucking chips after your shooting spree."

"Don't do this, Trav," Alex said, his voice low and stern. "Don't let the kid go."

"It's over, man," Travis said. "It's fucking over."

Alex gripped the handle of his knife, hesitated, then drew it from its sheath. "Like hell it is. We're still in control."

"Have you not been paying attention to *anything*?" Travis said, eyeing the blade. "The ship is coming apart. If Tin hadn't patched that bladder, we would have already crashed to the surface."

"Bullshit. I don't believe a damn word Ash or anyone on her crew says." Alex tucked his scarf into the top of his shirt and flipped the knife end-over-end in the air.

Brad and Ren took half a step closer, their eyes roving uneasily back and forth between Travis and Alex.

"I knew I never should have followed your plan," Alex said. "I knew this would never work. You're weak, Travis. You always were—just like your brother."

Travis lunged forward and tackled Alex so quickly that Tin flinched. They crashed to the dirt in a heap. Ren and Brad, their backs to the clean room, followed the brawl anxiously, neither one interfering.

"You son of a ... !" Travis yelled. He climbed on top of Alex and started punching. The blows were audible even above the emergency sirens and the excited barks from Silver and Lilly.

"I told you not to shoot anyone!" Travis yelled, swinging again. "We were never ... never supposed to hurt anyone!"

Alex kicked under the weight of Travis' body, struggling to knock him off, holding up his arms in an effort to deflect the blows, but Travis continued the barrage.

Two sharp whistles cut through the other sounds, and Tin saw the silver flash of the arrows streaking through the air. They caught Brad and Ren, one each in the back. The two men slumped to the ground holding the arrow tips protruding through their hearts.

Behind the livestock fence, a fuss erupted among the hens as Militia soldiers aimed their crossbows. The armored men and women hurdled the fence one by one.

"Secure the hostages!" a guard shouted.

By the time Tin looked back to the fight, it was already over. Travis remained on top, looking in Tin's direction and grasping the slimy red shaft of a knife sticking through his side.

"I'm sorry," Travis mouthed. Blood trickled from his mouth, and his eyes had that resigned gaze Tin remembered seeing on so many lower-deckers.

"I never meant for this to …"

Alex pushed the body off him and staggered to his feet, blinking rapidly as if trying to comprehend the reality of Brad's and Ren's corpses.

"No!" Alex shouted. He pulled his blade from Travis' side and spun toward the squad of Militia soldiers still rushing across the farm with the weapon out front.

"Drop the knife!" one of the soldiers yelled.

Alex raised it in the air, shouting, "You fucking assholes!"

Those were the last words that left his mouth before two arrows ripped into his chest. Looking astonished, he staggered a couple of feet before toppling face-first into the dirt. The sharp steel arrowheads sticking out of his back glistened under the bright LEDs.

The stress of the past few days finally hit Tin. Shivering, he sank onto his back, staring at the ceiling, blinking slowly, his mind drifting. A helmet swam into view, then another, as Militia surrounded him. A soldier knelt by his side and put a hand on his arm.

"You okay, kid?" the man asked.

Tin could hold on to only one thought. "Is X back yet?"

The man shook his head. "I don't know, son. Just hold on. We're going to get you help."

Tin ran a hand through his hair. "Do you see my hat anywhere?"

"Don't worry, kid, I'll find it."

Tin closed his eyes, smiling. He couldn't wait to tell X how he'd patched the bladder and helped save the ship.

TWENTY-FIVE

The domed concrete warehouses were different from those X had raided on other dives. From a distance, they looked like clutches of giant eggs surrounding the ITC towers. Weaver pointed to the building in the center.

"That's it," he said. "According to your map, the cells and valves should be inside."

The tower, larger than the others, loomed above them. The divers huddled in the mouth of the access tunnel, waiting there as a flight of Sirens sailed overhead and disappeared beyond the skyline.

After their cries had faded away, Weaver said, "Now's our chance. Follow me."

X went back to Murph, who was slumped against the wall, hands pressed against his stomach. He pulled away fingertips stained with blood. There was fear in his eyes. And exhaustion.

"You good to go?" X asked.

Murph managed a nod but waved X away when he tried to help. "I'll be okay," he said unconvincingly.

"I'll take rear guard," X said. "Katrina, cover our nine o'clock. Magnolia, you got three o'clock.

Weaver, stay on point. Murph, you just stay alive."

The engineer coughed wetly, and X saw, behind the visor, the rash forming on his face. It was an early sign of radiation poisoning. The gash in his suit had allowed the invisible poison inside. Murph didn't have much time, and by the look on his face, he knew it.

"You guys coming, or what?" Weaver said.

The four divers pushed out into the snow and followed Weaver in a wedge formation across the field. They were in the open now and exposed to the elements. Lightning streaked through the muddy clouds, spreading a fleeting curtain of blue over the industrial zone. The entire place gave X the creeps.

The relentless sound of thunder echoed overhead as they moved. Weaver set a quick pace, and X worked hard to keep up. He walked backward, his rifle trained on the access tunnel. The storm had covered the area beyond the embankment with a fresh layer of snow.

He took a pull from the straw in his helmet. The chems from the drink flooded his system, and his body accepted the energy greedily. He could almost feel his pupils dilating.

"Almost there," Magnolia said.

X sneaked a glance over his shoulder. The central ITC building's shell had been stripped of paint, exposing the windowless metal surface. It rose ten floors and ended in a curl of twisted metal that looked a bit like Tin's hat. The sight filled X with dread. The kid was waiting for him to come back, just as he had waited so many times for his father. And the deeper X trekked into this frozen wasteland, the less likely he was to return home.

It wasn't fair, but X had a mission to complete.

"Over here," Weaver said, waving them toward a set of rusted steel doors at the base of the central building.

"Where's the security panel?" Murph asked, clutching his gut.

"You okay?" X asked. It was a useless question, of course. Murph was far from okay. But he nodded and trudged over to the box that Weaver was busy wiping off.

"I doubt this is the kind you guys have seen on other dives," Weaver said. "Never seen anything like it myself."

"Oh, yeah?" Magnolia said. "I've seen it before. On the *Hive*. There's a security panel just like this outside the armory."

Murph nodded. "Very hard to hack into."

"Don't I know it," Magnolia said.

"Well, can you do it?" X asked. Sirens were nowhere in sight, but they were out there somewhere. Every second that passed increased their odds of being discovered.

Murph opened up a pocket on his tactical vest and pulled out a second minicomputer. Reaching for another pocket, he doubled over in pain, coughing.

"Let me take a look," Magnolia said.

"No," Murph said. "I can do this." Uncoiling the cable with great care, he plugged one end into the security panel, and the other into his computer.

X gazed out at the stark landscape. Gusting wind kicked up fresh powder in the distance. Behind the embankment, the snow rippled like waves. A few miles away, a pair of whirlwinds scudded toward the city. He watched them dissipate as they moved into the heart of Hades.

"How you coming along with that, Murph?" X asked.

"Just need a couple of minutes."

X pulled out his binos and studied the gated access tunnel they had come from. He half expected to see Sirens pouring out of the passage, but he saw only the two divers' corpses they had passed on their way out.

The snow above the embankment continued to drift in the wind. X zoomed in for a better look, and his breath caught at the sight of bony fins slicing through the powder. The spikes were moving fast, kicking up snow into the air. Beneath the surface, an army of Sirens was racing toward them.

"Murph," X said. "You—"

"Still working."

"You better do it fast," X said. "We're about to have company!"

Numbers rolled across the engineer's computer. A five and a six had solidified, but three more digits still had to line up.

X looked back at the hill just as the first Sirens climbed over the wall of snow. They tumbled down the side and streamed onto the field, some of them breaking into a gallop, others taking to the sky.

"Murph, you got thirty seconds, tops!"

The third and fourth numbers were in place.

"Oh, my God, oh, my God!" Magnolia grabbed the door handle and rattled it. "Open it, Murph!"

X felt a stab of fear as he raised his rifle and picked a target. But there were too many, and he had only one magazine left. The only hope for survival was inside the building.

"Got it!" Murph finally yelled.

Magnolia yanked the door open and burst through, with Weaver and Katrina on her heels.

"Go!" X yelled, shoving Murph through the door. X grabbed the handle, then hesitated. The sight took his breath away. Sirens stampeded toward the building, kicking up snow behind them, as others formed up in a large flying V. X slammed the door and threw his weight against it. He couldn't hold the monsters back now, but somehow, leaning against it made him feel better. Their only hope was to power down and pray the Sirens would move on.

Glancing over his shoulder, he saw that the other divers had already removed their battery units. Their helmets were angled up to where the roof should be.

But his team wasn't looking at the sky. They were looking at the bulblike nests lining the walls of each floor. Hundreds of them.

X took a hand off the door and pulled his battery from its slot. They had made a strategic error in assuming that the Sirens wouldn't be *inside.* The building housed not only the cells and valves the *Hive* needed—it was also home to the Sirens.

*　　*　　*　　*　　*

Tin took his foil hat from the soldier who had carried him from the farm.

"Thanks," he said.

"You bet, kid," the soldier said, grinning. He

patted Tin on the shoulder and hurried off to join the growing crowd of gray uniforms outside the farm entrance.

Tin carefully folded the hat and tucked it into his pocket. He was surprised at how different he felt without it now. When he was inside the gas bladder, he hadn't thought about the hat. For a few moments, he felt odd, but he quickly realized it was a good "odd," a good "different."

He held the pack of ice from the medic against his head and closed his eyes. It brought some relief to the throbbing of his swollen forehead.

"Tin? Is that you?"

Tin pulled the ice away and saw the stern, youthful face of Lieutenant Jordan. The officer scanned him with a flashlight beam.

"Looks like you got dinged pretty good there."

"I'm okay," Tin replied in his most confident voice.

"Good," Jordan said. He gestured with his hand. "Follow me. Captain Ash is waiting for us on the bridge."

Tin hurried after Jordan, through the dark passageways. The emergency message continued to crackle from the ancient speakers overhead, and the splash of red from the emergency lights told him the divers weren't back yet. The *Hive* was still on lockdown.

Thinking about Travis, he remembered something his father had said after the food riots two years ago. *There's a difference between fighting for what you believe in and killing for what you believe in. Violence is never the answer.*

Tin smiled, finally understanding what his dad had meant.

Jordan stopped when they got to the doors outside the command center. He spoke quietly with two soldiers standing guard. Both men acknowledged Tin with a respectful nod. He heard a chirp, and the doors whispered apart.

"Those guys heard you patched a gas bladder by yourself," Jordan said.

Tin felt his heart pound with excitement as he walked into the busy command center. He laid his bandaged hands on the metal rail overlooking the levels, taking it all in. He had been here only a couple of times. This time was different from the others. The space was alive with movement, electronic chirps, and raised voices. On the bottom deck, Captain Ash held the oak wheel, her gaze locked on the main display. He felt a thrill at being in the middle of it all.

Jordan motioned for Tin to follow him down the ramp. A skinny officer with black-rimmed glasses looked in Tin's direction for a brief moment, and Tin thought he saw the man nod.

Approaching Captain Ash, Tin stood as straight as he could. When they were a few feet away, she regarded them with a smile, one eye still on the display.

"Tin …" The captain paused, her lips pursing as if she was unsure what to say. "Thank you. Thank you for being so brave. If it weren't for you, the ship would already have crashed."

Tin swelled with pride.

"You're welcome, Captain."

"When this is all over—"

The ship lurched before Ash could finish her sentence. She put her other hand on the wheel and shifted her gaze back to the monitor. Tin, still a little woozy, lost his balance, but Jordan caught him by the elbow.

"What was that, Ryan!" Ash shouted.

"Pocket of turbulence," the skinny officer with glasses shouted from the second deck. "The storm's gaining on us!"

"What's our altitude?" Ash shouted back.

"Twenty-four thousand feet and climbing."

Ash wiped a bead of sweat from her brow and said something Tin couldn't quite make out. She cocked her chin at the captain's chair. "Get Tin buckled in. Things are going to get bumpy again."

Jordan motioned for Tin to sit, but he stood his ground. "Is X back yet?" he asked.

"Not yet," Ash said. She turned for a split second to look at Tin. "But he will be. If anyone can make it back, it's X."

Tin saw the confidence in her eyes and knew that she wasn't lying. He took a seat in her chair and reached in his pocket for his hat as Jordan buckled him in. On the main display, the mud-colored clouds churned like dark cake batter. The sight terrified him, but he had to be strong now. For the first time since his dad had given him the hat, he didn't feel the need for it.

*   *   *   *   *

The divers were frozen in place inside the ITC building. The crack of thunder overhead provided a reprieve from the wailing of the Sirens searching for them outside. Lightning cracked above the roofless tower, and in its glow, X saw the creatures flapping away.

His gaze shifted to the nests hanging from the walls. So far, he hadn't seen any movement inside the egg-shaped cocoons. If Sirens were inside, they were likely sleeping.

Seconds ticked by and became minutes. After a while, X wasn't sure how much time had passed. Without his HUD online, he couldn't see the mission clock. Murph trembled a few feet away, his hand pressed against his belly.

X wished he could take away Murph's pain. Something about seeing another diver suffer made him want to shoulder the burden. These were his brothers, his sisters. Their pain had become his.

At last, the shrieks died away, and X let out an icy breath of relief. The Sirens, it seemed, had given up their search.

He waited a few more minutes, just to be sure. When he couldn't hear anything but the wind, he flashed a hand signal toward a set of doors across the atrium. Using the intermittent flashes of lightning to guide them, the divers crossed the space. They fell into a simple routine: Scan the walls and ceilings. Take a step. Freeze for a minute. Repeat.

Every motion was strenuous. The lack of movement made their body temperatures drop even further, and without the battery units on, they would soon be hypothermic. Murph wouldn't last much longer. He was dying. There was no time to rest.

They had to keep moving.

A flash from the storm illuminated the layer of ice that had formed over their black matte armor, so that the divers looked like the statues X had seen in pictures of Old World parks.

He checked the doors ahead. Something had forced them apart. Drawing nearer, he saw where claws had raked across their surface. Four agonizing steps later, he reached the opening. The weak light in the lobby obscured the hallway beyond.

X waited. Listening, probing. He could make out the dim outlines of a few doors along the right wall. There was no trace of motion or any sounds to indicate that the Sirens were inside.

A tremor rippled through his chilled body. He flexed his forearms in an effort to keep his blood flowing. The shadows in the hallway suddenly shifted. Or was it just his eyes playing tricks on him?

Get with the fucking program, X.

He wedged his way through the opening in the door and shuffled forward on feet that felt as if they were someone else's. Reaching the wall, he shouldered his rifle and swept it from side to side. He could see only vague shapes in the blackness: door frames and windows, maybe a chair—he wasn't sure. Without his optics, he was all but blind.

He shuffled back to the doors and waved his team inside the passage. They huddled around him and he pointed to his chest, signaling for them to reinsert their batteries. His teeth chattered as he locked his unit into place.

The other divers inserted their battery units, and cool blue light glowed across the hallway. Warm relief flooded through X as his heat pads kicked on. He took a piss that burned like acid. Grimacing, he sucked down more of the chem water.

Only minutes later, X felt surprisingly refreshed. He patted the vest pocket that held the paper fortune Tin had given to him, and remembered the final sentence: *Face your future without fear.*

X motioned for the other divers to come closer, and they crowded around, lit by the glow of their batteries. Murph was holding back a cough. X could see it in his shaking chest.

"This is it," X whispered. "We're almost to our objective." He threw the strap of his rifle over his back and punched the screen on his minicomputer. A map with their location emerged on his HUD. He fingered the nav marker of the supply crate they would use to send their cargo back to the *Hive*.

"Once we retrieve the cells and the pressure valves, we haul ass to the crate. Looks like it's about a quarter mile from here."

"Got any idea where the loot might be?" Katrina asked, looking at Weaver.

He shook his head. "Like I said, I've never been in here before."

"Only one way to find out," X said. "Let's move out. I'll take point. Katrina, you got rear guard. Weaver, keep close to Murph. Magnolia, with me."

"I think we should split up," Weaver said. "This place is huge."

X considered the suggestion. The building stood ten floors high, with dozens of rooms on each level. The cells and valves could be anywhere. He didn't like it, but Weaver was right and they were running out of time. It could take hours to search the building.

"Okay," X said. "Magnolia's with me. We'll take even-numbered floors. Katrina and Murph, you're with Weaver. You got odd-numbered floors."

He checked the hallway a second time. The doors were unmarked, the labels lost to time. He unslung the rifle from his shoulder and gripped the stock. Frost ran down the length of the barrel. Magnolia raised her rifle, and they started down the passage. X bumped his comm pad and opened a private line between them.

"You've done well, kid," he said. "Still think this beats prison?"

She shot him a quick glare. Their glowing battery units provided just enough light to show the worry lines around her electric-blue eyes. "I'm scared, X."

"I'm scared, too. But we're going to make it through this. Just keep breathing."

She acknowledged him with the weakest of nods.

X took another sip of water and ran his tongue along the roof of his mouth. The hallway ahead curved with the tower's elliptical floor plan. An open door led to an old stairwell. By the time they reached the entrance, X could feel the blood tingling in his extremities again. He took a cautious first step into the stairwell, aiming his rifle up toward the first landing. It looked clear, and he waved the other divers up the steps.

"All right, this is where we break off," he said. "We'll start on the second floor. You guys clear this one."

Weaver and Katrina nodded, but Murph simply stared ahead.

"Good luck," Katrina said.

X caught her gaze in the blue glow from their battery units. In that moment, he felt something he wasn't sure he understood.

"Good luck," X said after the briefest pause. He continued up the stairs without looking back. Magnolia followed closely, her footfalls ghostly silent. Even with the heavy armor, she moved like a shadow. He considered sending her ahead, then remembered how she had frozen every time they got attacked. She was good at sneaking into places, but he didn't trust her in combat.

"Should we use our headlamps?" Magnolia whispered.

"Negative," X said. He stopped at the next landing to listen before creeping around the right edge. The faint blue light from his pack showed the passage clear. He hustled up the next flight and stopped on the landing.

Placing a hand on her armor, he said, "You good?"

In a shaky voice, she said, "I'm the goddamn best."

TWENTY-SIX

Ash cringed as the edges of the storm expanded on the main display. With both hands on the wheel, she stared at the weather monstrosity racing toward them. The clouds in the center swelled and surged outward.

The *Hive* was at twenty-five thousand feet now, and she still couldn't see an end to the storm racing after them. She didn't need navigation to tell her they weren't going to clear it. She had to take drastic action.

Ash felt as if she had a gun to her head as she tilted the bow into a fifty-five-degree angle upward. It would push the ancient ship to its limits, but she needed the precious few seconds it would buy them to sail above the storm before it gobbled them up.

"Thirty thousand feet!" Jordan called.

"Brace yourselves!" Ash shouted. She risked a glance over to Tin. The safety harness formed an X over his chest. He flashed a weak smile, as if giving her the go-ahead to do what she must to save her people.

The outer edge of the turbulence caught the stern before she could pull them above it, and the *Hive* lurched forward as if it had been rammed.

Ash lost her grip on the wheel, and a second jolt knocked her to the deck. In her mind's eye, she got a glimpse of what was likely happening belowdecks. She could even hear the frantic screams of passengers and imagine the crackle of random fires breaking out under her feet.

There was a voice shouting at her now, but it took her a few seconds to comprehend the words.

"Captain, are you okay?"

"I'm fi—" Wailing sirens drowned out her response. She reached up and grabbed the wheel with her left hand and fought her way to her feet. Her eyes instantly locked on the display. "Come on, old girl, I know you can do it," she said, unsure whether she meant the ship or herself.

"Almost clear!" Ryan yelled. "Thirty-two thousand feet and climbing!"

The ship groaned and creaked, slewing violently from port to starboard. The flash of fire and death belowdecks raced across Ash's mind. She closed her eyes, snapped them open again, and gripped the thick wooden spokes with both hands, pulling slightly to starboard. The aluminum guts of the ship screeched in protest as the *Hive* split through the clouds. They were almost above the storm, but she could feel it pulling the ship apart. She had never pushed it this hard before, but like Captain Willis, she was doing what she must to save her people—to save the last people on Earth.

For a moment, Ash reflected on the fear Willis must have felt in his final moments. In her experience, there were two types of fear: the fear of death and the fear of letting others down. The latter was worse. She was afraid now, not just of letting the *Hive* down, but also of letting down every human who had ever lived. The future of her species depended on her. The *Hive* was treading along the edge of extinction, and Ash was terrified she couldn't stop it this time.

"We're going to make it," she whispered over and over again. "We're going to make it."

*   *   *   *   *

X inched the door open with his palm. He searched the passage's green-hued walls and ceiling first, then the floor. Something lay on the dusty tiles, but it wasn't big enough to be a nest.

Thunder rumbled throughout the building, sending flakes of ash wafting down from the ceiling. He propped the door open with his boot and wedged his body halfway into the hall.

"Come on," he said to Magnolia.

There were more of the frozen, reddish-black things halfway down the passage. He continued cautiously, keeping his rifle muzzle trained on the mysterious objects.

"What *are* those?" Magnolia whispered.

X paused and bent down for a better view. It looked like frozen flesh, meaty and thick. He took a guarded step forward, squinting. Another step, and he froze.

"Look away," X whispered.

"Why?"

"I said *look away*, kid," X repeated.

He had thought the team had endured everything Hades could throw at them: first the dive, then the snowstorm, then the Sirens. He hadn't thought things could get any worse. As he stood there shaking, he realized he had been wrong. He couldn't stop staring at Cruise's ruined body. His helmet was gone, his mouth frozen open in a scream. Both eyes were wide and dead beneath icy eyelashes. The creatures had torn him apart. Broken ribs protruded from his sundered chest, and the frayed coils of frozen intestines hung from his belly. Only one stump of a leg remained attached to what was left of his body.

Magnolia whimpered. "Is that ... oh, my God."

X reached back for her and took her hand. "Close your eyes, kid." He guided her down the hall, looking away as they passed Cruise's remains. He didn't want her to remember the man this way.

The next body was so badly disfigured, X didn't even know whether it was male or female. It wasn't one of theirs, though. The armor was green, not black like those from the *Hive*. The third corpse was in even worse shape. He had assumed that the divers perished from the electrical strikes, not at the claws of the Sirens, but the mask of horror on Cruise's face told X he had still been alive when the Sirens found him. He had survived the jump only to be brought to this place by the monsters and torn apart.

X halted a few feet from the double doors at the end of the hall to check on Magnolia. Tears streamed down her face, making her black eye makeup run in spidery lines down her cheeks. "Was that Cruise? It was Cruise, wasn't it?"

"He was probably already dead before they got him," X lied.

"But their bodies … We can't leave them like that."

"We can't do anything for them now. We have the living to think about."

Magnolia sniffled and nodded.

X had never realized how much Cruise meant to her, but he had been her lead before she joined Team Raptor. Seeing Cruise like this had her rattled—hell, X was rattled, too. He needed Magnolia to keep it together, and he considered his next words carefully.

"I haven't told many people this, but when I lost my wife, I felt like the whole world stopped. I drank until I blacked out, picked fights, took risks on every jump. I think I wanted to die. But you know what kept me going?"

She stared at him blankly, more tears welling around her eyes.

"My duty to the *Hive*. I dive …"

"So that humanity survives," Magnolia finished.

"So you with me? Can I trust you to have my back?"

She nodded. "I'll be okay. And the next time I see one of those fucking things …"

"Just stay focused," X said.

Once past the corpses, he approached the doors slowly. The left was open just a hair. He propped a shoulder against the wall and peeked through the round window at shelves stocked with cases.

X chinned his comm. "Katrina, do you copy? Over."

"Roger," she replied. "We found the valves!"

"Excellent. We have eyes on cells. Regroup on second floor."

"Roger that."

"Wait," X added. "We found Cruise and two others. They're pretty torn up—better prepare yourself."

"Roger that."

X looked back through the window and noticed a hole in the ceiling at the other end of the room. Two of the bulblike nests hung from the exposed joist. Now he knew where the Sirens were that had fed off his friends.

"Shit," X breathed.

Magnolia quickly peeked around his shoulder and pulled away. "I don't see any movement," she said. "Maybe I can get in there and grab a few cases without them ever knowing."

"Those things weigh thirty pounds apiece," he said. "I'm coming with you."

"No," Magnolia insisted. "I'm faster and quieter. I can do this. I didn't come all this way to have my hand held."

X took another look inside. There was no hint of movement. He checked his mission clock. Fifteen and a half hours left. It was a lot of time, but they still had to make it back outside, avoid the Sirens, and launch the loot into the sky.

"Okay," he said. "I'll cover you."

"I can do this," she repeated.

He wasn't sure whether she was trying to convince him or herself. He patted her on the shoulder and slowly inched the door open. She slipped through the gap and disappeared into the shadows.

An impressively short time later, she was back with the first case of cells. She set it down at his feet.

"See?" she whispered.

"We still need more," X said.

She moved back into the room as the other divers made their way down the hall. Weaver and Katrina gingerly placed the forty-pound pressure valves on the floor, next to the cells. He glimpsed their faces behind the visors. They had seen the bodies. Murph stood a few feet behind them. He was still holding on, but X could see the life slowly ebbing away from him.

"Weaver, Katrina, you two hold security," X whispered.

They raised their rifles and took a few steps down the hallway to stand guard. Magnolia returned a few moments later with another case.

"One more to go," she said. Then she was gone, melting into the darkness of the room. She was good; he'd give her that. Fast, sneaky, and cocky— the perfect thief.

Hearing a thump, X turned. Murph had collapsed to his knees. He pawed at his visor and flipped it open, cupping his mouth with one hand to hold back a cough. Fresh blood oozed from the gash in the midsection of his suit. Murph wheezed into his hands. His lungs sounded as though they had fluid in them, and he struggled to breathe.

"Weaver, help him," X said.

Weaver crouched down by him and pulled something from his vest. It was a foil packet about the size of a credit voucher. Tearing it open, he shook out a couple of pills and offered them to Murph.

"Here. I was saving these. Strongest painkillers aboard *Ares*."

There was a hint of reservation in his voice, and X wondered whether he had actually been saving them to end his life should it come to that.

Murph held the pills in his palm, eyeing them skeptically.

"It's okay," Weaver said. "They'll help."

Murph knocked back the pills and took a swig of water from his helmet straw. A moment later, the tension in his face eased.

"You're going to be okay, Murph," Katrina said. "It's almost time to go home." She massaged one of his arms softly.

X winced at her words. There was little chance Murph would ever see the *Hive* again. Whatever Weaver's pills had done to dull the pain, they couldn't fix the internal injuries. Even if they could get him back, he would endure a slow and painful death from the radiation poisoning. With as many rads as he had been exposed to, there was nothing the ship's doctors could do to save him.

When X moved back to the window, Magnolia was carrying the final case across the room. But something else was moving, too. Blurred flesh, bristling with spikes, climbed out of the wall nests and plopped to the floor. The pair of Sirens perched there and let out angry squawks.

Magnolia's luck had finally run out. The creatures darted after her.

"Run, kid!" X yelled. He kicked the door open and followed the monsters through the sights on his rifle. One of them climbed onto a shelf and tilted its deformed skull in Magnolia's direction.

X pulled the trigger and sent the creature whirling into the darkness. A second lurched up to take its place, and he took off part of its head with the next shot. More came from the left, knocking over shelves and trampling the contents.

The flash from his gun lit up the room for a split second, illuminating long limbs and spiky prominences. Magnolia was halfway to the door, but her hands were full and the heavy crate was slowing her down. A Siren lunged from the shadows. X waited for her to get clear, then squeezed off a shot that sent the creature crashing into a wall.

"Come on!" X yelled. He squared his shoulders and squeezed the trigger until his gun clicked empty. Magnolia burst through the open door and spun as X punched in his last magazine.

"Duck!" she shouted.

X dropped to the floor, and Magnolia vaulted over his back and slammed the case of cells directly into the face of the Siren that had crept up on them. The metal crate shattered the creature's teeth, and it let out an agonized shriek. She dropped the crate, pulled her pistol, and shot the monster through its scabby skull.

Two more Sirens had perched behind a fallen shelf. They swooshed talons through the air, testing Magnolia. These were smarter. Behind them, two others lurked.

X threw the strap of his assault rifle over his shoulder and drew his blaster. "Turn off your night vision!" He flipped his off, aimed at the floor between the first two monsters, and fired a flare. It whistled and exploded between them, sending the creatures screeching away.

He had bought some time, but not much.

In a few minutes, every Siren in the building would be out of its cocoon and searching for them. X rushed over to Murph and bent down to help him up.

"No! I'm not coming with you," Murph wheezed. He fought out of X's grip. "I did what I came to do. Now it's time I joined my family. My girls are waiting for me." He cracked a painful grin and pulled a small bundle from his vest pocket. "Still got one more trick up my sleeve."

A screech directed X's eyes to the open door. The flare had fizzled out, and the distorted shadows of the Sirens were creeping closer.

X eyed the explosive that Murph held in the crook of his arm, and nodded. A moment of realization passed between the two divers. No other words were needed.

Murph jerked his helmet toward the exit and shouted, "Now, get your asses outta here!"

It was the only time X had heard the man raise his voice to anyone. Swallowing his emotions, he scooped up two cases of cells. Magnolia grabbed the third. Katrina and Weaver picked up the pressure valves and cradled them in their arms, and they left Murph there to die, just as they had left Tony in the street.

The four remaining divers ran down the stairs, through the corridor, and into the lobby, where they skidded to a halt. The walls were crawling with Sirens.

The creatures dispersed across the interior of the building, their faceless heads homing in on the divers.

"Come on!" X said. He made a dash for the front door and jammed it open with his shoulder.

Weaver slammed the door shut behind them just as one of the creatures rammed the other side with its thick skull. The area was clear, but it wouldn't take long for the monsters to fly out the open roof.

On his HUD, X found the nav marker for the supply crate. He set a breakneck pace, pushing through the wind and weaving around the domed warehouses, the cases and his rifle clanking against his armor.

The crate was a quarter mile away—less than three minutes if they ran. X led them around the last building and continued across a flat, snowy field that stretched as far as he could see.

Crunching across the snow, he scanned the whiteness for any sign of the crate. He ignored the screeches as long as he could, then finally glanced over his shoulder to see the first of the Sirens soar out the top of the tower. There was no way the divers would make it to the crate in time. He bumped his comm pad and said, "Murph, if you can hear me, now would be a good time to—"

An explosion as loud as a near lightning strike cut him off. A bubble of fire bloomed out of the sides of the building and mushroomed up from the top, engulfing the Sirens that had made it into the sky. Their smoldering bodies fell lazily back to the surface.

The building trembled, folded in the middle, and collapsed in a cloud of smoke and dust. The other divers stopped and stared in astonishment.

Murph's sacrifice looked as if it had killed every creature in the tower.

"Come on!" X shouted. He pushed on across the white landscape, his eyes alternating from the beacon on his minimap to the ground, until they were on top of the nav marker. But the storm had buried the crate. They were going to have to dig.

"Watch our six, Weaver," X yelled.

"On it."

"Magnolia, Katrina, start digging!"

X set the cases on the snow and began shoveling with his hands, tossing clump after clump frantically to the side while glancing skyward every few seconds.

"I think I've got something!" Katrina shouted.

X scrambled over to her and wiped off the edge of a box with the white arrow symbol of the Hell Divers. He'd never been so happy to see the marking in his entire life.

"Help me," he said. He uncovered the surface and then tugged on a handle to free the box. Katrina took the other side, and together they hoisted it out of the snow.

Flipping the lid, X wasted no time. He tossed the supplies and weapons into the snow to make room for the cells and valves. Weaver stooped down and picked up one of the extra boosters. After locking it in, he retrieved spare magazines and stuffed them into his vest.

"Hurry," X said, stowing the cases inside. Then he set the valves over the top. Using the straps, he secured the goods.

"We got a problem," Weaver shouted. "A big fucking problem!"

X glanced up and followed Weaver's rifle muzzle to the east. Dozens of winged Sirens flew across the industrial zone, moving in a V formation straight toward the divers.

"Grab a gun," X said. He flipped the lid shut and punched in his key code on the security panel. With a loud pop, two balloons shot out of the external boosters, expanding as they filled with helium. The crate rose into a sky alive with Sirens.

"Clear a path, but don't shoot the crate!" X shouted. He stood beside Katrina and aimed his weapon. They came together back to back, moving as one. Magnolia and Weaver took up position a few feet away.

The crack of gunfire rang out in all directions. Bullets shredded wings, sending the fliers spiraling down. Some swooped away, but others soared directly into the incoming fire, shrieking their high-pitched cries. Lightning flashed overhead as the sky rained monsters. X grinned in spite of himself.

Eighty yards out, a single survivor landed and folded its wings into its back. "Someone shoot that one!" X shouted as it broke into a gallop. He pulled an empty magazine and reached for another.

Weaver fired two rounds into the creature, and it somersaulted and lay still in the snow.

X watched the crate vanish into the clouds. It could take a lot of abuse, but he still found himself praying it got back to the *Hive* in one piece, and that the *Hive* was still up there to retrieve it. He had put the gunshot he heard during the first seconds of the dive out of his mind—until now.

"That's the last of 'em," Weaver said. "What's your plan now?"

X continued to look skyward. Hades had killed a lot of Hell Divers today, but despite the odds, they had completed their objective. Life would go on in the sky, at least for a while.

He turned away from the clouds to look back at the frozen city behind them. Hundreds of black dots rose above the skyline. The intermittent lightning flashes revealed a swarm of Sirens sailing away from the buildings.

X had never really imagined he would get to utter the words that left his mouth next. "Time to get the fuck out of here and go home."

* * * * *

The *Hive* shook fiercely. The storm had completely engulfed the ship. Captain Ash clung to the wheel, but her throat burned so badly, she could hardly concentrate. It felt as if someone were holding a flame against her esophagus.

"Thirty-five thousand feet, Captain!" Jordan shouted.

The walls screeched in protest, and LEDs flickered overhead. Amid the chaos, Ash heard a familiar voice in her earpiece. "Captain, I'm not sure how much more of this she can take!"

It was Samson, and he sounded defeated.

"Do whatever you have to, to keep us in the air," Ash said. "I don't care if you have to climb outside and flap your arms."

"I've done everything but that," he said. "I'm sorry, Cap. This is it."

"God damn it," Ash shouted into her mic. "I need you, Samson. Screw your head back on straight. You're a fighter!"

She pulled up on the wheel as far as it would go. The bow was at sixty degrees now. An explosion burst from a far corner of the room. Screams broke over the wailing sirens.

"We're almost clear of the storm!" Jordan yelled. "Another two thousand feet and we're home free!"

Ash scrutinized the main display. It blinked as if taunting her.

"Captain, I'm picking up a signal over Hades," Ryan shouted.

She turned, scarcely daring to allow the thought. Could it be X? Could the divers really be on their way back?

"It's a crate!" Ryan yelled. "The divers have sent back one of the crates!"

Ash felt a tentative wash of relief, but they weren't out of this yet.

"Plot me an intercept course as soon as we get above the storm," she replied.

"Captain Maria?"

Ash ignored the voice and concentrated on the main display. The data had solidified: they were two hundred feet from clearing the storm.

The voice came again. "Captain Maria?"

The glare of annoyance faded into a soft smile when she saw Tin looking back at her from the captain's chair.

"What is it, Tin?" she said in a voice loud enough to be heard over the sirens.

"Is X coming home?"

"I hope so," she replied. "Hang on tight, okay? I have a special surprise for you."

"What kind of surprise?"

"I'm going to show you the sun."

TWENTY-SEVEN

Everywhere X looked, the ground was littered with the smoldering bodies of Sirens. The divers had killed those in the industrial zone, but the explosion from the ITC building had attracted the creatures from the heart of the city like vultures to a kill. Wave after wave sailed across the horizon in a mass migration of beating wings that seemed to block out the skyscrapers behind them.

"Get in the sky!" X shouted. He peered up into the maelstrom. Even if they could escape the Sirens, they would still have to make it through the lightning. They were trading one hell for another, but they had no choice. There was only one way home, and that was up, into the soup.

X watched the approaching monsters with mixed dread and fascination. For a moment, their unearthly shrieks sounded like a warning for the divers to stay away from the raging storm—a warning that X didn't heed.

"Deploy!" X shouted. "Deploy your fucking boosters right now!"

Weaver didn't need to be told twice. He punched

his booster, yelling in a hysterical voice about hell and leaving the wretched place. Katrina followed Weaver into the air, but Magnolia hesitated, staring at the Sirens soaring toward them.

"I said GO!" X yelled. He swung her around, but she had already punched own booster. They locked gazes for an instant—enough time for him to see the raw terror in her eyes. Then she was gone, lifted into the air, screaming at the top of her lungs.

X pivoted away, raised his rifle, and aimed at the first wave. Beyond it, a dozen more V formations were sailing in over the industrial zone. There must be hundreds of the monsters, and judging by their energized screeches, they didn't want the divers to leave Hades.

X fired into the first wave. The rounds lanced across their flight path, catching the Sirens out in front by surprise. Several died instantly, their lumpy bodies spiraling toward the snow. Others took their place at the front of the line and climbed above the spray.

X squeezed the trigger selectively, focusing his fire on the nucleus of the formation. He killed three more before he was forced to replace the spent magazine. Katrina's panicked voice crackled in his earpiece as he reached for another.

"X, get in the air!"

"I'm right behind you!" he yelled. He had to kill as many of them as he could before he hit his booster, since shooting when airborne was much trickier. He slammed another magazine into the gun, pulled the slide, and fired into the next wave until he had broken the formation.

The monsters spiraled earthward as X prepared to take to the sky. Letting out a deep breath, he reached over his shoulder and activated his ride home. The balloon exploded from the canister, filled with helium, and catapulted him toward the storm.

Letting his rifle strap dangle over his chest, he grabbed his toggles to steer away from the second wave of Sirens. He caught a draft of wind and rode it toward the other divers. It took only a few seconds to catch up with Katrina and Weaver, but Magnolia had disappeared in the low clouds.

The pop of gunfire pulled his gaze two hundred feet eastward, where he saw the weak glow of her battery unit rising. Flashes from her rifle lit up the clouds. The comm channel flickered in and out, but in the breaks from static, he could hear her screams.

"Pull up, Magnolia!" X yelled. "You're heading …" Thunder clattered above, cutting off the transmission. Glaring up at the swirling purple beast, he realized that their possible doom might also be their salvation. The lightning strikes could fry the divers, but they would also fry Sirens.

"Head into the storm!" X said. "Hurry!"

Weaver was already using his toggles to pull himself up faster. He was gaining altitude, and so was Katrina. They rose toward the low, bulging clouds.

"Magnolia! Pull up!" X repeated. In a blink, he saw that it was already too late. The second wave was only a thousand feet away. Even if she pulled away, they would hit her within thirty seconds or less.

The Sirens' screeches morphed into a steady high-pitched blare. X tried to block out the noise.

As he raised his rifle, a network of lightning speared overhead, and in its glow he saw the snarling eyeless faces homing in on Magnolia. Their membranous wings seemed to glow in the brilliant light.

The blue residue quickly faded away, and X raised his rifle with one hand and kept his other on a toggle. The kick from his rifle lurched him backward with such force he lost his grip on the toggle. He spun out of control, his harnesses twisting.

X fought back into a stable position, one eye still on Magnolia. The second formation had maneuvered into an intercept course. He centered his rifle on them, but she was directly in his line of fire.

"Magnolia, pull up, God damn it!" X yelled.

Her reply was a frantic scream. Two of the Sirens drove forward from the front of the wave. They exploded away from the others, their wings beating the air so fast, everything else seemed to move in slow motion.

X tried to find a target, but the world had ground to a screeching halt. The tug of his harnesses seemed weaker. The whistle of the wind and the shrieks of the Sirens seemed faint, distant. In the brief moment of peace, specters of everyone he had ever lost rose into his thoughts. Rhonda was there, the perpetual scowl on her once-pretty face softening into something that was almost a smile. There was Rodney, Will, Sam, Cruise and Tony, standing shoulder to shoulder. Murph waved sheepishly, his eyes hidden behind orange goggles. Aaron grinned and nodded, and X realized for the first time how much Tin looked like his father.

X had outlived all of them. Somewhere up above, Tin would grow up to be a strong, honorable man like his father, but X knew in his heart that he wouldn't see it. With the crate on its way back up to the ship, he and the other divers had ensured that the boy and everyone else on the *Hive* would survive. They had completed their mission. Humanity would go on, at least for now, but if X didn't help, Magnolia would never see the inside of the ship again. She was young, with her life still ahead of her. X, on the other hand, had already lived his, and even though most of it had been lousy, he had survived far longer than most.

I should have died a long time ago, X thought.

Magnolia shrieked again. "Help! I can't ... I can't get away!"

"Hold on!" X shouted. Letting his rifle hang across his chest, he grabbed both toggles and steered toward the Sirens. He wasn't going to let Magnolia join the ranks of dead divers, not when he still had some fight left in him.

She angled away from the Sirens' claws while X shot toward them. The two that had broken off from the pack were a hundred feet away now, their gangly arms already reaching up for Magnolia.

"No!" Katrina shouted over the comm. "Don't, X!"

X imagined she was looking down at them, watching as he soared through the sky toward Magnolia and the monsters. But he didn't have time to console Katrina or explain what he was doing. The clock was ticking, and he had time for only one message.

"Make sure Captain Ash takes care of Tin," he said. He bumped off the channel and caught Magnolia's terrified gaze for a split second as he rocketed past her.

With his left hand on a toggle, X raised the rifle in his right. He aimed carefully, knowing he had exactly one chance to save his friends. The other formations were five hundred feet away, but maybe if he could kill the front two, it would buy the other divers enough time to escape into the storm.

The Sirens' vacant faces jerked in his direction. He closed one eye, then fired just as they changed course. The bullet hit the first Siren right between where its eyes ought to be. It dropped like a rock, and he squeezed off another shot that hit the second one in the chest. The bullet jolted the creature, but it fought to stay in the air and angled toward X.

He fired two more shots into its mass, veering it from its trajectory. The Siren torpedoed past X, narrowly missing him. An ear-splitting screech followed, waning as the monster tumbled into the dark void. When X looked back up, the heart of the formation was almost on him. They reached out with ropy muscles, maws chomping and wings riding the wind.

They were so close now, he could see their scarred flesh coming apart as the bullets hit. Blood ballooned into the sky. For a moment, he thought he might actually have enough bullets to kill them all—that maybe he would make it back to the *Hive* after all. He had killed six of thirteen before his magazine clicked dry.

X let the rifle drape from its sling. Then he let go of the left toggle and grabbed his pistol and his knife.

Letting out a guttural scream that rivaled even the Sirens' shrieks, he extended his arms, brandishing both blade and gun at a bulky Siren at the front of the second formation. Its wrinkled flesh was covered with scars. Well, X would give it some new ones. He managed to fire a shot into its neck before they smashed into each other. He plunged the blade into the monster's torso as they collided. The pistol flew from his hand, and air exploded from his lungs. He was spinning now, his knife still stuck in the Siren's lean muscles.

It flapped its wings, screeching and tearing at him. Claws scratched over his chest armor, and he felt the hot burn as one of the talons ripped through his layered suit and caught the flesh in the gap beneath his armor and his belt.

X wrenched the blade from its neck. Blood spurted out, half covering the outside of his visor. He plunged the knife back into the monster again and again. Piercing shrieks, filled with rage, answered each thrust.

The field of view beyond his visor blurred with scabrous, wrinkled skin. He could see leathery wings and little else. A moment later, a pair of wings wrapped around his body, and darkness enveloped him.

"No!" X shouted as the dense weight pulled him downward. Fear gripped him as he squirmed in the membranous shroud, struggling to move his helmet. Through a hole in the cocoon of tattered wings, he glimpsed three flickers of blue from battery units above. In the blink of the eye, they vanished into the storm clouds. While the other divers rose to salvation, X fell back into hell.

*   *   *   *   *

Weaver had flinched at the sound of a single gunshot below. He watched in shock as X crashed into the Sirens. They swarmed him, flapping their wings like prehistoric flying reptiles. In a heartbeat, the diver plunged into the darkness and disappeared with the roiling mass of monsters.

In that instant, Weaver had considered helping X, but a gust of wind sent him and the thought spinning away. There was nothing he could do to help. He had known X for only a few hours, but his courage and sacrifice had reminded Weaver that diving wasn't a job or an obligation; it was a duty and an honor.

He stared at the storm as the balloon pulled him through the sky. Flash after flash of blue lanced through the muddy clouds. The panicked screams of the other two divers broke over the distant clap of thunder.

He glanced down to see Magnolia pulling frantically on her toggles and scanning the clouds below her feet for X. Katrina was doing the same thing. It seemed unfair that X had led the divers through hell, only to perish at the very end. Katrina and Magnolia might not understand his sacrifice now, but they would if they would just get back to the *Hive*. Life in the sky was harsh but precious, and X had spent his life protecting it. The moment of his sacrifice would forever be embedded in Weaver's memories.

Another torrent of lightning flashed above, arcing out like blood pumping through veins. Low, dull thuds boomed as his balloon pulled him toward the heart of the storm.

Until now, Weaver hadn't even thought about their ascent, but the booming thunderclaps reminded him that Hades hadn't let go of him yet.

His HUD was flickering now. In a few seconds, the storm would knock it out entirely. They were nearing eight thousand feet. *If* the *Hive* was still up there—and Weaver seriously doubted it—then the divers were almost halfway there.

He searched the clouds for any sign of escape—for a place that he might squeeze through. There, maybe a hundred feet to the west, he saw an area where the clouds seemed lighter.

"Come on!" Weaver shouted. He waved at Katrina and Magnolia with one hand and pointed with the other toward the paler clouds framed on both sides by denser bulging masses.

As he rose into the sky, he found himself trying to remember the words of Jones' prayers, but the thunder all around him made it hard to think. He still didn't know why he had survived while his family and so many others had perished. Finding a divine reason seemed disrespectful to the memories of everyone else who had died. Why was he so lucky? Why would God save only him?

There was no simple answer, nothing to explain the air in his lungs or his beating heart. There was no time to think at all. Lightning zipped overhead, raising the hair on his neck. He tensed and eyed his balloon, his heart skipping. The ball of precious helium continued its ascent. He exhaled a sigh of relief. The aftermath of the strike shook him, and he lurched in his harness, glimpsing a view of the clouds below. The air hadn't even left his lungs when the roar of thunder came crashing in.

Weaver blinked away beads of sweat and tried to focus. Using his toggles, he directed his balloon toward the break in the storm. Magnolia and Katrina were still right below him. Lightning backlit their outlines, each flash making his heart pound faster.

They had to be around twenty thousand feet up now. He couldn't see anything on his HUD, but his mind could estimate his location by habit.

Tendrils of electricity reached out toward the divers as they scaled the clouds. The subsequent cracks of thunder rattled his body again and again.

He was in the heart of the storm now. The electricity arced to his left and right, below and above. He was floating in a stew of lightning bolts. Before he knew what had happened, one of those streaks licked him. He saw the bolt in the corner of his eye before it passed through him. The strike jolted his body so hard, it felt as if he had landed without a chute.

There was no pain at first. That was good—it meant that the layered suit had protected him from the brunt of the electricity. The burning didn't start for another five thousand feet. It began under his skin and spread from his toes to his face. His entire body felt as if it had been burned from within. His insides felt as if they were melting. The raw burn worked its way into his bones, the pain shooting through his skeleton.

Distant voices called out. Or maybe it was the thunder; he wasn't sure anymore. His body had caught fire, and he imagined flames consuming him as he climbed higher into the storm.

You're not dead, Rick. You're not dead …

But he sure felt as though he was *going* to die. He repeated the mantra through the grid work of electricity, his body hanging limp in his harness. He was aware that he was holding on to a toggle, but his hand wouldn't respond to any mental command.

Below, Weaver caught a glimpse of Magnolia and Katrina. They vanished in the clouds a moment later. Lightning cut through their flight path. He sucked in a breath, holding it in his chest. Their balloons remerged a moment later, and he exhaled the air from his burning lungs.

A wall of red crept into both sides of his vision. The deep burning continued to rip and boil through him. He closed his eyes and chomped down on his mouth guard in response to the pain. The burn slowly faded away into numbness, and a moment later, yellow light washed over the red in his vision. But this light was different. Through his thin eyelids, he could see a golden glow.

He snapped his eyes back open and looked skyward. Rays of light penetrated the thick clouds above.

But that had to be an illusion. Or perhaps he was just dead.

Weaver's balloon pulled him out of the darkness,

and he looked down to see the churning storm clouds below his feet. He spit out his mouth guard in shock. He had made it through the Sirens and the storm. He had actually made it through!

When he looked back up, he was surrounded by puffy white clouds. At first, he thought maybe Jones had been right about heaven. Maybe he was dead. Maybe this *was* heaven. He blinked the final bits of red away as the yellow light strengthened. He fought to raise a hand and shield his eyes from the golden glow.

Blinking rapidly, he tried to focus on the sphere of crimson in the center of the light. It was so intense he could see only the radiant edges of the flaming ball. There was something else up there, too. A single black dot crossed the horizon. He squinted into the light, and the sleek, beetlelike outline of an airship came into focus.

What he was seeing was impossible. *Wasn't it?*

The voices were back again. But he couldn't tell whether it was one of the other divers or himself talking. He forced his rattled brain to concentrate, finally realizing it was neither. They were the words of his wife, Jennifer.

You're almost there, Rick. You're almost safe.

Warm tears streaked down his face, and he sobbed like a child as the *Hive* came into focus. The ship looked so much like *Ares* that for a moment, he thought he was staring at his home. And then it hit him. Yes, he was staring at his new home.

As the ship grew bigger, it blocked out the sun. The light danced around the metal edges as the flames had around *Ares* when it crashed. But the *Hive* wasn't burning. It was basking in the glow of the sun.

A pair of doors under the hull parted and opened, revealing the inside of the unfamiliar ship. Part of him wanted to pull away, to fall back to the surface and join his family. He wasn't sure he could make a new life without Jennifer and the girls. Instead, he let go of his toggles and stretched his numb arms to embrace the final ascent.

He let out a laugh that sounded a bit unhinged, even to himself. But that was okay. Maybe he was a bit crazy now—crazy, burnt, and ...

Alive.

The balloon pulled him into the recovery bay a moment later. Katrina vaulted through the doors, doing a quick somersault to burn off her momentum. She hung on to the rungs of a ladder, her helmet still searching the clouds below. Magnolia entered less than a minute later. Weaver could see the tears streaming down her cheeks through her visor. She trembled as she hung there, her gaze examining Weaver's face and his tears. He touched her on the shoulder.

"It's okay, kid," he said, remembering X's words. "You're home now."

TWENTY-EIGHT

Sunlight greeted Ash when she arrived at the launch bay. She hurried toward a crowd of yellow suits swarming around the plastic dome that covered the reentry bay. Tin was with her, his hand clasped in hers.

"Is X back?" he asked.

"I hope so," Ash replied.

As they walked, Tin scanned the porthole windows, his eyes wide with awe. Normally, the sight would have mesmerized her, too, but she didn't have time to stop and stare. Halfway across the room, she noticed something else.

"Where's your hat?" she asked Tin.

"I don't need it anymore," he said. "Hell Divers don't wear hats."

"Hell Divers?"

He looked away from the windows and found her eyes. She saw strength there beyond his ten years.

"I don't want to be an engineer anymore," Tin said. "I want to be a Hell Diver, like X and my dad."

She smiled and squeezed his hand.

"Captain," a voice called out. Jordan came running from the crowd of technicians. He slid to a stop a few feet in front of Ash, his boots squeaking across the floor. "We recovered the crate and three divers."

"Just three?" Ash said, dread rising in her voice.

"Afraid so," Jordan replied. He glanced back at the dome. Ty motioned for the technicians to step back and yelled, "Repressurizing!"

A hiss sounded as air flooded the reentry bay.

"Sterilizing for contaminants," Ty said.

Mist filled the inside of the dome, swirling and churning like the storm over Hades. Ash tightened her grip on Tin's hand. Finally, the plastic clicked and unsealed, and a grappling hook pulled the dome away.

Floor vents sucked away the white cloud, and three divers staggered out. One of them dropped to both knees, dented armor shining in the sunlight. The other two stood, their visors roving this way and that as if they couldn't believe they were indeed back on the ship. It took only a moment to see that X wasn't among the group.

Tin pulled away from Ash's grip. "Where's— where's X?"

The diver on the ground removed his helmet, and a man Ash didn't recognize looked up. He wore green armor, and his layered suit was subtly different from those her own divers wore.

"Where's X?" Tin asked again, his voice cracking.

"I'm sorry, kid, but he didn't make it," the man said. "Bravest damn diver I ever saw, though. What he did for Magnolia …" He shook his head and pushed himself to his feet. Extending a trembling hand, he said, "Captain Ash, I presume. I'm Commander Rick Weaver from *Ares*."

Ash didn't know what to say, so instead of saying anything, she shook his hand. Then she grabbed Tin's hand again. She looked to the other divers as they removed their helmets. Katrina and Magnolia, their faces streaked with tears, wrapped their arms around each other.

"What do you mean, 'he didn't make it'?" Tin asked. "He promised he would come back." Ash squeezed his hand, but he pulled away. "Where is he?"

Katrina shook her head. "He's gone, Tin. I'm so sorry."

Tin glanced back at Ash. "We have to go back for him!"

Magnolia cupped a hand over her mouth and sobbed.

"I'm sorry, Tin, but X is ..." Ash considered her words, then said, "He's dead, Tin. We can't do anything for him now. I'm sorry."

"Captain," Jordan said.

Ash turned and saw the look on her XO's face. They were out of time. They needed to move the ship. She nodded, feeling her heart break, and Jordan hurried away.

"No!" Tin said. "We can't leave without X!"

"We have to, Tin," Ash said. "I'm sorry, but X would want this. He gave his life so you and everyone else could be safe." She grabbed Tin and pulled him close as Samson and his men entered the room. The engineer nodded at Ash and motioned his team of blue suits to the crate. They rummaged through the contents for the power cells and valves that so many Hell Divers had died for.

"X said he would come back," Tin sobbed. "He promised he would do everything to return."

"He sacrificed himself so that you and everyone else could live," Ash said. Her voice was low and soothing. "He wanted you to grow up. He wanted you to become an engineer."

Tin tilted his head back and wiped a string of snot from his nose. "He promised he would take care of me."

Ash hesitated, considering her next words carefully. Thoughts of Mark, her cancer, her duty to the *Hive,* and her dream of finding them all a new home surfaced in her thoughts. It was overwhelming, but she was Captain Maria Ash. She was a fighter and always would be. She could still fight her cancer, pursue her dream of finding a home, and look after Tin with what time she had left.

"I'll take care of you, Tin," she said. "You can stay with Mark and me. How would you like that?"

The boy glanced up and met her eyes but didn't say a word. Nothing she could say would make Tin understand why X had given his life—at least, not right now. All she could do was console him. She pulled his head to her chest and patted his back. "You can even sit in my captain's chair if you want."

Tin snorted—a cross between a grim laugh and a sob. He nodded, and hugged her. A tense silence followed the heartbreaking moment, and everyone in the launch bay worked quietly. Medics attended to Weaver, Katrina, and Magnolia while Samson's engineers unloaded crates and whisked the precious cells and valves away.

Ash considered making a statement—something that would honor the sacrifices that X and the other Hell Divers had made on this day. But there was still work to do, and she knew that any words she said would ring hollow. Everyone in this room—everyone aboard the *Hive*—would know the names of the divers who had saved them. But first, Ash had to save their ship.

*   *   *   *   *

X opened his eyes to red-hued darkness. That was the first surprise. He wasn't dead, but his entire body hurt—every muscle and bone and nerve. And he was cold—colder even than he had been without his heat pads. He knew that the chill came from loss of blood.

Even now, when facing certain death, he fought. He struggled to sit up, and when he couldn't do that, he squirmed from side to side. The snow had hardened around him.

First things first. You have to get free.

X inhaled a raspy breath, trying to focus. He blinked heavy eyelids until his vision had cleared enough to see that it was a Siren's wings, not snow, that had him trapped. The leathery shrouds covered him from neck to feet. Now he knew how he had survived the fall back to Hades: the creature that had tried to kill him had ended up padding his fall.

If he had survived, then maybe the Siren had, too. The realization filled him with energy that he didn't know he had left. He wiggled and used his arms to push the tangled wings off him. When he was free, he scrambled across the snow, right into another dead Siren. He climbed over it and saw another. There were three—all limp and unmoving, riddled with bullet holes. These were the creatures the divers had killed before they deployed their boosters.

The smoke from the burning ITC building filled the horizon to the west. He smacked his helmet on one side until the flickering HUD solidified. The nav marker for the crate was gone, but he still remembered where it had been. If he could get to the supplies he had dumped, maybe he could use one of the extra boosters to get back to the *Hive*—if it was even still there.

The harnesses attached to his balloon pulled him back when he crawled away from the bodies. He reached for his knife, which wasn't there. Then he remembered plunging it into the Siren.

Pushing himself to his feet, he gritted his teeth in anticipation of the wave of dizziness he knew was coming. Darkness washed over him, and he collapsed back onto the snow. The worst of the pain seemed to be coming from his stomach. He pulled a slimy hand away from his gut, warm blood steaming off his fingers. The wound was bad, but the threat of radiation poisoning was worse.

He had to get moving. The *Hive* wouldn't wait forever. He doubted it was still up there even now, but he clung to the spark of hope. The spark grew as he pushed himself to his feet and worked his way carefully back to the first Siren. It lay on its back, wings outstretched. A halo of frozen blood surrounded the knife hilt protruding from its rib cage. He watched its chest for any hint of breath, but the bloody flesh was still.

X took a guarded step toward the monster. Certain it was dead, he bent down and plucked his knife from its chest. He staggered backward as a coarse tongue plopped out of its open mouth.

With one eye on the creature, he reached over his shoulder and cut the harnesses away. Then he yanked the useless booster from the slot in his armor and dropped it in the snow.

Ignoring every stab of pain tormenting his body, he struggled to a trot. He stumbled after a few strides, nearly toppling over in the snow. The crackle from his raspy breathing echoed in his helmet.

In an out, X. Focus. You can do this.

The eerie call of a Siren broke his concentration. Two others immediately answered its call. These screeches weren't coming from the sky. They were coming from the ground. He didn't need to turn to see the monsters advancing across the snowy landscape.

He reached for his weapons, but his hand came up empty. He had lost both the rifle and the blaster in the fall. There was only one thing to do: run—and pray that he reached the supplies in time. Pain shot up his legs and burned through his gut as he fell into a jog.

The sight of Sirens loping across the snow energized him. All at once, their screeches seemed to collide in a wavering, electronic-sounding whine that shocked him into motion. He could see still more of them behind the first wave, fighting through gusts of snow in the distance. They rushed toward him, closing in from all directions. He pushed harder through the deep drifts, gasping for air, running on adrenaline and little else.

The supplies weren't far now. He could see them just a few yards away—boosters, weapons, boxes of extra ammunition—lying in the snow, where he had tossed them to make room in the crate.

X launched himself in a headlong dive for the gear. The uncontrolled slide ripped at the wound and packed it with dirty, radioactive snow so cold it ached. Swallowing the pain, he searched frantically for a weapon beneath the light coat of powder that had fallen.

He gripped the stock of a blaster and brought it up to meet the four Sirens galloping in from the north.

Without thinking, he fired a flare at the cluster. A split second later, he realized his mistake. As the flare exploded in the snow between the creatures, he chinned the pad to shut off his night-vision optics. The Sirens squawked away, darting off into the gusting snow.

X scooped up a new booster, slid it into the slot on the back of his armor, and secured it with a click. Then he grabbed one of the assault rifles and turned to see two dozen Sirens stalking him.

He could power down and pull his battery unit, but he would never survive the trip back without the heating pads in his suit. His only option was to fight.

X planted his boots in the snow and struggled to shoulder his rifle. His arms shook as he raised the weapon. The crack of his own gunfire was a welcome sound, blotting out the encroaching wails. He fired in short bursts that punched through leathery skin and shattered bone. Four bodies pitched into the snow. He killed three more before ejecting the empty magazine and shoving in another. Smoke curled from the muzzle as he trained it on the six Sirens drawing closer. He squeezed the trigger, moving his sights from target to target.

Between the cracks of gunfire came a shrill cry above. He looked up to see three Sirens cutting through the sky in a nosedive. Swinging his rifle skyward, he fired single shots into the mass. One of the creatures veered away, wounded, but the other shots went wide as panic threw off his aim.

X concentrated this time, aiming with greater precision, knowing that each round was precious. He closed his eyes and flinched as the two Sirens crashed headfirst into the snow around him, sending up a cloud of white. He didn't check to see if they were dead. Now was his chance to escape. He changed out his magazine, then reached over his shoulder to hit the booster. The balloon shot out of the pack and launched him skyward.

Two converging Sirens bashed into each other right where he had stood a moment before, throwing up more snow. He angled the muzzle toward the ground as soon as he was in the air. Ten of the creatures writhed just under his feet, their eyeless faces turning this way and that, as if confused by the cloud of snow.

Not wanting to waste the stolen moment, X squeezed the trigger at one of the monsters as it looked skyward. Several of the rounds punched through its skull, spraying the others with fresh blood and sending them into a frenzy.

One down.

The next shot left another flopping spastically in the snow, with a shattered leg.

Two down.

He mowed down three more with a single controlled burst, but the rifle's recoil pushed him higher into the air in erratic jerks.

The remaining Sirens locked on to his position from the ground, squawking furiously. He dropped three more with calculated shots before the final two got airborne.

X centered the weapon on them, but the stock felt light in his hands, and when he went to squeeze the trigger he realized his fingers were almost completely numb. His entire body shuddered. Shock and blood loss were taking a toll. The wind whistled over his armor as he rose toward the clouds.

Even with numb fingers, he managed to fire off another volley, ripping through the wings of the Siren to his left. It tumbled away before smashing into the ground. He focused on the other now, holding the rifle as steady as he could.

The monster soared through the sky. It was almost elegant, the way it caught the air currents. Even as it closed on him, X found himself marveling that somehow these creatures had survived in this harsh environment. Maybe it was the next step in evolution on earth. Maybe humans' time was indeed over.

No. We still have time.

Holding in a breath, he lined up the sights and

fired into the creature's torso, knocking it off course and sending it spiraling out of control. He pulled the trigger again, but the gun wouldn't fire.

X reached for his final magazine just as a crosswind knocked the rifle from his hands. He watched helplessly as it disappeared into the clouds. All he had left now was his knife. If the Sirens returned, he would have no choice but to use the blade.

He searched the darkness for any sign of them. His vision was tinted red, the field growing narrower, the images dimmer.

Almost there. Almost home.

He pressed against the wound on his belly and groaned at the stab of pain. Ascending higher, he drifted closer to unconsciousness. He fought it, but this wasn't a foe to be vanquished with grit and a tactical knife.

Lightning shot across the clouds to the west, and ten seconds later, he heard the dull roll of thunder. X had drifted to the east, his balloon pulling him away from the storm.

He grabbed his toggles and focused on the flashes. Watching them helped him concentrate, kept him barely present. Despite his injuries, he began to relax. There was something serene about the darkness. He imagined that it was a lot like death: infinite and everlasting.

As he coasted away from the storm, his HUD solidified. He was at ten thousand feet now.

Were the Sirens still searching for him?

He listened for their high-pitched shrieks but heard only wind and the echoes of thunder.

X closed his eyes, he wasn't sure for how long— maybe just a moment, maybe much longer. But when he opened them again, the brightest, most beautiful light he had ever seen flooded his vision.

A carpet of yellow stretched across the horizon. White, fluffy clouds drifted across an ocean of blue. And there to the east was a black speck that might just be the *Hive*. Above it all, sat a flaming ball so bright, it hurt his eyes. He had seen the sun only a handful of times in his life, and never so clearly as this.

X squinted into the sunlight, shielding his visor with a shaky, bloody hand. Could it be? Could he really have made it back?

He shifted his gaze back to the tiny black sphere and bumped his comm pad. "This is Commander Xavier Rodriguez …" He broke into a cough, then sucked in deep gasps to control his breathing. Stars floated before his vision, encroaching on the beautiful view. "Does anyone copy? Over."

Static rushed out of the speakers in his helmet. He blinked away the fuzz and watched the only home he had ever known fly slowly away. He pleaded that someone would hear him and come back for him. Several minutes passed, and he tried again.

"This is Commander X. If anyone can hear me, I'm drifting east with eyes on the *Hive*. Anyone copy? Over."

White noised crackled in his ear.

The *Hive* continued gliding through the blue, carrying its precious cargo to safety. X felt his lips curl into a smile. They had made it. Captain Ash was steering the ship away from Hades, leaving the death and despair behind while his balloon pulled him toward the sun.

X let out a sigh and searched his vest pocket for the fortune Tin had given him. He pulled it and read it in the sunlight.

"Handle your present with confidence. Face your future without fear," X said. Tin had taught him what it meant to live again, and even more importantly, what it meant to be courageous. In the end, it was with the boy's help that X had fulfilled his promise to Aaron. It didn't matter that X wouldn't be there to see the boy grow up; he'd given Tin the chance *to* grow up.

He let the wind take the piece of paper from his fingers and watched it swirl away. *Ares* was gone, but the *Hive* was still flying. Maybe Captain Ash really would find a place to land someday—a place where the survivors of the human race could finally start over. The fate of humankind was now in the capable hands of others. He had done all he could. He didn't need to fight anymore. His battle was finally over. X loosened his grip on the toggles and let the balloon pull him into the warmth of the sun.

ACKNOWLEDGMENTS

It's always hard for me to write this section for fear of leaving someone out. My books would not be worth reading if I didn't have the overwhelming support of my family, friends, and readers.

As many of these people know, far more than writing goes into creating a book. The time it takes to edit, format, print, and market a book can take just as long as the actual writing. For that reason, I'm grateful for my new publisher, Blackstone. They believed in my Extinction Cycle books enough to take a chance on *Hell Divers*. Working with their staff has been wonderful. It's been refreshing to see a traditional publisher thinking outside the box and taking risks. They spent countless hours on editing and marketing *Hell Divers*. Without them, this book would not be what it is.

A special thanks also goes to David Fugate, my agent, who provided valuable feedback throughout the many drafts. I'm lucky and grateful to have his support and guidance.

I would be remiss if I didn't also thank the people for whom I write: the readers. I've been blessed to have my work read in countries around the world by wonderful people I will probably never meet. If you are reading this, know that I truly appreciate you for trying my stories.

To my family, friends, and everyone else that has supported me on this journey, I thank you.

ABOUT THE AUTHOR

Nicholas Sansbury Smith is the bestselling author of the Orbs and Extinction Cycle series. He worked for Iowa Homeland Security and Emergency Management in disaster mitigation before switching careers to focus on his one true passion—writing. A three-time Kindle All-Star, several of Smith's titles have reached the top 50 on the overall Kindle bestseller list and as high as #1 in the Audible store. When he isn't writing or daydreaming about the apocalypse, he's training for triathlons or traveling the world. He lives in Des Moines, Iowa, with his dog and a house full of books.

Newsletter: http://eepurl.com/bggNg9
Twitter: https://twitter.com/greatwaveink
Facebook: Nicholas Sansbury Smith
Website: www.NicholasSansbury.com

To personally contact Nicholas Sansbury Smith, email him at GreatWaveInk@gmail.com. He would love to hear from you.

COMING SUMMER 2017

HELL DIVERS: GHOSTS